Tears of Heaven Series

HEAVEN AND HELL

Tears of Heaven Series

HEAVEN AND HELL

The Journey of Chris and Serena Davis

Kenneth Zeigler

Destiny Image® Publishers, Inc.
P.O. Box 310 Shippensburg, PA 17257-0310

"Speaking to the Purposes of God for this Generation
and for the Generations to Come."

This book and all other Destiny Image, Revival Press, Mercy Place, Fresh Bread, Destiny Image Fiction, and Treasure House books are available at Christian bookstores and distributors worldwide.

For a U.S. bookstore nearest you, call
1-800-722-6774.

For more information on foreign distributors, call
717-532-3040.

Or reach us on the Internet:
www.destinyimage.com

ISBN 10: 0-7684-2503-4

ISBN 13: 978-0-7684-2503-1

For Worldwide Distribution, Printed in the U.S.A.

3 4 5 6 7 8 9 / 16 15 14 13

Dedication

I dedicate this book to my mother, Gladys Marie Zeigler, whose commitment and faithfulness to our Lord Jesus Christ was an inspiration to me. She has long since gone to be with the Lord; and one of my greatest hopes, indeed, anticipations, is to be with her in our Father's Kingdom at the end of my life on Earth.

Preface

SINCE his earliest days, man has been incessantly curious about the world around him. What mysteries might lie beyond the next mountain, up the treacherous jungle river, or across the vast unexplored seas? His curiosity has carried him far from his home. From the deserts to the poles, from the depths of the oceans to the depths of space, man has pushed back the frontiers of his universe.

Yet one realm, one frontier remains unexplored, hidden beyond the impenetrable curtain that we know as death. To some it is no frontier at all, but rather a vast nothingness, an eternal sleep from which we shall never awaken. To others it is a wondrous land filled with endless and eternal possibilities. There is one certainty—we shall all embark upon an expedition into that mysterious realm.

So what lies beyond this life? Does something of us remain beyond that last breath? Is death the end, or just the beginning? To the Christian, the answer is clear; death is the beginning of a journey that extends beyond the vanishing point on the horizon, through eternity into infinity.

But what is life after death like?

The earliest writings of the Old Testament did not confront the issue of life after death directly. Later, events like Saul's encounter with Samuel's spirit through the incantations of the Witch of Endor (see First Samuel 28:4-25), suggest that an afterlife exists. Yet in the Book of Ecclesiastes, Solomon seems to suggest that there is no life after death, and that the dead know nothing.

> *For the living know that they shall die: but the dead know not any thing, neither have they any more a reward; for the memory of them is forgotten* (Ecclesiastes 9:5).

Even at the time of Jesus, the Jews were strongly divided on this issue. The Pharisees believed in the existence of spirits, angels, and the resurrection of the dead. But the Sadducees believed in none of these things.

> *For the Sadducees say that there is no resurrection, neither angel, nor spirit: but the Pharisees confess both* (Acts 23:8).

Jesus spoke extensively about the Kingdom of Heaven, as well as about outer darkness, a place of wailing and gnashing of teeth. In the parable of Lazarus and the rich man, He even gives us a glimpse into that realm (see Luke 16:19-31). Yet, even in the New Testament, our glimpses of Heaven and Hell are vague and fleeting.

In the middle ages, the poet Dante Alighieri (1265-1321) gave a detailed account in his *Divine Comedy* as to the nature of Heaven and Hell. Was his a vision, a divine revelation, or just a satirical commentary on the state of the Church? My personal feeling—it was a little bit of both.

Divine revelation, from God's Holy Spirit, must travel from our spirit, through the filter of our own experience, and onto paper. Along the way, it can potentially lose something in translation. Likewise, it can also pick up extra baggage. This is why we must not be too quick to accept the words of a modern-day prophet or visionary at face value. We must first take a long hard look at the fruit of that person's spirit. That which is flesh is flesh, and that which is spirit is spirit. Spiritual revelation does not come from the flesh.

In the last few years, several prominent books on the subjects of Heaven and Hell have been published—books inspired by divine revelation. I will not be so bold, or so foolish, as to judge the merits of these works based on my own experiences. I can only attest as to where and how this work you hold in your hand arose. As you read through it, you might encounter startling similarities between it and other works. There are many ministries, but only one Spirit.

I am a scientist, schooled in the discipline of the scientific method. My encounter with Christ came in the fall of 1972 when I was 18 years old. Before that, I openly admit to being most cynical when it came to spiritual matters. Through an amazing near-death experience, I became a new creature through Christ Jesus. But, that didn't mean that I abandoned the scientific method; far from it.

There is no conflict whatsoever between my faith in God, and my studies in astronomy, physics, and quantum mechanics. Indeed, through the melding of these influences, I have received a most unique perspective on the universe. That perspective will become clear as you read this book. Through it, I hope you will come to see the places called Heaven and Hell in the grand scheme of a multidimensional universe.

Do I truly believe that Heaven and Hell are as I describe them here? Absolutely, yes. The elements of this book emerge from my studies of the Bible, the divinely inspired Word of God. Others emerge from my studies in science. Even the study of history plays a role.

As a man who loves God, with all of my soul and all of my heart, I try to maintain a healthy and vital prayer life. Yet some of the questions I ask God in prayer are, to say the least, unusual. They have included questions about the nature of space time, the fabric of the universe, and cosmological constants. And, yes, they have been answered, though it may take me some time to comprehend those answers. God is a loving Father, but His thoughts are far above ours.

And, yes, I have experienced powerful visions that have shaped the chapters of this book. I have tried to reproduce them faithfully. This book is a work of fiction, viewed against the backdrops of a Heaven and Hell that are very real. I hope that the story that unfolds before you will be a blessing to you and that it will bring glory to our heavenly Father.

chapter one

A flurry of snowflakes swept around their car, as Chris Davis and his young wife, Serena, sped down the dark country road toward home. Serena placed her arm around her husband as she gazed out into the swirling snow, illuminated in the glare of the headlights. To her it seemed like a sort of magical fantasy, a grand dance of snowflakes played out against a darkened stage as large as nature itself. It was a special performance, just for the two of them.

She was still dressed in the medieval garb she had worn to the ARS banquet. How she loved to dress up—the long, flowing lace dress was an escape from the realities of the technological present. She often thought about being part of a simpler time and place, how wonderful it must have been.

Chris smiled broadly as he glanced toward his lovely wife. They'd had a wonderful evening of food, laughter, and good company; still, Serena suspected that Chris played the part of a medieval scholar at these dress-up events more to please her than anything else.

Another ten minutes and they would be home. They would slip into something more comfortable, and curl up together in front of the fireplace. After all, tomorrow was Saturday; they had the whole night to play.

Chris didn't see the patch of ice on the curve of the darkened highway until it was too late. When they had passed this way three hours before, only a trickle of water was melting from a roadside snow bank. Now, it formed a deadly sheet of ice.

His eyes grew wide with fear as the small car slipped across the solid yellow line and into the opposing lane of traffic. He battled for control as the tires slid wildly back and forth. If they'd had the road to themselves, it would have been scary enough; but then they saw the headlights of an 18-wheeler that appeared out of nowhere and was bearing toward them. It was the dark essence of a nightmare, a possibility neither of them had ever envisioned. Now they stared at it head-on.

The car hit the guardrail first, then bounded into the path of the oncoming leviathan. The impact ripped through their world, as the sheet metal of their small import bent and twisted like cardboard.

"Oh Chris!" cried Serena, trying her best to brace herself. She was propelled toward the windshield because no seatbelt restrained her.

Chris slammed into the steering wheel and then against the driver's side door. The car spun; then tumbled over and over again, crashing through the guardrail and into a power pole where it finally came to rest, wrapped about the stout pillar, a steaming mass of twisted metal. For a moment, there was nothing but silence.

With difficulty, Serena picked herself up from the cold, snowy ground. She was still shaking as she rose to her feet. She was disoriented, surprised not to be in pain. She remembered being tossed about in the tumbling car, or did she? The past few minutes were a blur. Perhaps she was in shock, injured beyond the point of pain. She looked at herself and discovered that she had sustained not a single bruise or cut. Even her dress had survived the impact without so much as a rip. Somehow she'd been thrown from the car and landed in the soft snow.

She glanced back at the car and saw that the passenger's side door was crumpled, but very much closed. The window was closed too. She thought that the door must have flown open during the crash, just long enough for her to have been thrown free. She looked more closely— was that blood on the window? She couldn't be sure from where she was standing, it was too dark. No, it couldn't be. She looked at her arms and legs and felt her head once more to verify that she was fully intact. Not a scratch.

"Unbelievable!" she gasped. Had luck been with her or what? Then a wave of horror swept over her like a dark shroud. Maybe it is blood, but not hers. "Chris! Where are you? Oh God, are you all right?"

Serena was filled with dread. What if her love was still within that twisted wreck, perhaps horribly crushed? Suppose he was dead! How could she go on?

"I'm OK," Chris said.

Serena turned to see Chris rise to unsteady legs on the other side of the car. He seemed dazed, but unharmed. His eyes met Serena's.

"Are you all right?"

"Yes, I am now," she said.

Chris looked at the mangled car, took a step toward it, then stopped. "Serena, do you smell that? It's gasoline—it might explode!"

That was a thought she hadn't considered. It would be indeed ironic to miraculously survive the crash, only to be killed in an explosion. Serena ran as fast as she could through the snow, crossing the guardrail, and meeting Chris along the side of the road, about 50 feet from the car. They embraced.

"Thank you Lord Jesus," Chris said, wrapping his arms about his shivering wife. "I thought for sure I'd lost you. That old car can be replaced—you can't. Maybe our next car will have airbags."

He looked back at the 18-wheeler which had finally managed to stop about a hundred yards down the road. The driver had jumped from his rig and was running toward them. Chris waved his arms in the air. "I bet we scared the begebers out of that poor guy."

"And don't forget me," Serena said, managing a slight chuckle. "You'll have an interesting story to tell in church this Sunday." Serena turned toward the car that was twisted around the power pole and shook her head. "People just don't walk away from these kinds of accidents, but we did."

"Maybe a guardian angel saved us," Chris said, taking her hand and walking toward the truck driver. "It's very possible. With God, all things are possible."

That response didn't surprise Serena in the least. Chris often spoke of heavenly matters. Actually, she was surprised that he'd never become a preacher himself. He would have made a good one. Perhaps it was her lack of spirituality and religious conviction that had hindered him. She hoped not.

They stopped about 20 feet from the car. Amazingly, the right headlight was still shining, illuminating their surroundings. The glare of the lone headlamp prevented them from getting a really good look at the full extent of the damage. They'd been so concerned about each other, that they hadn't given the condition of the car much thought. It was totaled, that much was certain. Chris hesitated for a moment, apparently considering if it was safe to draw any closer to the twisted hulk. There was no sign of a fire, and only a trace of steam rising from the shattered radiator. The only event in this car's future was a journey to the scrap yard.

"We're OK!" yelled Chris, waving again at the approaching truck driver. It seemed strange that he didn't respond.

"Wait here," Chris said, stepping from the glare of the headlight and toward the contorted hunk of metal and glass.

"Maybe we should all wait for the state police," Serena said. "The car could still explode.

"It's OK," Chris said to his wife. "If it was going to explode it would have done so already." He turned toward the car again. "This is strange; the driver's side door is still closed. So is the window. How in the world was I thrown clear?"

"Oh Chris, I wish you'd wait," repeated Serena, as her husband approached the driver's side door. "I have a really bad feeling about this."

Chris dismissed his wife's warning, and looked in the car window. His expression spoke of his horror. He blinked, rubbed his eyes, yet the apparition remained.

"Serena, come here! This, this can't be!"

Serena hesitated, then joined her husband by the car door. "Chris, no, oh God, it's us! How can we be in there and out here at the same time?"

Now, the truck driver, too, stood at the driver's side door. His flashlight revealed two contorted and blood-soaked figures, a young man and woman. He did not notice the uninjured doubles standing by his side.

Serena stepped back and into the glare of the lone headlight, as she witnessed her husband's hand pass through the driver's shoulder like some sort of phantasm. Then she noticed that her body cast no shadow on the snowy landscape. "No," she whimpered.

Chris retreated to his wife's side, speechless. It was Serena who spoke the unthinkable.

"Chris, we're dead, we're ghosts." Her voice was quivering and uncertain. "But we can't be, I mean, I can still feel and think. My body is warm, I'm breathing." Serena reached for her wrist, searched frantically for her pulse. She was relieved when she found a fast but strong rhythm. "My heart is still beating, how can I be dead?"

Chris didn't respond. Something else had caught his attention, something that hadn't been there just an instant before—a warm breeze was blowing from somewhere, driving away the cold of the winter night.

Serena turned around to see a bright point of light floating in midair. It looked like a beautiful, white star, adrift some 30 feet away. It grew brighter, becoming an increasing disk of luminance, pushing back the darkness of the snowy night. No, not a disk, a portal with depth and substance, a softly glowing tunnel, and at its end, a light that now appeared as bright as the sun. No, brighter even than that.

The distraught truck driver took no notice of the wondrous spectacle, as he struggled to open the twisted driver's side door of the car. Why should he? This luminous phenomenon was part of another world, another reality. It illuminated Chris and Serena in its radiance, yet its light seemed not to affect anything else around them.

Chris hugged his wife and gazed into the light. "It's so bright. I know that it should hurt my eyes, but it doesn't. And can you feel it, Serena? Can you feel the love coming from the light? Did you ever feel anything like it?"

Serena shielded her eyes from the light. It was so bright. She too sensed the love it emanated, yet she felt fear as well. She seemed frozen in time, unable to move. She'd read about this sort of apparition. It was the ever-present constant in all near-death experiences—the tunnel of light. It was real. But this was no near-death experience—this was real, a one way tunnel from this life to whatever existed beyond.

"Come on," Chris said. "That's where we've got to go."

"I don't know about this, Chris," warned Serena. "You don't know what's at the end of that tunnel. It might not be what you think."

Apparently Chris hadn't heard her, or hadn't wanted to, because he began walking toward the light, drawing her with him. She walked by his side, drawing strength from his touch. Without his help, she was certain that she would not have been able to move at all. She squeezed his hand. Yet his touch was becoming ever more tenuous. It wasn't that his grip was weakening, it was her ability to feel his touch that was fading. It was almost as if he were, somehow, less real. He didn't seem to notice as he walked boldly toward the portal.

They were at the very threshold of the tunnel, when her hand slipped from her husband's grip. A moment later, he vanished into the soft glow, leaving her behind. She tried to follow him, but no matter how hard she tried she couldn't move. Why hadn't he returned for her? Didn't he realize that she was no longer beside him?

"Chris!" she cried, yet her voice was barely above a whisper.

She stood there, paralyzed and weeping. She had been forbidden entrance. It was a force greater than her will that had decreed it, and it was not within her power to disobey.

The brilliant light at the end of the portal faded from sight, even as the warm breeze ceased. It was replaced once more by the cold darkness of the winter night. Then the apparition vanished completely. A chill swept through Serena, a chill that went beyond the coldness of the night. She'd been denied the right to enter the next life, if that was indeed what lay beyond.

She was gripped with fear. Minutes passed, minutes of near total paralysis, giving her ample time to ponder her fate. Was it her destiny to become a ghost, a lost and restless spirit doomed to wander Earth forever? She had read more than her share of books on the topic as a youth. Her inability to move? Some experts insisted that ghosts remained close to the place of their deaths for years. Perhaps, like her, they experienced some form of spiritual paralysis that kept them there.

Sure, there were lots of people who had claimed to have had visitations from the dead, and some of them were pretty scary, but there was no documented proof for their claims. She had come to dismiss such things as hoaxes, perhaps results of a natural phenomenon compounded by an overactive imagination. The current circumstances, though, were compelling her to reconsider her previous conclusions.

In the midst of her contemplations, her ghostly existence was interrupted as another unearthly portal materialized out of the emptiness, not far away. Yet this one was very different from the first. It was an undulating violet-colored corridor, pulsing with arcs of blue electricity. It seemed endless and foreboding, a dark passage leading into infinity.

No sense of love emanated from this dark abyss; indeed, it seemed the incarnation of despair. It was brooding, sinister, yet irresistible. This was her portal, the gateway to her destiny.

"No, please, I don't want to go in there," she murmured.

But what she wanted didn't matter. She slowly stepped toward it as in a trance, and felt as light as a snowflake as she was swept off her feet and into the void of the portal. She felt its electric presence, like an army of ants crawling over every inch of her body—it was cold, far colder than the winter night.

She became nothing more than a weightless and inconsequential vapor as she tumbled down end over end into a bottomless pit. It was a helpless, sickening feeling.

Tenuous clouds of red and violet against a dark gray background swept past her. Was she really falling or just being swept along by some invisible current? She couldn't tell. The experience was totally disorienting and absolutely terrifying.

She looked at her hand and discovered that it was nothing more than a translucent form. She gazed down to see that her body was also transparent—like one of those plastic models she pieced together when she was in junior high school. Being the model was not nearly so much fun.

She screamed, yet she couldn't hear her voice over the roar of the ethereal winds that swept her along. She wondered if there was a destination. Perhaps she would be swept along through this ethereal realm throughout all eternity.

She thought of Chris. Where was he? Was he experiencing anything like this? She hoped not.

How long or how far she was carried, she couldn't say. In this realm there were no constants, no frames of reference for either time or space. Even existence itself was tenuous, measured only by the extent of her fear.

She felt a jolt, as if her course had been abruptly altered. There was light ahead, shining forth like a lone beacon into this realm of eternal twilight. A moment later a new world seemed to materialize around her, replacing the ethereal nothingness of the tunnel through which she had passed. She stood in the middle of an arching corridor, perhaps a dozen feet wide, where the floor, walls, and ceiling were composed of the finest, cultured white marble.

She was whole again, a physical entity with weight and all of her senses intact. She turned around, surprised to discover a blank wall, not the formless passageway through which she had just traversed. She touched the wall, caressing its cold smooth surface, as if to verify that this wall was indeed as substantial as it appeared. It was.

Twenty feet ahead, the corridor opened into a chamber of brilliant white vastness. Slowly, deliberately, she walked toward it, unable to resist.

The chamber beyond was like nothing she had ever seen. Before her was something of great brilliance, that she could not immediately distinguish. Its radiance caused the white-tiled marble floor to glisten brightly.

Serena spun around and saw many tiers of seats descended in a square pattern toward the central arena in which she stood. In those seats sat a great multitude of people, all dressed in pure white. Standing in the central arena, she was separated from them by a shimmering marble wall, perhaps 8 feet or so in height. All eyes were focused on her, which gave her a very uneasy feeling. She was the center of attention. What did they want from her? What did they expect her to do?

She gazed up to see that this place had no ceiling in the conventional sense. Although the perimeter of the vast arena was replete with many towering marble columns, they appeared to serve no purpose beyond a decorative one. Above her, great billowing clouds towered toward an azure blue sky. It was awesome, yet frightening.

Again her gaze turned toward the bright radiance before her. She could perceive a great white throne, upon which sat a being who appeared to be the source of the radiance. She could not see the figure clearly, nor could she see what lay beyond the throne. Perhaps it was nothing more than the fourth wall of the arena, but maybe it was something else.

The impression she felt now was not so different from that she had felt emanating from the portal that her husband had vanished into. There was an overwhelming sense of love here, as though love itself could take on a physical form. Yet there was something else—fear. The fear did not originate from the being upon the throne, but rather was generated from within her own soul as a result of his tremendous presence.

Out of the glare stepped a slender being, standing well over 6 feet in height. Its pallid flesh took on essentially human contours, though unusually smooth and exceptionally symmetrical. It wore white sandals upon very human feet, and was clothed in a long and flowing white robe. From its waist, hung a long sword, its blade hidden beneath an intricately crafted golden scabbard.

Yet this being's most striking feature was a pair of enormous white wings, which arched outward and upward from the back of its shoulders. If fully extended, Serena was certain they would have easily spanned a dozen or more feet from tip to tip. She was unsure as to whether they were composed of individual feathers, or even whether they served anything more than an ornamental function.

Its eyes were blue and piercing, and its golden hair long and glistening. It was difficult to determine the being's gender, and Serena wondered if gender was even relevant when dealing with an angel.

The awesome yet beautiful being watched her every move carefully. Its expression betrayed no emotion.

"Welcome, Serena," the being said in a voice that did not reveal its gender. "Come with me, child. The time of your judgment is at hand." It motioned with its right hand toward the brilliant being behind it.

"My judgment?" gasped Serena, turning suddenly pale. "I don't understand."

"It is appointed once to a man or woman to die, then to judgment," was the reply.

"But where is Chris? He was with me but we got separated."

"He is not here," replied the angel, placing a gentle hand upon the young woman's shoulder, guiding her on the way. "It is not the time to speak of such things. It is your moment to stand before God, your creator, and give an account of your 28 years on Earth."

"God?" repeated Serena. "You mean God, like in the Bible?"

"The only God," confirmed the angel, who hurried Serena across the marble courtyard. "He whose will holds sway over the entire universe, over all things."

Serena felt confused and increasingly fearful as she was guided toward the very heart of the immense glow whose brilliance dominated the entire arena. She was taken to within a few dozen feet of the great being upon the throne. At the urging of the angel, she fell to her knees.

Amidst the great luminance, Serena did her best to make out the features of He who sat upon the throne. Serena wondered if it might be sacrilegious to even make the attempt. He was clearly of enormous stature, at least 10 feet in height. Like the angels, He was robed in white, yet every part of this being glowed, especially His eyes. He seemed to have long golden hair, but not the long beard she had often seen in paintings. For a time, His gaze seemed focused upon the kneeling woman; then it shifted to one side.

"Let the books be opened," He announced in a voice like thunder.

Serena turned to her right to see another angel robed in white. This one stood behind an ornate crystal podium that faced the being who sat upon the great white throne. Atop the podium was a large open book. He seemed to be studying it intently, turning page after page.

Serena directed her gaze once more toward the figure upon the throne. This time, instead of the figure, she saw an image of herself as a young child playing with her friends amidst a cloud of blue. Events that brought back fond memories, as well as those she would have sooner forgotten, swept through the vision before her. She saw herself learning sign language to befriend a deaf girl she had known in her youth. A 12-year-old Serena collected a thin and tossed away kitten from behind the mall and nursed it back to health. She saw herself as a teen reading to her grandmother in the hospital. She remembered the love they shared.

Yet all was not goodness and light. She witnessed once more the dreadful arguments between herself and her mother; heard the harsh and angry words. They had argued about so many things—clothes, friends, schoolwork. Her mother had been a rigid disciplinarian who seemed to lack the ability to see a situation from any perspective other than her own. The strong-willed youth's rebellion was inevitable.

In the end, their war of words had escalated in directions Serena had never expected. It was her mother who had finally resorted to committing her to a mental hospital at the age of 14. Rebellious, mentally unstable, and a danger to herself; is how Serena's mother described her daughter to the hospital administration. Nothing Serena said altered the fate her mother had selected for her. Her background as a youth probation officer for the county gave her more credibility and more contacts within the system than a confused teenage girl. Eventually, committing her daughter to a mental institution was a simple matter.

Serena had been confined in that nightmarish realm for more than three months. Those were the darkest of the dark times. The drugs, the incessant testing, the mind games that they referred to as counseling, broke her will. In a world of profound isolation, she was compelled to conform to her mother's will and admit her own failings. Anything else was self-destructive.

She remembered night after night praying for deliverance from that dreadful place. As time passed and her prayers went seemingly unanswered, her mind descended into a sort of fantasy realm, a place of escape from the unpleasant reality around her. She imagined herself as a fair maiden imprisoned in a dark and foreboding dungeon by an evil wizard. Her surroundings, though far from the stereotypical medieval dungeon, reinforced her fantasy—locked doors, cries in the night, constant heavy-handed supervision.

In the end, it was her stepfather who had been her knight in shining armor. It was he who had finally brought her home, against her mother's wishes. In the ensuing years, he was the diplomat who had managed to keep their home in a state of uneasy peace. Yet the rift between Serena and her mother remained until her mother's death nine years later.

Still the dark times continued.

Although she was an exceptional student in school, well-mannered and well-liked by her teachers, the fearful months in the mental hospital had marked her both socially and emotionally. She had become very quiet and withdrawn, making few friends of her own age in school. Most of her classmates stayed away from the thin, plain-looking youth who had spent time in the "nut house."

All sorts of stories about her mental state were rumored throughout the school. Because of her good grades, she was inducted into the National Honor Society, yet even this accolade gave her no status among her peers. When the school day came to a close, she withdrew into a world of her own.

Now, standing in the arena gazing toward the throne, she saw herself at home, in the midst of reading book after book on the occult. They had seemed harmless enough at the time, yet they had inevitably led her down a twilight path to paganism, tarot card reading, and magical rituals that gave her the illusion of power. They replaced the all too familiar sense of helplessness. She found escape in a variety of dark pursuits, imagined ancient gods and goddesses, and other fantasies that seemed preferable to the realities of her existence.

Somewhere along that path to perdition, her moral fiber had become tattered and frayed, as her affair with a married man 20 years her senior had demonstrated. She was 18 at the time—a wild fling with one of her former high school teachers. The affair lasted only a few months, and as far as she knew, no one had been the wiser. After all, these things happen—no one is to blame.

But now in the vision she saw it all very differently. There had been suspicions, innuendoes, talk of impropriety. Inevitably, the rumors had reached her lover's wife through a variety of channels. Serena had been instrumental in weakening an already strained marriage, a marriage that eventually and inevitably dissolved.

"All lives in the world touch all other lives," announced the angel who stood behind the podium. "It is within our power to influence them for the better, or for the worse. Your actions, your sins, brought about the latter."

Serena's life rushed forward in a dizzying collage of imagery. She witnessed her first marriage. She'd known Kevin since high school. He had been one of her few friends. Like her, he was an outsider and interested in the fantasy world of renaissance festivals and occult powers. It seemed a perfect match.

They'd had such noble goals. They would put each other through college, and in time, live the good life. They worked so hard, yet life seemed to have conspired against them. Demoralized and discouraged, Kevin had retreated into a world of computer-generated fantasy. Sitting in front of a video monitor for hours at a time, he became in cyberspace what he could not be in reality, a success, even a hero. At a time when she needed his support the most, Serena was ignored. Her attempts to become closer to him, to even be noticed, earned her a new name—a high-maintenance wife. That's what Kevin had called her.

In the end, Serena had found the comfort she so desperately needed in the arms of other men, and at one point, another woman. In their company, she explored her darkest fantasies. She became the submissive, the slave, the witch, and the wench; whatever pleased her partner. At times she took some terrible risks, once allowing herself to be strangled to the point of asphyxiation.

Kevin knew of her nightly dealings, if not the specifics, at least the generalities. Yet, it didn't seem to bother him. At least when she was out, she wasn't disturbing his game. With Serena and Kevin pulling in two different directions, their marriage had lasted less than two years. When it was over, Serena descended into a deep depression that several times brought her close to self-destruction. Yet in the midst of her despair, had come the birth of new hope.

She first met Chris at the health food store where she worked. A few brief conversations with this charming man led to lunch at a downtown coffee shop, then to a more formal date. When she was with Chris, she was lifted from the depths of despair. He was charming, thoughtful, and amusing. He spoke of such wonderful ideals. He talked about God's love, about trying to make a difference in the world. She even went to church with Chris, more to please him than to seek out his God.

After all, if God did actually exist, where had He been these last nine years as her life had gone from bad to worse? If He was so merciful, why had He allowed her grandmother to suffer so much during her last year on Earth? Her grandmother's faith had remained strong to the end, yet to Serena, it seemed as if God had abandoned her. No, her life's experiences had hardened her heart when it came to believing in the existence of a loving and merciful God.

Chris seemed to realize that Serena had no real interest in his church or his faith, though she did a good job at pretending she did. But it didn't matter. He had fallen as much in love with her as she had with him. Their love led Serena to the altar one more time. This marriage was different—Chris was an attentive, compassionate husband, and Serena was absolutely faithful to him.

For the first time, love was more than sex, deeper than a physical sensation. Love was caring and nurturing, and in the arms of Chris, it grew stronger as the years passed. Chris claimed over and over that it was Christ within him that allowed him to love her as he did. At first, Serena wasn't so sure that she was buying that explanation. After all, how could the spirit of a long dead prophet live inside of her husband? Still, there was clearly something wonderfully different about Chris. He had a sweet spirit about him. It was that aspect of his character that had initially attracted her to him.

To please her husband, Serena continued to go to church with him. That was the goal foremost in her mind. She even became involved in the charitable activities of her husband's church.

For Serena's sake, Chris had done his best to take an interest in some of the things that motivated her, short of compromising his own relationship with his God. Therefore, attending renaissance fairs and the like became an integral part of their lives, and had given rise to the medieval scholar character Chris played at the events. To him, it was a small price to pay for his wife's happiness.

Those five wonderful years passed before her quickly—the sweet Serena lived once again. Her husband had become her whole world. His love had changed the course of her life. Yet somewhere along the road she had missed something crucial, her husband's love for God. Now she feared that omission might separate them for all eternity. She hoped against hope that she was wrong. After all, she had changed so much during these past five years, did so much good.

Surely, God would realize that, it was in the vision that played out before the courtroom for all to see. She wasn't the woman she had been. Through her husband's church she had clothed the poor, fed the hungry, and visited the sick. She had done all of these things cheerfully and without complaint. Didn't Jesus say that whenever you did these things for even the least of God's children, that you had done it for Him? Maybe, just maybe, it would be enough.

It was difficult to say how much time had transpired when the images before her finally faded. She gazed up at the figure sitting on the throne; He seemed deep in thought. Then He turned His gaze toward the angel who stood behind the podium. "Does her name appear in the Lamb's Book of Life?"

The response was immediate and definitive. "No, Lord, her name does not appear in the book."

God's eyes turned toward the woman kneeling before Him. "Then the time has come to pass judgment upon you, child. Serena Farnsworth, the books have been opened, your life's deeds have been reviewed, and you have been found wanting. Do you have anything to say in your own behalf before judgment is cast?"

Serena was shaking all over. Somehow she'd hoped that these proceedings would have gone a little better than they had. Chris had warned her about this day, he'd practically pleaded with her to utter those few simple words. Why hadn't she been able to put her belief in that pagan goddess aside? The goddess wasn't here to save her now. Only Jesus could have done that. How easy it would have been to avoid all this, to have said the prayer of faith with Chris, but now it was too late.

But what about her husband? God had just addressed her by her maiden name, not her husband's name. What could that mean? Her fate was sealed, she knew that. Her concern now was for Chris. She gathered up her courage.

"My husband," pleaded Serena, tears flowing down her cheeks. "What's going to happen to him? Please, Lord, please tell me."

The mighty figure upon the throne gazed into the eyes of the distraught woman. There was compassion in His eyes.

"Peace, be still, child. He of whom you speak is no longer your husband. That is why I call you by your maiden name. Years ago, he accepted the gift that I had offered him, the gift I offer to all humanity. My only Son was sent into your world to prove to all the reality of my love. He became the perfect sacrifice, paying the penalty for the sins of all humanity. Through His sacrifice, all people gained the right to be called my sons and daughters. Chris is now my son, through an act of faith. He dwells even now with a great multitude in Heaven. Let your heart not be troubled, he is in my hands now and forevermore. But you, child, you are no daughter of mine. Nor are you any longer the wife of my son."

The radiant figure rose slowly to his feet. All the while His eyes remained fixed upon the woman before Him.

"Even as you go into outer darkness, know that My mercy endures. I know how dearly Chris loved you. To realize that you were in the hands of satan would burden him with grief for all eternity. Surely, you would not desire such a destiny for him. For this reason, I have removed all memory of your existence from his mind and from the minds of all of the saints. For them it will be as if you had never existed. You shall remember the love you shared, but he will not. It is best that things are this way, for his sake."

Serena's despair deepened, as she felt a gentle hand upon her shoulder. She looked over to see the angel who had guided her to this place. He motioned for her to rise to her feet; she complied.

"Miss Serena Farnsworth, you shall be removed from my presence and that of the saints," commanded the mighty being before her. "In outer darkness you shall abide, a place of wailing and gnashing of teeth, there to dwell with satan and his angels until the day of final judgment. Let it be done."

The angel guided Serena to the left, away from the judgment seat of God. Before her, a great amber vortex opened. Serena could sense the vast void, the emptiness that was a place without the presence of the Spirit of God. The swirling undulating corridor arched downward, downward into the eternal abyss reserved for the damned.

For an instant, Serena turned to behold the face of God one last time. She was surprised to see sadness upon the face of the Creator of the universe. Even now He grieved for her.

"Come, child," bid the angel, taking her hand in his. "We must go."

Serena watched the great courtroom fade into the mists as she was drawn into the vortex. She sensed she was falling as she and the angel plunged headlong toward places unknown.

chapter two

SERENA felt a sense of profound nausea as she plummeted through a confusing corridor of swirling turbulent clouds, occasionally illuminated from within and without by ragged bolts of lightning. She heard the low rumble of thunder and felt static electricity coursing around her as she plunged into the netherworld. As she proceeded ever deeper into the abyss, the environment grew darker, more sinister. The glowing clouds around her seemed to lose their luminous energy, fading to gray ragged masses of oozing vapor. Then she saw what looked like a tunnel suspended in space, a portal leading to the realm of the damned.

Gray clouds swirled into the tunnel like waters descending into a drain; and as they were swept in, they vanished into the darkness. It was a terrifying sight to behold, like a special effects expert's version of a black hole. Yet, unlike a black hole, the walls of this tunnel appeared not to be composed of swirling vapors, but rather of dark shadowy rock that faded away to a realm of total darkness the deeper they went.

It didn't make any sense, it was surreal, and yet its form was unmistakable. How could such a thing be? It was like an enormous cave, miles wide. Near its mouth, something caught Serena's eye. It was there for but a moment; then gone. A long slithering form like a titanic snake emerged from its lair and into the light, then retreated to lurk in the shadows, just out of sight.

She looked to the angel who continued to firmly hold her hand in his. The angel's wings were fully extended now. He turned and pivoted, navigating his way amidst the turbulent clouds and swirling eddies of this eerie realm. He drew her closer to him as the turbulence increased, as they grew closer to the dark and chilling passageway.

Again the form appeared, much closer this time. It was not so much like a snake as it was like a winged dragon. There were frills around its neck, and coarse scales covered its long sinuous body. It turned, rolled, and pirouetted about the entrance to its lair. Only then did Serena see the others—a myriad of tiny forms, dwarfed by the mighty serpent, being swept along with the clouds into the darkness. They were humans, a great multitude of them, caught up in the ethereal winds and swept into the darkness. The great dragon watched them, every last one of them, as they tumbled helplessly into his lair. Here and there she saw a few who had angelic escorts, like herself, but most of them were alone.

It was then when Serena realized that the dragon was watching her. His gaze did not leave her for a very long time as she was swept toward him. Her heart was filled with terror at the sight of this netherworld behemoth, whose form now filled her entire world. It was more than just his appearance or size that frightened her, it was his aura. She could sense his evil—as though evil itself was incarnated in this fleshly form. A scream froze in her throat as he loomed closer. Then he abruptly turned away, focusing his attention on others.

As she and the angel passed into the realm of darkness, they were swept into the great tunnel, descending ever deeper. The thundering turbulence faded away to a dead quiet calm. It was an eerie blackness, vast and lonely that surrounded them. The other souls she had seen but a moment before had vanished into the darkness of this realm beyond God's universe. Only the radiant angel, who held her close to himself, lent any illumination or warmth. Serena was certain that without him, this would be a place of unimaginable cold.

And there was something else about this place—an emptiness that penetrated to the depths of her soul. Never had Serena felt such a thing. It went beyond a sense of emotional depression; it was a somber melancholia that emanated from the very darkness itself. She couldn't shake the terrible feeling; something fundamental to life was missing from this place.

The flight continued. Though the angel's wings swept back and forth to a slow but steady rhythm, there was not a breath of wind left in their wake. Perhaps there was no air here at all. In that case, these appendages upon the angel's back were not wings at all in the conventional sense. Perhaps they were some sort of exotic propulsion system. No, what was she thinking of? This couldn't be a vacuum, she was still breathing, or at least seemed to be. No, she wasn't thinking straight.

Serena's attention was drawn to a point of light ahead. It looked like a star, the only star in a vast universe of total darkness. Though it seemed infinitely far off, it was growing steadily brighter.

Within a few minutes it had come to dominate her world, pushing back the dark nothingness, bathing her in an eerie amber illumination. The bright point of light became a phosphorescent disk, an expanding ball of radiance surrounded by the nothingness of the void. She could feel its growing heat. It was indeed a star, a lone sun, the only source of heat and light here in this dismal realm.

A moment later, a dark spot appeared near its center. This sphere of darkness grew rapidly, eventually swallowing up the great luminary, and plunging them into darkness once more. Yet as the disk loomed closer, Serena could see that it was not a true realm of darkness like that which surrounded it. Its growing rim was bathed in a halo of color, a yellow inner ring transitioning slowly to green and blue, with a violet fringe that faded into the blackness. Upon its gray disk, flashes of lightning swept through swirls of mists, while dull red illumination blanketed the landscape below. There was so much to take in. It was both frightening and awe-inspiring.

The strange new vista vanished, obscured by swirling clouds of gray. There was a return of gravity; and an instant later, Serena felt the floor beneath her feet. The angel's wings folded and they were walking. The mists around them parted, and Serena found herself walking down a hewn stone stairway cut into a spiraling rocky corridor. It was an almost claustrophobic environment, illuminated from above by shimmering oddly shaped crystals of fantastic size.

"Where are we?" gasped Serena, trying to take in the unearthly environs around her.

"A small island in the realm of outer darkness," replied the angel, glancing only momentarily at his frightened companion.

That wasn't much of an answer. To someone who was new to this whole state of affairs, it was no answer at all.

"What is outer darkness?" asked Serena, who wanted to hear another voice just as much as she wanted to hear the answer.

"It is a spirit realm beyond your universe, beyond the creation of God," came the reply, "a void, a place largely untouched by the hand of the Creator. Before the Father spoke the universe into existence, there was only a sea of nothingness. Outer darkness is the manifestation of that primal state."

Serena looked around again. She didn't fully comprehend all that the angel told her—everything was happening so fast.

"And into this sea of nothingness came the fallen, those who rebelled against He who had created them," continued the angel.

"Lucifer and his angels?" asked Serena.

"Among others," confirmed the angel. "Lucifer was the name given to him by God, but he long ago rejected that name, so great was the enmity between him and his Creator. He took onto himself a new name, as did the angels who followed him."

"He became satan," Serena said.

The angel nodded. "Here, he and his legions were to be exiled for all eternity, separated from their Creator. Here, they might ponder forever the bitter fruits of their savage disobedience. Even still, God was not without mercy. Amidst the sea of nothingness, He had spoken into being an island, this island, a place where one could stand upon solid ground, breathe life-giving air, and feel the warm orange sun. It was here, that lucifer and his wayward followers came to dwell. This was to be their prison until the day of final judgment. Only in this place would they be able to manifest a physical presence. Beyond this island, they would become but wandering spirits, without form or substance."

"Believe me when I tell you, that existence as a disembodied spirit is not a pleasant alternative. Still, more often than they would like, lucifer compels many of his minions to go forth from this place. They wander your Earth, to spread what influence they can, to beguile humanity, to lure them here, into the hands of their master. Nonetheless, they much prefer to remain here. To them, the world beyond is as a wasteland in which they find no rest."

"I remember reading something like that in the Bible," noted Serena. "Jesus was casting a whole group of demons out of some possessed man. The demons didn't want to be cast out. They pleaded with Him to allow them to go into a herd of pigs, or something like that, rather than be sent out into the world. They had to be in some sort of living creatures, even a herd of pigs."

"This is true," said the angel. "Only their dedication to their master, and his purpose, would motivate them to travel from here and into the spiritual wilderness beyond. Yet, they have been at work here as well, doing their master's bidding. Over time, they have desecrated this world, transformed it into a realm that better suited their needs. You see, even then, they knew that their efforts on Earth would be largely successful, that humans—such as yourself—would one day join them in their exile. They transformed their prison into a world of their own, into an empire that satan could rule. This empire became the place you know as Hell."

"Then this is Hell?" asked Serena, her voice faltering.

"Yes, as far as the eye can see and beyond. This is but a small part of an island prison, lost in the vastness of the sea of nothingness. More than infinity separates it from everything you ever knew. It is a place from which there can be no escape."

Serena was overwhelmed. A sea of nothingness beyond creation? An island prison, an inescapable prison, separated by more than infinity from all she had ever known? Her frightened mind refused to grasp the concept. To her, this angel was speaking in riddles.

Serena and the angel had reached the bottom of the stairway. Before them was a long, level corridor hewn from the surrounding gray rock. On either side of the corridor, were a multitude of small dismal cubicles, each closed off by a set of thick metal bars. From the cells that lined the corridor, Serena heard the pathetic whimpering and crying of many wretched souls. The mournful cries sent a chill through Serena's soul.

The angel paused for a moment, pointing toward the corridor before them. "This is a temporary holding area, one of many, where some of those cast out from God's presence await the pleasure of their new master."

"And what will he do to these people?" asked Serena, who was only beginning to realize that she would soon be among them.

"Do you really want to know?"

Serena only nodded.

"I cannot say what his specific plans are for you," replied the angel, "but it is nothing pleasant, I can assure you. All I can tell you is that I was directed to bring you here, to this place, to await your sentencing."

"Directed by God?" asked Serena.

Only silence answered her question. Then she realized the answer. "No, it was that terrible dragon at the mouth of that portal of darkness, wasn't it? He somehow told you to bring me here, didn't he?"

The angel nodded.

"And you listened to him? Did what he asked?"

Again the angel nodded.

"But why? Answer me that."

"Because that is the way God would have it," replied the angel. "Satan and God are adversaries, but they are, as you might say, on speaking terms. There are agreements, arrangements made between them, even now."

"No way," objected Serena. "How can that be?"

"It is, nonetheless, the case," confirmed the angel. "Have you never heard the story of Job?"

Serena had heard of it many times, but had never actually read the Old Testament book. She knew the basic premise, however. The Book of Job tells how God allows the devil to afflict His faithful servant Job with all manner of curses to test his faithfulness to his Creator. Why? Because the devil had challenged God, claimed that if Job faced true adversity, he would not continue to be faithful to his Creator. By Serena's way of thinking, it implied that God made a bet with the devil, at Job's expense.

The angel continued. "Then you realize that there are lines of communication between the Creator and satan. Satan is, apparently, quite interested in you. The Father agreed to turn you over directly to him."

That sent a chill up Serena's spine. "But why is satan interested in me? What am I to him?"

The angel's answer was slow and deliberate, well rehearsed, as if he'd spoken it a thousand times. "Satan is interested in all of humanity. Satan's envy, his hatred of God knows no limits, child, and it deepened with the passing of time. He cannot strike out at God directly, however he can vent his wrath upon that thing which God loves most deeply, humankind. That is his interest in your kind. However, in your case, his interest would seem to be even greater. You are to have a sentencing hearing before satan himself. I do not know why."

"That isn't normal?" asked Serena.

"No, it isn't," confirmed the angel. "Satan does not have the time to review the case of every human condemned to this place. Some of the lost are dealt with by his many minions who take them to their predetermined place of eternal punishment, there to become just another soul among billions. There is no hearing, no trial, only quick retribution. Still others are never found by his minions at all. They drift through outer darkness as disembodied spirits until the terrible Day of Judgment. For you to have been brought to this place tells me that satan has something special planned for you."

"Then God has thrown me to the wolves. He put me exactly where satan wants me. He did it to all of the people here. He has played right into satan's hands, given him what he wanted. I was delivered to the devil on a silver platter. How can a loving God condone such a thing?" Serena asked.

The angel scowled. "God didn't do this to you, you did this to yourself. God offered you a means of escape from this place, but you rejected it. By your own actions, your own rebellion, you chose to dwell in this place." Again the angel looked down the corridor. "Come, we must get you to your cell. Time is short."

Serena felt the firm grip of the angel's hand on her shoulder. She considered resisting, but realized that it was futile. After all, where could she run, even if she did manage to evade him?

As she was ushered along down the corridor, she glanced into some of the cells. They were all the same, about 8 feet on a side. They contained neither beds nor chairs, and no comfort facilities of any kind. They held not so much as a rock to set upon. They were totally barren cubicles, and only a few were empty. There were men and women of all ages and races here, representing every region of the world. They cried out in many languages yet to a common theme, lamenting a life lost, and an opportunity gone forever.

"This place is like some sort of medieval dungeon," Serena said.

"Of course," replied the angel. "Most of those who have occupied it are from times past. They were better able to relate to its architecture, and the dread it engendered. Your history is replete with such places. Satan knows this well, and has utilized it to prey upon your fears."

Again, Serena gazed about this dreadful place, breathed in the atmosphere of gloom and despair, then looked at her hands, her feet. "I don't get it, why does it all have to be so real? I mean, I'm dead, my body is probably laying in a morgue somewhere back on Earth." She pinched herself, felt the tiny prick. "I have a heartbeat; I still feel; I have a body; how can that all be? I've got to be nothing more than a disembodied spirit, a ghost."

"Yes, this is all true," confirmed the angel, "you would be no more than a disembodied spirit were it not for the mercy of God. It is God who has allowed you to retain a state of consciousness. He has given you the body you now inhabit, a body that, in appearance, is much like the one you possessed in life."

"You also said that most of outer darkness was a zone of nothingness, right?"

"Yes, we traveled through it on our way to this place," confirmed the angel. "Very little of it is otherwise."

"But it just doesn't make sense. God is supposed to be merciful, right? You said there were some souls that satan couldn't find, souls that were allowed to drift free in outer darkness until the Day of Judgment. Wouldn't it be more merciful to just leave me as a disembodied spirit, allow me to drift in this outer darkness of yours? At least I'd be at peace. Was I that bad, that sinful in my lifetime? Why give me a body that satan can torture, and then drop me off right at his doorstep?"

"Because it has been decided that this is how it shall be," replied the angel. "That should be enough for you. Nonetheless, as I said, a countless number of spirits do drift through outer darkness, for it is a realm of spirits. Those spirits of the dead wander aimlessly through the abyss in a sort of dream state, a sleep that shall last until the day of their final judgment. They are hardly conscious of the darkness that engulfs them."

"But not me."

"No, not you," continued the angel. "You are different from those who sleep. In this place you have retained a physical form. The body you seem to possess is similar in many ways to the one you possessed in life, yet in other ways, it is very different. If you are to remain conscious in this realm, you will need a physical form for the sake of your own sanity. God has provided you with that. All of your senses still function. In this new body, you can still enjoy the pleasures of eating and drinking, as well as the bliss of sleep. You can feel warmth and cold, pain and pleasure, sense the odors and tastes of the world around you, just as you did on Earth. God, in His wisdom, has given you this body to make the transition into the realm beyond life less traumatic, more akin to your Earthly experiences. Yet, unlike your Earthly body, this new body is incapable of a second death. No matter how severely it might be injured, it will mend, and do so with astonishing rapidity.

"In Heaven, these aspects of your new body would have become a blessing, but here, they are a curse. As to why you are here, I do not know. I do not understand why some sleep until their final judgment, while others are condemned to this place. I am not so bold as to question my Creator's motives." There was a moment of hesitation. "I did that once, but not again. Now, I exist to serve. I do what I am told, and no more."

That last comment struck Serena as being quite odd. Yet, she did not feel at all inclined to probe into this angel's relationship with God. No, right now, she had troubles enough of her own.

They passed two intersecting corridors, containing still more cells and more souls, whose eternal future held nothing but pain and remorse. These corridors seemed to extend for miles. Serena could only imagine how many people were awaiting their terrible fate in this place. Serena was startled by a loud mechanical clanking emanating from a cell to her right. As she watched, the crude cell door opened, making clear her entrance into the small chamber.

The angel motioned toward the empty cubical. "You will enter your cell now, my child."

Serena couldn't seem to resist the angel's voice, and quietly walked into the small enclave. The massive cell door closed behind her, locking her in. The angel turned to depart.

"Wait," pleaded Serena, moving to the bars of her cell. "Do you have to leave right now?"

"What would be accomplished if I remained?" he asked. "It is not within my power to intervene when satan's minions come for you. Over the years, so many of your kind have pleaded with me to do just that."

"Please, that's not the reason," replied Serena. "Could I at least know your name? Angels do have names don't they?"

The angel turned toward Serena, his expression spoke of his curiosity regarding the nature of her question. "Yes, child, I have a name. It was given to me by God Himself. I am Aaron."

"When this is all over, you will be going back to Heaven, won't you?"

"Yes," replied Aaron.

"Aaron, I would be eternally grateful if you would carry a last message from me to my husband."

Aaron looked at the young woman incredulously. "Child, you don't have a husband. This thing you must accept."

Serena caressed the golden band about her finger. "Aaron, I wish to differ with you. I do have a husband."

"Not in the sight of God," Aaron said, who at this point felt the need to depart. "That is the standard I must uphold. You have become a non-entity. All memory of your existence has faded from Heaven and Earth. The relationship you shared with this man, this son of God, no matter how real it may seem to you, does not exist."

"No," insisted Serena, pointing defiantly to her heart. "It exists here. The love we shared is not dead so long as it still dwells within me. Nothing can take that away."

"I do not wish to be cruel," Aaron said, "please understand. But you must face facts. You do not yet comprehend the relentless agonies of Hell, and what they shall do to you. In a tragically short time, this love you speak of will be ripped from your heart. In the end, this place will leave you with little more than your most primal animal instincts."

"All the more reason for me to give you this message now, while the love within me still lives," insisted Serena.

"You understand that Chris will have no recollection of you, or the love you shared," said Aaron. "Even if I approached him and spoke of you, which I may not, it would mean nothing to him."

"But perhaps, someday, he will remember," replied Serena, tears welling up in her eyes. "I know I will never see him again. I will never get out of here. But you might see him, and if one day, by some miracle he remembers the love we shared, I want to entrust you with a message for him. Will you be able to remember it?"

Aaron smiled slightly. He knew the utter futility of this poor woman's hopes. Nonetheless, he would humor her. It seemed the most humane course of action. "I remember every word I have ever heard. What would you have me tell him, child?"

"Tell Chris that I'm so sorry that I can't be with him now. For the first time I'm beginning to realize the true extent of his love for me. He tried so hard to get me to believe, to get me to accept Jesus as my personal Lord and Savior. He wanted so much for us to be together in paradise, for eternity. He wanted to save me from this."

Serena hesitated, wiping the tears from her eyes. "Tell him that it's not his fault that I'm here, its mine. Though we might be separated for eternity, my love for him will never die, not ever. But I don't want him to mourn for me. I want him to remember us as we were, in the stone house in Oregon. I want him to remember how wonderful life was. Tell him not to think of me as being here."

Serena turned from the bars. "God, maybe it's better if he doesn't remember me." She leaned against the cold stones of the back wall of her cell, weeping softly.

Aaron said nothing.

It was over a minute before Serena turned away from the wall. She was surprised to find Aaron still there, his eyes full of sympathy.

"I'm sorry to make such a scene," said Serena, walking toward the bars. She extended her hand between the bars.

Aaron took her hand in his. "It's all right, child, I understand. I promise that if one day Chris does remember you and the love you shared, if he does seek me out, I will tell him all that you have told me. I will speak of your courage, and of your love for him. After all, our God is a God of miracles."

"Thank you," replied Serena, as their hands parted. "Goodbye Aaron."

Aaron only nodded as he turned to leave. As he walked down the corridor he reflected upon the fate of this poor soul left behind. A single tear welled up in his right eye. How he wished things could have been different.

Serena stood by the bars, watching Aaron walking away until she could see him no longer. She wondered just how much time remained before the demons would come for her.

"Hello," came a greeting from the other side of the corridor.

Serena turned to see the man in the cell across from hers. Amidst the intense emotions of the moment, he had gone unnoticed.

"Hello," she said, not quite sure what else to say.

The slender middle-aged man walked up to the bars of his cell. His dark eyes focused upon his comely companion across the corridor. His gray business suit was wrinkled and dusty. The top several buttons of his white shirt were open, and his black tie hung loosely from his neck. From his appearance and accent, Serena figured him to be of Indian descent.

"You are from my time aren't you, 2007?"

What a strange comment. At first, Serena didn't understand what this man was talking about. Then she glanced at her medieval attire. She managed the slightest of smiles. "Yes, I'm from 2007. I mean that's when I, well, died." She realized that her statement was no less strange than that of her companion. She'd have to learn to think in entirely different terms here. "I'd been at a banquet, an ARS banquet, just before I died."

"Oh, the American Renaissance Society, I've heard of it. Interesting organization," replied the dark-skinned man, nodding his head. He paused, apparently searching for the right words. "I couldn't help but overhear your conversation with the angel," he continued, in a soft voice. "I'm sorry for your loss." He reconsidered his words. "Or is it a separation? How indeed do you define our situation?"

"A nightmare," Serena said.

"Yes," confirmed the man, "would that it were that simple. I fear, however, that this is no simple nightmare. It is a reality beyond the veil of death, a reality that, I must admit, I was not quite prepared for." The man paused. "Oh, but forgive me, I have not introduced myself. My name is Nari Patel, but all of my friends call me Benny."

"I'm Serena Davis. That's who I am, really. But they insist that I'm actually Serena Farnsworth. Farnsworth was my maiden name, you see. I guess they've annulled my marriage, or something like that. I remember my husband, but he doesn't remember me. That's what they tell me. I guess he doesn't love me anymore either. How can you love someone who doesn't exist for you?"

Serena's words had taken on the rambling, disoriented aspect of one whose mind was teetering on the brink of a terrible precipice. She felt so helpless.

"Yes, I heard," replied Benny, his tone soft and understanding. "It's terrible what has happened to you. I only wish that I had some words of wisdom, something that might help."

Serena couldn't continue on with this subject. "How long have you been here, Benny?"

"I'm really not sure," Benny said, fully understanding why his companion had changed the course of their discussion. "Long enough to have become very hungry and very thirsty. Room service here is not so good, in fact, it's nonexistent. It has been, perhaps, two days. When I arrived, this place was mostly empty, but many people have been brought in since then, I think."

"It's almost full now," Serena said.

"Then, perhaps, it will not be long before something happens," noted Benny. "I don't know if that's good or bad."

"I don't think its good," said Serena. "Benny, how did you come to be here?"

"I think the simple answer is that I died." Benny did his best to add some levity to their situation. It didn't work. "I'm sorry, Serena, I know it's not a laughing matter."

"It's OK."

Benny nodded. "Yes, let me start again. I think I got off to a bad start. I guess it all boils down to this; I hadn't put my faith in Jesus, the Christian's Savior. That is what I was told at my judgment. I did my best to put up a good defense at my trial. I explained that I had little exposure to the faith of Christianity until I came to your country. It really isn't a major religion in my native India. How was I to know that it was the correct faith, the only faith? Now I'm here, separated from my wife and children forever, and for what? How was I supposed to know? Tell me that."

Benny turned from the bars and walked to the back of his small cell. There was a long silence.

"Benny, are you OK?" asked Serena, fully realizing after she said it, that no one here could truly be OK.

"No, I don't think so," Benny said with a trace of anger in his voice. "Look, I don't claim to have lived a perfect life, I certainly had my faults. I have a temper for one thing, I admit it; but I do my best to control it. I've never touched my wife, or my children, in any manner other than a loving one. I've been known to twist the truth now and again, especially with the IRS. But I'm not a thief, a murderer, or an adulterer. I've done my best to teach my children right from wrong. I think I did a pretty good job of it."

Benny returned toward the bars, his face was flushed.

"So, at 47, in my office at Motorola, I have a massive heart attack. They rush me to the hospital, but I never make it there. I find myself sitting along the freeway, the pain is gone, and so is the ambulance. I try to wave down a car or two but it doesn't work; no one sees me. Suddenly this dark vortex appears right in front of me. I didn't want to go into it, but I couldn't stop myself."

"It was like that for me, too," Serena said.

"It took you to that huge arena?"

Serena nodded.

"Well, I'm here to tell you, that after that wild ride through that vortex, I was pretty disoriented. I wasn't at my best during my judgment. Still, I wonder if there was anything I could have said there that would have made a difference."

Benny's train of thought was interrupted as an angel marched down the corridor, with a squirming youth in his arms. The young man appeared to be about 16 or 17 years old and was dressed in a white tee shirt and black baggy pants. He was struggling wildly and crying loudly. Neither Benny nor Serena understood what the young man was yelling, it sounded like he was speaking Spanish. His voice faded slowly into the distance. The whole experience sent a chill up Serena's spine.

Benny shook his head sadly. "I've seen a lot of that sort of thing in the past two days. Not everyone goes quietly. It goes on constantly, night and day. That is, if there is a night or day here."

"It's so unfair," said Serena, her voice quivering ever so slightly. "How were we to know?"

"I know," said Benny, his voice soft and understanding. "I wish I could tell my wife and children about what lies beyond death. I want to warn them, to tell them what they need to do to avoid what has happened to me, to us."

"There's a parable in the Bible that's sort of like that," Serena said. "It's about a wealthy man and a poor beggar named Lazarus. The wealthy man had it easy in life. He lived in the lap of luxury. In his day-to-day affairs, he barely took notice of the poor leper. But then, both the wealthy man and Lazarus died. Lazarus went to his reward in Heaven, but the rich man was sentenced to eternity in Hell. The rich man was very thirsty, he begged for a drink from a nearby angel, but was refused. Then he saw Lazarus, far off in Heaven. He begged that if Lazarus could just dip his finger in a cup of water and place a single drop on his tongue, he would be eternally grateful. But the angel told him that there was a great void between him and Lazarus that could not be bridged. Then the rich man asked the angel to go back to Earth on his behalf, and warn his brothers of the terrible fate that might lie ahead of them if they didn't mend their ways. But the angel told him that his brothers had the words of the prophets to warn them of what might lay ahead. If they didn't heed the prophets, why should they heed a message from beyond the grave?"

"But there have been so many people who claimed to be prophets," objected Benny. "So many of them preached conflicting messages, how were we supposed to know which ones to believe?"

"My husband used to say something about the sheep recognizing the shepherd's voice, or something like that. I'm not the person to ask about such things. After all, I'm here with you. I sure didn't recognize the shepherd's voice."

"One thing did truly frustrate me at my trial," complained Benny. "God spoke of my shortcomings, my 'sins' as He called them. Apparently any sins, anything we did wrong, made us unacceptable. Without accepting Jesus, we were pretty much done for. He demanded that I be taken from His sight and into outer darkness, there to dwell with satan and his angels forever."

"I just don't see how my sins compare to those of satan. If I understand Christianity correctly, satan actually challenged God's power, went to war with Him." Benny stepped back and spread his arms. "Picture this, Serena, the rogue's gallery of history, enemies of God and humanity. We have Nero of Rome, who horribly and sadistically killed tens of thousands of Christians in the Circus Maximus, in the name of entertainment. We have Adolph Hitler, author of the holocaust, the murderer of six million Jews in the death camps. There's Miguel de Torquemada, who tortured to death thousands during the Spanish Inquisition. Oh, excuse me; he tortured them in the name of God, so that's OK. Perhaps he is not here at all. And last but not least, we have Benny Patel, who knowingly cheated on his taxes. All are sentenced to the pains of Hell for all eternity. What is wrong with this picture? Am I missing something here?"

His odd discourse might have been mildly amusing, had it not been so very tragic.

"Remember, I'm here too, Benny," Serena said in a soft voice. "I'm as guilty, no, more guilty than you. I practiced witchcraft, dishonored my mother, worshiped a pagan goddess, and committed adultery. Then I refused to accept God's salvation through Christ, because I had become so bitter and sarcastic about how the world had treated me that I couldn't see God's love. Maybe I got what I deserved. Maybe Hell should be my home."

Benny lowered his arms. He felt so very small. His careless words had just made things all the worse. "I'm sorry, Serena."

"I wonder what it's going to be like," said Serena, whose mind had already wandered elsewhere. "Hell; that is. Is it a lake of fire, a huge dungeon filled with cruel and ingenious devices of torture, or what?"

"I'm afraid we're going to find out soon enough," replied Benny, "There's nothing we can do about that. Why should we continue to dwell on it? Let us agree to speak of it no further. Why don't you tell me a little bit about yourself, Serena? I'd really like to get to know you better, even if we never meet again. Regardless of God's judgment, I believe that anyone who loves her husband as deeply and sincerely as you do, is a person worth knowing."

Serena smiled slightly. Right now, she was really thankful to have someone like Benny to keep her company. They both sat down on their cell floors and spoke of their lives—their aspirations and hopes, philosophies and attitudes, life and love, as if it still mattered. After a long time, they both curled up and fell asleep on the cold floor.

chapter three

CHRIS felt no fear as he boldly stepped into the glowing ethereal tunnel. Yet, for an instant, there was a sense of confusion; a sense that something was missing. He glanced at his right hand as if expecting to see something within it. It was empty. It wasn't empty just a few seconds ago, he was certain of it. What had happened? The Earth behind him, and his life upon it, had become a blur. Why couldn't he remember?

That wasn't important right now. No, he would try to put all of that together later. Right now, he was positively overwhelmed by the vastness and beauty of this place. The light ahead of him was bright, and was becoming brighter by the second. It was magnificent. Yet, his eyes were easily adapting to the changing illumination.

He looked around and saw a cylindrical wall of gray clouds, slowly swirling. Here and there, diffused ribbons of light threaded their way through the billowing mists. He was convinced that he was witnessing the subtle glow from hidden bolts of lightning traveling through the depths of the clouds, yet they were not accompanied by any auditory sensation resembling thunder.

He looked down to discover what he already expected; there was absolutely nothing beneath his feet but empty space. He was floating free, weightless. But he experienced none of the vertigo that he certainly would have experienced had his earthly body been placed in the midst of such vastness.

He never cared much for flying. When the captain turned on the "fasten seatbelt" sign, and warned of impending turbulence, he was inevitably the first passenger to go for the little bag in the seat pocket in front of him. Yet, this time he had no problems at all. Actually, this flight was sort of fun.

Stranger still, there was no fear. The sense of indescribable love and peace that he had felt at the entrance to the tunnel was far greater now—it had become all encompassing. If these emotions could be transformed into a tangible entity, they were present within this tunnel. He knew that he was not alone, though he could see no one. He knew he was in good hands, so why worry? For now, he would simply enjoy the ride.

He looked around again, this time with a more analytical eye. How wide was this tunnel of light? He could hardly imagine. There were no points of reference. It was obviously much wider than the 10- or 12-foot portal he had entered just a minute ago. Perhaps it was a dozen miles across, maybe even wider than that. There was so much to take in.

He was in motion, of that much he was certain. He was being carried along by some sort of ethereal wind. He could feel it blowing around him. It was not unlike an earthly wind; yet, it was so much more. It was refreshing, even invigorating, and it seemed somehow alive. It was a crazy thought, but that was his impression of it; a living wind, the breath of God. He was like a sailing ship, carried by steady unerring breezes, to a distant and exotic port. What would that port, that final destination, be like? And how long would the journey take? He could only guess. He figured he had the time to spare.

Beyond the wind, there was no physical sense of acceleration or movement. Still, he was moving toward the light. He had no problem with that. Minutes passed and Chris settled in for the voyage, much as any passenger might do on a long trip. The light at the end of the tunnel was becoming brighter, even as the clouds around him were transformed from gray to white.

Looking at his hand, he discovered that he could see straight through it to the clouds beyond. "Weird," he whispered, though he quickly realized that he could not hear his voice. No, he heard it only within his mind. *This is so cool*, he thought.

For a time, he didn't know how long, he was transformed into a state of pure spirit, free from the limitations of any physical form. In this state of being, he felt indeed close to God. As far as he was concerned, he could have remained in this state forever.

Then, all too soon, physical reality returned. It materialized all around him in the form of a great white antechamber of glistening grandeur. Towering marble columns supported a ceiling of dazzling light, and beyond that, a soft white billowing mist extended as far as the eye could see. There was music too, the most wonderful music he had ever heard. It seemed to be coming from everywhere. Was it real, or was the music simply a manifestation that existed within his mind? He could not say for sure.

Then he beheld something more awe-inspiring than the architecture, more beautiful than the music. A man in a long white robe stood about 20 feet in front of him. Chris realized that this was the man he had seen at the end of the tunnel, the great luminary who radiated not only light but love. There had been no formal introduction, no band of angels gathered about Him, yet Chris knew Him from the instant he first saw Him. This man was Jesus. It should have been no great surprise; after all, He was the light of the world, and the light at the end of it.

He had the appearance of a man in His mid-30s, handsome and solidly built, with light brown hair and a well-trimmed beard. Even now, His form was practically radiant, yet it was His deep blue eyes that caught Chris's attention. They were so kind, so very deep, they seemed to gaze into the very depths of Chris's soul. His face held a loving smile as He looked at Chris. He stretched out His hands, revealing barely discernable scars on both wrists.

"Welcome home, Chris."

Tears of joy welled up in Chris's eyes as he stepped forward to embrace his Savior. After a moment, Jesus spoke again. "Chris, I need you to be of stout heart, for your trial is at hand. Like all men, you must stand before God to be judged."

For a moment, Chris was fearful. He was not proud of everything he had done during the course of his life. How could he possibly stand before God?

"Don't be afraid," Jesus said, His tone and smile reassuring. "I bore the penalty for your sins already, your debt is paid, remember?" Jesus took Chris's hand in His. "I know you Chris, better than you realize. For years you have placed your faith in me, placed your hand in mine, even as I now place mine in yours. Place your faith in me now, and lay your fears to rest. You are in my hands, I assure you. I shall be by your side every minute of the trial."

They walked side by side into the great judgment hall, a vast arena, surrounded by men and women robed in white. Chris took little note of his surroundings. There were many people here, yet Chris's attention was drawn to the figure upon the white throne before him. It was a human figure, as bright as the sun, yet His radiance didn't hurt his eyes. Instinctively, Chris knelt before the figure upon the throne. He was unsure as to whether it was proper to look into the face of God as he did; yet he could do nothing else. What he beheld was magnificent beyond description.

The being upon the throne appeared ageless, with no wrinkles or imperfections. Chris fully realized that, in this case, age was a meaningless concept. Chris remembered that God was a spirit, perhaps He only took on a familiar form for Chris, one that he could relate to.

The white-robed being was of enormous stature, and yet Chris was not as afraid as he thought he might have been. Yes, having Jesus at his side helped a lot, but the Being before him, the Creator of the universe, was the Creator of Jesus as well, the ultimate Father of all. He had so loved the world; that He had sent Jesus to redeem those who lived in it.

A white-robed angel, who stood before the throne, opened a large book. And in that moment, Chris beheld his life, amidst the blue mists of a divine vision. At first he was fearful, ashamed of what might be revealed, yet those things never appeared. He witnessed himself as a child praying the prayer of faith with his mother. He witnessed his own baptism at the church in Eugene, Oregon.

He'd had a little trouble on that day. He'd swallowed some water on the way up from the baptismal pool, and had choked on it off and on for the better part of a minute. It was definitely an embarrassing moment, and here it was for all to see. Had he heard traces of subdued mirth from the vast audience around him? He wasn't sure, but he thought so. He looked nervously toward the angel who stood by the great book, their eyes met. He was surprised to see the expression of mild amusement upon the angel's face. He was unsure as to whether that was a good or a bad sign.

Chris saw himself as a young man, proclaiming his faith in his Savior before his friends at school. He spoke boldly of God's love to them. Some laughed at him, even made fun of him, but most listened. Yes, he had planted a seed in their hearts, more than he had thought. Some of those to whom he had spoken had gone on to accept the good news he had shared with them. This, too, was revealed in the vision.

The vision continued, and he witnessed happy times with his parents at their home, gatherings around the dinner table, in the back yard, in the park. There were so many happy memories.

A tear came to his eye as he saw himself praying with his mother in the hospital during her last days on Earth. Yes, there were some sad times, but nothing for which he should have felt ashamed. Somehow those things had been erased from the record. Somehow? He knew how, didn't he? It was the blood of the Lamb, the blood of Jesus, shed on Calvary. The Bible spoke of the cleansing blood. Now Chris truly understood the meaning of those words. It had to have been the blood that had washed his sins from the record before him, the record that God now reviewed.

When the vision came to an end, and the time came to speak, Chris did not have to defend himself before the judgment seat, for it was Jesus who spoke in his behalf. He spoke of His love for Chris, of faithfulness, and devotion, of the debts He had already paid. When He had finished, God turned to the angel who stood before the judgment seat.

"Does the name of Christopher Alan Davis, appear in the Lamb's Book of Life?" He asked.

There was a pause, a shuffling of pages that could not have lasted for more than a few seconds, yet, to Chris it seemed far longer.

"Yes, Lord," replied the angel, pointing toward an entry made in the great volume before him, "his name appears in the book."

God turned to Chris. There was a broad smile upon His countenance. "Well done, good and faithful servant, well done, my son. Enter into the eternal joy that I've prepared for you."

"Thank you, Lord." A tremendous weight had been lifted from his soul.

Jesus bid Chris to rise. They walked together from the judgment hall, across the white marble floors of the outer courts.

"What now?" Chris asked Jesus. "I mean, where do we go from here?"

Jesus stopped momentarily, looking into His companion's eyes understandingly. He smiled broadly. "Where? That is totally up to you, Chris. A long journey lies ahead of you, as it does for all humanity. The end of life is not the end of man's sojourn, far from it; it is but the beginning. The first steps in any journey are the most difficult and important ones. Those are the ones that you took on Earth. When you accepted Me into your heart, and as you followed Me throughout your life, you decided which direction your personal voyage would take you. You chose the narrow path. Too few people find it, for the world is full of cares and concerns that obscure the way. Though I offer to carry their burdens, most reject me.

For the wide highway that leads to destruction, to Hell, is so much easier to find and travel. They find the pleasures it offers along the way too sweet, too tempting to pass up. But you rejected the easy way; you searched out the narrow path. And it has taken you to the threshold of a wondrous land. You will learn much there, and along the way, you will grow in wisdom as well. God's judgment and mine are now behind you. We are both very pleased with you."

For a moment, Chris seemed confused, "Your judgment, Lord?"

"Yes," Jesus said. "Did you not know that judgment begins in the House of the Lord? For you, judgment is over; but for those who rejected my sacrifice, a final judgment is ahead for them, a judgment at the end of time. But don't be afraid. Today, I have weighed you and the fruit of your faith in Me in the balance. I am very pleased with what you have accomplished. I am very pleased with you. You have fought the good fight. Now the road to eternity lies open before you."

"Lord, I can never thank you enough for opening this road to Heaven for me. I wouldn't have made it without you."

"And you were worth the sacrifice," replied Jesus, placing a compassionate hand upon the young man's shoulder. "Our Father sent me into the world, that you might have everlasting life, that you might have communion with Him, as I do."

"But now that I'm here, what do I do?" Chris asked.

Again Jesus smiled. "Continue the journey. You've done a pretty good job so far, stay the course. I urge you to get to know the Father better, love Him as He has loved you, and love those around you, even as God has loved you. These are the two greatest commandments that I gave you on Earth. Nothing has changed. It is the same in Heaven, as it was on Earth. You followed these commandments on Earth, and I am proud of you. Stay the course, Chris, let the love within you flow to all of those around you."

Chris couldn't help but smile at that comment. It meant a lot to him to hear it coming from Jesus. "Thank you, Lord."

"But there is something else," Jesus said, his tone somewhat more serious. "Chris, you need to stop worrying so much. Worry does not add so much as a minute to your life, or an inch to your height. Take one day at a time. Don't worry about tomorrow because our Father has everything in control. But I know that you are still searching for a starting point, and I shall give it to you. From there the rest will be up to you."

Jesus led Chris into the bright mists beyond the great pillars at the threshold of the outer court. For a moment, they seemed to be walking on air, yet it was neither scary nor confusing. After all, Chris was with Jesus.

They walked a few seconds before they materialized on the grounds of a great mansion. The mansion sat in the middle of a rolling grassy lawn, interspersed with flowers of a variety of colors. They lent a pleasant odor to the cool air. Beyond the wide lawn, a forest of tall trees in full summer foliage surrounded the estate.

The mansion itself was of two-story, Southern antebellum architecture, with four grand white pillars supporting a wide porch in front. Several wooden chairs were scattered about the wide wooden porch, and across the arm of one of them was draped a partially completed knitting project. A single strand of yellow yarn ran from the chair and across the porch, ending in a somewhat dismembered ball near the front door of the house. Not far from the ball, a sleeping black cat was curled up, its head facing the two visitors.

Jesus motioned for Chris to proceed toward the house, and they walked toward the four wide steps leading to the front porch. They were nearly there when the cat opened one eye, then two, to inspect the approaching visitors. The cat stood up and moved toward them.

"No, wait," Chris said. A look of astonishment was on his face as he gazed intently at the yellow eyed cat. "This is incredible! Ebbie?"

The cat's ears perked up, and she came running straight to Chris. She purred loudly as she moved around Chris's legs, the way she always had in life. There were tears of joy in his eyes as he picked her up and held her close. Her purring grew louder.

"It's a miracle," whispered Chris, with his head next to Ebbie's.

Chris remembered the last time he had held her, on that terrible spring evening. He had come home from a movie to find her lying along the road dying after being hit by a car. The cat that had brought him so much joy in his youth, the cat that had mourned with him at the passing of his mother, lay alone in the dark. Yet somehow that night, she had hung onto life, gripped it in her tiny paws until he had come home, if only to say good-bye one last time. She died in his arms that night.

The God who loved all of humanity had shown His loving mercy to a small ball of black fur, uniting them once more. Here, two good friends would never have to say good-bye again.

"Thank you," Chris said, turning to Jesus.

"But, there is more," Jesus said, motioning to the door.

Chris looked up to see a woman in a green print dress standing by the front door. "Mom?"

His mother, Jennifer, stood there in wide-eyed wonder. This was not the pale, weary woman he watched die in a hospital bed 12 years ago—she looked as she did when Chris was a child, young and full of life, no, even better than that, she looked positively angelic.

Jennifer came running across the porch, down the steps, and into a three-way embrace with her son and his cat. "Oh, Chris, I've missed you so much."

Jesus stepped back to watch the happy reunion, a broad smile on His face. It was more than a minute before emotions subsided enough for words.

"Thank you, Lord," Jennifer said. "Thank you for saving my son."

"You taught him well, Jennifer," replied Jesus. "I'm happy for the two of you." Jesus turned to Chris. "Here is your starting point. I leave you with a beautiful mansion and wonderful company to share it with. I'm sure that the two of you have much to talk about."

No, please stay for a while," urged Jennifer. "I have a freshly baked apple pie cooling on the windowsill, all ready to eat. Please, Lord, join us."

Jesus smiled broadly. "How could I possibly refuse an offer like that? One of your wonderful pies and such excellent company are not easily turned down."

The three friends, and their feline companion, retreated to the house. Inside, Chris discovered a mixture of old Southern-style furniture and modern conveniences. It was magnificent.

"Having been born and raised in Alabama, I always dreamed of having a home such as this," said Jennifer, setting out slices of pie on three plates on the kitchen table for her son and special guest. She placed her arm around her son. "It's so wonderful to have you here, still, I expected that I would go many more years before seeing you again. I wanted you to have a long life." There was a moment of hesitation. "And what is it with those clothes? Have fashions changed that much while I've been gone?"

Chris laughed. "No, I joined an organization, a club. One of the things we do is help present renaissance fairs. We have a lot of dress-up events. I'd been at a banquet before, well, before I ended up here."

Jennifer smiled. "My, your interests sure have changed. I seem to remember that you were not all that thrilled with the renaissance festival your dad and I took you to when you were growing up. You were bored. About the only thing that caught your interest was the food, especially that big turkey leg, and that Galileo tent show. Why the big change?"

"Oh," said Chris. "I'm still not all that interested in it; but, you see, I met this special friend, who…."

"Yes, go on," urged Jennifer.

The smile vanished from Chris's face. "I don't remember. I really don't. It all seems so distant now, my life on Earth, that is. I know it was only just a few hours ago, but, right now, it seems like forever ago and a billion miles away. There is so much I don't remember. That bothers me." Chris turned to Jesus.

"Don't be concerned, Chris, it is normal. It is part of our Father's plan. You see, there are parts of your life on Earth, memories that could cause you pain here, things that you had no control over. Until you have the inner strength, the spiritual maturity, to face them, you will not remember them. Some things will come back to you over time, others will not."

Chris had to think about that one for a moment. "I'm sorry, Lord, I don't know that I totally understand."

Jesus took Chris's hand in His. "When I walked upon your Earth, I spoke to all who would hear my voice. I spoke to people around the dinner table, at the temple, even on the road. Many times, I addressed thousands, bringing to them the good news that there was hope of eternal life. They didn't have to be separated from God anymore. They could come directly into His presence, commune with Him, even as I did. My heart went out to every one of them. I loved each and every one of them. I died for all of them, anyone who would accept and believe what I had to say. I showed all the way out of their sins, the way out of Hell. Do you understand?"

"Sure," Chris said. "I heard and believed."

"Yes," confirmed Jesus, "you did, but many more did not. I knew the content of their hearts from the moment I saw them. I knew that many would not accept the good news, but I had to give it to them anyway. They had hardened their hearts. Even as I spoke to them, I knew what they would do. I loved them so much, but knew that they were on the road to eternal separation from our Father. Can you understand what that feels like?"

Chris nodded.

"I cannot tell you how many times I wept over that very thing. I didn't desire for them to die in their sins, but even I, the Son of Man, was powerless to prevent it. What the Father has done for you is to spare you from this pain."

"I think I understand now," said Chris. "I'm not going to remember loved ones who are not coming here to Heaven, those sentenced to Hell."

"That is true," said Jesus. "Still, the time may come when you desire to know all that transpired during your life on Earth, that you might profit from the experience. That is a big step, and it can be painful. Most people never come to that point. They decide that they don't really want to know. If that day does come for you, the knowledge is yours; our Father will not forbid it. You will know of those lost ones, but that knowledge will not stir within you the feelings that you had for them on Earth. You will be spared that pain. You will know of them without truly knowing them. Even still; that knowledge carries with it a burden. Do not enter into such a decision lightly. I believe that your mother has sought some of that knowledge in her short time here."

"I have," Jennifer said, "but only a little bit, and not for years. I had to know what was going on with my family, my son, back on Earth. But it can be painful; I found that out really quickly. Chris, honey, once you get to feeling just a bit more comfortable here, I'll show you how. But get settled in here first. It's an entirely different world; you need some guidance at first. My own grandparents were my guide, I will be yours."

Chris was starting to feel a bit uncomfortable with this subject. He realized that there were many adjustments to make. "You know, I was just thinking, I didn't realize that people ate food in Heaven. I didn't think they needed to."

"We really don't," Jennifer said. "But I suppose old habits are hard to break."

"Especially when we are talking about your mother's wonderful apple pies," said Jesus. "During my time on Earth, the Pharisees often criticized Me because I loved a good meal, a good glass of wine, and the pleasant company that went along with it.

Some called Me a glutton and a drunkard. There will always be those who will find fault with what we do. Many saints here in Heaven have abandoned eating because it is no longer necessary to sustain life. They wish to spend that extra time seeking a closer relationship with the Father. I understand their reasoning, but I have not given up the partaking of food. I have found that conversations held over a dinner table tend to be among the most sincere. That is when people are the most likely to open up to you."

"My son will be well fed and well looked after here," said Jennifer, a broad smile on her face. "I'll see to that."

Jesus glanced over at Jennifer. He laughed openly. "I'm quite certain of that." Then he returned his gaze to Chris. "Your mother will take good care of you, now that you are here. She loves you very much. Listen to her Chris, consider all that she tells you, I know that her council will be sound. She has much to teach you." There was a brief pause.

"But understand this; Heaven is not a final destination for humankind. In your modern era, you have places for the older members of your society, some call them rest homes, others rehabilitation centers. Heaven is not a place such as this. It is not simply a place of rest. As I told you before, your spiritual growth has just begun. Here, with a closer, more intimate relationship with the Father, you will grow greatly in knowledge and wisdom. You will develop God-given gifts that you cannot yet imagine. Many are called, but few are chosen. Chris, you are one of the chosen; that is why you are here. One day you and the other children of God living here, shall be called to God's highest purposes."

Now, Chris was really intrigued. "Which is?"

"One of my dearest servants, the one I personally called on the road to Damascus, told you a little bit about it in his letter to the Corinthians. He told you that you would judge the angels. It is a responsibility handed to you directly from the Father. You were created a little lower than the angels, but, in time, your wisdom and authority will far exceed theirs. For many here in Heaven, that is already true. Do you now see why satan and his minions hate you so much?"

"Yes," replied Chris, "but I don't think I ever really grasped it like I do now."

"And as time passes, you will understand still more," Jesus said. "Another thing, and this is very important; God needs from you your love and devotion. Some people feel that the Father literally feeds on your adoration and worship. Your generation might say that He is on a power trip. Let me assure you that this is not the case, far from it. Understand how much the Father loves you. Most of you can not even comprehend the depth of that love. He needs you to love Him just as much as you possibly can, as He loves you. It is not so much for His benefit as it is for yours. Coming into an intimate relationship with the Father is critical if you are to grow in mind, wisdom, and power. You need to one day become as I am now, and you will, if you come to know the Father as I do."

Chris was, to say the least, astonished. "Become like you?"

Jesus laughed openly. "Don't be so surprised that I tell you this. It happens to be true. I have no doubt you will succeed. It takes much work and perseverance, but the results are well worth the effort. You will see." Jesus rose from His chair, having finished the pie. "Thank you, Jennifer, that was wonderful. As I said, I have had many a pleasant and meaningful conversation over a good meal. I have enjoyed this one, but I must be on my way. Keep asking questions, Chris, don't hesitate. That is how we grow spiritually."

Jennifer and Chris accompanied Jesus to the door. It was then when Chris worked up the nerve to ask his last question.

"Lord, I suspect that there is something else, something that you are not telling us. What happens when we finally become like you? God has a plan for us, doesn't He?"

Jesus turned to Chris. The twinkle in His eye, His broad smile was almost magical. "Yes."

There was a moment of silence. It was Jennifer who pursued her son's question. "And that would be what? I don't know either."

"Along the way to that goal, you will be given growing responsibilities. Some of you will reign with me over Earth for a thousand years. You will gain valuable experience."

"And after that?" asked Chris.

Jesus walked about half way across the porch before turning once more. "That is a conversation for a later time. You are not as yet ready for that answer. But I will tell you this much; it will be challenging, yet glorious beyond your comprehension. When the time comes, you will be ready. My blessings on you both. We will speak again, many times, I promise you."

Even as Jesus descended the stairs, a twinkling sphere of starlight appeared before Him. He stepped into the midst of it and quickly vanished.

"Wow," was all Chris could say.

The remainder of the day was spent in touring the house and the grounds and talking. The house was truly enormous, with a formal dining room, five huge bedrooms, a well-equipped kitchen, and, of course, a sewing room. The house had the heavenly equivalent of electric lights and appliances, although there were no cords. Apparently, each had its own internal power supply.

"They were all here when I arrived," explained Jennifer. "They have never failed, and the bulbs in the light fixtures have never burned out, not a single one of them. I suppose that's a good thing, since I haven't located any replacements if they did. Please, don't ask me exactly how they work, I don't know. I just accept it as a gift from God, and leave it at that. He has gone to great lengths to make me feel at home and comfortable."

"But where is the TV?" joked Chris. "There are a lot of good programs on Saturday. I think the Trailblazers are playing at home tonight."

"Sorry, Chris, didn't I tell you that the tube wasn't all that good for you. You need to get out more instead."

Chris smiled. "Actually it isn't really a tube anymore, Mom. I have a 40-inch plasma HD TV at home."

"Oh," Jennifer said, pondering what her son had just told her. "You have a plasma HD what?"

Chris laughed. "I guess I'll have to bring you up to speed on what is going on back home."

Chris and his mother had so much to tell each other. There were a lot of holes in Chris's recollection of his life on Earth, especially during the last five years. That was indeed odd, but he tried not to allow it to trouble him. After all, Jesus Himself had said that such things were to be expected. The important thing was that he was here, he was thinking more clearly than at any other time in his life, and he had been reunited with his mother.

As day slowly faded, the fireflies lit up the lawn and the forest beyond. Chris and his mother watched it all from the porch swing, chit chatting the way they used to so long ago. How he had missed her since then.

"I wasn't sure that there would be a night in Heaven," said Chris, gazing out into the fading twilight.

"It all depends where in Heaven you are," replied Jennifer. "We have day and night here, but they don't in the City of Zion. There it is forever day. It always feels like early afternoon there, at least to me."

"Zion?" asked Chris.

"Yes, I guess you could call it the capital city of Heaven, the dwelling place of God. It is really amazing, you'll see. I'll take you there in a few days, but I wanted you to get acclimated to your new home first."

"OK, Mom," said Chris, placing his head on her shoulder the way he used to as a young boy. "Whatever you say. Right now, I just want to stay home with you."

Chris was greeted by a sky full of the brightest stars he had ever seen. It was several hours later when a feeling akin to tiredness began to overtake him. "It would seem that our bodies still need sleep," he said, stretching out his arms wide.

"You think you do," Jennifer said, "and sleep is a good thing, even here. You're used to the cycle of sleep, so am I, even after all of these years. But, believe it or not, you could go on without it. Your glorified body really doesn't need to sleep. There are people here who have matured completely past the need for sleep. Maybe we all will, with time. But for now, I still sleep, but not as much as I used to. I'll take you to your room."

Chris's bedroom was on the first floor of the great mansion, a huge room that seemed immediately familiar. Within the walk-in closet, Chris found a complete wardrobe of clothes, everything he would need.

Following a good night kiss from his mother, he was ready for bed. He truly felt like a kid again, and he loved it. As he sat there alone on his grand bed, he took a moment to offer his thanks to God. So far, Heaven had met or exceeded all of his expectations. He could hardly wait to explore it in greater detail; and explore it he would, for he had all of the time in the universe.

chapter four

SERENA tried her best to get some sleep. For a time, she dreamt of Chris, and the rock house in Oregon. In her dreams, she was lying in bed by his side, his arm wrapped around her. She could hear his gentle breathing, hear him call her name in the night, feel him gently caress her. Sadly, it was an illusion, a phantasm, a ghost of a time that would never be again. Her dreams were all too frequently interrupted by a commotion in the hallway, as yet another damned soul was ushered through to await their fate. The pattern of sleep and rude awakenings was repeated at least half a dozen times, before a different sort of disturbance caught Serena's attention.

She rose to her feet to hear screams from somewhere far down the corridor. It was not just the screams of one or two individuals, but those of a great multitude. She stumbled to the bars of her cell to find out what was happening. The commotion had attracted Benny's attention as well, for he already stood by the bars of his cell, doing his best to peer into the corridor beyond.

"Something's happening," he confirmed, turning to Serena. "This might be it."

"Oh God!" gasped Serena, taking a step back. She knew this moment was coming. She had tried to prepare herself for it, but she realized now that she wasn't ready for the reality. It was now. It was time.

If only she could get out of her damnable cell, run, hide, do something, anything but wait helplessly. She wrapped her hands around the cold metal bars in frustration, testing them a final time, with all too predictable results.

Serena turned away from the bars and paced back and forth several times. She wanted to pray, but God wasn't listening, was He? Prayers were for Earth and Heaven, not this place. Nonetheless, she found herself on her knees.

"Lord, God, I know it's too late for prayers, too late to plead for your mercy. If you're listening, all I ask is that you give me the strength to face what is to come." Serena hesitated before continuing. "Lord, look after my husband, Chris. I know that now he's only my husband in my own mind, but please watch over him. Shower him with your love, even though I can't. In Jesus' name..."

"Amen," came the response from across the hallway.

Serena looked up to see Benny, his hands folded, his head bowed. He looked up, their eyes met.

"I know, it's pointless," he said. "But doesn't it say somewhere, the day will come when every knee shall bow, and every tongue confess that Jesus Christ is Lord?"

"Yes, it does," Serena said. "A strange time for us to realize it, isn't it?"

Benny nodded.

Serena turned toward the source of the commotion. "Do you think it's getting closer?"

"Yes," confirmed Benny. "But it might be some time before it gets here, whatever it is."

"I hope I get to see you again," said Serena. "You've made my time here more bearable. Thank you."

"The honor has been all mine. It has been a privilege, and a pleasure, to be in your company."

For a time, the two stood there in silence. Yes, the commotion was drawing nearer, and at a faster pace than either of them wanted. Whatever it was, its presence was beginning to permeate the cell block. The large glowing crystal protruding from the ceiling in the corridor just beyond Serena's cell seemed to be changing. It was fading. Its previously blue white glow was acquiring a more somber amber hue. The stage was being set for them. Soon, very soon, the curtain would rise on the next act of tragedy. There was absolutely nothing they could do to stop it.

Minutes ticked by, measured only by Serena's rapidly pounding heart and heightening fear. Again she peered into the hallway from her cell. Though nothing out of the ordinary met her eyes, a sudden terrible wailing from a nearby cell drove her back against the wall. She was shivering as she looked at Benny. He stood there stoically, facing the bars, arms at his side. He looked toward the source of the cries, then back to Serena; his eyes were kind and understanding. He whispered something, though Serena couldn't hear it above the loud lamentations that apparently arose from the man in the cell next to hers.

Quite abruptly the cries died away to a soft pitiful whimpering. Serena heard the poor man muttering something in an undecipherable tongue. She wasn't sure what language it was, but the tone was unmistakable—indescribable terror.

The awful thing creeping down the hallway toward them had grown frighteningly close. Serena listened more carefully. There was another sound, though she couldn't quite make it out. Perhaps it was the result of shifting winds sweeping through the corridors? No, it wasn't that. It was a sort of screeching sound, like nothing she had ever heard. It reverberated from every wall, emanated from every quarter of the subterranean hallway. It authored even greater fear within Serena as it grew closer and louder.

Amidst the fading amber light, perhaps 20 feet down the corridor, she saw the swift movement of a nebulous dark form. No, not one, but many forms, swirling like black ragged cloth caught in an ethereal whirlwind, yet there was not the slightest breeze. In the midst of it, Serena was certain that she saw at least one pair of glowing orange eyes. She quickly retreated back to the wall, her heart pounding loudly. She wasn't ready for this. She was frightened, nearly to the point of hysteria, yet she held her peace.

"Be brave, Serena," Benny said, standing at the bars of his cell, gazing at her. It was becoming difficult to see him in the fading light. Even his voice seemed strangely distant. "You're going to get through this. You're a woman of courage, whether you realize it or not. I know you have it in you to face whatever is ahead."

The whimpering from the next cell grew momentarily in volume, then faded completely.

In the corridor, black vapors swept past the bars obscuring the far wall from view, and then the entire hall vanished into the mists.

"Benny?"

No answer.

"Benny?" she repeated loudly.

Still no response. But wait, she heard voices, deep and guttural. They seemed to be coming from everywhere and yet nowhere. They were too deep to be those of a human. Serena felt a chill as she realized that she had been somehow separated from all of the others in this place; left alone to face the unknown. Never in her life had she experienced such fear.

Again she heard a deep guttural voice. This time it was a single voice, one very close.

"Serena Farnsworth."

Serena turned to see the dark hooded figure step toward the bars, materializing out of the mists. The being was tall, every bit as tall as the angel was. His body was cloaked in a jet black robe, his face veiled in shadows. Only his glowing amber eyes and the gaunt bony hands beyond the long, loose sleeves of his robe were visible.

He was the substance of a thousand nightmares. Serena felt the strong desire to scream, to release a portion of the terror penned up within her, but she managed to stifle it. She thought back once more to the Scriptures. The devil had the ability to appear as an angel of light. That might be convenient, in the event that he wished to beguile some foolish mortal with his beauty. But if that were the case, might he, or his minions, also appear as anything they wished? Might they take a more sinister form with the intent to invoke fear? Perhaps, but she wouldn't yield to fear. If fear is what he wanted, it would be the last thing he would get. She did not back away from the thing; she stared it in the face, what little she could see of it.

"Yes, you are a pretty thing," it continued, "in your own human sort of way. It would seem that God has discarded you, thrown you into the cold darkness, what a shame. But be not concerned, I have come to bring you to your new master. Yes, you should feel honored, for satan himself has summoned you. It is he who shall hear your case. This is a rare privilege. He shall not abandon you as God has; no, he will keep you throughout all eternity as one of his own. It is he who shall decide your fate, the precise nature of your punishment."

"But first, you must be appropriately dressed for your meeting with your new master," continued the dark being. A gray pile of cloth was pitched into Serena's cell, catching her by surprise. "Remove the clothing you are wearing, and put those on. They are far more appropriate for what is to come, for your new station in existence. This garment is quite utilitarian."

Serena hesitated; then cautiously reached out to examine the filthy garb that had been tossed at her. Its fabric was as coarse as burlap. There were two parts to her infernal wardrobe. One was a short, dirty skirt. The other was a halter top, tattered and roughly cut. They were disgusting. Serena considered refusing, resisting the demands of this demon, or whatever it was. Would that be an act of courage, defiance, or simple stupidity? Did courage or cowardice matter in this place?

The demon noted Serena's hesitation. The tone of his response spoke of his amusement. "I see that I will have to encourage you to obey. So be it."

Quite suddenly, Serena's dress began to yellow and disintegrate. Within seconds it had decomposed to decaying rags that fell from her body and became a pile of swirling ashes scattering across the floor. Even her shoes decomposed into dust at her feet. Serena turned from the dark being, trying to cover her nakedness.

"I am not the least bit interested in your body," said the demon, his impatience obvious in his tone of voice. "Your form is disgusting to me, I assure you. You are an obscenity, a pale mirror image of the Creator, molded in flesh. Only He could be so egotistical. Now put those rags on—cover yourself, woman, before you make me ill."

Serena reluctantly complied. Had she decided to obey out of her own human modesty, or had this thing somehow compelled her obedience? It was an outlandish thought, but she wasn't so sure that it wasn't true. After all, this was Hell, she'd have to get used to doing things, and experiencing things, that she didn't like, and she'd be doing and experiencing them for all eternity. Her heart sank even more.

Serena picked up the tattered skirt, and stepped into the dirty, primitive garment, pulling it up around her hips. For a moment she was certain that it was too small for her, that it would rip, yet it molded itself to fit her perfectly; the uneven hem of the skirt was scandalously short, barely covering her intimate parts.

Then she picked up the top and slipped it over her head. Like the awful skirt, it too seemed initially too tight. Yet, as she pulled it on, it conformed to fit her perfectly. It was unnatural.

The fabric had a foul stench—a strong odor of decay and death. Serena felt ill in it. As much as she might have dreaded appearing before some sort of tribunal naked, it might well have been preferable to what she now wore.

Somewhere in the New Testament, she had read that our righteousness is as filthy rags before the Lord. She also recalled a parable about a man who came to the Lord's banquet table in rags. When the Lord asked the man why he was dressed so, he had no excuse. That man had been bound and cast out into outer darkness, hadn't he? Could those Scriptures have been alluding to this? She couldn't say.

"Yes, better," said the demon, scanning his victim carefully. "That garb is most unique. It will endure the harshest environments Hell has to offer, as you shall soon discover. In time, it will become almost a part of you." It was then that his glowing eyes focused upon her hand. "Your wedding ring—remove it!"

The words hit Serena hard. "But it's all I have left of my marriage, beyond the love I feel for Chris in my heart. Please, let me wear it. If there is any mercy within you, please let me keep this one thing." Serena's voice was faltering, pleading.

"You don't have a husband, wench," retorted the dark figure, his tone cruel and taunting. "This Son of God, of whom you dream, is only a husband of your lurid fantasies. You're pathetic. Surely you must realize that you are not so much as a fading memory to him. Even if you were, why would he desire the likes of you? You're a whore, unclean, nothing more than fuel for the eternal flames of Hell."

A slight chuckle emanated from the dark form. "Ah, alas, you have not so much as a single mourner. In the end, none beyond this place will so much as remember that you ever existed. But we shall not forget you. We shall see to it that you receive everything that is coming to you. Now, remove the ring!"

Tears appeared in Serena's eyes as she reached for the band of gold. The tears had turned to sobs by the time the ring cleared her finger and fell to the floor. She heard the clink as the ring hit the stone. Such a cold sound, and with its last reverberation, her previous life vanished into the mists of the dead past.

"Much better," commented the dark being.

There was a loud clank, as a pair of jet black manacles connected together by a short, but formidable chain, struck the floor at Serena's feet. They appeared heavy and crude, the sort of thing that one might have seen upon an Earthly prisoner of the distant past.

"These shall be the bands you wear now. Pick them up, wench!" commanded the shadowy form beyond the bars. "They will fit about your wrists, restraining your hands behind your back. Now, get them on!"

Serena whimpered as she picked up the manacles. Examining them more closely, she discovered that while the outside surface of the manacles were smooth, the inside surface, that which would be in contact with her skin, was brutally rough, covered with tiny needle-sharp barbs. Yet, the manacles appeared to have no locking mechanism, or even a catch to hold them shut around her wrists.

"If you continue to delay, wench, I promise that I will make this all the more uncomfortable for you," said the demonic being.

"Believe me; you don't want to know just how uncomfortable things can get."

Serena placed one of the manacles about her left wrist and began to close it carefully. It was obvious that it would be very tight when completely closed. The two halves had nearly met when the thing seemed to suddenly come alive. Snapping shut as if powerfully magnetized. She winced in pain as the metal barbs dug into her flesh.

The meeting point of the two halves of the manacle became momentarily red hot. Serena cried out in pain as she saw a cloud of smoke and heard the sound and smell of sizzling flesh seep from beneath the glowing irons. She struggled to control herself, to stifle her screams, but to no avail. The cell reverberated with her cries of agony. After a moment the glow and the pain faded, to reveal a single band of uninterrupted metal wrapped tightly around her wrist.

"Place your hands behind your back, and place the other manacle around your right wrist," commanded the dark being.

Serena looked toward the demon incredulously. After experiencing that pain, how could she willingly submit to it again? The answer came more swiftly than she could have imagined, as she was struck by crippling stomach cramps.

"Do we really have to continue with this, or are you going to obey?" the dark being asked.

Almost without thinking, Serena thrust her arms behind her back and searched blindly for the open manacle. All the while the terrible pain in her stomach intensified. She had fallen to her knees now, struggling to thrust her right wrist into the remaining open manacle. Her animal instincts had taken control, as she sought for any means to escape the horrible pain wrenching in her gut. The sharp bite around her right wrist, followed by the agonizing heat, told her that she had succeeded. The pain in her stomach vanished, replaced by a new agony.

Serena twisted and stretched her arms as far behind her as she could in an attempt to move the red hot manacle away from her bare back. Tears streamed from her eyes, and she gasped pathetically as the searing pain exploded her senses. Never had she experienced such agony. By the time the manacle had begun to cool, her body was drenched in perspiration, and her face in tears. She could only imagine what her damaged wrists looked like.

"Very good," said the dark form, drawing closer. "You're a relatively smart wench; I thought you'd see reason eventually."

For the first time Serena saw his face. It was gaunt and terribly thin, with sunken cheeks and deep-set eyes. It was like the face of a corpse with a devious smile. Quite unexpectedly, the door to her cell swung open wide.

"Rise," commanded the dark being, extending a slender arm in her direction. "Your audience with the master, your sentencing, is at hand."

With difficulty, Serena rose on unsteady legs, and nearly stumbled from the cell into the misty corridor. She saw that Benny's cell was empty and the corridor was quiet; everyone was gone. How could this be? Had that much time passed?

"Where are the others?" she asked.

The dark being scowled, "Who do you think you are? No one here owes you any answers. Now, move!"

Serena was grabbed roughly and pulled toward her captor. She felt cruel hands and cold metal around her throat as a heavy black collar was thrust around her neck, a long chain trailing from the front. She was almost relieved when she heard the metallic click of the latch as the collar locked into place. There was no glowing metal, no searing heat to fuse the band together, only a conventional lock. She felt a hard tug on the chain as she was quickly dragged down the corridor by the tall hooded figure, past row after row of empty cells.

A swirling vortex of deepest crimson materialized before them. She tried to pull away, but it was a futile gesture. The dark hooded figure before her seemed to dematerialize at the threshold of this other worldly tunnel, flowing into the turbulent corridor, like a curling black mist caught up by a whirlwind. An instant later, Serena was jerked by the neck chain into the highly charged environment of the vortex. She was swept off her feet by gale force winds, even as cold, blue electricity arced around her. In this turbulent tunnel of elemental force, she discovered a new definition of pain. She felt the electricity coursing through her body and experienced the terrible nausea.

She prayed for an end of it, but it seemed to go on and on, carrying her through swirling clouds of kaleidoscopic vapors, whose icy touch made the coldest winter wind feel balmy by comparison. Then there was blackness, the deepest and most profound night she had ever experienced.

Through it all, the chain linked to the collar around her neck stretched out before her, glowing and pulsing with static electricity—extending into infinity. Though she could no longer see the dark being at the other end, his presence was betrayed by the tautness of the chain and the irresistible force that propelled her onward, viciously choking her.

Ahead, a faint point of light materialized like a dim star amidst the inky blackness of the void. It was becoming larger and brighter by the second. It grew to become a portal of light, perhaps a way out. She felt a sense of abrupt deceleration, then falling.

Serena slammed face first into the hard stone floor. With her hands chained behind her back, there was no way for her to break her fall. She lay on the cold floor, unable to move. She was still in pain, but thankful to be out of the horrible vortex.

After a moment, she lifted her head and looked around. The floor was shimmering black marble, reflecting the amber light of the hundred blazing torches mounted along the gray stone block walls. Hanging from the walls were large, intricate tapestries depicting dark skies with swarms of demons, terrible astral battles between great armies of angels, and grotesque acts of mayhem and torture. Serena was certain that the tapestries told some sort of story. Perhaps it was a pictorial account of the fall from Heaven.

Standing near the fringes of the room was a great throng of beings with an astonishing variety of forms. There were horned demons with bat-like wings, small and muscular imps with barbed tails and sharp horns, while still others looked like tall, pale women with cloven feet and claw-like hands. It was a nightmarish company whose presence brought terror to Serena's soul.

She turned her attention from the motley crew of bipeds and strained to look behind her. She saw a large ring of metal that looked to be made of copper or brass. It stood upright upon a finely fashioned golden support. Through the open ring, Serena saw not the wall beyond, but blackness, a void of infinite depth, the void of outer darkness. Around the inner edge of the ring, Serena could see an occasional arc of blue lightning. It was a gateway, most likely the means through which she had entered this chamber of nightmares.

Serena turned her head to look forward. The dark figure stood before her, her chain in his hand. Several yards beyond him, three wide marble steps led up to a large platform, covered by a crimson red carpet. At the center of the grand stage was an ornate golden throne, whose dollar value on Earth would surely have been incalculable. Upon the throne sat a tall figure draped in deep blue velvet. In his hand he held a golden scepter, upon the end of which was a finely cut, fist-sized gem, with a center that glowed with a crimson light. Serena felt a terrible chill in his presence. It didn't take a theological scholar to realize who was seated before her.

She had heard much speculation over the years regarding the devil's appearance; red suit, horns, cloven feet, and a forked tail, were among a few of the features traditionally attributed to him. Yet the appearance of this prince of darkness was not quite what she had expected. He was as tall as the angels, yet his physical appearance was far more akin to that of a human male. He was in all aspects well proportioned, moderately muscular, and his flowing dark hair bore just the trace of gray around his temples. His eyes were brown, and his tan skin was flawlessly smooth without wrinkles.

Had she not known better, Serena might have guessed his age as early forties. The only traditional aspect of his appearance was his small dark goatee. All in all, he was darkly handsome. In fact, Serena was certain that he was the most handsome man she had ever seen. He had a powerful animal magnetism that any woman would have found most difficult to resist. Perhaps that was his intent.

Yet, beyond his physical appearance, he projected a regal bearing—a confidence in his authority and power, all without saying a word. Now, he was scanning the woman before him very carefully. He seemed to like what he saw. Serena resolved to be careful about what she said and did before the prince of darkness. How she conducted herself here could have far-reaching consequences. This being held her destiny, indeed her eternity, within his hands. Perhaps, just perhaps, he might be inclined to be merciful if he liked her.

Satan rose to his feet and took several steps in Serena's direction. The dark figure holding her chain moved toward Serena.

"Kneel before the master!" he commanded, roughly pulling Serena by her collar, lifting her from the floor, forcing her into a kneeling position facing the prince. She winced in pain.

"Gently, Marlock," instructed satan, who brushed the bottom of his goatee with the index finger of his left hand. "We don't wish to damage her, at least not yet." Satan turned his attention to a dark robed figure to his left, one who stood at the bottom of the steps, holding a thick black book in his hand. "Now, who do we have here?"

"Her name is Serena Farnsworth, my Lord," was the reply.

"And what were her sins?" continued satan, looking back toward Serena. "Why is it that the Most High God condemned this woman to outer darkness, relegating her into our custody?"

"Her sins are many indeed," assured the hooded figure, "adultery, fornication, dishonoring her father and mother, and worshiping pagan gods, even as she took the Lord God's name in vain. Yet her sins did not end there, they also included theft, bearing false witness against her neighbor, idolatry, fortune telling, witchcraft, and the sexually deviant act of lesbianism."

Lesbianism? Serena felt like raising an objection over that one. It had only happened once, and afterward, she had very much wished it hadn't happened at all. It had been an incident that had taken place in her darkest and most confused days. But what could she say of the other charges? They were all true. She kept her head bowed; deciding that not looking directly into the face of this megalomaniac might earn her some points.

"An impressive list for one so young," satan said, taking a better look at the bound woman before him. "Yes, you have certainly earned for yourself a place in my kingdom, doomed to partake in the eternal cycle of agony and despair that is mine alone to bestow. The only question is, exactly how shall I deal with you?

With so very many agonizing possibilities; what form shall your destiny take?"

Serena glanced up momentarily. She searched for the right words, anything that might help her case, yet she could find none. Perhaps what was to happen was inevitable, perhaps nothing she said would make a difference.

There was a sudden twinkle in the dark lord's eyes. "Ah yes, of course, I know how I shall deal with you, Miss Farnsworth. Still, it is customary that I listen to the groveling and pleading of my guests before I pass sentence upon them. Do you have any last words, before judgment is passed upon you? Think carefully, for this opportunity shall never come your way again."

Serena felt ill to her stomach. There would be nothing she could do to lessen her sentence, she knew that now. She could cry, she could beg for mercy, but it wouldn't help. The words that came out of her mouth surprised even her. "Sir, if you please, I would like very much to ask a question before these proceedings continue."

There was a twinkle in satan's eye. Most people who knelt before him were too terrified to speak beyond a few groveling pleas for mercy, but not this one.

"Ask what you will, I am listening."

"Thank you, sir," Serena said in the most sincere tone she could muster. "I don't understand why you are doing this. The same God that banished you to outer darkness did it to me as well. Why do you have to torture me? It seems like we have something in common."

Satan couldn't help but laugh at that remark. It was a bold comment. He'd heard that line before, but rarely so eloquently spoken. "Do you really think that you can compare yourself to me in the same sentence?"

Serena knew that she was on very thin ice. It was all too clear, that this being could make her eternity here far worse, if he was inclined to do so. She thought about the attributes that the Bible ascribed to satan. She did her best to appeal to those.

"I wouldn't be so bold as to compare myself to you, sir. I mean, I admire what you've accomplished. You've become the master of outer darkness, brought order to chaos. Surely, only a great leader could have done all of this. Why torture humanity? If we're all outcasts, why can't we work together to create a wonderful new world, one where you are the master—revered, honored, even loved by a grateful people?"

Satan began to smile. He was so weary of listening to pleas for mercy, hearing about the problems and sorrows of these worthless humans, problems that he was about to greatly compound. But this one, on the threshold of her eternal torment, wanted to talk about him. He was impressed with this female. "You're very perceptive, little one. When the Great God cast my minions and me into outer darkness, this place was a vast realm of nothingness, an empty void, but a void awaiting the hand of creativity to transform it into something greater. I became the god of this new realm, and I fashioned it into a form that served my needs."

The smile dissolved from satan's face at the very thought of his arch nemesis. "God, the Creator was a tinkerer, nothing more. He played endless games with the universe. He was like a child with a grand creation that He had fabricated with His new set of building blocks. It was so intricate, so vast, so perfectly balanced. He wanted everyone to see it. Yet He was alone, there was no one else to appreciate the work of His hand. He desperately needed to be praised for his accomplishments. He needed to know that what He had done was good, that He was good."

Satan paused momentarily. Silence fell upon the audience chamber. Even the other beings there became still in his moment of contemplation. The dark prince looked upward for a moment. His eyes took on a distant stare. Serena's nervousness grew. She wondered if she might have asked the wrong question.

"He loves praise," continued satan, looking once more toward Serena. "Did you know that? That is why He fashioned the angels, not merely to be laborers and messengers, not even to be His companions, to deliver Him from loneliness. No, He needed sentient beings who would proclaim His greatness. He created me to lead the other angels in that praise. Though, in time, I came to question why we did this thing, I did my job with consummate perfection. Day and night, we fed an ego as big as the universe itself, but that wasn't enough, He needed more. After a time, He decided that our worship wasn't what He wanted at all. Understand this; we were created with all of the knowledge God saw fit to give us, and we worshiped Him because He created us to do just that. It was our function. We did it because we were commanded to."

Again, satan paused to consider how best to express himself, before this human female. "The people of your time might say we were preprogrammed with a set of instructions. But God wanted a race of beings who would worship him because they made the conscious choice to do so. He desired a people whose minds were virtually a blank slate at their birth. They would experience His universe most intimately and through that intimate contact come to love Him. Their praise and worship would proceed naturally and willfully from their lips, and thus He created humanity."

The intensity in the dark lord's face grew. "I had never questioned God's motives, no angel questioned God, not until that moment. We loved Him, all of us, even I loved Him. But it seemed as if He had become weary of us, in much the same way as a child grows weary of playing with an old toy. He needed a new distraction. It was then when I confronted Him; never had I done such a thing. I spoke of our concerns. Had we somehow displeased Him? He assured me that this was not the case. He in no way loved us less; He simply desired the creation of a new sort of being, one created in His own image, His own likeness. He had already selected a world upon which He would bring humanity into existence. I pleaded with Him to reconsider, but His mind was made up."

Satan abruptly turned from Serena and looked to the others in the great room. "Many of you remember that fateful day, I'm sure. I was the visionary, and you shared in that vision. We saw then the threat humankind represented. The ascent of man had to be prevented. The time for change was at hand, and you turned to me as the instrument of that change. God's plan, His rule, had to be brought to an end. And who better to bring about that end than I? Our rule, my rule, would have been the beginning of a new age, the age of an enlightened angelic empire. We would have brought stability to the universe, it was our birthright."

Satan pirouetted slowly, his hands raised to the sky. Serena watched in stunned amazement.

"But our brethren would not listen, their minds had been dulled by God's promises, they refused to see the truth. So we alone took up arms against the creator. You all fought bravely, all of you, but we were too few. In the end, our defeat was inevitable. But even then, God showed weakness. Even when we were brought before Him for judgment, He could not bring himself to destroy us utterly. Instead, He cast us out into this place, beyond His precious universe. Perhaps He thought that this would be a far greater punishment than bringing us to utter destruction.

"But He was wrong, we not only survived, we thrived. It was difficult at first, but slowly we established a new order, a new universe. And from that universe, we struck out against the upstart, man and woman. We have brought low God's great experiment.

And one day soon, very soon, when we have grown strong, we shall return to God's universe, not just as spirits, but in physical form. On that day, we shall depose God and His angels, and a new order shall be brought forth."

A loud cheer rose from the multitude throughout the room. It grew in intensity and enthusiasm. "All hail, satan!" they shouted, over and over again.

Satan's speech reminded Serena of old films she had seen of Adolph Hitler's great rallies, during the 1930s. There was the ranting of a megalomaniac, followed by the rhythmic chanting of people caught up in the passion of the moment. For beings that resented humans so much, they acted a lot like them.

Satan turned abruptly toward Serena. Within his eyes, the mirror of his dark soul, Serena could see madness.

"Then, when you humans began to stray, when God's great experiment began to fail, as I knew it would, He cast great multitudes of your kind into outer darkness, and we were waiting for them." The dark lord was becoming agitated, his thundering voice becoming ever louder. "You wonder why we hate you, why we torment you. It is because an arbitrary and irresolute God offered unto you a glory greater than ours, a privilege of which you are wholly unworthy. In the end, you were to become the judges of our deeds, the authors of our fates. Yet, you are the usurpers. Your kind will never be accepted here! We will confine you, desecrate you, and drive you insane with pain! We will hurt God by hurting you. Do you now understand?"

Serena battled to control her terror. "Completely," she replied. "I'm just sorry that it had to be this way."

"I'm certain that you are," said satan, his tone almost mocking. His remark met with a round of cruel mirth from his loyal disciples.

"There is so much you could teach us," continued Serena, determined to make one last desperate appeal. "I mean, you've accomplished so much out here. I'd hoped to witness, to experience, what you've created. I'd hoped to learn from you. It is, well, scientific curiosity." Serena realized how lame that excuse sounded. She had angered the devil, and fully expected to be on the receiving end of an even greater portion of his wrath.

Satan laughed openly. "Science; yes, I understand the methods of human science. Allow me to enlighten you. Scientific curiosity; and the observations that flow from it mean nothing, if you are unable to share your results with others of your kind. I assure you, that you won't be doing that. In fact, you're about to become a part of the experiment."

Satan's comment precipitated another round of laughter from the multitude of demons that surrounded him. Serena, however, wasn't laughing; but she wasn't groveling either. She fought to maintain her emotional ground.

Satan's attention once more turned to his kneeling victim. Both his tone and his expression had changed. They seemed far less menacing than before. His oral history highlights hadn't achieved their desired effect.

"You truly wish to know more about my realm?"

Serena nodded.

For a moment, satan seemed to ponder Serena's request; then he spoke again. "Nearly all of my guests are taken by my minions directly and without fanfare to the special place of torment chosen for them; the place where they shall spend eternity. They know nothing of the rest of my vast empire, for they are trapped by their own unique situation. They don't have much time to ponder the nature of my realm; their own agony leaves them little room for such higher thoughts. This is not a place of learning, wench; it is a place of torture, pain, and pandemonium."

The prince of darkness paused. Perhaps he would grant this wench's request, give her a true appreciation of his power, of his creative genius, before she entered her own place of torment.

"Very well Serena; I will give you twelve hours to wander freely about this world of mine, unhindered, unbound, and in no pain."

Quite abruptly, the shackles fell from Serena's wrists and the collar fell from her neck—she was free. She slowly moved her wrists and saw that they were scarred from the barbed interior of the shackles, but the burns had already healed.

"Your new body heals with great rapidity," confirmed satan, seeming to reading Serena's mind. "It has to."

Quite abruptly, a pair of brown leather sandals materialized on the floor in front of her.

"Put them on!" commanded satan. "If you are to wander about my realm, you might as well walk in comfort. You see, most of my guests don't need such things. They aren't going anywhere."

Again, there was a subdued chuckle from the odd crowd that had gathered around her. Perhaps it was considered necessary to respond to the master's dry and sadistic humor.

Serena fumbled to put the sandals on, as the prince of darkness walked down the three steps to stand before his human captive. He crossed his arms as he took a closer look at his comely guest.

"Rise," he commanded.

Serena did as she was told. It was difficult, though, because her muscles were quivering in fear. She tried to control them.

"Extend your open palm."

Again Serena complied, stretching out her right hand, upturned and open. Satan placed a very small hourglass into her palm.

"Look at me, little one," he continued.

Serena looked up, their eyes met. To be this close to the prince of darkness was nothing short of terrifying. She felt overwhelmed by his evil.

"You can not stop the flow of sand through this hourglass," he said, pointing to the tiny glass. "It will always flow in the same direction. It will require twelve hours to travel its course. During that time, you may travel as you please, and observe what you wish, with but two provisions. One, you may not intervene in any way in the torments of any of my guests. Two, when the last grain of sand has traveled its course, you must be atop the cliff overlooking the great sea of fire. There you shall throw yourself from the precipice, to begin your eternity of burning torment."

Throw herself in? That was too much to ask.

"If you are late for your appointment, or attempt to aid one of my guests, I shall send my minions out to hunt you down. Believe me when I tell you, that it is within my power to make your torment here far worse. Do you understand?"

"Yes," Serena said.

"Then go," replied satan, pointing to the portal behind Serena. "Follow your shadow. It will lead you to your eternal destiny."

Serena turned to discover that the portal displayed an image of a barren desert. Yet it seemed three dimensional, holographic. It was her doorway, her gateway to Hell. She glanced once more toward the hourglass in her hand. Its sand had already begun to flow. Serena took a trembling step toward the portal; then stopped.

"I will give you a gentler journey through the portal this time. I do not wish to confuse or dull your senses. I want you to experience my kingdom with a clear mind, behold it in all of its grandeur."

Serena still hesitated.

"Go before I change my mind!" commanded satan in a demanding tone.

Serena took five quick steps. The fifth carried her through the portal, and into the realm of the damned.

chapter five

THE journey from the audience chamber, through the portal, and into the barren landscape beyond was instantaneous, more like walking through a doorway between rooms. It was hot and dry here, perhaps 90 degrees or so, and the air held a faint odor of sulfur. A great red luminary, far larger but dimmer than the Earth's sun, illuminated her surroundings with a somber, amber light. Serena turned around to see nothing but the desert and the barren, craggy mountains beyond; the portal through which she had traveled was gone.

Serena stood there for a moment taking in the unearthly landscape. She was situated near the edge of a wide, boulder-strewn valley, at least a few miles wide. Its length was indeterminate, extending in both directions as far as the eye could see. The rocks and ground were rusty brown, and the sky was filled with billowing gray clouds of smoke and dust that swept swiftly across the face of the swollen sun, yet here at ground level there was hardly a breath of wind.

So this was Hell. Serena wasn't really sure what she had expected, but somehow this was not quite it. It sort of reminded her of the Mojave Desert, perhaps Death Valley. Hell was not a series of subterranean passageways winding their way through the deepest recesses of the Earth. No, Hell was an entire world unto itself, a world circling a lone red star in a region beyond the known universe. That much she had deduced from her conversation with the angel. It seemed like science fiction.

Serena looked at the small hourglass in her hand. It was scarcely an inch long, and no matter how she held it, the sand flowed in the same direction. It was as incongruous as the rest of this place.

What now, follow her shadow? That wouldn't be too difficult, her shadow stretched out before her, at least a dozen feet long. It occurred to her that she hadn't asked how long or difficult a journey this might be. Such questions hadn't been on her mind at the time. Maybe it would have been better to have simply been cast directly into the sea of fire and get it over with all at once. What was she going to accomplish out here during the next twelve hours?

"Delay the beginning of eternal agony," she said out loud, answering her own question.

Almost unconsciously she began to follow her own shadow. The way she figured it, her route would take her directly down the valley, through a lonely realm of hard packed clay and rocks. At least it was preferable to scaling the steep mountains on either side. That would have been a considerable task for anyone, short of an expert climber with all of the right equipment.

She paused for a moment, again gazing at her bleak surroundings. As far as she could see, she was the only traveler upon this barren landscape. That in itself surprised her. Where were all of the tormented souls? Did she really want to know?

Perhaps she was going about this all wrong. Perhaps she should have taken off in the other direction, up the valley, perhaps into the hills. But could she really hide from satan in his own realm? Perhaps satan would lose track of her, perhaps forget her. After all, there had to be billions of souls in this place. Did he keep tabs on every one of them? No, now she was trying to delude herself. There wasn't so much as a chance of that happening. She continued on with her scientific expedition.

A scientific expedition? There was a time when such concepts had held a very strong appeal. She had had such a passion for science in high school. She had hoped to major in science or engineering in college. But there were financial considerations. Her parents hadn't seen science or engineering as proper professions for a young woman. With no support from home, she and her first husband had attempted to put themselves through college, working as a team. It had sounded like a good plan, yet she'd been forced to drop out of community college after only two semesters to get a full time job. That had been the end of her academic career and her dreams of becoming a scientist. That was, until now.

The journey before her was, in a way, a sort of scientific expedition, a journey of discovery. She looked at her clothes. She was not very well outfitted for an expedition. Nonetheless, she would see and experience things that no living human had ever seen or experienced before. It was an incredible opportunity, if only she had a camera, a tape recorder, even a notebook.

No, Serena realized that she wasn't thinking straight. She wondered if she was in the midst of some emotional condition akin to shock. This wasn't some sort of research project. At the end of this excursion into the unknown was an unimaginable fate. Yet she couldn't allow herself to think of such things. Better to exist in a state of denial for now, create in her mind some sort of fantasy. Perhaps she would find Chris at the end of the road. Perhaps God would grant her a last minute pardon, a reprieve. Perhaps He was just testing her, seeing if she would surrender to the devil's will, or find a new faith in her Creator. It was a hope that she would cling to, cling to until the flames of the sea of fire burned it to blackened ashes.

Serena saw not a single sign of life as she carefully navigated her way around the rocks and boulders strewn randomly about the barren valley. Not even a trace of lichens adhered to the brown angular rocks. In the absence of life, it was amazingly quiet, only the sound of wind in the hills disturbed the silence.

Quite suddenly there was a sound. Amidst a realm of silence it seemed greatly magnified. It was a distant screech, like that of a bird of prey. Serena turned in surprise to see it flying swiftly through the air not too far to her left. It was a large dark bird, perhaps an eagle or a vulture. Its wings beat swiftly against the hot air. It was apparently in a hurry to get somewhere. Serena followed its course with her eyes, and in the distance saw still more of them, many more, pirouetting upon the thermals, diving and soaring, as if they had discovered a source of food amidst this barren land. The place of their gathering lay directly in her path. She figured that she would soon discover the object or objects of their interest. She quickened her pace.

It was about ten minutes before she heard the distant sounds of distress from someplace up ahead, the dreadful sounds of the screaming and wailing of a great multitude. As yet she couldn't see the source of the distress, for it lay hidden beyond a ridge of rubble that ran the entire width of the valley, but it had attracted a vast armada of the large birds. In places the sky was visibly darkened by their presence. Never had she seen such a multitude of birds in one place, especially ones of this size.

Serena scrambled up the low ridge of rocks and gravel. The wailing beyond grew ever louder. Reaching the top of the rise, she beheld the source of the terrible commotion. The land before her had been cleared of boulders and leveled. Stretching across the entire width of the valley and as far down the valley as she could see, were millions of rectangular black altars arranged in orderly rows. All appeared to be identical, perhaps two and a half feet high, two feet wide, and three feet long.

Upon most of the altars were human forms, men and women, dressed in the same filthy attire. Stretched across the altars in unnatural positions, their heads and legs hung over the ends of black stone slabs. Their feet dangled a few inches above the ground, held by a pair of ankle shackles mounted by short chains to the base of the altar. A tight, heavy chain looped around their throats forced their heads back. Their wrists were also secured in shackles mounted to the left and right sides of the slab, rendering them totally helpless. They screamed, cried, and cursed in a chorus of agony that echoed across the barren landscape. They wiggled and squirmed wildly, yet in total futility, as the armada of large vultures feed ravenously upon their prone human prey.

It was a ghastly sight as the large black birds, perched upon the hapless victims, digging into their flesh with their long beaks, and pulling forth chunks of meat and lengths of entrails. Blood pulsed from severed arteries, and oozed from deep wounds drenching the altars in crimson essence. Some of the blood dripped down the sides, while even more was lapped up by the merciless black vultures. No less than two or three of the winged tormentors at a time would feed upon a victim. As one bird would leave with a bloody piece of stringy meat in his beak, another would quickly replace it, and the feast would continue.

"Oh God!" gasped Serena turning away in disgust. What sort of sick mind would come up with such nightmarish torment? Yet she knew the answer to that one, a being full of hate and jealousy.

If there were only another way around, a means by which she might avoid this field of agony. There wasn't. After a minute, Serena made her way down the small ridge of crumbling rock and into the midst of a nightmare.

At first she was afraid that the birds might turn upon her; but they were too preoccupied with the easy pickings upon the altars to concern themselves with a victim who might resist. She went virtually unnoticed.

Physically, it wasn't difficult to make her way through this place. The ground was hard and level, and there was at least a half dozen feet of open space between each of the altars. She tried not to look at the horror around her, tried not to hear the moans and screams of the tormented. But how could she not? Perhaps she would go unnoticed by the victims, but those around her cried out to her, pleading in a hundred different languages for mercy. She could hardly ignore their pleas, yet she knew she could do nothing. Tears streamed from her eyes as she made her way through the field of carnage.

The tormented victims around her existed in many different stages of dismemberment. Some were almost fully intact, while the flesh of others had been almost completely ripped from their bones, leaving little more than indigestible sinew and unpalatable organs. Yet, even the most horribly desecrated continued to moan and cry in pain, for there was no death beyond death, only eternal existence.

From above, a new commotion arose, a terrible scream. Serena looked up to see two demonic beings with leathery wings, robed wholly in black. Their skin was dark gray, their faces ancient, wrinkled, and contorted. Their hands were not at all like human hands. No, they were as much claws as hands, with sharp glistening nails at the end of each slender finger. Between them, they held a rag-clad woman.

Within seconds they had landed, scarcely 50 feet away. Serena came to a halt, surprised that they took no notice of her. Instead, one roughly pushed the poor woman toward a vacant altar. The middle aged woman turned toward the dark being, a look of horror upon her face.

"Your altar awaits you, wench," said the demon in a deep gruff voice. He motioned to the shiny black monolith. "Lay down upon it now, the vultures are famished."

The woman looked about frantically, as if searching for any means of escape, yet there was no place to run, no place to hide. "Please, no," she pleaded, tears in her eyes. "It's inhuman!"

"But as you may have noticed, we are not human," said the other demon. "Let me make it simple for you; you can lay yourself down upon this altar, or we can do it for you, perhaps breaking some of your fragile bones in the process. Choose!"

Weeping bitterly, the woman sat down upon the edge of altar, then after a few seconds she leaned back. Her shoulders met the warm stone, never to leave it again, while her head and legs hung over the stone slab.

The demons went quickly to work, placing her arms and legs in black manacles. The spiny manacles closed decisively, welding themselves together with a horrible searing heat that Serena knew all too well. Amidst the smoke of burning flesh, the woman cries were temporarily muted, as one of the demons brought the chain around her throat and locked it in place. Her head swung backward; as she struggled to reduce the brutal pressure its links applied to her soft pulsing throat.

The demons wasted no time in departing, leaving this wretched woman to the ravenous vultures. She pulled at her manacles, but the chains that coupled each of her restraints to this abominable altar gave her little mobility. Already several vultures had noticed her plight, and circled downward toward her.

"Oh God!" she cried, yanking again at the formidable chains that restrained her.

A large vulture, with a wingspan of at least 3 feet, swept within inches of the poor woman as she wept bitterly. Up to this point Serena had stood there motionless, fearful to intervene, but not anymore. She rushed to the woman's side waving her arms wildly in the air.

"Go away you horrible thing, go away!"

The startled vulture veered sharply away, climbing back into the turbulent sky. The dark haired woman looked at Serena incredulously, at first not understanding what was going on.

"Who, who are you?" she gasped, gazing up at her unexpected benefactor. "How'd you get here?"

"I'm just like you," began Serena, "a damned soul abandoned by God, doomed to this place." Serena did her best to quickly explain her situation. Considering this woman's shattered state of mind, she wasn't so sure just how much of it registered with her.

"Then you weren't sent here to rescue me?" asked the woman. "I'd hoped that God might have reconsidered my case and pardoned me."

"I'm afraid not," replied Serena, "But I'll try to protect you, as long as I can."

Serena didn't want to give this poor woman false hope, but what else could she say? Right now, her presence had somehow produced an island of temporary calm in this sea of agony and terror. The birds seemed to avoid her, but she couldn't stay here long, and when she left, this poor woman's torment would begin. Serena would remain as long as she could, despite the devil's warning.

She closely examined the woman's shackles, hoping that there might be a weakness that she could exploit in an attempt to free her, but there wasn't. The burns left around the woman's wrists were dreadful, the worst she had ever seen. Her skin had actually been charred beneath the seams where the shackles had welded themselves together. What a cruel and barbaric method of restraint. Then again, what purpose would a lock and key have served on shackles that would remain closed for all eternity? From satan's viewpoint, it was infinitely practical.

Serena looked at the countless others. She didn't care what they had done in life, no crime warranted this sort of cruelty. If only there was something she could do; yet she realized that she was just as damned as any of these, only the means by which she would be punished was different.

The woman seemed somewhat calmer now. "My name is Karen, Karen Collins."

"Serena Davis," replied Serena.

"I'm sorry that we had to meet like this," continued Karen.

"Me too," Serena said. She hesitated; she wasn't sure how well her next question might be received. "Do you have any idea why you're here? I mean, why this?"

Karen closed her eyes for a moment. "My heart attack was my ticket here," she said bitterly. "It isn't fair, I mean, I'm only 42…42. I quit smoking eight years ago, hadn't had a sick day in years, for God's sake, I went to aerobics three times a week. A heart attack shouldn't have happened, no, not to me, but there it was."

"I don't think any of us were safe from death," Serena said. "I was only 28."

Karen didn't seem to notice Serena's comment. Her head swung from side to side, as she stared in disbelief at her seared wrists, which incredibly, had already begun to heal. "Oh God, this crazy itching in my wrists, its driving me nuts," said Karen, trying to twist her wrists in the manacles, to somehow alleviate the awful discomfort. Her efforts were rewarded by a trickle of blood as the barbs within the shackles dug into her still tender flesh. Her wrists went still.

"I was getting ready to go to work," Karen said. "You see; I'm a full partner in a large law firm in Atlanta. It had taken me years of hard work to get to where I was, but it was finally paying off. I had so much to live for. There was no warning; the pain started suddenly, the worst chest pain I'd ever felt. It was like there was a ton of weight on top of me. There was no one at home to help me. My husband had already left for work, and my son was on his way to school; I was alone. I stumbled to the phone, managed to call 911, but I could hardly speak. If they came, they came too late. The next thing I knew, I was being sucked into this violet tunnel. It was horrible."

Serena only nodded. She was getting to know the procedure pretty well.

"I was taken to the grandest courtroom I had ever seen, where I was forced to kneel before God," said Karen, who seemed to be more agitated again. "There was a huge audience in the gallery, as I watched my whole life flash before my eyes, in some sort of vision. I didn't like what I saw. It was biased, it wasn't fair. I mean, I did a lot of good in my life. I raised a loving son, saved more clients from being run over by the system than I can remember. I saved lives! But in this courtroom, I wasn't even afforded the opportunity to seek council, or even argue my own case. When it was all over, I was told that my name wasn't found in the Lamb's Book of Life, and that was the end of it. God condemned me just like that, sentenced me to outer darkness. What kind of justice is that? It wasn't fair."

Tears streamed from Karen's eyes, as she gazed upward at the circling birds, awaiting the coming feast. "Why can't they at least give me a fighting chance? Why do I have to be shackled and help-less? I can't stand it."

"I was dragged away by an angel, carried into Hell," continued Karen. "Everything happened so fast. Next thing I knew, the angel had thrown me into some sort of hellish holding cell. Believe me, I've seen a lot of horrendous holding tanks, but this was the worst." Karen again paused. "But I guess you know about all of that."

Serena nodded. "That was the way it was for me too."

"They forced me out of my clothes, and into these horrible smelling rags, dragged me off to be sentenced by satan himself. Satan accused me of being uncharitable, of serving self and money. He said that since I had failed to do service to God, since I had not sacrificed anything of myself, that I myself would be sacrificed to the birds of the air on this altar for all eternity. It's insane! How can he do this to me?"

Karen was becoming far more agitated. Her voice increased in volume, yet trembled at the same time. She again yanked upon the chains that restrained her. "I'll never see my husband or son again; I'm going to be on this damn altar forever! They're going to eat me forever! I want out of here! Let me loose, let me loose! Help!" she screamed.

Serena tried to calm her, but it was no use. Karen flailed about wildly, screaming and cursing at the top of her lungs, cursing both God and satan. Serena stepped back.

Within seconds one of the birds was upon Karen, scratching at her left leg with its sharp talons, pecking viciously at her bare belly with its large pointed beak. Blood began to spill. Karen howled and flailed about wildly, but it was to no avail, the execution of her sentence had begun.

Serena ran, tears streaming from her eyes. She ran like a frightened animal, driven on by pure adrenaline. She felt like she could run forever. She tried to block out the screams around her, tried to focus on the ground in front of her, but in vain. There was no escape from the terror, not in Hell.

Serena wasn't sure how far or how long she had run when exhaustion finally took its toll. Apparently, there was a limit to human endurance, even here. She collapsed to the ground amidst the blood-stained altars, amidst the cries of torment that echoed from every corner of her world, and there she wept.

"Please don't cry," came a voice from nearby, nearly masked by the din of agony all around. The voice was strained, the voice of one in great pain.

Serena looked in the direction of the voice, to discover a man shackled to the altar. In reality, he was little more than a collection of bones, torn muscles, and shattered organs. The birds had apparently abandoned him in search of better pickings; yet, like any victim of Hell's fury, his body was regenerating. New muscle was growing, spreading over blood-stained bones, while within his chest, his vital organs and blood vessels were repairing themselves at a phenomenal pace. It was a thoroughly unnatural and grotesque process, one that sent a chill up Serena's spine.

Again the tormented being spoke. Only the timbre of his voice told Serena that this lump of flesh and bone was, in reality, a man. "Where are you going, child?"

"The sea of fire," replied Serena.

"I'm sorry," he replied, his voice full of genuine sympathy. "I guess there aren't any pleasant destinations in this place." His head turned slowly toward Serena. She gazed into a face that was as much bone as ravaged flesh. The eyes were set deep in the dark sockets of his skull, and Serena wondered if they might not have been there at all just a few minutes ago. His nose was little more than a bloody stump, but it too seemed to be regenerating. "Please excuse my appearance. I know it must be frightening to you."

"No, no it's not," replied Serena. She lied.

"The birds will be leaving me in peace for a time," continued the man. "That is, until I am whole once more. Then the entire ordeal will begin anew. As best I can figure; it takes about four hours for the birds to pick one of us clean. Then it takes about an hour or so for our bodies to reconstitute. It is an endless cycle, as endless as eternity itself."

"Who are you?" asked Serena, trying to dry the tears from her eyes.

"My name is Thomas Allen Stanford," was the reply. "Not that names mean a great deal here."

"I'm Serena Davis," replied Serena.

"I'm sorry that you're here," continued Thomas, "though, I appreciate the opportunity to talk to you."

Serena smiled slightly; this man's kind voice had calmed her. She really needed someone to talk to. "May I ask how long you've been here?"

"You can ask," came the reply, "I don't think I could tell you. You see, after a while, time is a thing that can get pretty blurred here. "I passed into this world in 1938, just before Christmas. How long has that been?"

"A long time," said Serena, doing the math. "It's 2007 now."

"Sixty-nine years," interjected Thomas, almost immediately.

"Your math skills are sharper than mine," noted Serena.

There was a slight sound that came from Thomas. Serena thought it might have been a chuckle. "I had to be good with numbers; you see I was a banker, a bank president to be more specific. I was in the banking business for over 30 years, through good times and bad. I was a good businessman, and I did my job well. My small bank was one of the few that survived the stock market crash of '29, and it continued to thrive on through the depression that followed. Yes, LaSalle National continued to serve the greater Chicago area with courtesy and efficiency through those dark days. But it was such a long time ago. I sometimes wonder if that dependable old bank is still there today."

"I really don't know," admitted Serena.

"Well, I guess it doesn't matter, does it? At least not to us, not here. I doubt that we will be taking out a home improvement loan anytime soon." Thomas pulled weakly upon the chains that bound him. "Nope, this altar and these shackles are as sound today as they were on the day they were fashioned. All of our needs are seen to here. We want for nothing, except possibly an end to our torment." Thomas paused. "I'm sorry. I know that outburst was uncalled for. I didn't want to upset you. I guess my etiquette has become a little coarse over the years."

"It's OK, really," Serena said, hesitating to ask the next question. "But why are you here?" She regretted asking the instant she said it.

"It's all right," assured Thomas, "I don't mind talking about it. I'm paying the price for my affluence, pride, and arrogance. You see, the board of directors of my bank had blessed me with a very generous salary. After all, my brilliant financial strategies had pulled our institution through a crisis that had crushed many of our competitors. We even acquired several of those competitors during those dark years of the depression.

"I showered my family with the blessings of our wealth. My wife and two daughters wanted for nothing. We lived in a large, beautiful home in one of the most affluent areas of the city; threw lavish parties; became part of Chicago's elite society. My daughters attended a prestigious private college, and their weddings were large and important social events. Life was beautiful—at least for us.

But somewhere along the line I had forgotten one thing, charity. In the midst of our affluence, we had forgotten the millions of suffering people around us. Socially, we had nothing to do with those less fortunate than ourselves; after all, what would our friends say? In my business affairs, I made loans only to those people whom I counted as good risks, and that meant persons that I considered at least socially acceptable. I wasn't afraid to foreclose on an overdue mortgage, just because the client was out of work. After all, my bank wasn't a charity. We were a business, and we were in it to make money."

Thomas paused. A grunt of pain emanated from his lips. Flesh now covered virtually all of his face, and his nose was nearly whole. His rib bones were rapidly being covered with new muscle tissue and his internal organs were nearly restored. Yet, the pain associated with the entire process was apparent upon his countenance, and in the abrupt jolts that occasionally racked his body as nerves reconnected, once more transmitting pain from ravaged regions of his desecrated body.

"I thought of the poor as being inferior. There was only so much money to go around, and 'a fool and his money were soon parted.' Most of the money came to rest in the hands of those who used it most wisely and effectively, hands like mine. In such hands, money attracted more money. But, you see, I had never been poor, never considered the circumstances under which those in poverty lived. All that many of those people needed to get back on their feet was a helping hand, perhaps my hand, but I never extended it to them. I was in a position to make a difference, but I didn't.

Serena, we are our brother's and sister's keeper. In all of my 68 years of life on Earth, I never came to realize that simple fact. I realize it now, but now it's too late. Once, my world was my wife and children, the house on Ventnor Drive, and my office on the 16th floor. But now this is my world, an altar of pain amidst the eternal heat and harsh sun of this barren valley. The sun never sets on this place, you know. It beats down on you constantly, unremittingly. What I wouldn't give for a night, even a shadow.

Oh, to feel the rain upon my face, even a drop of water upon my lips, but all of that is gone, part of another life."

Thomas turned to gaze upon the pain and misery that surrounded them. "I often wonder if my wife, Susan, is somewhere here among us. I guess I'll never know." Thomas turned once more to Serena. "Oh, she was such a beautiful woman, a loving wife and mother. I hope and pray that she isn't here. I pray that today she dwells with God in Heaven. In that case, she wouldn't remember me at all, would she? Perhaps that would be for the best. Perhaps our two daughters are there with her by now. I hope so. I want so much for them to be happy. They don't deserve to be in this place."

Serena stumbled to her feet. She walked to the altar, knelt by his side, and took the hand of Thomas in hers, in an attempt to lend to him some measure of comfort. Thomas was now almost fully regenerated. Only a few scars remained to attest to the suffering he had most recently endured. He had the appearance of a man in his late 30s, and a handsome one at that. Yet decades of pain had etched its mark around his sad eyes.

"You can't realize just how good it has been to talk to you, Serena," continued Thomas. "None of those around me speak English. I suspect that fact is courtesy of satan himself."

Thomas strained to gaze toward the sky, toward the great hoard of buzzards circling overhead. Experience told him that his time was indeed short. "I'm afraid that I've been doing all of the talking. Time in Hell is eternal, but moments like this, moments without pain and in good company, are precious. I know that you will need to leave me soon, and we will never meet again, but I would like to know a little about you, about your life. That is, if you don't mind."

Serena didn't mind; she so desperately needed to talk to someone. She told Thomas about her all too brief existence among the living, about the rock house in Oregon, about Chris. It was when she spoke of her love lost, that tears came once more to her eyes. What was she going to do?

"I'm sorry that you've lost someone so wonderful," said Thomas, "but I'm sure that there are many heartbreaking stories to be heard here. It might have been better for us all if we had no memory of our lives on Earth."

"Thomas, do you think there's any hope for us?" asked Serena.

"I fear not," was the response. "In the great judgment hall, God himself sentenced me to outer darkness until the day of final judgment. What will happen after that, I can't say, but I fear our fates are sealed. I only wish that I could give you another answer, a more optimistic one. I fear that Jesus was our only hope of escaping this place, and we both rejected Him."

Serena shook her head sadly. "If we only had another chance."

Thomas squeezed Serena's hand. "If I knew then what I know now, I truly believe that I would have changed my ways. But you see, at the time, I believed that the only thing beyond death was eternal sleep. One had to live life to its fullest, for all too soon it would be gone. Now understand, I took my family to church from time to time, but I guess that I just wasn't listening to the sermons very carefully."

Again Thomas looked skyward. The terrible black birds were gathering above him. His body was whole once more. It was time for the cycle to be repeated, as it had countless times before. "Serena, it's time for you to go now."

"If I stay I might be able to protect you for a while," replied Serena, who couldn't bear to think of her newfound friend in agony again. "Maybe you could get some rest, a break from all the pain. I'd be happy to watch over you, shield you from the sun; protect you from the birds. It would be no trouble at all, really."

"You are such a dear sweet person," replied Thomas. "It makes your presence here all the more tragic. But if you stay, things might be all the worse for you. Remember what satan told you about helping others here? Now go, please, and don't look back."

Serena rose to her feet; then leaned down to kiss Thomas on the cheek. "God bless you, Thomas."

Thomas wasn't so sure that such a thing was possible, yet he smiled back at this young woman who had brought a brief moment of respite from his eternity of pain. "And you too, Serena."

Serena turned to leave, then hesitated.

"Go quickly, Serena," warned Thomas, the volume of his warning increasing. "Run, get away from this place."

Serena walked and then ran. She never looked back. She couldn't bear to look at what was destined to happen.

"Good-bye Serena," whispered Thomas, as he strained to watch her diminishing form vanish into the distance. A terrible shadow swept across his body as one of the huge birds passed by inches above. It climbed and pirouetted in midair before swooping back in his direction. Shackles rattled as he closed his eyes and prepared to experience the next chapter in the eternal tragedy of the late Thomas Allen Stanford.

chapter six

THE dominion of black altars and swarming vultures went on for miles. Serena could hardly imagine how many tormented souls were trapped here, nor did she care to attempt the computation. It was like a great city, the altars set up with mathematical precision like homes along well-planned streets and avenues. There was only one industry in this great metropolis, one product—the eternally regenerating raw flesh of its unwilling citizens. And there was no lack of consumers for that product. The ravenous birds of prey consumed everything that the city's inhabitants could produce, and still hungered for more. It was an economy, indeed, an ecosystem like none other.

How Serena longed for an end to it all. She could bear the screams of agony no longer, the terrible sounds of pecking and pulling, and the dreadful caws and cries of the birds in the midst of their feeding frenzy. Was there ever an end to it all, or would it extend all the way to the sea of fire?

At long last, Serena beheld it, the final row of altars and a great levy of rock and soil beyond it, not unlike the one she had scaled on her way into this terrible place. At the very heart of the city, virtually every black altar had been occupied by a desecrated soul. But here in the suburbs, most of the altars were vacant, shiny slabs of obsidian awaiting the arrival of eternal victims.

Then the strange irony struck her. Like most earthly cities, this one was growing like a beast, claiming more and more of the countryside around it. Land was cleared and new altars were fabricated to make room for the steady stream of unwitting inhabitants who were sure to come.

"Oh, if only there was some way to warn them," whimpered Serena. "If only they knew what was ahead."

What was it like to be eaten by birds again and again while you lay there, shackled and helpless for all eternity? It was an unimaginable concept. How did one keep their sanity amidst all this destruction? Thomas Stanford had. His kind words had pulled her back from the brink of hysteria. He had been a friend when she desperately needed one. If only she could have repaid the favor in kind. She felt so helpless. Just thinking of that brave soul now brought even more tears to her eyes, then open sobbing. Did one, in time, get used to the eternal cycle of pain? She hadn't thought to ask. She wouldn't have.

She paused, sitting down upon one of the vacant altars for a moment, trying to compose herself. Right now she was so tired, more mentally than physically. She heard a round of screeches and cries from the birds circling above. She turned her gaze upward, then to the instrument upon which she sat, to its glistening surface shimmering in the red sunlight, to the chains and barbed shackles securely anchored on it. She considered its purpose. She thought better of her decision and quickly jumped to her feet. To sit here was sacrilegious, perhaps even obscene. She would only rest her feet when she was well clear of this place. She moved on, eventually passing the last row of monoliths and scrambling over the ridge and into the rocky terrain beyond.

She thought back upon the stories she had heard in high school, stories of the world's greatest human atrocities. She considered the concentration camps of Nazi Germany and the killing fields of Cambodia, the most terrible acts of human barbarism of the last century. But this experience went beyond acts of genocide—this was eternal torture in the guise of execution for *billions*. As totally evil as those who masterminded these terrible holocausts were, satan, the architect of this city of pain, was far more nefarious. The beautiful angel who had led the praise to the Most High had become creation's greatest villain, humankind's most vile adversary.

Serena couldn't explain why she turned one last time to look at this realm of horror, yet as she did, a new aspect became apparent. For the past hour she had focused her eyes on the ground in front of her, hardly daring to scan the width and breadth of the dreadful valley, but now she dared. She focused her attention on the hills about a quarter mile to her left. There, just beyond the level expanse of the field of agony, she saw thousands upon thousands of wooden crosses set into the steadily rising terrain, each one held a victim of satan's hatred. Here too, the black vultures swarmed and fed, adding a new dimension to the horror of this ancient form of execution.

Through the sacrifice of Christ, the Cross had become the instrument by which humankind had been offered redemption. But in satan's hands, it had become just another form of torture, a route to eternal agony, inspired by the twisted mind of man.

"Oh God!" gasped Serena, quickly turning away. She had no idea as to what horrible sins these poor souls might have committed, but she wasn't about to go up there and investigate. Instead, she moved on, venturing into the rugged boulder-strewn valley beyond the monoliths.

The cries of agony slowly faded away, yet deep within her mind the screams continued. What she had beheld had profoundly affected her. No doubt, her own coming experience would affect her even more. She cried, not only for herself, but for all of the people who had turned their back on Christ's love. God hadn't sent her here, she had. She thought of all of the sins in her life, of all of the people she had hurt, intentionally or inadvertently. There were so many things in her brief existence on Earth that she now so desired to make right, but she no longer had that power.

Her mind wandered back to that green rich Earth. By now, she imagined, her earthly body rested in a coffin 6 feet beneath the Oregon sod, filled with formaldehyde. She wondered how many people had attended her funeral. She and Chris would have been buried side by side in Holly Hillcrest Cemetery, in his family plot; at least she hoped so. There, at least, she and Chris would reside together for eternity.

She tried to imagine that place in spring. She and Chris had gone there to place flowers upon his mother's grave last May. It was so green and peaceful, a hilltop overlooking the small Oregon town and the farms beyond. Was Chris with his mother now? Serena thought so. She had never met her husband's mother, she had died when he was only 15, but she had been the wellspring of her husband's faith. She had educated him in the ways of the Lord, in the ways of caring, and she had done her job well. Their reunion was most assuredly a blessed occasion. It would help him deal with her loss. Then Serena remembered; he would never remember that loss. There would be no pain, only joy. Serena wept all the more. Hell was more than pain; it was the separation from God and all of those she had loved on Earth. It was the realization that she was totally forgotten by all who had ever loved her.

Serena stopped. Reaching for the mystical hourglass that she had slipped into the tight upper hem of her loincloth, she stared at the enigmatic device. Yes, there was still plenty of time, only a small fraction of the sand had run its course. But what horrors lay ahead of her, how far did she have to travel? Maybe this wasn't such a great idea. Maybe she hadn't been so clever after all. Being thrown quite suddenly and unceremoniously into that fiery pit might have been more merciful than this.

Serena was startled as a long dark shadow swept across her. She turned to behold a tall figure, engulfed in darkness. Satan's countenance bore a slight but devious smile.

"So, Serena, what do you think of my realm so far? Or may I assume that your tears have already answered my question?"

"Sir?" she answered awkwardly, trying to gain control of her emotions. She wiped the tears from her eyes. "I'm sorry, I didn't see you coming."

Satan laughed openly. "Most people never do, until it's too late. You didn't."

Serena looked at the prince of darkness with puzzlement. "I'm sorry, sir, I don't understand."

"Of course not," replied satan, "For years you played your futile spiritual games, Tarot cards, palm reading, rituals to honor a goddess of ancient Celtic mythology; so many games."

"But the Tarot readings were so often right, as were the palm readings," objected Serena. "I really thought that I had psychic abilities. Maybe I did."

Again satan laughed. "Of course the readings seemed to work, my minions and I went to considerable effort to create that illusion to deceive you. It was a diversion. In doing so, we led you and many others away from the truth; and down the road to my kingdom. As to you having psychic abilities; no, little one, I don't think so."

That revelation caught Serena off guard. "But why have you taken so much time and effort to get me here, why not someone else?"

Satan sat on a nearby boulder. "Don't flatter yourself, child. I am a deceiver of nations, of multitudes, yours is just one of my many success stories."

"But, sir, why did you grant to me the privilege of walking free in Hell for these 12 hours? You said that you would do it to satisfy my scientific curiosity. You also said that it was something that you rarely do. Excuse my boldness, but I suspect that there is something more to it than that."

Serena knew she was pushing her luck with that comment. After all, this wasn't just a casual conversation with some stranger on a busy street corner; this was satan, the devil, the villain of eternity that she was addressing.

There was a momentary pause; then satan's expression broke into a wide grin. "I like you, Serena, at least as much as I could like one of you loathsome humans. I believe that I am coming to understand why God, the Creator, liked you so much."

That one threw Serena for a loop. "He did?"

"Most certainly," replied satan. "He spoke of it openly to me, on several occasions. That is one of the reasons that I became so interested in you. Oh yes, I believe that the Ancient of Days had great expectations as far as you were concerned, and even grander plans. Taking you from Him was a particularly sweet victory. You are clever and persuasive, gifted of speech. You might have lead many people away from the path to my kingdom during your days on Earth, given the opportunity. Thankfully, you won't have that opportunity in the sea of fire. It will keep you quite preoccupied, as you will see."

Serena was absolutely stunned. Yes, she had heard this before, from the angel Aaron, yet, somehow, it hadn't quite sunk in. "You are still on speaking terms with God, after all that has happened?"

"Don't be so surprised; of course I am, little one," laughed satan. "Surely, you must have figured that out by now, a woman as bright as yourself. You have heard of the trials of Job, have you not? Did you think that was just a myth? And did you think that the story of Job was an isolated incident? No, there have been many Jobs during the course of history, so many. Surely, you must realize that. The Creator has always valued my opinion. He does even now. I widen His horizons, open His eyes to His own failings. In a manner of speaking, I am His conscience. No one knows Him as I do, nor manipulates Him so effectively. I am the tempter of humanity, the accuser of the brethren, and I shall bring to naught the plans of God."

"But you spoke about me, you and God?"

"Among other things, yes, your name has come up. Is there some reason that I need to tell these things to you twice?" Quite abruptly the direction of the conversation changed. "But Serena, what has happened to your scientific curiosity? You have been granted a rare opportunity and you are squandering it. You hardly conducted a meticulous scientific study of the altars of agony, did you? It was both a brilliant and clever feat of engineering, if I do say so myself, an expression of my infinite creativity."

Satan turned back to the great city of altars, though it was not directly visible from their current location. "I made full utilization of the space available. I'd first thought of making the altars larger, draping the victims across them, shackling their wrists and ankles at the four corners; but that would have been such a waste of space. By making them smaller, I can fit so many more of them in the limited space this valley affords me, and my guests are so much more uncomfortable with their head and legs hanging over the edges. Oh yes, sometimes I even surprise myself with my creativity."

Serena was speechless. Never had she known something so cruel and conceited.

"As for the hills of crucifixion, well, you turned your back upon them completely. I thought you wanted to learn, glimpse a morsel of my genius, before joining the others in their eternal agony. Once you become part of the experiment, a true subject of my realm, I doubt that you will be in much of a mood to study it objectively."

Serena searched desperately for an excuse; trying not to show weakness before the prince of darkness. "There wasn't enough time. I didn't want to be late in arriving at the sea of fire." Somehow, she realized that satan saw through her lie. Why was she still trying to promote this deception? It was pointless. Before her stood the master of deception himself, the prince of lies, surely she did not expect to beat him at his own game.

"Ah, I see," satan said, gently twisting the bottom of his goatee between the fingers of his left hand. "Aren't you even the least bit curious as to what crime I was addressing in crucifying them?" He didn't wait for a reply. He rose to his feet, and extended his hand to the young human. "Come with me, little one."

Serena hesitated then took two steps toward satan. She placed her hand in his. She was surprised to discover that it was soft and warm like a human hand, but there was something else. She could feel the powerful sphere of darkness about this mighty being, a loathsome oppressive spirit. It sent a chill down her spine.

"See, I don't bite, at least not this time," chuckled the devil. "Come, I have things to show you."

Before them, a large circular portal outlined in a shimmering violet aura appeared. Within the ring of luminescent glow, Serena beheld another landscape, another place. Together they walked through, with no more effort than one would expend in walking through a wide open doorway between two rooms in a house. They emerged amidst the rolling hills high above the valley of altars. Serena gazed across the valley, across the vast expanse of pain and despair.

"Magnificent, is it not?" proclaimed satan, stretching his arm out toward the valley below. "There are over 2 ½ million altars at this site alone, 72 percent of which are currently occupied. And there are 93 other sites similar to this one throughout Hell, some larger, and others somewhat smaller. The largest has a capacity of over 12 million. Imagine that, this is eternal torment on the grandest of scales."

Serena was speechless—no words could describe the magnitude of the atrocity being perpetrated here. How might the knowledge of the existence of such a place as this affect humanity in its day-to-day dealings? Would it compel people to be kinder and gentler with one another? Would it persuade people to make peace with God and accept His terms of salvation? She wondered.

"Come, Serena, I have still more to show you." Satan led his stunned companion across the rocky ground toward a nearby pair of crosses. He pointed toward the tall wooden instruments of agony before them. "I was inspired by the mind of man when I created this masterpiece, but as you can see, I have improved upon it as only I could. This means of inducing eternal pain is not as often utilized as the altar, oh no. There are less than 8,000 crosses on the hills surrounding this valley. The victims that call them eternal home are a special group, united by a common thread. During their lives they willingly chose to worship me. Some of these humans actually accepted God's plan of salvation at one point in their miserable lives, yet they were like grains of wheat that fell amidst the thistle. As they grew, so did the thistle, and, in the end, that thistle choked them out." Satan stopped momentarily, turning to Serena. "Do you understand the parable?"

"Yes sir, I think so. It's in the Gospels. The thistle represents the cares and evil pleasures of the world."

"Exactly," satan said. "But these souls didn't just turn their back on God, oh no, nothing so simple, they turned to me. Imagine that. You humans are so marvelously fickle. I have rewarded their devotion by allowing them to suffer for me, in my name, in much the same manner as Jesus suffered for you."

Satan yanked once more on Serena's hand, drawing her toward the two crosses, which faced out across the valley. Their victims, one a young man, the other a young woman, hung from the crosspieces by their nailed wrists, blood oozing from the wounds. The stout wooden crosses stood at least 15 feet tall, and the nailed feet of the victims hung better than 8 feet above the ground.

The young woman was dressed much as Serena was dressed, in a ragged gray skirt and a tattered top. Yet her attire was rather more revealing than Serena's, especially in the position in which she found herself. The young man wore a small gray loincloth that scarcely covered his manhood. Their scant clothing offered virtually no protection from the elements, and the torn and shredded condition of their flesh told Serena that those elements extended far beyond the harsh sun and torrid breeze. It was obvious that the birds circling overhead frequently took the opportunity to feed upon their tortured bodies as well.

Around both of their necks hung a leather cord; and dangling from that cord was a golden amulet in the form of a five-pointed star. One vertex of the star pointed downward, while two others pointed upward. Serena recognized this sign as the inverted pentagram, the sign of satan. Drool oozed from the corner of their mouths and their breathing was exceptionally labored, as their arms were stretched to the limit by their own weight. Occasionally they would push upward on their nailed feet in an attempt to take some of the strain off their arms and chest. In this way they were able to breathe once more, but only at the cost of a different sort of pain. Their wide eyes followed the approach of the prince of darkness.

"Please, have pity on me, master," said the young woman in a hoarse voice. "I served you as best I could during my life. I even sacrificed to you. Haven't I suffered enough for you? Please, let me down!"

"What more do I need to do, master?" pleaded her companion. "I was loyal to you. You know I was. Why do you have to do this to me? Lord, what have I done that offended you?"

Satan stepped away from Serena and toward the crosses. "You have not offended me, but I require your worship, my children. Show me that you love me, tell me that you would suffer anything in my name, or I shall make your agony far worse!"

Satan began to raise his hand toward the two, yet the very threat of his wrath was sufficient to produce the desired response.

"Hail satan, our lord and master!" cried the woman, tears in her eyes. "All hail to the most high!"

"We worship you, master!" the young man said. "You are the only one for us, our only god."

In their debilitated condition, they hardly seemed capable of lifting their voices in honor of he who had placed them upon their crosses, the author of their pain. Yet their praises echoed through the hills, for over a minute, a disjointed hymn of agony to their torturer.

"You are the great one!" cried the woman, fearful of being outdone by her companion, fearful of the consequences of being second best. "We worship your name. I would gladly suffer anything for you!"

"So would I!" her companion said. "I would suffer even more for you than she. Don't you see, lord, I'm the one who is the most loyal to you."

"No, I am," objected the woman. "I would do anything for you, give you anything. I would suffer anything for your pleasure."

Satan smiled broadly as his two victims each sought to outdo the other. "And so you shall," he replied, turning to depart, "for all eternity."

Serena looked on in horror, tears in her eyes. Satan's cruelty kept reaching new extremes. Why had he taken such an interest in her?

"While they lived, I gave them a vision of grandeur. I promised them a kingdom, a kingdom of millions that they could look out upon for all times." Satan stretched out his hand to the countless altars below. "As you can see, I kept my word. They shall look over this valley forever, to behold their many subjects, who lay prostrate before them.

Serena gasped. This was an irony that only satan could appreciate. If anything, those who had faithfully served him were all the more subject to his wrath.

"There are others here who openly admitted to having no belief in me whatever," continued satan. "Their worship was no more than play, an excuse to indulge themselves in their own lurid fantasies, for their own fleshly pleasures. Nevertheless they worshiped me, built ornate altars in my name, and conducted elaborate rituals to honor my own greatness. In light of all of that, their current situation is really quite humorous."

"Humorous?" gasped Serena, astounded by satan's choice in words. "Tragic might be a better term."

Satan's smile widened. "But that would depend upon your point of view, wouldn't it?" Satan once more took Serena's hand. "Let us move on, there is still more to see before I must leave you."

Serena cautiously took the hand of the dark prince as a portal, similar to the one she had seen in the valley, opened before them. Walking through, they were immediately transported to another region of Hell. They stood near the base of a sheer cliff, towering 500 feet above them, overlooking the rough, rocky valley floor. Even as Serena watched, she was alarmed to see a human figure plummet from the top of the cliff to the valley below. He hit the ground with a terrible thud and a cry of excruciating pain. His cry blended in with the moans and lamentations of a multitude of others. Then another, a woman this time, was thrown from the precipice and slammed into the rocks below a few seconds later.

"We are only a few miles from where you began your journey," satan said. "Your route to the sea of fire would not have taken you by this place, but I wanted you to see it, nonetheless. Let us take a closer look." Satan roughly pulled Serena toward the impact point at the bottom of the cliff, even as a third and fourth victim were cast down from above.

Before them a great gathering of rag-clad bodies crushed and mutilated by the long fall, crawled and dragged themselves away upon shattered and twisted limbs. The presence of heavy shackles about their wrists and ankles made their journey all the more difficult.

They were urged along by the prods and whips of a multitude of devilish taskmasters. The horned demons who ruled over them were large and covered in coarse brown fur. They had sharp claw like hands and feet, and large black eyes. To Serena, their glistening eyes appeared almost insect-like. Their large mouths were filled with black, razor-sharp teeth, and their ears were exceptionally large and pointed. They were truly like something out of a nightmare.

The pathetic mounds of flesh before them moved as best they could amidst the clanking and rattling of their ponderous chains. They moved in a great barefoot procession along a treacherous yet heavily traveled pathway that led from the base of the cliff into the hills beyond.

"After their unfortunate fall from that cliff, these poor souls are urged by my minions to climb back up to the high precipice," satan said while watching yet another victim of his wrath plunge from the heights. "It's a difficult journey at first, with so many broken and shattered bones, ripped and bruised muscles, and severed tendons to contend with. But along the way, they heal, reconstruct themselves. Yet, that process of reconstruction is agonizing in itself, especially when the victim must use those bones and muscles quite vigorously in order to escape the whips and prods of the taskmasters. It takes nearly two hours to traverse the trail to the top. By the time they arrive, they are whole once more and ready to take the plunge again. Each one repeats the process without rest, throughout eternity."

"It's inhuman," gasped Serena. "What did these people do to deserve such a horrible fate?"

"I wondered when you were going to ask," laughed the devil. "They committed unnatural sexual acts. Men lusted after other men and women after other women. It is a futile pursuit, unable to bring about the miracle of procreation. Therefore, they who have committed it will spend the rest of eternity in this futile gesture of plummeting from the cliff, only to climb to the top once more and plummet from its heights again."

Satan looked carefully into Serena's eyes, then smiled. "You had perpetrated such an act as they, if only once. Perhaps you would like to join them, give this thing a try, just one or two rounds to get a feel for the routine. After all, the best way to understand a thing is to experience it first hand. Who knows, perhaps I could even be persuaded to adjust your sentence, condemn you to this place for all eternity rather than the sea of fire. You might prefer this. What do you say? Want to give it a try?"

Serena heard footsteps behind her. She turned to find one of the large hairy demons towering over her, a pair of open ankle and wrist shackles in his claw-like hands. Apparently, satan's terrible offer hadn't been a spur of the moment proposal—it had been well-planned.

Satan's smile grew even wider. "See, all is in readiness, you just give the word and we can have you on the trail in no time."

Serena struggled to remain in control. Yet, despite the intense heat of this place, a chill as cold as ice, swept through her body. Satan made it sound like an invitation, but would she be afforded the right of refusal? "Thank you, sir, but I think I'd rather not."

Satan shrugged. "You might have found it an interesting experience, but as you wish, little one." He motioned to the demon before them to go back to his assigned task. "You know, do you not, that you are only delaying the inevitable. The 12 hours of grace I have afforded you are as a flickering candle amidst the great darkness of eternity that lies ahead. When those fleeting hours have passed, you will be compelled to face your inevitable future. That future holds in store for you pain, an eternity of unimaginable agony. Pain will become your reality. It doesn't really matter if it begins now or nine hours from now."

Satan paused for another moment to watch two more poor souls fall to what would certainly have been their deaths anywhere else; but not here. "I never grow weary of the parade. Sadly time grows short, but there is one more thing I want you to see. I have saved the best for last. I suspect that you might appreciate what you shall witness next."

Again a portal opened up before them, and a moment later the two vanished beyond it.

Serena felt the pleasantly cool air the instant she passed through the portal. A brisk wind was blowing at her back, while before her was a fantastic panorama of jagged mountains and valleys. Beyond the mountains was a level plain that ended in what appeared to be a great glowing sea of red that stretched to the distant horizon. The view was partially obscured by clouds of dust and smoke sweeping across the landscape below. She turned around to see still more mountains and the great red sun low in the sky.

They stood on the summit of what appeared to be the highest peak around. Overhead the sky was violet. For an instant, the memory of the horrors she had seen during the past hours faded, replaced by a sense of awe.

"Incredible!" gasped Serena.

"See, I told you that you would like it," replied satan. "We are over a mile above the valley floor. From here you gain an entirely different perspective of my creation, a perspective that few of my guests ever experience." Satan watched in amusement as the young woman scanned the horizon of the starkly beautiful environment.

"From here, who would possibly suspect what horrors lay below? From time to time, I come to this place, and other places like it, to get a breath of fresh air, to behold the world my hands have made." There was a momentary pause. "What do you see, little one?"

Serena turned to look at the bloated red luminary hanging in the sky; then she turned to satan. "Sir, I see a barren dry planet circling a small red star, maybe the only planet and only star in all of outer darkness. It is its own small universe."

Satan was rarely surprised, especially by a human, but this was one of those rare moments. "You see all of that from the top of this mountain?"

"Yes, sir," Serena said, "You see, I studied a little astronomy in my time on Earth."

"Speaking of time, my time is so very precious," interrupted satan. "I have enjoyed your presence. I would like nothing better than to spend the entire day with you, and at its end, escort you to the sea of fire myself, where I might bid you a final farewell. It would be a date, as you humans call it, an opportunity for you to get to know me a little better. However, that is not to be." There was a momentary pause.

"I have personally revealed to you the realm I have created. Who else could have done such a thing as this?" Satan raised his arms and turned slowly about to view the work of his own hand. "Surely, Serena, I am worthy of your worship; for truly, if I am not now your god, who is? Fall to your knees, little one, and do me homage—worship me."

Well, there it was. Serena had feared that this moment was coming. Since the experience at the crosses on the hill she knew this time of decision was inevitable. This megalomaniac thrived upon worship, whether he was deserving of it or not. What was she to do now? Perhaps diplomacy?

"Sir, please understand, I'm very impressed with your accomplishments here; they are stunning. I respect your abilities."

Satan shook his head in disapproval. "Here, all beings refer to me as lord satan or just lord; for in this place, I am lord. Only you persist in calling me sir."

"I call you sir out of respect," countered Serena.

"But that is not sufficient," replied satan with a trace of growing anger. "I require your worship. Kneel before me."

Serena's knees were shaking; she had run out of options. "Sir, throughout my entire life, I failed to worship God, the Creator of a hundred billion times a hundred billion stars, the Creator of the entire universe. I should have, but I didn't. Now you ask me to worship you." Again there was a pause. "Sir, if I failed to worship God, the true god, I cannot worship you."

"Ah, but you worshiped a pagan goddess," retorted satan. Then his anger ebbed once more and his expression softened. "Oh yes, I see that I have been going about this thing in the wrong way. How forgetful of me. Let me make this easier for you."

Suddenly, satan's form was in a state of metamorphosis. His skin color faded, his raiment became as white as snow. In a few seconds he had been transfigured into the form of a stunningly beautiful woman with long golden hair. This was the form that Serena had always associated with the goddess; the long flowing gown, the glowing countenance, it was all there.

"Now, you may worship me, Serena," said the goddess, her voice soft and feminine. "I am here before you, the author of spring, the bringer of the harvest, the creator of all nature. Fall to your knees, and yield to me the honor that I am due."

Serena was awestruck by the beauty, the majesty, of the goddess. For years she had been at the center of her life; yet now, for the first time, she understood the futility of such worship. She wasn't real; she was a lie, a fabrication of the prince of lies. She had always been so. "I'm sorry, I can't do that."

"I could force you to worship me," retorted the goddess, her voice suddenly angry. "I could cause you such agony, that you would do anything to bring it to an end."

"I know you could," replied Serena.

"And you still won't worship me?"

Serena hesitated. Wasn't the object here to reduce the pain as much as possible? "No, sir, I can't."

The imposing form of satan swiftly replaced the image of the goddess. Serena was surprised to find him smiling. "I believe you would resist me, for a while at least. Unfortunately, we don't have the time to put you to the test, at least not right now. But answer me this; did you really believe in this goddess of yours? Answer me truly."

Serena hesitated. In her youth she had performed rituals in the name of the goddess, burned incense to her, but had she truly believed? Did she have the same faith in the goddess that Chris had in his God, the true God, or was she just playing games? In more recent days, she had abandoned the rituals, beyond the occasional burning of incense. She looked toward satan who was still patiently awaiting her reply. "No, I don't think I did."

"So you surrendered your eternity for a thing you knew to be an illusion? You humans never cease to amuse me." Satan once more extended his hand. "Come, little one." Serena took his hand, as yet another portal materialized before them.

The trip through the portal brought Serena back to the very spot where her journey with the prince of darkness had begun.

"Here our paths shall part," announced satan, releasing his companion's hand. "You are indeed a strong-willed woman. I am relieved that you failed to respond to God's calling. In His service, your courage and determination might have hindered some of my enterprises, but here, your courage means nothing. For now, you are brave and defiant, but I wonder how brave and defiant you will be a year from now, or ten years, or a hundred. Time is a thing we have in abundance. Will the agony that awaits you in the sea of fire make you more pliable? I think so."

Satan turned to depart, then hesitated. "Oh, there is one final thing. We had a deal, you were not to interfere with the torments of any of my guests, remember? You have already violated that agreement once. I do not wish to see a repeat of that violation, least you suffer the consequences. Do we have an understanding?"

"Yes sir, I'm sorry," Serena said, quivering in fear.

"Very well, then. Enjoy what remains of your precious freedom, little one."

A portal of shimmering light appeared before the dark lord. He stepped through it, vanishing from sight. Shivering, Serena looked once more at the hourglass. Her time was running out with the sands. She had to continue the journey.

Serena was on the move once again. If she had ever held any hope in the depth of her heart, it was utterly gone now. How pliable would a year, or ten, or ten thousand in the sea leave her? Satan was right; in the end, she would probably do anything to be free of just a portion of the pain she would soon experience. How long would her ethical and moral fiber last? She feared that she would inevitably learn the answer.

chapter seven

FOR over an hour, the journey through the boulder-strewn valley was uneventful. No large birds of prey, no cries of pain, and no sign of a living thing met Serena's senses. Yet things around her were changing nonetheless. The rocks and boulders had taken on a darker more porous nature, and the odor of sulfur had become perceptibly stronger. Here and there, traces of yellow elemental sulfur could be seen adhering to the dark rocks.

Serena claimed no expertise in geology, but it seemed all too obvious that she was approaching a volcanically active region. She thought back to her panoramic view from the lofty mountaintop. She had attempted to put what she had seen there to memory. There had been signs of smoke, perhaps some sort of volcanic venting in this area. It might well extend all the way to the sea of fire. It was, no doubt, a dangerous region to travel.

She pondered the possibility of hiding out, trying to evade satan and his minions. There were so many souls here; despite satan's boasts, he and his legions couldn't possibly watch everyone all the time. She recalled the haste with which the demons had restrained poor Karen to the altar. They had been eager to depart. Had they said something about being in a hurry to move on to others, about not having the time to mess around with her too long? She wasn't sure. From what Serena had seen, they kept most of their human victims restrained by one means or another. Perhaps it was to keep them from resisting their tormentors, but perhaps it was something else. Perhaps it was to keep them in one place and accounted for.

There had been no demons watching over the valley of altars, at least Serena hadn't noticed any. Perhaps she should have paid closer attention. They probably weren't needed. After all, the victims of the altars weren't going anywhere, were they? But maybe there was more to it than that. Maybe satan couldn't spare the manpower, or in this case, the demonpower, to patrol it. Sure, there had been quite a hoard of demons at the cliff of falling souls, but perhaps that was an exception.

It seemed like a slim hope, but volcanic areas often held caves, lava tubes, that ran for miles underground. Perhaps she could find a place and hide out there. Perhaps satan would get sloppy, assume that Serena had leapt into the sea of fire and turn his attention elsewhere. Sure, spending a good part of eternity in a dark musty cave would be no picnic, but it would be better than spending eternity in the sea of fire.

Then again, satan had found her once, hadn't he? He'd spent quite a bit of time showing her around. He had a special interest in her, of that much she was certain. In fact, he might be observing her at this very moment. Would he eventually lose interest in her? Probably, but by then she would be in the sea of fire. The devil would have her exactly where he wanted her, in a place from which there was no escape.

In the midst of her contemplation, Serena walked into an open area, free of large boulders. It was a bowl-shaped expanse of sand and small rocks, perhaps 100 feet wide, and at its center was a roughly circular pool of crystal clear liquid. Water? Oh, could she be so fortunate? Her ordeal of the past hours had taken her mind off her thirst, but it was there nevertheless. She cautiously ventured toward the pool, being vigilant of her surroundings, yet no dangers met her eyes.

She knelt down by the pool's edge and slowly extended her hand into the liquid. Was it really water? Perhaps. The area around the pool had that special odor and feeling of moisture. Her hand penetrated the surface. It was warm but offered no burning sensation. She withdrew her hand and rubbed her fingers together. The liquid wasn't slimy. She touched it to her tongue; it didn't burn. She took a deep breath and cupped her hand to take a sip. The water had a slight taste of sulfur, but it wasn't bad, after the long walk it was wonderful. She drank handful after handful until she had her fill. She had convinced herself that she would never again savor the wonderful taste of this nectar of life.

She undid her sandals and waded barefoot into the pool. It was a fantastic feeling. At the pool's center, was a narrow tunnel that led into the depths. It confirmed Serena's cave hypothesis. Too bad this one was underwater. She sat down on the sand in the knee-deep water, allowing the refreshing liquid to wash over her. It was like a warm bath. Perhaps she would manage to clean the putrid rags that clothed her.

Almost as an afterthought, she noticed that a froth of small bubbles was rising from the small dark cave at the bottom of the pool. "A hot spring," she said while splashing herself with warm water. "I could open a resort here—a five star hotel, the best accommodations. The marketing brochure would read: Serena's Hot Spring. Get away from the cold winters, right here in the heart of Hell. That has a nice ring to it. But, the trouble is—everyone here is shackled or otherwise restrained, and the demons are too busy tormenting them to take a vacation. Too bad."

It was several minutes before Serena again glanced over at the bubbles rising from the cave below the pool. There were more of them now, and they were bigger. The water was becoming warmer, and that warmth was coming from the cave. She rose to her feet to take a better look. The water above the cave was becoming frothy with effervescence. Serena sensed danger and backed away. She reached the shoreline, and was in the process of putting on her sandals when the real eruption began. Water burst from the depths, spouting a dozen feet in the air for the better part of a minute. Serena stepped back as the pool grew to nearly twice its volume. Then, as abruptly as it had begun, the eruption ceased, and an uneasy calm returned to the now steamy pool.

Serena cautiously dipped her hand into the now turbid water, to discover that it was indeed very hot, much hotter than before. Had she not escaped the pool when she did, she might well have been severely scalded.

She figured that, like the geysers of Yellowstone, this one probably erupted on a regular schedule. Another useless scientific observation to the credit of the explorer who would never return to the world of the living to recap the wonders and horrors she had beheld in this strange world.

Serena left the misty pool behind, continuing her trek down the dismal valley. Here the terrain seemed less rugged. There were fewer large boulders, so she made better time, and she had a more unobstructed view of any dangers ahead of her. In the distance, she saw vast clouds of vapor rising from the valley floor, probably steam from other geysers. A large portion of the valley floor seemed to abruptly drop off as if a section of the valley had collapsed. As Serena drew closer she could hear the now all too familiar sounds of a multitude of tormented waling souls.

"What now?" she said, walking cautiously toward the source of the commotion.

Before her was a great pit. It was several miles in diameter, and perhaps 50 feet deep, surrounded on all sides by shimmering, slimy, nearly vertical walls of rock and mud. The bottom of the pit was covered with a roiling, turbulent lake of brown mud, whose heat and stench was so great that Serena was overwhelmed, even from where she stood. It was like a mammoth cesspool. Within this horrible pit was a great multitude of men and women, reeling, swimming, and splashing about, their flesh as red as fire. The scene reminded Serena of lobsters boiling in a pot. Serena had always hated that because it seemed so cruel; but to see it happening to human beings was unimaginable.

As Serena watched, she noticed that some regions of the pit were deeper than others, for the victims in those regions were compelled to swim through the viscous boiling mire; while in other places, the mud was scarcely ankle deep. Realizing this, the great throng of rag-clad humans struggled to reach the shallows, battling each other savagely, striving to occupy the most prime locations of the great pit. It was a constant struggle for those fortunate few to maintain their stations of least agony, for always there were those within the surging crowd who sought to take it from them.

Still others clawed at the sides of the pit with bloody, lacerated fingers, searching for any handhold that might allow them, if not to escape the pit, to at least pull them up and out of the boiling mire. All were futile attempts. Though some managed to climb some distance above the roiling filth, the slopes were too steep and slippery. Inevitably they too were pulled back into the foul cauldron by others seeking escape. And so it continued—an eternity of struggling and pain.

Even as Serena watched, a dark figure swooped out of the sky. In his arms he held a squirming, screaming man. He descended over the great pit like a mighty bird of prey, then cast the poor soul into the boiling lake of squalor below. With his burden shed, the dark figure soared into the misty sky and out of sight.

"Do you wish to know what their sin was?"

Serena turned abruptly to see an angelic being, very handsome, robed totally in black. His deep blue eyes looked into Serena's with such intensity. His dark wings were folded tightly to his back. Were it not for the darkness of his apparel and the circumstances of their meeting, Serena might have mistaken him for one of the angels who allied themselves with God, the Creator.

A look of concern appeared on his face. "I hope that I have not startled you, for that was not my intent."

He had startled her, quite thoroughly, but Serena was not about to admit to it. "It's OK," she said, quickly regaining her composure.

"Lord satan has commanded that you be treated as an honored guest until such time as the sand within your hourglass runs its course." The dark angel motioned to the great pit. "This is a place for those who took advantage of the less fortunate, the poor, the downtrodden. It is a realm of those unethical individuals who advanced themselves at the cost of others, who forgot kindness and mercy, and thought only of their own gain. Now and forever, they struggle to escape the boiling foulness that is the scourge of their world. They pull, push, claw, shove, and strike one another in an attempt to escape the scalding caustic slime, if only for a moment. Sadly, all of their victories are temporary…and in the end, meaningless."

"Ghastly," gasped Serena.

"But so was the way in which they lived their lives," retorted the dark angel. "Cruel were their methods and cruel are their rewards. You humans like to think in such complex terms; but in the end, it is just that simple."

"But the tortures here are so extreme," objected Serena. "I mean, these people committed these sins for, what, 60 or 70 years? But you torture them for eternity. How is that fair?"

"It is the nature of things," explained the dark angel. "Your few years on Earth are the most important ones of your eternity. They determine your path forever, your destiny." The dark angel motioned to the right. Here the great pit seemed to meet the high cliff wall that formed the edge of the valley.

"That is the best route around the pit. Stay to that side of the valley, the south side, on your way to the sea of fire, it is the safest way."

Serena nodded. "Thank you."

The dark angel smiled a devious smile as he bowed before the young woman in a mendacious courtesy. Then he turned, spread his dark wings, and leapt into the sky. His great wings created a virtual whirlwind as he climbed swiftly away. Serena was knocked to the ground by the blast. For a moment she feared that the blast might actually cast her into the terrible pit behind her, yet the powerful gale was short-lived. She turned to see the demonic form decrease in size as it climbed into the mists. She suspected that the entire incident was not a careless oversight, but a very deliberate act.

Serena continued on her journey. Making certain to leave a safe distance between her and the edge of the pit, she was forced to take a significant detour. Occasionally she glanced into the huge stinking caldera to see the eternal struggling within. What a terrible fate—perhaps worse than the black altars. The constant cries depressed her, reminding her of where she was and her eternal future.

The great chasm spanned the entire width of the valley, leaving only about 20 yards of level terrain between the yawning precipice of the pit and towering mountain cliffs at the narrowest point. It was well over an hour before she finally left the terrible chasm behind.

Before her was a great field of mighty geysers that were scattered across the entire width of the valley. Towering plumes of water thundered up from a valley floor encrusted with salts of white and yellow. This place made Yellowstone pale by comparison. There were hundreds, perhaps thousands, of geysers.

At any given time several of them roared with activity, thrusting water high above the steamy plain. Some took the form of narrow pillars of vapor and liquid, while others threw a wide fan of water across the barren landscape. There were plumes that possessed a trace of blue, green, or brown, bearing witness to the presence of local minerals. One geyser would erupt, then another, some distance away. There seemed to be no discernable pattern to the eruptions.

Traveling through this geothermal field might be a trick akin to traversing an earthly minefield. If Serena was near one of the vents when a geyser erupted, thousands of gallons of boiling hot water would engulf her. The receding flood might even sweep her into the vent as the eruption subsided and the geyser reclaimed its boiling hoard. It was a frightening prospect, but there seemed little choice; she was off.

She moved quickly, keeping a close eye on her surroundings. She had never been to Yellowstone and wondered if there was any warning before a geyser blew its top. She might just find out the hard way.

The ground shook frequently as she continued, and the air was full of the rumble of water and steam thundering up from the depths. Here and there, she spotted dark forms in the sky, flying in apparently random patterns above the valley floor. Occasionally they seemed to dive at the ground and then pull up before hitting the surface. At first she figured them to be large birds, like the ones she had seen around the black altars, but as one flew almost directly overhead, she realized that they were large-winged demons. What were they up to? She couldn't say; but whatever it was, it consumed their interest. Serena disregarded the demons, focusing her full concentration on the path ahead of her.

During the next half-hour, Serena's route did not carry her particularly close to any of the geysers, for which she was most grateful. The most active region of the field seemed to be along the far side of the valley. That was fine by her. She preferred to view these geothermal wonders from a respectable distance. Perhaps that was why the demon she had encountered at the edge of the pit had steered her in this direction, out of concern. Sure it was; these demons were deeply concerned for the humans under their charge. It was all the more reason to be suspicious of their advice.

Serena discovered a lone vent directly in her path. The slightest trace of steam issued from the salt-encrusted opening. She swallowed hard. She had kept a careful eye on her selected route, and this particular geyser hadn't erupted in the last half hour. She wondered if that increased or decreased the danger. She looked for a detour, but other paths would only lead her closer to more active vents. There was no way around it, she had to continue.

As she drew closer, her sandals made a grinding sound on the wet, briny salt deposits. She saw small pools of water here and there confirming that this geyser had erupted in recent times. Judging from the distance to the vent, when it erupted, it threw scalding hot water over a wide area. This was not good. She hoped that there would be some warning before the next eruption.

She was less than 50 feet from the vent when she noticed a coal-black chain coming out of the mouth of the geyser. A chill swept through her. "Oh God, not again," she gasped. Once more she considered taking another route, steering as far from this vent as possible, but in the end she stayed the course. What horrors were within the geyser? She had to know; she had to better understand her adversary.

Serena drew to within a few feet of the mouth of the geyser. The formidable chain was firmly attached to a heavy stone block set into the ground. From there it led into a roughly circular vent, less than a yard in diameter. The chain seemed under tension, as if holding a considerable weight. From the depths of the vent, Serena heard moaning. It was a woman's voice, she was certain of it. Cautiously she approached the hellish well and peered in. All she saw was darkness, so she dropped to her knees to get a better look—a foolhardy act.

Perhaps 15 or 20 feet down into the semi-darkness she saw the form of a young woman about her own age. She had long, brown hair, wet, and matted, a slender yet muscular build, and a pale complexion. She hung limply from the chain by her shackled wrists, which were extended high above her head. For a moment she looked lifeless, yet sensing the presence above her, the woman slowly lifted her head. At first what she saw didn't seem to register; then her eyes opened wide with surprise.

"Who are you?" she gasped.

"My name is Serena."

"No, you're just an illusion, you can't be real."

"I assure you, I am," Serena said, glancing again at the black chain. She remembered satan's warning about assisting the victims of Hell's fury, but right now she didn't care. "Look, I'm not that strong, but maybe we can work together and get you up out of there. At least we can try."

"What a kind offer," replied the woman, her voice languid and weary. "But there's a problem with that." She swung her shackled feet back and forth, revealing that they were not only chained together but linked to three other chains that radiated downward and were mounted securely to the tunnel wall at three places, perhaps a dozen feet farther into the depths. "It didn't used to be like this," she continued, "but I guess I was a bad girl."

"How long have you been here?" asked Serena, leaning farther over the dark opening.

The woman shook her head slowly. "I really couldn't tell you. I died in October 1983. How long ago was that?"

"Twenty-four years and two months," replied Serena.

Again the woman shook her head. "Has it been that long? After a while here, time seems to lose its meaning."

"I only wish that there was something I could do for you," lamented Serena.

"So do I. By the way, my name is Gwen, Gwen Thomas. And let's see, I guess I'm 44 years old."

"How can you go on?" Serena asked. "How do you stand it? How do you keep from losing your mind?"

"You go on because you have to," replied Gwen. "I don't know how others react to this place...you see, I'm sort of isolated. I guess many scream and curse and cry, but what good does it do? After it's all over and you've screamed yourself hoarse, or cried your eyes dry, you're still here. All you can do is take it, and somewhere deep in your soul, hope that someday there will be an end to it all." Gwen hesitated.

"But tell me, Serena, how is it that you are wandering around loose up there? I can hardly imagine satan letting the likes of you run free. That sadistic pig loves to put women in chains and torture them."

"I'm not as free as you think," lamented Serena. "I guess satan has just given me a little time to think about it before he starts working on me, before I begin my eternity in the sea of fire."

"Sea of fire...that sounds nasty," Gwen said, staring up at Serena.

"I guess I'm going to find out," replied Serena.

"No, we don't want to talk about things like that, I want to hear about you," said Gwen. "I so desperately need to hear another human voice. I haven't heard another human voice in so many years. I want to understand who you are. I want to hear about anything but this place."

Serena did her best to describe her life on Earth, and the situation that brought her here to Gwen. When it was over, Gwen shook her head sadly.

"Being separated from your husband must make it all the worse. As for this little slice of freedom satan granted you, I don't think the pig did you any favor." A momentary groan emanated from Gwen's lips as she pulled upon her chains. "I really didn't leave anyone behind. Maybe it's better that way."

Serena's next question was natural enough. "Tell me about you, Gwen. I've been doing all the talking."

"I'm not much for talk anymore," said Gwen, "but, in a word, I was a prostitute."

"Why?" asked Serena, who only now realized how potentially offensive her question was.

"Because it meant escape and money," replied Gwen. "I thought it was the only way I could support myself. Life had screwed me over pretty bad growing up, so I decided to screw it back, and I didn't come cheap. If men wanted me, fine, but they paid. You see, I had dreams, Serena, and I wasn't afraid to take chances to reach them."

"What kind of dreams?"

"I was a gymnast, and I was very good. The rings, the parallel bars, the horse, I did it all. My greatest dream was to make it to the summer Olympics, to bring home the gold. From white trash to Olympic gold—there's a dream. But it takes more than talent, it takes money to do all that. I paid for it by selling off my dignity, my self-respect."

"Did you ever get to the Olympics?" asked Serena.

"No, I never got the chance. Maybe I should have quit my night job sooner, maybe I got a little greedy. I had enough money, and more. It was right there, all tucked away in CDs. Maybe that's why this all happened to me. Maybe that's why I'm here."

There was a pause. Gwen gasped, pulling on her shackles. A trickle of blood flowed from beneath her left wrist restraint and down her arm. Serena could only imagine the strain on Gwen's arms and legs especially because of the barbs that lined the inside of her shackles. It had to be pure agony.

"I was always a high class girl, and I was an outlaw, through and through."

"An outlaw?" asked Serena.

"Yeah, what I mean is that I didn't have a pimp, I ran the whole show myself. Men only want women for what they can get out of them. No male pig was going to run my life; take all the profits, while I took all the risks. No, I was calling the shots, choosing my own clients. And I catered to the best. You know, I always figured that if something did happen to me, that it would be one of my clients that would do it, but it wasn't.

"No, it happened to me on my way back to my car after a particularly busy night. I was tired, sore, ready to get a few hours of sleep before a long day at the gym. It all happened so fast. To this day I don't know exactly what went down. All I know is that this guy pulled me into an alley and slit my throat wide open. It was a horrible feeling, a sickening pain. The rest is history."

Serena only nodded. What could she say that would make any difference?

"Satan took great pleasure in sentencing me to this hellish hole in the ground," continued Gwen. "He was such a pompous ass sitting on his throne; lord of all he surveyed. Forget anything noble I might have done during my life; he focused only on my months of prostitution. He acted as if I had been doing it my whole life, as if I had enjoyed it. He said that because I had tried so hard to hide my sins from the light of society, that he would torment me for it in a hidden dark place, where I would feel the heat of his wrath. He sentenced me to this place. Two of his dark demons carried me here. They shackled me hand and foot, and threw me into the throat of this steamy hot geyser."

"I'm sorry," said Serena.

"Not as much as I am," retorted Gwen. "When the chain went tight that first time, it nearly pulled my arms out of their sockets. They told me all about this place as I hung there— about the game."

"Game?" asked Serena.

"Oh yes, game," confirmed Gwen. "The rules are quite simple, really. They told me about the eruptions, about the scalding hot water that exploded out of this geyser every few hours. When it happened, I'd more than likely be thrown out by the sheer force of the eruption. But you see, the throat of this geyser was my prison, and my sanctuary. To be safe from the demons, I had to remain inside, always.

"If the erupting waters threw me out, I was to scramble back in as fast as I could. If they managed to catch me outside, they won, and got the pleasure of hacking me up with their claws, before throwing me back into the geyser again. There I'd hang by my chain, healing, waiting until the next round, the next eruption. If I managed to get back in before they caught me, I was safe, but I still lost, if you get my meaning."

Serena got it. Then a terrible thought hit her. "How often does this thing erupt?"

"You don't have to worry," assured Gwen. "As best I can figure, there are about five or six hours between eruptions. Most of the time, I just hang here in this steamy heat and suffer, alone. I get a lot of time to think down here, between eruptions. I don't know, maybe that's the worst part. But the eruptions; they're terrifying. Believe me; you don't even want to know what that feels like. The rumbling starts about a minute before the scalding water reaches you. The heat increases, you can hear it coming, a roaring sound from far below, growing louder and louder; it's terrifying as the boiling water works its way through the narrow cracks in the rock below this cauldron I hang in.

"There is a blast of scalding hot air and steam that hits me first; then I can see it, a frothing boiling mass, bursting out of the darkness. If engulfs me in seconds. The violent turbulence tosses me against the walls, cutting me up real bad, before it pushing me up and out of the vent. I quickly run out of chain and am yanked hard, thrown to the ground, showered in boiling hot water. It lasts for about a minute, but it seems so much longer."

Gwen began to gasp as she flailed around at the end of her chain. Serena could see the pain in her eyes as she pulled in futility upon her bonds. She grunted and groaned as tears came to her eyes, shimmering in the faint light. Then she went still again.

"Are you OK?" asked Serena.

"Not hardly," said Gwen. "It's just cramps, that's all, they'll pass." It was over a minute before she could continue. "I remember that first eruption. When it was over, I was left dazed and confused, out there on the plains. I looked like a lobster—red and covered with boils. It was horrible. I was in such pain. The gritty salt all around me made it all the worse. Then I looked a little ways away to see another poor soul who had also been thrown from her geyser. For a moment she laid there, just like me.

"Then, one of those black demons pounced on her. He came out of nowhere. He clawed at her, ripping huge chunks of her flesh away with his sharp talons. Blood and guts were flying everywhere. The whole time she just screamed. What else could she do?

She couldn't die again. Then, he threw what was left of her into the vent of her geyser, and turned to me. I scrambled for the still steaming vent. I barely managed to plunge back in before he arrived. He cursed at me, taunted me from up there for the longest while, then he left."

Serena shivered as she pictured that horrible moment, and she could picture it only too well.

"I hung there for a long time," continued Gwen. "Then I decided to do something, I put my skills as a gymnast to work. I reached for the chain attached to my wrist shackles and began to climb. It wasn't easy, but slowly I made my way up the chain to the surface. Reaching the top, I looked around; no demons in sight, I crawled out. I looked for any way that I might release these shackles, or bust the chain anchored into the rocks, but I couldn't figure it out. All the while, I kept an eye out for the black demons. I could see them in the distance all right, but none of them came anywhere near me. They focus on the erupting geysers to find their victims, there was no point in checking up on the quiet geysers because their occupants were trapped inside, hanging from the end of their chains. They are all women, former prostitutes, hardly the sort who were going to find the strength to climb up the chains to get out. And hauling them out was against the rules."

"So, what did you do?" asked Serena.

"For a time I just sat there, trying to keep a low profile. Eventually I felt the rumbling of the geyser as it prepared to erupt again. I tried to get as far away from it as I could, which wasn't very far. Still I was able to escape the worst of the spray. Sure, I got burned some, but nothing like the first time. When the eruption was over, I made for the vent. Sure enough, there was one of those black demons on its way toward me, but I was able to duck into the vent before he got anywhere close. I hung on to the chain, watched him from just inside the vent until he turned away in search of other victims. After a few minutes, I was out once more.

"During the next few days, the cycle repeated again, and again, a game of cat and mouse. It was tiresome, stressful, and often painful, but it sure beat the alternative. It was then when I began to think of eternity in a different way. Like rainfall wearing down a tall mountain, might I wear down my chains, given enough time? There were plenty of rocks, very hard ones, all around. The chains between my wrist shackles gave me about 2 feet of play, enough to wield the rocks.

"At first I tried to use them as a hammer. I decided to work on the chain between my ankle shackles first. After all, if I couldn't run, I'd have no chance. I decided to work on what I thought was the weak link in the chain, where it met the shackle. For weeks I struck that link. I managed to bend it way forward and way back time and time again. That's supposed to break a link eventually, right?"

"But aren't your shackles barbed on the inside?" asked Serena.

"Yes, and that made it hurt all the more," replied Gwen. "With every blow of the rock, those barbs dug into my ankles, but I didn't seem to be getting anywhere. If I couldn't remove the shackles from my leg, well, there was only one solution, wasn't there?"

Serena realized where this conversation was leading. "Oh my God, you thought of amputating your foot?"

"Exactly," replied Gwen, "it was the only way. Cut the foot off, pull the shackle from the stump, then reattach the foot. Sounds simple, doesn't it? I just wasn't all that sure that I had the guts to do it. I knew my foot would grow back together in an hour or so, but how do you do such a thing to yourself. I thought of stories of desperate animals who chewed off a leg that was caught in a trap. It is a lot easier said than done. Nonetheless, I started working on a large narrow rock, sharpening it into a blade. Still it took me a long time to work up the nerve to do it."

Serena shivered at the very thought, it was ghastly. Only in this place would anyone possibly come up with such a scheme.

"I don't think I'll go into the details, of cutting off a foot and then reattaching it. It can be done, but believe me, you can't imagine what it's like. Cutting through flesh, and then bone; it was horrible. And when you start, you've got to see it through to the end, no matter what. I don't cry easily, but I did then. Those two days were the worst days of my eternity, but somehow, I got through it. When it was over and the healing was complete, I just stared at my bare feet. It was wonderful to have them free again, but what I wouldn't have given for a pair of shoes. I buried the shackles beneath some rocks and prepared to do my wrists."

"Had you thought any about where you planned to go when you finally got free?" asked Serena, looking for a moment around the valley. "I mean, where could you go? This place is so open, surely you'd be seen."

"I'd thought a lot about it," was the reply. "I wasn't about to go through all of this, just to get caught again. There was a way; I'd thought my way all through it. But I guess I didn't think about it quite enough. Anyway, I never got the chance to make the break. It was after I did my left wrist that the black demons caught up with me. I'd slipped back into the vent, was waiting until the coast was clear, when two of the demons showed up. They grabbed my chain and pulled me out. I think they knew what had been going on for quite a while. Maybe they'd just been playing with me, waiting for me to almost get free before catching me. They clawed me up real bad; then they put the shackles on me again and threw me back into the vent. But they didn't stop there. They climbed down into the vent, crawling along the walls like some sort of insects. They added extra chains to my feet, shackling them to the walls to keep me inside the vent. They said that because I didn't play fair, that I wouldn't be allowed to play the game at all. And that's the way it's been ever since."

"I'm sorry," said Serena. "I know that doesn't mean much, but I am."

"And do you think you're any better off than I?" asked Gwen, a crazed anger in her voice. "I don't know what you'll experience in the sea of fire. I don't even know exactly what the sea of fire looks like, but I think I'll take this over that any day."

Serena drew back from the gaping hole in the ground. Gwen might be right. What was the sea of fire? She wasn't really sure. Continually being burned alive might make Gwen's ordeal seem like a picnic by comparison.

"We're both damned, you and I," continued Gwen. "I can offer you only one consolation, for whatever it's worth. The experience of continual and unending pain has a dulling effect on your senses, you'll see. Eventually your mind learns to block a large portion of the pain out. It's still terrible, don't get me wrong, but not quite as bad as you might imagine. It becomes a part of you, like breathing. You come to forget what existence without it is like. Life without pain might even seem empty. You'll understand." There was a pause, then suddenly Gwen's voice took on an alarmed aspect. "I can't do it, I can't! Run, Serena, run! This geyser is going to erupt, I can feel it! I can't keep you here. I don't care what he does to me, run!"

Serena rose to her feet. She was confused and didn't know what to do.

"Run, Serena!" gasped Gwen. "You've gotta get out of here!"

Serena backed slowly away from the vent, then turned and ran.

It was less than a minute before she felt the rumble beneath her feet, followed by the roar behind her. She turned to behold the tower of scalding water rising high into the sky. Had she stayed a moment longer, she would have been engulfed in its fury. What was Gwen talking about? Was she under orders to delay her? Serena quickened her pace. She felt as if she had been set up. The dark demon had directed her down this path, perhaps anticipating her meeting with Gwen. Had he been behind it all, or might there have been higher powers at work here? She figured that she would never know.

Yet one thing was certain; there was no escape from her fate, no hiding from the prince of darkness. He held absolute sway over his realm, and nothing happened here that he was unaware of. Hell was as much about hopelessness as it was about pain. Soon she would know both.

chapter eight

SERENA'S journey through the realm of the geysers continued for nearly two hours. Under different conditions, it might have been a fantastic experience. Yet, she knew the dark secret these deadly fountains held, the human tragedy locked up in this wonder of nature. She could only imagine how many of these vents contained souls in torment, souls waiting helplessly for the blistering hot fury from below to be expelled, only to be compelled to scramble once more into their dark prison to escape the demons above. It was a nightmarish cycle. Now and again, she could hear the muted, mournful cries of the inhabitants of this defiled natural wonder.

Eventually the field of the geysers came to an end, and the valley opened into a vast featureless plain, an expanse of flat nothingness that extended to the horizon. She had seen this region from the mountaintop, through the mists and smoke that dominated this wretched land. The way she figured, the sea of fire was not far off. She had come a long way. She glanced at the small hourglass. She was dismayed to discover that more than half of the sand had run its course. Her time was running out.

"No hope," she sighed, as she continued on.

Serena discovered that the plains before her were not as featureless as she had at first thought. Scattered here and there among the rocks and gravel were white-bleached bones. Certainly not mountains of them, but bones nonetheless, cast helter-skelter across the landscape. So scattered and fragmented were these remnants that Serena was unsure as to whether they were of human or animal origin. The source of the carnage was a mystery, but it was obvious that it happened a very long time ago. In the absence of rain or insects, it was hard to say just how fast animal remains might deteriorate here. Human bodies would regenerate, and Serena suspected the same was true for the fallen angels. So, what about these bones? It was a question with no answer.

Looking up from the bones, Serena saw an orange glow on the horizon. At first she thought it might be the edge of the sea of fire, but as she grew closer it took on the appearance of a myriad of campfires, spaced at regular intervals across the landscape. It seemed to be an encampment of a mighty army that stretched as far as she could see. Above the fires, a multitude of large dark forms flew through the ragged skies.

"What now?" moaned Serena, who was weary of the pain and suffering she had witnessed on her tragic journey.

She looked for a route around whatever lay ahead, but there appeared to be none. All she could do was continue to follow her shadow into oblivion.

Eventually, she had drawn close enough to see the true nature of the fires. They were bowl-shaped pits, perhaps 4 or 5 feet deep and twice that wide. The walls and floor of the pits were lined with glowing red hot rocks, and the air held the intense stench of brimstone. Most of the pits contained the writhing forms of the damned—moaning and screaming, many fully engulfed in flames. Their forms rippled and quivered amidst the waves of rising heat. So great was the heat of the pit, that their bodies had been reduced to nothing more than skeletal remains. The flesh that sought to regenerate was swiftly swept away, dropping from their bones and into the pit, where it was swiftly incinerated within the blazing inferno. Even the eyes of these damned souls had been swept away by the flames, leaving nothing but dark empty sockets staring out at the world.

Within their rib cage and surrounding the bones of the legs and arms, a gray turbulent mist swirled like smoke, yet never escaped. Was it smoke from their continually vaporizing flesh, swirling in the eddies created by the intense heat? Or was it something more substantial, something more precious? Perhaps it was the physical manifestation of their eternal souls?

Still, the most incongruous aspect of these damned souls was the worms. The porous, light gray bones were teaming with white worms that seemed totally unaffected by the intense heat. They crawled in and out, as if feeding upon the slim remains of these skeletal apparitions that had once been human beings.

Serena had seen many horrible things since her arrival here, but this was the most ghastly of them all. With no flesh, no lungs, and no tongues, how could these people scream so? Serena was amazed that the bones of these hapless individuals remained assembled in the form they had taken in life. With no muscle or sinew to hold them together, why didn't these scorched skeletal members fall to the ground, to become no more than a pile of litter scattered across the bottom of the pit? And the worms, how could they possibly survive under conditions such as these?

The pits emitted such heat that, even from a distance of 10 or 15 feet, their radiance was absolutely brutal. She could hardly imagine what it must be like from within. Surely the laws of reason, of physics, no longer applied here. They had been indefinitely suspended at the whim of the prince of darkness.

Overhead, hundreds of demons cloaked utterly in black guarded the pits. Well, so much for her theory about a shortage of demon power. Satan seemed to have no lack of resources.

The walls of the small pits were steep, but not insurmountable. So what force held these poor souls in their primitive crematoriums? Was it the fear of the dark horde above them, or were they so weakened by their ordeal that they had no strength to escape?

The pits before her were widely scattered enough to allow her easy passage, at least physically easy. Emotionally, it was another story entirely. Her fortitude and courage were failing her. As pointless as it might have been, she offered a brief prayer before she took another step toward the plain of tormented souls. It was not only a prayer of mercy for her, but for them. It was a prayer for strength that she, the condemned prisoner, might be able to continue on her final journey. She moved forward.

Serena tried to focus on the path before her rather than the carnage around her. Surprisingly, none of the damned souls called out to her as she passed by. Perhaps they lacked the ability to see or hear her. Perhaps all they could sense was the searing pain carried upon the flames that leapt up from the embers beneath them. Perhaps their personalities, memories, and consciousness had perished in the flames, leaving only their primal urge for survival. No, that would be too merciful.

Serena's attention was caught by a commotion not far away. Turning, she discovered that one of the skeletons had scrambled from his pit, only to encounter a black demon in the process. Already, the skeleton had started to develop internal organs and the beginnings of flesh.

"I can't stand it anymore!" he screamed, flailing wildly in the demon's grasp. "You gotta let me out." His cries quickly turned to sobbing pleas. "I'll do anything you want, but please, don't put me back in there, please!"

The demon effortlessly picked him up by his bony neck, held him out at arm's length. "So you can't stand it?"

"I can't," cried the man. "Please, it hurts so much. I'm going out of my mind! Please, let me out of here, please!"

The demon cast the poor man back into the pit, but not before ripping a skeletal leg from him. The small quantity of flesh that had formed on this poor soul's bones, virtually dissolved as the pit erupted in flames that towered 10 feet into the sky. When the flames died down once more, Serena witnessed a bare skeleton, flailing around upon the coals.

"So, you can't stand it," said the demon, in a sadistic sneer. "OK, let's see how you like laying in your pit rather than standing in it. It will take days for that bony leg to regenerate in there. That should be enough time for you to ponder the consequences of trying to escape. And if you do try to escape again, I'll rip you into a dozen pieces, and scatter them across the desert. I'll show you a new aspect of pain."

Serena looked fearfully toward the dark demon, yet he gave her but a passing glance before returning to the sky with the prize leg in tow. The mystery of the bones in the desert had been solved, though Serena could have lived without that knowledge. It was best that she moved on, putting this place behind her as quickly as she could.

As the minutes passed, it became apparent that at least some of the skeletal beings around her sensed her presence, for they cried out to her as she passed, begging for help. But what could she do? If she managed to pull a tormented soul from their pit, one of the demons circling overhead would simply cast them back in, perhaps doing the same to her in the process. Right now, the demons seemed unconcerned by her presence, but if she interfered that might quickly change.

"Please, have mercy upon me!" cried a skeleton nearby. Only the nature of his voice told Serena that this was a human of male gender, and from his accent, she deduced he was of Spanish or Hispanic descent. "Oh please, save me!"

Serena turned to see him, and was sickened by the multitude of white worms crawling in and out of his bones, like maggots.

"Won't you please help me?" he pleaded.

Serena gazed into his vacant bony eye sockets. The man wept in dry heaves, as he knelt in the middle of his glowing hot pit surrounded by searing waves of heat. His skeletal hands reached for the worms that infested his bones, in an attempt to dislodge them; but it was a futile effort, for they were quick to retreat into the many holes only to emerge elsewhere. It was a dreadful sight. Serena's heart went out to this poor soul, yet she knew that she was helpless to intervene. She remembered only too well satan's warning about the penalty for interference. "I wish that I could, believe me."

"The pain," he wept, "it hurts so much. Oh please, you've gotta help me!"

"I can't, don't you see?" replied Serena. "Even if I tried, those demons would only throw you back."

"Please," pleaded the man, all the more insistently.

"Do you not see, she can't?" objected another, in a pained male voice. "'Tis no hope for us—not now, not ever."

Serena recognized the distinctly Scottish accent. She turned to see a skeletal form standing in the middle of the pit across from the one where the first man knelt.

"Young woman, I know not what fates have conspired to bring you among us, but 'tis a place most dire that you've come to," said the Scotsman in the pit.

"You can see me?" asked Serena, looking into his empty eye sockets.

"But vaguely," he replied, pain in his voice. He moved a couple steps toward Serena. "Even without my eyes I can perceive your form. 'Tis with the eyes of my soul that I see thee. From the way that you appear to be dressed, I suspect that you're not here by choice."

"No," replied Serena. "I'm like you, condemned by God, sentenced to the sea of fire by satan."

The living skeleton nodded. "I've heard tell of this sea of fire, but I can not say, with any certainty, that I know exactly what you're in for. Certain am I that it's nothing pleasant. 'Tis not but an act of cruelty that has brought satan to send you upon this sojourn, to reveal to you a small bit of his realm, before he compels you to join us in our suffering."

A look of surprise swept over Serena's face. "How do you know all of that?"

"It's happened before," he replied, yet he seemed reluctant to comment further.

"How long have you been here, I mean, what year?" asked Serena.

"After 48 years of life, I came to this place in 1703," was the reply. "My name is Kyle McCandish; in life I was a blacksmith. But here I'm just another tormented soul beyond the realm of God's grace."

"My name is Serena, Serena Davis"

"A pretty name," noted Kyle, "a pretty name for a pretty girl. I'm sorry that it had to come to this, lass."

"And you've been here over 300 years?" gasped Serena.

"Sure 'tis a long time," noted Kyle, "but there be far more years ahead than there are behind, of that I am most certain."

Eternal torment; it was a terrible prospect. Again, Serena scanned the scene around her, witnessing the crying and moaning, the helpless writhing of so many tormented souls. Then she looked to the turbulent skies. Yes, there were demons there, but not hordes of them, not compared to the multitudes of humans in the pits. Surely, there were millions of people here, if these pits extended as far as she suspected. What would happen if there were to be a general uprising? She wasn't thinking of just a few frightened pain-crazed souls here and there making a futile break for freedom, but a rebellion of countless thousands, even millions. Could the few hundred demons circling overhead really combat such a throng? They were large and undoubtedly strong, but were they that strong? Again she gazed at the hourglass; she figured that she had two or three hours left.

"Kyle, have you ever tried to escape?"

"Only once… 'twas a long time ago. The pain had brought me near madness. I could feel the flames from without and the worms crawling from within. I could stand no more. I looked skyward to see that none of the black devils were nearby. Perhaps I could be free of the pit for a few minutes, just a few minutes. What a fine thing it would have been, to be a whole man once more. I gathered my strength and managed to crawl from the pit, yet it took all of my strength. You see, with no muscles, no sinew, we are so very weak. I laid at the pit's edge and as I did, I could feel my body returning to me. Oh, that it might have continued, but one of those black devils spied me from above. He threw me back into the pit, but not before ripping me arms off, and carrying them away. Many days passed before new limbs of bone grew in their stead. Those days were my worst. I was ne'r foolish enough to try to escape again."

"But there's gotta be a way out of here!" objected the man who had first pleaded with Serena. His tone was becoming increasingly agitated. "I can't stay here forever. I can't stay here."

"He's tried to crawl out of that pit more oft than I care to remember," Kyle said. "Those black devils have ripped him asunder many a time, but he'll not give up."

"No, they can't keep me here, I won't stay here!" he cried.

"You can't escape, Luis," objected Kyle. "This is Hell, why can you not understand that?"

Luis turned to Serena. "And you, I heard what you said. Are you going to walk into the sea of fire just because satan tells you to? That's insane!"

That comment brought back to Serena's remembrance the reason she was on this journey. She wasn't like Dante, being given a tour of the infernal regions that she might warn all of humanity about what lays ahead. She was here to stay, and when this journey was over, her torments would really begin.

"Answer me! Will you go quietly into the sea of fire, like a lamb to the slaughter, or will you fight?"

By now Serena was visibly shaking. To one degree or another, she had managed to exist in a state of denial for much of the trip. There would be a last minute reprieve, Chris would come to rescue her, or she might wake up from this dreadful nightmare. But none of that was going to happen, was it?

"Look at me!" demanded Luis. "Do you want to look like this? Well, do you? Do you know how much this hurts? If I was where you are, I'd do something."

"'Tis pointless, Luis," objected Kyle, "you'll make things worse for you and Serena."

"I'd expect as much from you, Kyle!" roared Luis. "All of these years you have simply stood there and accepted all that the demons dished out to you, but not me. Those demons had one hell of a time getting me into this pit, and even more trouble keeping me in it. I didn't go quietly, I fought them every inch of the way, and I'll continue to fight them, continue to be a pain in their side. But you, you're different, aren't you? You've accepted it all; you've given satan your consent to torture you, without objection, without even so much as a whimper. You're gutless, Kyle. You make me sick."

"That will be enough," Kyle said, turning to his heckler.

"No, I'm only getting started," cried Luis. "You have no right telling Serena what she should or should not do." Again, Luis turned to Serena. "Now, I'm depending on you, help me out of here and we shall change the course of history, start a revolution that will topple satan himself."

"No, Serena," warned Kyle. "Luis is in the pit of brimstone, his bones are searing hot; his very touch would be as fire. You would be horribly burned. Even if that frightens you not, you've no idea what the demons charged with the task of guarding us would do to you. It matters not what we say and do now, neither he nor I merit saving. We had no time for God during our lives, now He has no time for us, 'tis just that simple."

"Serena, you've gotta help me," insisted Luis. "You and I together, might be able to fight them off. If we stood up to them, others would join us, I know it. You could be the catalyst. We must stand together. This is your only chance! Did you ever think that you might be here for some higher purpose? You could be the start of a rebellion that would change the very face of Hell."

Luis had given a voice to the thoughts that had tormented Serena for hours. She was tempted to go along with his plan. Perhaps Luis was right. Satan had told her that she might have made a difference on Earth had she wanted to, if she had listened to the call of God. Could she make a difference here? She looked toward Luis, then gazed skyward. Several of the black demons had taken an interest in what was transpiring below. They wouldn't stand a chance. A moment later, Serena backed away from Luis.

"No!" screamed the skeletal form. "You can't leave! I need your help! We all do!"

Luis threw himself at the side of his pit, crawling and scratching his way to the top, as the winged demons watched from above. Luis stumbled onto the ground beyond his pit, where he rose to his feet and moved toward Serena. Serena took yet another few steps backward as the skeleton approached.

Luis swung around screaming all the while. "Listen to me, brothers, sisters, all of you, it's time to fight for our freedom! Death to the demons! Get out of your pits and join me now! They can't fight us all! Our strength is our numbers."

Again, Serena looked to the skies. The demons were still there, but for some reason, they took no action against this raving skeletal man. Serena gazed about at the others in the pits, surely some of their inhabitants would answer the call, but they didn't. They continued to cry and moan, paying little attention to Luis and his ranting.

Again Luis turned to Serena. Serena was amazed to see a pair of eyes within the bony sockets, and there was madness within those staring globes.

"Cowards!" raved Luis, spinning around to address them. "All of you! Why don't you do something? Fight back, this is our chance!"

Still the others did nothing. Perhaps they didn't even hear him, or perhaps they were too beaten down, too frightened to respond.

Luis turned to Serena once more. Within his rib cage, internal organs were swiftly growing to fill the emptiness. It was a sickening sight, one worthy of the best special effects people in Hollywood. Within his mouth a tongue was growing, and upon his bones, muscle tissue. Luis clenched his fists, obviously in pain. Serena took yet another step backward.

"Why wouldn't you help me, Serena?" he said, taking a step toward the young woman. "Getting out of there would have been so much easier, less painful, if you had only helped me."

Serena was terrified. She felt like turning and running, yet she held her ground.

"Come here, young woman," demanded Luis, beckoning with his right hand.

"Leave her alone!" cried Kyle.

"Stay out of this, Kyle," shouted Luis, turning to face the skeletal Scotsman. "Or even better, climb out of that pit and make me. Come on, Kyle, make me. You want a piece of me? Well, here's your chance!"

The Scotsman grew silent and still, his arms at his side.

"No, I didn't think you would, not you." Again, Luis turned to Serena.

Serena still stood motionless. It was fear, more than bravery that kept her feet planted upon the ground as if rooted.

"Do you know why I was sent here, Serena?"

Serena held her peace, not knowing how to respond to this madman.

"I was a bad boy," he laughed. "My father was Juan Ramirez, the head of the most powerful drug cartel in all of Columbia. He was not one to be trifled with, and neither am I. After my father's death, my older brother took over the family business, but he was weak. It was I who ruled our drug empire from behind the scenes. I have never been afraid to take chances or make decisions. I had my own fiancée executed for her unfaithfulness. I made certain that her death was slow and painful. No one crosses me, Serena, not anyone, not then, and not now. One day I will get a piece of satan himself for what he's done to me, I swear it. But for right now, let us talk about you."

Luis was regenerating at a fantastic rate. His skull was rapidly vanishing beneath a veneer of new flesh, and the bones of his arms and legs were already enshrouded in a layer of dark red muscle that glistened in the light of the bloated amber sun.

"We are not so different, you and I," continued Luis. "I stood where you stand now, whole, without pain, 18 years ago. My rebellious and bold spirit, to say nothing of the fact that I wasn't afraid of him, fascinated satan. He granted me half a day to see this operation of his, before I was to be thrown into this pit. You see, during my life, I had done a lot of horrible things to those I didn't like for one reason or another, but hey, it was just business. Isn't it nice when business can be mixed with pleasure? I guess the devil and I sort of dabbled in the same craft. I think satan wanted to show me that he could do me one or two better. I'll admit that he had developed some pretty incredible ways to torture people, but hey, he had the budget for it."

"Oh my God," gasped Serena, turning suddenly pale. "You tortured people?"

"In my line of work, a certain degree of fear had to be maintained to keep the locals in line, to say nothing of the competition. Hey, it came with the territory. In my special chamber, beneath the family estate I loosened up plenty of purse strings, silenced many a tongue, and saved the family business a lot of money and trouble in the process. I made a lot of people vanish. That sort of thing happens in Columbia. You gotta do what you gotta do, and if you enjoy it, well, all the better. I won't go into all the details about my methods, but they were unique. A lot of terrible things happen in the mountains of Columbia."

Serena was horrified. She couldn't imagine how anyone could find pleasure in physically harming another. "But now, you're the one on the receiving end of the torture," she noted. "Hasn't that made you understand how your victims felt? Hasn't it caused you even a little bit of remorse about what you did to them?"

"No, not really."

"Are you telling me that you like what happens to you in that pit?" asked Serena.

"No, that's crazy, you must be as stupid as you look," Luis said. "I prefer to give rather than to receive. As I already told you, when it came my time to enter that fiery pit, I fought tooth and nail. I didn't go quietly. So, I ask you again, will you?"

Luis glanced at a vacant pit to Serena's right. "Yes, that will do nicely. Perhaps the time has come for you to realize the nature of my suffering, Serena." Luis pointed toward the glowing pit. Just kick off your sandals and jump in."

Serena's eyes grew wide with terror. She looked into the pit. She saw the luminous red rocks, the shimmering waves of heat, it was unimaginable. "What? You can't be serious!"

"Don't question me, woman, do it!" demanded Luis. "I want to watch you squirm, see the flesh burn from your bones, and it won't take long, seniorita. It won't take long."

"No," gasped Serena, taking a step backward.

"Why, what's wrong, Serena? You were going to jump into the sea of fire for satan, why not jump into this pit for me? Look, let me make this simple for you. You can jump in yourself or I can throw you in, it's your choice."

"Luis, please, leave her in peace!" pleaded Kyle.

Luis took no notice of the Scotsman's plea. He was no threat.

Luis kept advancing toward Serena. By now, his ribs had been completely closed in by muscle and sinew, and skin had nearly covered the muscles of his face. Even the first signs of hair were appearing upon his scalp. "I want you to know what it's like to be down there in the pit as I was, nothing but scalding hot bones infested with worms that can't die, and in such terrible pain. I want you to be looking up at someone whose body is whole and beautiful. Then I want you to beg, to plead for mercy. Don't worry, I might pull you out, after a while, if you beg pitifully enough and long enough. Don't you see? You're mine. Now, do it, get in!"

Luis lunged toward Serena, yet he never reached her. He was caught in midair by three huge demons. They swept around him like a terrible dark cloud. Serena could hear the dreadful screams, the curses, the sounds of ripping flesh. That was the last she ever saw or heard of Luis.

Serena was on the run, running as fast as she could. More than once she narrowly missed tumbling into one of the hellish pits. A state akin to madness had descended upon her, and now it would not lift. The world around her had become unreal, distant, little more than a nightmare. Perhaps stumbling into one of the broiling pits would accomplish nothing more than shocking her back into the world of consciousness. She might find herself in her own bed, Chris at her side.

Perhaps her dream had begun earlier than that. She might awaken as a child of ten, her whole life having found its genesis in the raging fever that had nearly killed her that spring. And still she continued her headlong flight. Her lungs and legs ached, yet she didn't break stride. She didn't have to stop or even slacken her pace. There was no such thing as pure exhaustion here, how could there be? Exhaustion was for mortals, she was an immortal, a being of eternity, so she ran.

Time had become a blur. Her pain was continual, she just had to stop, but she didn't. Surely there was a limit to her endurance, but it never came. It hung out there in the imminent future, yet, like a desert mirage, like the end of the rainbow, she never reached it.

In the end, it was her own haste that brought an end to her flight. The half-buried, football-sized rock caught her left foot, and in a fraction of a second, she was airborne in a headlong plunge. She felt the harsh radiant heat, saw the glowing rocks of the pit before her, then beneath her. Her head was awash in adrenaline, she plunged downward. Her toes caught the far edge of the pit as she landed flat on her face. She pushed herself up, spun around to see the pit that she had virtually leapt over. She hadn't leapt over it at its widest point, but it was still quite a jump. She had caught the full attention of the skeleton who sat at its center. He gazed at the rag-clad human who had flown over the crematorium that was his eternal home.

"Chi sei? Dove stai andando?" he asked, in a trembling voice that spoke of his pain and anguish.

"I'm sorry," said Serena regaining control of herself. "Really I am."

He rose to his feet, facing the only stranger who had wandered into his eternity in a very long time. He stared at her, or at least she figured that was what he was doing. He seemed so pitiful. Serena rose once more to her feet, extended her apologies, for all they were worth, and continued on, this time more carefully.

For a moment, the stranger remained completely motionless, standing like some hanging skeleton in a biology lab. Then he sat down within the pit once more, with only his pain to keep him company.

Serena had regained control. She couldn't allow herself to lose it like that, not again. She looked back, trying to figure out just how far her headlong frenzy had carried her. She was surprised to discover how much more distant the mountains appeared now than before. She pulled out the small hourglass. It was difficult to tell just how many minutes had passed based on this strange chronometer, but it couldn't have been more than half an hour, probably less. Then there was the issue of the pit. She had jumped completely over it. How fast had she been running? She was still winded, but quickly recovering. A Scripture verse came to mind, probably remembered because it was also part of a song sung at her husband's church.

"You will walk and not be weary, you shall run and not faint," she said, quoting it as best she could. That was a description of the glorified body of a saint in Heaven.

No, this wasn't Heaven. In Heaven she would not have been winded at all, but apparently, this new body that healed so very rapidly also had other abilities. The fact that she had sailed over the pit said that she must have been running very fast. Yes, her muscles hurt, there was a limit to her strength, but her endurance; well, that might be another matter. This body she now had was God's final gift to her before He cast her into outer darkness. Satan depended on this gift. In order for the souls in Hell to suffer, they had to have endurance, didn't they?

Serena continued on, wondering if there truly was an end to the pits; there was. Not ten minutes had passed when she left the last of them behind and stepped out into a vast plain with few rocks. Only cracked, sun-baked soil stretched before her. No, there was something else. It was almost on the horizon, nearly lost in the haze, a glowing sea of red—the sea of fire?

Her journey was almost at an end.

chapter nine

SERENA continued on, following her long shadow much as the proverbial mule might follow the carrot hanging by a stick in front of him. Yet in this case, the end was now in sight. It was no longer a mirage retreating eternally before her. It was difficult to say how long it would be before she reached the infernal shore, but she suspected that she would arrive there well before the appointed time. Perhaps she should slow her pace. There was no hurry. Perhaps it was best to arrive just in time, rather than to wait around for her time to be up.

After all, this wasn't a flight at the airport she was rushing to catch. She wouldn't be expected to check in at the gate two hours before departure. She wouldn't have to go through security or wait in line to check her baggage. She didn't even have any carry-on. Nope, she could step right to the head of the line. Serena shook her head in disbelief, why in the world did that crazy analogy pop into her head?

Serena continued to scan the hazy horizon before her. Here and there she could make out flashes of light. It had the appearance of a distant thunderstorm. Did it actually rain in Hell?

She thought back to her days as a child, watching the summer thunderstorms roll over the Cascade mountains. How she had loved the thunder and the lightning, the ever-changing shape of the white towering clouds against the deep blue sky. It was a thing of power, of wonder. Back then, she had pondered over the wonders of creation. She thought about the Creator of the thunderstorm and the lightning, of the One who ordained the coming of the rain; that brought such a wonderful fragrance of freshness to the meadows.

Then there was the rainbow. Her grandmother had said that it was God's covenant with man, the promise that He would never again destroy the world with a terrible flood, as He had done in the days of Noah. She thought of her grandmother. It was she who had spoken about the wonderful God who had made all of creation. She had often looked after the young Serena when her mother and step-father were at work. She had read Bible stories to Serena, spoken of God's love. She had so wanted Serena to believe, yet she had died. She was only 61 when the Lord took her away.

Through her prolonged illness, she had spoken of going to be with Jesus in Heaven. Serena had no doubt at all that she was there with Him, looking down on the world. But, she wouldn't remember Serena any longer, would she? Her memories of Serena, and the love that accompanied them, would be swept from her mind, so that she might not mourn for her. Still, Serena remembered her Grandma Sylvia, and as long as she did, their love would not truly die.

Serena's mind snapped back to the here and now. In this place there was no room for love, caring, mercy, or compassion. There was only fear, hate, pain, and remorse. One's only encounters here were with those most dismal emotions. And the hate? Most of that was furnished by encounters with satan and his minions, and it spread out from there. She hoped that she would have no more other worldly encounters between here and the sea of fire. She had seen enough suffering, encountered enough crazed souls for one day. Yet she expected that she would not be so fortunate.

Nonetheless, there didn't seem to be anything going on out here, no circling demons, no flaming pits or thundering geysers, no odor of death, just a vast flat expanse of loneliness. Even the traveling was easier here.

Now that the sound of the wailing souls in the pits behind her had faded into the background of nothingness, it had become very quiet. Only the slightest breeze stirred the hot dry air, an acrid breeze that swept in from the great sea before her. Serena watched her shadow pass across the parched ground that knew neither a green plant nor a drop of rain, as she followed it to disaster.

She was becoming so hot, so thirsty. It had been many hours since she'd had a drink of water or rested her legs. She doubted that she would have the opportunity to do either anytime soon. Indeed, she might never have that opportunity again.

The trek continued without incident and without any remarkable discoveries. The red sea was growing closer, and the distant lightning was becoming brighter and more distinct, as the haze above the plains slowly cleared. Yet, something else, something odd did attract her attention. Here and there, small sections of the land had been disturbed, for the flat radiating pattern of cracks that dominated this region was interrupted by a small mound of smooth earth, hardly more than a few inches high. It might well have been a natural phenomenon, but Serena doubted it.

It was many minutes before Serena stopped. She was certain that she had heard a sound coming from parts unknown. At first, she thought it might be the cacophony of wailing souls in the pits, echoing off the distant mountains behind her, yet she quickly dismissed that possibility. No, this sound was coming from close at hand, muffled and faint, yet very nearby.

She looked about her, then at the ground beneath her feet. Could it possibly be coming from somewhere below? A chill swept through her soul. It was not a single voice she was hearing, but many; and they were in anguish. She dreaded to even consider the nature of the distress. She moved on, hoping that the muffled cries would fade, but they didn't. The voices were different from moment to moment, yet they were still there. She recalled the disturbed plots of earth. Had satan buried people alive beneath her feet? She dropped to one knee, listening carefully. The voices were there; and they were coming from the ground. They were too muffled for her to make out individual words.

"Oh God," she gasped. "Oh Lord; how can you let something like this go on?"

There was nothing more to say. Serena figured that God wasn't listening, not to people here, anyway. Why should He? They were lost forever, beyond redemption, as she was. She rose to her feet and moved on.

The mournful cries that arose from the ground below drove Serena to despair, as the great sea before her grew closer. Above it, along the horizon, she witnessed towering clouds, not unlike those of the Oregon summer, rising above the glowing sea. Reflecting the light of the low sun and crimson sea, the turbulent clouds held an amber hue, highlighted by bright threads of electricity that arced around and between them. Slowly, a great vista of infernal grandeur was unveiled, stretching across the horizon. Before her the ground seemed to drop off precipitously, even as a low roar gradually masked the cries from below. Within minutes, she stood at the precipice of a great cliff, rising 30 or 40 feet above the turbulent fiery mass below.

What lay before her was a vista like none she had ever seen before. No, this was not a lake, but a great sea, with mighty waves pounding at the base of the cliff, as if seeking to drive it back to the mountains. In the back of her mind, she had envisioned the sea of fire to be an enormous sea of red hot lava. Nowhere in the

Bible was such a thing inferred, but somehow, that was the picture that was ingrained within the depths of Serena's mind. Her lofty vista from the mountain top had only strengthened this view. Yet, now that she was here, at close range, she realized its true essence.

Its surface was black and shiny, and its nature slimy and viscous, like crude oil. Much of it burned with a terrible intensity that Serena could feel even from the top of the cliff. Here and there great fountains of super hot liquid erupted from the depths, scattering their scalding essence into the black sea of ooze. In other places, pillars of fire burst forth, rising high into the sky. The evil black mass swirled with incredible fury, as if being churned from below by unseen forces. Amidst it all was the dreadful roar, the pounding of waves against the nearly vertical cliff, the bubbling, the swirling, and erupting. In her most terrible nightmares, Serena had never imagined that it would be like this—was she to be cast into this vast cauldron?

"Oh God, no!" she whimpered. "No!"

She was trembling as she picked up the mystical hourglass. So little time left. Of all the things she had seen here, this was the most horrifying. What had she done to deserve such a terrible fate?

"Glorious, is it not?"

Serena turned to behold the prince of darkness himself. Upon his face was a broad smile. How long had he been standing there? She couldn't say.

"My crowning achievement," he said, stretching his hand toward the horizon, "a great sea of turbulent thundering fury that extends farther than you can possibly imagine. It extends far into the darkness beyond the horizon. It is the black heart of Hell itself, and it will be your new home. I wanted to be here to bid you farewell before you took the plunge to meet its hot, wet embrace." Satan turned to the lifeless plains behind him. "Still, we have some time before you must begin your eternal service to me. Yes, time to see another example of my creative genius."

Serena had seen enough. "Please, no more," she begged.

Satan cocked his head in feigned surprise. "This couldn't be the inquisitive Serena, who knelt in my chambers less than twelve hours ago. Where is the young woman who was so bold as to instruct me on the finer points of governing my dark empire? I thought you wanted knowledge."

"I can't bear to see any more," she whimpered, her honor and dignity long forgotten.

"But see it, you shall," retorted satan. "It is my will." He extended his hand to Serena. "Now, come."

With little choice, Serena placed her hand in his and walked with him away from the edge of the cliff. Almost immediately she noticed a dark figure standing in the distance. He seemed to be leaning over a pit dug into the dry soil of the plain. He must have been standing there all along, yet, in her agitated state, she hadn't noticed him until now.

"I couldn't have you missing this," continued satan. "I've arranging this little drama for your benefit. I wanted you to witness yet another example of how I deal with your kind."

"Why me?" asked Serena, her voice stressed. "Why do you have to show all of this to me?"

"I've already answered that question once," replied satan glancing toward Serena. "Really, little one, you need to listen more carefully. I told you that you were special to God. I know His plans, and I have worked tirelessly to thwart them. This time I succeeded. If you had taken a different path, if you had followed Him rather than me, you would have deprived me of more guests than you can imagine. You would have caused me much trouble. But now, little one, you are here, and I shall take good care of you. I shall put you where you can do me no harm."

As the thunder of the great sea faded, she could again hear the mournful voices rising from below and they added to her sense of despair.

"When I confer once again with the most holy God, you may be sure that the topic of Serena Farnsworth shall be brought up, if only briefly. You are but another sentence in my story of success. You shall be but one more example of the failings of the Creator's grand design, and this pathetic little creature called man. I will spare Him no details of your eternal torment. I want Him to realize just how pointless His love for your kind really is. When the final tally is taken, and the game over, I am confident that I shall possess far more souls than the most high God."

"You talk as if it were a game," retorted Serena, who no longer cared if she offended the prince of darkness.

"Oh, it is," assured satan. "And I do enjoy it so. Formulating punishments that befit the nature of the many crimes of mankind constantly challenges my creativity. Behold a case in point."

Satan stretched his hand forward, toward a mound of dirt and an elongated hole excavated into the dry ground of the plain. A demon dressed wholly in black stood over the pit, while an occasional spray of brown dirt issued from the hole before him.

"Be quick, or it will be all the worse for you!" He demanded, gazing downward toward some unseen individual.

It was then that Serena noticed the plain black coffin setting by the rim of the pit. It was of the oblong variety, a bit wider toward its middle than at its ends, the sort of coffin that might have been used several centuries ago. Its lid sat to one side, allowing Serena to view the inside of the box. Much to her horror, she discovered that it was lined on both its bottom and sides with a multitude of sharp nails, each over an inch long. Even the inside surface of the lid was lined with sharp barbs. The demon came to attention at the approach of the master.

"Is all in readiness?" asked satan, looking briefly at the project before him.

"Yes, my Lord," confirmed the demon. "You have arrived at a most opportune time; we have just finished with the dull preliminaries. We are prepared for the real drama to begin."

Now Serena could see into the pit. It was five or six feet deep, and at the bottom, a man clothed only in a gray loincloth labored tirelessly. He moved handful after handful of earth, his only tool; his bloody fingernails. He seemed totally exhausted.

"Now, get out of there!" demanded the demon. "Be quick!"

The thin, barefoot man scrambled from the roughly hewn pit. He appeared to be about 30 years of age and was both filthy and sweaty from his prolonged labors. There were telltale welts upon his back where the demon had apparently applied a lash to his hide as motivation.

The demon pointed toward the grizzly spiked box. "Now, get into your coffin, the master is waiting."

"Please!" pleaded the man, falling to his knees. "Please, no!"

The demon's wrinkled face scowled. "Believe me; it will be far better for you if you get in of your own volition."

Weeping, the man rose to his feet and walked to the edge of the coffin. He hesitated as if searching for some means by which he could enter in with a minimum of pain. How could one willingly step into a box filled with hundreds of sharp nails? Finally, sensing that the demon was about to lose patience with him, the terrified man sat upon the rim of the coffin. He tried to lie on his side, balancing himself on the rim, before attempting to ease himself into the menacing box. His efforts were for naught. He lost his balance and fell in, impaling himself on a hundred or more sharp nails. He howled as blood oozed from his back and down the nails. He tried to rise, but found he lacked both the strength and the conviction.

The demon reached for a large sealed jar by the side of the coffin and opened its wide lid. Serena was horrified as all manners of crawling insects poured from the earthen container and into the coffin. Some appeared to be large beetles, while others were more akin to cockroaches. Still others looked like giant fleas and ticks. They all lit ravenously into the defenseless man in the coffin, even as the demon swiftly closed the lid, sealing the hoard of insects and their human host within.

Serena endeavored to turn from the horrible tragedy being played out before her, but satan held her tightly by the arms, compelling her to watch. An instant later, the demon raised his arms, and the coffin was levitated from the ground and then lowered into the hole that its occupant had excavated. The dirt tumbled in behind it, as if cast down by a hundred invisible spades, covering up the coffin in a matter of seconds. In less than a minute, all that remained was a small mound of slightly darker soil and the muffled screams that emanated from the depths.

"Thus is the penalty of sin," announced satan, raising his hands. "Pity him not, little one. Do you think I have condemned an innocent man? I have not. He was an assassin, a killer for hire. Many were his victims, killed at the whim of his villainous employer. Men, women, even children; he killed without regard. Most of his victims never saw him coming, for he traveled in the shadows and attacked without warning. In darkness he lived, and in darkness shall he dwell for eternity, attacked by a voracious hoard he can not even see, never to know a moment without terror. So I have decreed, so it shall be."

Serena was horrified beyond words, this dreadful soul's crimes not withstanding. She could hardly imagine the torment of those countless souls buried in this cemetery beyond the grave. The nails, the darkness, the suffocation, the horrible insects; it was absolutely ghastly.

"Ah, but I've saved the best for last," promised satan. "I have planned a sort of family reunion. Yes, that is exactly what it is."

"A family reunion?" asked Serena.

"Yes," confirmed satan. "But I do not wish to spoil the surprise."

With the wave of his hand, the prince of darkness, caused a dark portal, the sort that Serena had become only too familiar with, to appear before him. He compelled Serena to gaze into its depths.

It was difficult to see beyond the threshold, for the rocky corridor was misty and dimly lit, perhaps subterranean. More than ever before, Serena dreaded to enter. Something horrible awaited her in that tunnel. She had seen enough. She tried to pull away from the prince of darkness, though it was a vain attempt.

Satan had little patience with this human wench. Yes, she amused him, but his schedule was indeed full this day, and there were so many other matters to see to. He grasped her arm firmly and dragged her into the ethereal gateway.

The first thing that hit Serena was the claustrophobic, hot atmosphere of this realm, an atmosphere that bore a trace of the stench of sulfur, combined with that of burning flesh and hair. Serena could hear the distant muffled roar of flames, like that of a mighty blast furnace. Yet the roar did not come from any specific direction, but from all around her.

The brown, rust-stained walls of the narrow corridor in which she stood extended into the dusty mists in both directions. The mists prevented her from accessing the true size of this place, though she suspected that it was huge.

The roughly hewn walls were lined with a multitude of heavy metal doors, spaced at regular intervals. To the left of each door, a trio of metal wheels, one large and two small, were mounted to the wall, obviously some sort of controls, for as yet unseen machinery. Each door was identical, sealed tightly to its metal frame, and held together by a multitude of large metal rivets. Each door had a small circular glass peephole at about eye level. A fiery orange glow radiated from most of these small portals, illuminating the otherwise dark corridor in stark flickering illumination. They attested to the presence of a roaring inferno, just inches beyond the metal door. It reminded Serena of a scene from an old horror movie, though she really didn't remember which one.

Serena had always felt uneasy in dark, close quarters. For her, this phobia only compounded the ghastly atmosphere of this place.

Satan allowed Serena a moment to breathe in the gloomy despair that dominated this place before speaking. "Behold, we are over a mile below the torrid sun-baked surface of this world, in a prison with no physical entrance and no route of escape. Above us, the eternal midday sun bakes the landscape at over 250 degrees. It would boil water, if there was water. But let us focus on this dark realm. It was devised by a group of my most skilled and inventive minions, over a century ago, in an attempt to make my kingdom more modern and relevant to the people of the time; a renovation of sorts. I suppose to you, its architecture must seem somewhat dated. Nonetheless, it remains quite an effective means of delivering fear and agony to our human clients."

"What happens here?" asked Serena, who regretted posing the question almost before she had finished saying it.

"I never thought you would ask," replied satan, an evil gleam in his eye. "Behind each of these heavy metal doors, fed by an ingenious network of pipes, vents, and shafts, are a series of indeed marvelous furnaces, furnaces fueled by hot volcanic gases escaping from the dark heart of this world. It is, indeed, a beautiful thing to behold."

The prince of darkness walked to one of the dark metal doors, pulling Serena with him. It was only then when she noticed the plaque riveted to the door, just below the small glassy port. It bore only a name embossed in bold letters: Karl Rienstadt.

Satan motioned to the small viewing port. "Go ahead, take a look. Tell me what it is that you see."

Serena hesitantly moved toward the peephole and gazed into the room beyond. It was very bright, making it difficult to discern what lay beyond the door. Slowly Serena's eyes adjusted to the brilliance. She saw a small room, perhaps six or seven feet square, the size of a walk-in closet. It appeared to be composed entirely of riveted metal, of that much Serena was fairly certain. The walls of the furnace seemed to undulate in the intense heat, even as brilliant flames of bright yellow, orange, and blue fire swirled wildly through a large grate on the floor, sweeping through the tiny room like a small but powerful cyclone. They vanished again through a similar grate in the ceiling, spiraling rapidly upward to who knew where. Never had she seen flames that looked or behaved like these, it was unnatural. Indeed, it had a beauty all its own.

Then Serena discerned a movement within the terrible furnace, something at the rear of the chamber, almost lost amidst the swirling flames. Her perfect, immortal eyes focused upon it, and it became clear. It was the form of a man, shackled hand and foot to the back wall, writhing in agony, clothed in a bright shimmering garb of kaleidoscopic fire.

Unlike the damned souls in the fire pits of the plains, his body had not been reduced to a mere skeletal form, but appeared to have retained most of its muscle and sinew. That muscle was encased in a blackened layer of charred bubbling flesh that fought an eternal battle against the fires that sought to consume it. Of all the sights Serena had seen in Hell, this one was the most ghastly. Serena turned away in horror.

"I call it a furnace cell," announced satan, a sense of prideful accomplishment in his voice. "It leaves its human victim's body and his nervous system largely intact, allowing him, or her, to better appreciate the essence of the flames. Imagine it, little one, being clothed in a luminous colorful garment of fire for all eternity. This wretched soul made his home on Earth a living hell for his wife and children. He imagined himself to be the center of his world. Therefore, in his afterlife, I have again made him the center of his own world, small as that world might be. I have placed him in his own private crematorium, shackled him in position, at the very center of the swirling fire. Here, he shall dwell alone forever, to feel and consider the consequences of his vile deeds."

Serena was speechless. Did the dark heart of this enemy of humanity know no limits in its depths of depravity?

"But I did not bring you here to meet Mr. Rienstadt. No, this is to be a family reunion. Come."

Satan continued down the shadowy corridor with Serena in tow, until they came to another metal doorway. Little light emanated from the small viewing port of this door, the room beyond was quiet and only dimly lit. The prince of darkness directed Serena's attention to the plaque on the door. It was hard to read amidst the gloom of the corridor; Serena drew closer. A surge of adrenaline swept through her whole being as she read the name engraved upon the plaque—Bedillia Farnsworth, her mother.

"No," she cried, collapsing to her knees.

"Why, I'm surprised," said Satan. "I thought you'd be happy to learn how I have dealt with your evil, abusive mother during these past eight years. You should be thanking me. I have avenged her cruelty to you many times over, and I have only begun."

Satan proceeded to the large wheel mounted upon the wall and began to turn it. Amidst the sound of a dozen clacking gears and squeaking metal rollers, the ponderous door slid slowly to the side, along its metal track. It had the sound of a mechanism that was seldom used.

The next thing Serena knew, she was being pulled roughly to her feet and escorted into the small chamber. The room still bore the awful odor of burned hair, as well as the odor of cooking meat. The horrible inferences of these sensations made Serena's mind whirl. The only light within the room was an orange glow that came from beyond the metal grates in the ceiling and floor.

Peering through the grate below her, Serena beheld the swirling kaleidoscopic flames, roaring through some sort of enormous glowing conduit, held back from the chamber by a force she didn't understand. Maybe it was some sort of clear barrier; perhaps something more exotic. Nonetheless, it was a fearful sight. Serena felt very uneasy standing in the midst of this terrible crematorium.

There was a smile of satisfaction on satan's face as he stretched out his hand toward the small room's lone quivering occupant. "Normally the flames would be roaring through this chamber, as they have for the past eight years, but I had commanded that the vents be closed about half an hour ago, to give Bedillia a little bit of time to compose herself. Not too much time, mind you. I did not wish to grant her an overly long respite from her agony. That action might be regarded as an act of mercy, and I didn't want to project that sort of image. I'm sure you understand."

Yes, Serena understood, though she said nothing. There were tears flowing from her eyes, as she gazed into the face of her mother, for the first time in over eight years. Her mother's arms were shackled together high over her head, and her bare feet were secured in some sort of gray metal stirrups that were riveted to the large metal grate on the floor. She was clothed in rags, even more inadequate than those Serena wore. She was covered in ash and soot from head to toe. Still, she looked younger than Serena had remembered her. She had the countenance of the Bedillia Farnsworth of Serena's early childhood, though she seemed far more worn and sad.

"I'm so cold," said Bedillia, in a quivering tone. She didn't seem to comprehend what was going on around her.

"Mommy?" said Serena, in a soft voice, barely above a whisper.

Bedillia looked up with dazed eyes at her daughter. At first she didn't seem to recognize her. Then her eyes widened. "Serena?"

"Yes, it's me, Mommy," replied Serena, the tears flowing from her eyes.

"Yes, Bedillia," announced satan, his smile growing, "it is true, your daughter is indeed here. It pleases me greatly to orchestrate this impromptu family reunion. But it is you, Bedillia, who is the author of it. It is your failure as a mother that has brought this little one to us. Your years of training, of abuse, have served my purposes well. They hardened her heart and dimmed her vision. Now both mother and daughter belong to me. My victory is complete."

"Oh, God, no!" wept Bedillia. "It's my fault that you're here. I belong here, but not you. Oh God, Serena, I'm sorry, I'm so sorry. Please, forgive me."

There was not a moment's hesitation. Any malice that had dwelled within Serena's heart these many years seemed to evaporate in the heat. Serena caressed her mother's cheek with her hand, then wrapped her arms around her. "Please don't cry. I love you, Mommy. I forgive you. I want you to know that. I still love you."

Bedillia could hardly speak; she was so full of emotion. "I love you too, Serena, more than I can say."

The devil stared at the two; he seemed stunned. Clearly, this wasn't what he had planned at all. "You don't understand," interrupted the devil, growing anger in his voice. "It is Bedillia's fault that you are here. Bedillia's abuse hardened your heart, started you on the road to my domain. How can you forgive her for that? I brought you here so you might enjoy some measure of revenge before your own suffering begins. Do what you wish to her, you have my permission. I will provide you with whatever you need to accomplish that end. What is your pleasure, Serena? This opportunity will not present itself again. Indulge yourself."

"No," retorted Serena. "My mother didn't do this to me, I did. I rejected Christ's love. I had my chance, and I rejected Him; I admit I did." There was a moment of hesitation. "If I could blame anyone, it would be you."

Serena expected satan to react with rage to her comment. She was not disappointed.

"Your flattery will gain you nothing here," he roared. "And I assure you, the fate I have planned for you is no better than that of your mother. You too will feel the touch of the fires soon enough."

With those words, satan pulled Serena from her mother, throwing her to the floor.

"Leave her alone!" cried Bedillia. There was unexpected anger, and even defiance in her voice. Satan grabbed Bedillia by the neck, turning her toward him. She gasped, barely able to breathe.

"Know this, Bedillia Farnsworth, I will take your daughter to the great sea of fire, there to swim forever, engulfed in its scalding blackness, caressed by its flames. And as for you, wench, you will remain here, clothed in your garb of fire, for all eternity. Only know that your daughter's suffering will be worse. And I will see to it that you have a front row seat at the festivities, her baptism in the sea of fire." Satan's grip grew tighter. Bedillia's wide, terrified eyes bulged.

"Stop it!" screamed Serena, who had risen to her feet again. With little concern for the consequences of her actions, she plowed into the prince of darkness from behind. She struck him hard, wrapping her arms around his legs.

Much to Serena's surprise, he released his grip from her mother's neck, and stumbled to the left several steps, before regaining his balance. He swung violently about, pulling Serena upward by her throat. She tried to hang on, but he easily dislodged her.

"How dare you touch me!" he screamed in a deafening roar. He lifted Serena into the air with one hand, then tossed her violently to the far wall of Bedillia's cell. She hit hard and slumped down to the ground. Satan moved forward then stopped. "No, I want you in one piece, conscious and fully alert; all the better to feel the hot caress of the sea of fire. I want no other pain to interfere with the experience."

Satan roughly picked Serena up from the floor, as a portal of light appeared before him. Through the portal they, and Bedillia, could see the cliffs that towered above the sea of fire.

"I love you, Serena!" Bedillia cried, even as satan pulled her daughter through the portal. Satan would see to it that the portal would remain open until Serena's sentence was fulfilled.

"Now," continued satan, standing a few feet in front of the terrible cliff overlooking the sea of fire, "let us turn our attention to you. You've had twelve hours to watch all manners of horrors happening to others, but now it's your turn, little one." Satan grasped Serena's wrist and gave it a slight twist. "You have an appointment to keep, and I don't want you to be late. I've even granted your mother the privilege of watching."

A tear trickled down Serena's cheek. If only it were simply death she was facing. How mercifully quick it would be. But it wasn't just death, was it? It was something far worse. What would it be like? What did she have to look forward to? Did she really want to know? "What will the sea of fire do to me?"

Satan laughed. "Why Serena, I don't want to spoil the surprise. You shall know soon enough. In time, the eddies and currents of this great turbulent sea will carry you to distant and fascinating places, into a realm of darkness, though I doubt that you will be in a mood to truly appreciate the grand journey."

Before her, Serena saw a narrow and treacherous peninsula of land, a ridge that jutted out about 30 feet from the sheer cliff. At its end, an almost surreal precipice overlooked a particularly turbulent stretch of the flaming frothing sea.

"Behold, your gateway to a new and terrible existence," announced satan. "From there, you shall throw yourself into the maelstrom. It shall be the beginning of an eternal struggle, the likes of which you cannot now imagine."

Serena struggled for control. The terrible moment had at last arrived. Now she would join the tormented souls she had encountered in their agony, no longer an observer, but a victim. Her mind was awash in emotion. She turned to see satan watching her intently, and a few feet away was the portal. Beyond it she could faintly see her mother. No, she had to be strong for her.

Satan waited. Surely this wench would break down, faced with the unimaginable fate before her. He waited, but nothing happened. Yes, she was quivering, but she didn't cry openly. He could wait no longer.

"Enough—the time for talk is at an end. Remove the sandals from your feet, for you shall have no further need of them where you are going. For you shall never again feel the solid ground beneath your feet. The moment has come for you to immerse yourself in your element. You shall walk to the threshold from whence you shall cast yourself into a sea of pure undiluted pain. Obey me, wench, I warn you, I will not ask twice."

Serena undid her sandals and rose onto trembling legs. Slowly, she walked out onto the narrow ridge. To either side of the treacherous pathway, she saw the burning swirling sea, a Dantesque parody of the pounding waves along the rocky coastline of Oregon. She tried to focus on the stony ground directly before her feet, yet all too soon it ended, to be replaced by empty sulfurous air. The precipice that loomed ahead gave her a frightening vista of the nightmarish sea directly below. It was a straight plunge down to the heaving turbulent inferno.

"Do you have any last words before the sea of fire engulfs you in an agony beyond your comprehension?" asked satan with a sense of satisfaction in his tone.

Serena looked back to see him waiting patiently at the edge of the cliff, watching her intently. His arms were folded across his chest, his eyes icy cold, filled with hate for humanity.

Serena said not a word to satan, but turned to the dark portal beyond. She couldn't see her mother anymore, but she felt certain that she was watching. "I love you," she whispered, hoping that her mother could see and understand. There was nothing more to say.

"Now, just lean forward and allow yourself to fall," said satan. "It is just that simple. Be quick, I have other more important tasks to attend to."

Serena turned once more to the burning shifting maelstrom below her. She could feel the intense heat. Even from here it burned. There were no other options, and no escape. She took a last deep breath and let go. There was an instant of weightlessness, of dizzying instability, as ground and feet parted company. At first she was falling headfirst toward the seething inferno. Her whole universe was encompassed by the swirling sea of fire. She felt the growing heat, saw the broiling mass hurtling toward her. She managed to swing around, to right herself, for whatever good that might do. She closed her eyes tightly. Then came the impact, the penetration. It was hot beyond comprehension, encompassing her entire body, as she plunged into the hot blackness, vanishing beneath its heaving surface.

Nothing could have prepared her for the intensity of the pain and terror of this ghastly experience. Despite her best efforts, the terrible black fluid penetrated into her body, through her nose, her ears, and between her lips. No part of her body was unaffected by the broiling touch of the black sea. It fried her tongue, and her eyes felt as if they would explode.

She tried to fight her way back to the surface, flailing her arms wildly through the thick, swirling inferno. She couldn't even be sure if she was moving in the right direction, yet she eventually burst to the surface. She howled in pain, as a mouthful of the black oil mixed with boiling saliva and blood erupted from her lips.

She opened her eyes, only to see a wall of pitted black rock looming directly ahead. The current nearly threw her into the cliff before sweeping her away once more. Again she was swept toward the rocks. Again she was drawn away. She vanished below the surface of the black sea once more, pulled downward by the powerful undertow. She kicked and flailed wildly before emerging again. An instant later, she was bounced mercilessly off the cliff. She was pulled back once more stunned and bruised.

Nothing in her experience could have prepared her for this. It was a pain beyond pain, an engulfing agony for which there were no words, for life could not offer its equal. She was tossed and swirled around again and again by the violence of a sea like none other, and through it all, she screamed as she had never screamed before.

For an instant, through the rippling waves of heat, she saw satan, standing at the threshold of the cliff; then he was gone. Serena fought against the pain and formulated a desperate plan. The cliff. If the waves threw her against it again, she just might be able to get a handhold. Yes, it was almost vertical, but its rugged, pocked surface was filled with small crevices and holes, potential handholds if she could just reach them.

Yet the current was sweeping her away into the open sea. She tried to swim, but the black slime was hot and unyielding. Her plan faded into a screaming realm of pain, which swiftly became the center of her world.

Her beautiful long hair burst into flames, burning to blackened stubble. She struggled desperately, to what ends she knew not. For a few seconds, her right arm emerged from the undulating sea—a steaming mass of scalded flesh oozed with bubbling dark blood.

"Oh God!" she cried, thrashing about, pushing upon the dark surface of the seething sea, trying to prevent herself from vanishing beneath the swirling mass. It took all of her effort to prevent it from swallowing her. The flesh above the dreadful touch of the searing sea was caressed by the flames, lending to it a different yet no less terrible pain than that below. Her face was soon covered with ugly red splotches. She could feel the intense heat penetrating her body, the pain plunging ever deeper. A growing cloud of steam and smoke erupted from the boiling black mass surrounding her, as her blood boiled and vaporized. Were she not immortal, Serena was certain that she would already have been dead.

Within a minute, the terrible searing pain had penetrated to the deepest regions of her body. Her lungs burned with a terrible agony, as the immense pressure of a heart attack struck at the very core of her chest. The red splotches on her skin swelled and pulsated, and the veins and arteries in her neck bulged. She gasped in terror; her blood was boiling within her! She coughed up volumes of her life's essence; it oozed from her nose and the corners of her eyes.

Her skin finally yielded to the growing pressure from within, and steaming blood issued forth from great rents. Surely she would pass into shock from the total collapse of her internal organs, but she didn't; if anything she was more alert.

She was tossed around in the turbulence as her body was reduced to a seething mass of desecrated flesh. She was swept into an erupting plume of black horror, swirled round and round before being cast into the torrid air, and back into the burning sea. Through it all, her tortured flesh still managed to cling to her bones, a ragged reminder of the smooth skin that had once been.

The incredible regenerative powers of this immortal body would fight an eternal battle with the great sea, preventing her from being completely consumed. Already it had reached an equilibrium in which destruction and regeneration struggled to reach diametrically opposite goals.

The nature and intensity of her agony also reached equilibrium as she watched the shoreline fade into the distance. Soon her horizon would hold only a lonely vista of fire upon black swirling fury. Thus it would be for all times. Surely there were others here, adrift in this sea of agony, but if there were, they must be scattered far and wide, for she had not yet seen them.

Hell was real, not a dream, not a fantasy, but a horrible reality, and it would be her reality for all time. With only her agony to keep her company, she would be tossed about forever amid the waves, forgotten by all those she had ever loved, save one. Perhaps she was even forgotten by God. Her eternity had just begun.

chapter ten

CHRIS Davis opened his eyes to sunlight streaming in through the great window of his bedroom. The white translucent drapes rippled gently in the slight breeze that blew in from the garden. Chris stretched his arms wide and sat up on his large, oak canopy bed. He'd had another wonderful night's sleep. He'd never been much of a morning person, but that was all in the past, on Earth.

Upon the white pillow beside Chris, Ebbie stretched lazily, apparently aware that her human friend was now awake. She looked toward Chris, at first with only one yellow eye, then two. Her mouth briefly opened, but no sound came forth. To Chris, it almost seemed as if his companion was smiling at him.

"Ebbie, you silly thing," Chris said softly, stroking his bedmate gently on the head and then down the back. His actions elicited a gentle soothing purr. "Are you ready for another beautiful day?"

Of course, there was no answer, yet Chris could sense that Ebbie was ready to go. Chris sat up in bed. His large bedroom seemed so familiar, despite the fact he had been here less than a week. The flower pattern of the wallpaper, the shiny hardwood floor, and many throw rugs, all reminded him of his bedroom in his parents' old home outside of Eugene, Oregon, only on a far grander scale. They'd moved out of that old house when he was

12. The house they had moved into in Salem was larger and newer, but it somehow lacked the distinctive character of the old home in Eugene. It was the memory of that old house that he treasured. Even the pleasant garden that lay beyond the white double French doors was reminiscent of that house, that era. He chuckled as he swung his feet out over the end of the bed.

"Lord, you said that there were many mansions here," said Chris, knowing that God heard the voices of all of his children. "I had no idea that the one you had prepared for Mom and me would be so wonderful." He glanced once more at the beautiful cat, standing on the bed at his side. "And you didn't forget a thing."

Wearing only his white nightshirt, Chris walked barefoot across the floor and through the French doors into the garden, followed by his furry black companion. There were so many different and magnificent flowers, and their aromatic fragrance filled the cool clear air. He looked around at pure green grass and a garden full of vegetables without a single weed. Surely, such perfection could not have been achieved on Earth.

Beyond the garden and the vineyard, beyond the great lawn and the hedge, was the vast forest. Perhaps he would go there again today, to wander through the handiwork of God's creation. Yesterday he'd had many a pleasant encounter there, both with other people who appreciated its intricacies and grand design, and with the wildlife, which neither feared nor posed any danger to him.

He smiled when he thought of yesterday and his encounter with a tiger in the depths of that forest. He hadn't even noticed the great beast until he was practically upon him. At first he was alarmed, yet the great animal had made no threatening moves. He just sat there, doing nothing more than swinging his long tail back and forth. Then he stretched out in the gentle sun with a look that showed Chris he had no reason to fear. He remembered a Bible verse that told of the lion lying down beside the lamb. That probably applied to tigers too.

Chris also remembered his encounter with a large, partially buried rock. He had been so caught up with the beauty of the colorful birds amid the trees, that he tripped over a round rock, and down he went, scraping his knee in the process. Yet, even as he dusted himself off and examined the minor scrape, it vanished before his very eyes. Within 30 seconds, it had totally healed—a testimony to the incredible regenerative power of a glorified body, a physical form without flaw, designed to last for eternity.

He would never have to concern himself with the ravaging effects of time. No more trips to the health food store for vitamins, antioxidants, or protein supplements. Back on Earth, he had spent a lot of his hard-earned money on those sorts of things. It was probably his background in health care that had made him so aware of the body's basic dietary needs. Quite abruptly, his thoughts seemed to run up against a roadblock. There was something significant about the health food store, something beyond the vitamins and mineral supplements. It was important, of that he was certain, yet it was also illusive, a sort of phantom memory.

It was like a jigsaw puzzle, this earthly life he had left behind. All of the existing pieces fit together fine, but there were gaps, missing pieces. One of those pieces had something to do with health food. No, not with health food, but with the store, a specific store. The New Life Center; yes, that was the place. He could picture the little downtown shop, wedged between the old theatre and the dollar store. It was just two blocks from the community hospital where he worked as an X-ray technician; and he'd walked there quite often. He even remembered the things he purchased, but that was where his memories ended.

He recalled the words of Jesus, when he had brought him here six days ago. He had said something about painful memories, about them being blocked, about loved ones he would never see again. The fragmentary nature of his remembered life during the past five years had something to do with that. It made him feel uncomfortable. Should he seek the answers?

"Chris, I do believe that you and that old cat of yours have fallen in love with my garden."

Chris turned to see his mother standing by the French doors, wearing a long white dressing gown. Her blue eyes practically sparkled. Chris walked to her and wrapped his arms about her, kissing her on the cheek. He felt like he could have hung on forever. Come to think of it, he did have forever. "Good morning, Mom, I hope you had a nice rest."

"Wonderful," said Jennifer.

"I can hardly believe that I'm here with you," said Chris. "I've missed you so much."

"I've missed you too, Chris," said Jennifer. "I'm so glad you're home."

"Meow." Ebbie looked up at her two favorite people, doing her best to join the circle of joy.

Jennifer glanced down to meet the glance of her yellow-eyed friend. "Yes, Ebbie, I missed you too." Ebbie seemed to understand. She walked around Jennifer's ankles, as she had so often done on Earth. Jennifer had always liked that, the feel of her soft fur.

"You know, when Ebbie first showed up here a few days before you did, I was confused. I was sitting on the porch swing, just daydreaming. The next thing I knew, she jumped up on my lap, and started purring away. I knew that it was her right away. I really didn't think I'd ever see her again.

"The Bible is rather silent when it comes to the topic of our beloved pets, and I'd never thought to ask the Father about it. But, then again, why shouldn't they be here? They were so much a part of our lives on Earth, why can't they be a part of our lives here? She was here because you were coming, and God knew just how much you loved her. She is a gift from God to you."

"Having the two of you with me makes my life complete," Chris said, smiling broadly.

Jennifer continued, "When our Lord saw fit to take me from the world, to deliver me from that terrible pain, I was so very thankful. But I quickly realized that I had lost you and your father. Here in Heaven, I had everything I could ever have wanted, except the two of you. You guys were my life. I missed you both terribly; still, I wish that you could have had more time on Earth, a larger portion of life. But, I'll not be questioning God's wisdom on that matter."

"I worry about Dad," said Chris. "He's all alone now."

"Your father is strong. His faith is strong. He'll get through this, you'll see. The day is coming when we'll all be together again, here in the loving hands of our heavenly Father."

Quite abruptly, the direction of the conversation changed. "Mom, how well do you remember your life on Earth?"

Jennifer looked into her son's eyes. That question didn't surprise her at all, yet she responded with another question. "Why do you ask, dear?"

"Well, I guess I've been trying to evaluate my life on Earth, sort of in retrospect."

"Yes?" Jennifer said.

"Well, the thing is, I'm having trouble remembering details. I was never like that. I mean, I seem to know everyone I meet here in Heaven. Yesterday, I ran into this wonderful white-haired man in the woods. We had a fascinating conversation. We talked just like we were old friends. I knew that I couldn't possibly have met him on Earth, he came here centuries before I was even born, but I did know him, felt very comfortable around him."

"Of course," confirmed Jennifer. "We are all brothers and sisters, children of God. We all recognize each other, even if we have never met before. I told you all about that on the first day, remember?"

"Sure, but I guess I'm having trouble accepting the fact that there are going to be things about my life on Earth that I won't remember. It makes me, well, uncomfortable. I don't know how to put it other than that. The last few years are the worst."

"And that troubles you?"

"Very much," Chris said. "Because I feel like something has been removed, something important." Chris hesitated. "Maybe it is someone important."

"Like who?" asked Jennifer.

"That's the thing, I don't know. Sometimes, in my dreams I can see this face, the face of a woman. I know that she should be familiar. No, more than familiar, but she fades away. I reach out to her, but she dissolves like a phantom. Three mornings ago, I awoke with tears in my eyes. I must have been crying in my sleep. I think I've dreamt about her most every night I've been here."

A look of concern swept across Jennifer's face. "Bad dreams…here?"

Chris nodded. "Mom, has anything like that ever happened to you?"

"Never, not like that," replied Jennifer. "I know what you mean about the blur, but it never troubled me. You remember what you need to remember. Now that doesn't mean that you won't remember some of the unpleasant things. Going through some of those experiences on Earth made us stronger people. Somewhere I once heard 'what doesn't kill you makes you stronger.' What you don't remember about your life on Earth are the things that would only bring you unnecessary grief. Jesus told you all about that, remember?"

"Yes, I remember."

"What I can't understand is why you'd have a portion of a memory," continued Jennifer, "something bouncing around in your head. Just give it to God, things will work out. They always do."

"Sure, Mom, I guess you're right," said Chris, a smile appearing. "If God has a purpose in it, I'm sure that it will become clear to me in time."

"Sure it will. Hey sport, why don't you get dressed and come out to the dining room. I'll make you and Ebbie some breakfast."

Chris smiled. He loved his mother's cooking, he always had; and she loved cooking for him. It wasn't work to her; it was part of the joy of Heaven. Far be it for him to interfere with that. "I'll be right there."

"What do you say we take a trip to the big city later? I think it's about time I took you there. I'll give you the grand tour."

"Zion?" asked Chris.

"Of course," giggled his mother. "Is there any other city? You haven't been there yet, and it's high time that we made the journey."

"I'd love to," Chris said.

"Well, put on your best clothes. By the time you get dressed, I'll have breakfast on the table. Then we'll head out after breakfast. And let's stop worrying about those dreams, OK?"

"Sure," Chris said, his smile growing.

Jennifer picked a few ripe peppers from the garden, along with a big red tomato, and headed back through the large French doors, leaving Chris and Ebbie to contemplate the world around them. And about the dreams, if there is something about the mysterious young woman, something to be learned, God will make it clear in His own time. After all, Chris certainly had an ample quantity of time.

chapter eleven

CHRIS pulled on a long white robe he found in his bedroom closet. It seemed the most appropriate attire for the journey ahead. His mother was also dressed all in white. At breakfast, the trip to Zion was the center of conversation.

"You can really lose track of time in Zion," Jennifer noted, as she poured Chris a second glass of orange juice. "With no night in the city, no darkness, things are just bustling all the time. A person could spend days there, and hardly realize it. Believe me, I know. I once spent nearly a week there. The time passed so quickly. There is just so much joy, so many things to experience and do."

"I'm really looking forward to it," Chris said. "It will be wonderful to go somewhere special with you, to go on an adventure with my favorite person in the whole world, again."

"Such flattery," giggled Jennifer. "You've gotten so much better with it over the years."

Chris only smiled. It wasn't flattery, it was from the heart. He meant every word of it.

"I should have taken you on this journey days ago," said Jennifer, as they were finishing their meal. "I suppose I was being a bit selfish. I wanted to have you all to myself for a while before introducing you to the wide world beyond."

"That's OK, Mom. I wanted to be with you. I've wanted to be with you ever since…well, ever since you died."

That sounded like such a strange statement to Chris; so very alien to his earthly experience. It would take some time to become accustomed to heavenly realities.

There was excitement in the air as the two walked out the front door, hand in hand. They stopped just beyond the front porch. Following closely behind them was Ebbie, "Ebbie, you're going to have to stay here. Mom and I will be back, I promise," Chris said.

Ebbie sat down, her eyes never turning from her best friend. It seemed as if she had understood every word—she probably had.

Jennifer looked toward her son approvingly. She couldn't get over what a man he had become in the years since their separation. "Well, are you ready to begin?"

Chris smiled broadly. "Whenever you are, Mom."

Jennifer turned her attention to a point just ahead of them, closed her eyes, and stretched out her hands. Almost immediately, a field of sparkling, star-like luminaries materialized, quickly growing in brightness and number.

Chris watched the entire process in amazement. Yes, he had watched Jesus do it, yet, to see his own mother perform the same act, filled him with wonder. Eventually, he hoped to be able to do such a thing himself. His mother had told him that it simply took practice. The power was not within her, but with God. Jesus had drawn upon this power when He entered a closed room where the apostles had been hiding from the Roman and Jewish authorities after His crucifixion and resurrection. God had granted that same power to all of His beloved children. The power is there, it comes down to a simple matter of faith and knowledge.

The lawn beyond the sparkling blue and green stars faded into a fog. Before them was a portal which led to the destination of Jennifer's choosing.

"Let's go, sweetheart," said Jennifer, who took a step forward, leading her son into the mists.

For a moment they were walking through a bright fog. Chris could feel the love that surrounded them; he was at peace. When the mists parted, they stood before a tall archway that allowed passage through a mighty wall of the whitest marble. Chris gazed up in awe. The glistening wall must have stood over 100 feet high, with the archway being about half that tall, and at least 100 feet wide. A great multitude of people dressed in bright white robes, swept in and out of the great portal. To the right and left, the wall extended as far as his eye could see.

"It's magnificent!" gasped Chris, who realized that simple words could not possibly describe the glory of what he saw.

"This wall completely surrounds the City of God. It marks the boundary of the most holy place in all of Heaven, the most holy place in the entire universe," explained Jennifer. "There are twelve entrances like this, one for each of the tribes of Israel. There are three of them on each of the four walls that surround the city."

For a moment, Chris turned his attention to the land surrounding the great city. The city itself sat atop a sort of high plateau, surrounded on all sides by the green forests and peaceful meadows of a wide valley. Beyond the valley were lofty mountains, many of whose peaks held great reserves of white snow, glistening in the sunlight.

"What a place!" Chris said, overwhelmed by the vista.

He turned his attention toward the great throng entering and leaving the city gate, some 50 yards away. People were materializing and dematerializing just outside the gate, making roads beyond the city unnecessary. Everywhere spirits were high and the praises of God echoed from all around.

"Well, lets head on in," Jennifer said. "There is so much to see. We won't have time to see it all during this trip, but there will be other days." Jennifer laughed. "Many other days."

Chris and his mother blended into the crowd entering the city. The group was amazingly friendly and relaxed. None appeared to be in any particular hurry; and all around, groups of three and four stopped to speak to one another. In fact, all those around had a friendly hello to offer the pair. Though Chris had never met any of them, he knew them by name, every one of them, and they knew him.

As they walked through the vast arch, Chris looked down to discover that the smooth roadway was glistening gold. It looked like gold, yet it had a strange translucent quality that gave the thoroughfare an almost glassy appearance. Chris couldn't help but chuckle as he thought back to his chemistry class in college. He seemed to recall the professor mentioning that gold was practically inert. It didn't tarnish or rust, it kept its luster even under the most grueling of conditions. Gold could lie at the bottom of a creek bed or ocean for a thousand years, and come out little the worse for wear. If it were plentiful, it would make an excellent material for building roads.

The streets were filled with people, and many of them were singing their praises to God out loud. No vehicles of any kind traveled the wide avenues, which were reserved exclusively for pedestrians. The architecture of Heaven was, to say the least, unique. The predominant building materials were blue and white cultured marble; gold, reddish brown tile; and glass, both stained and clear. The architecture bore some resemblance to that of the Greeks, yet there were evidences of Middle and Far

Eastern influences as well. Even aspects of modern architecture were evident in some of the buildings with vast amounts of glass.

No, maybe he was looking at it all wrong. This was the original architecture, developed by the original architect. Perhaps it was the mind of God that had inspired the world's many architectural forms in the first place. Perhaps the great creations of the past and present were simply reflections of God's creativity.

Above them, an occasional winged angel robed wholly in white passed over the streets. Jennifer had explained that the angels were servants, messengers, and guardians all rolled up into one. They rarely slept, and were constantly vigilant, a perfect army, holy, wise, and pure; and their dominion wasn't restricted to Heaven alone, but included Earth as well. On Earth they took on a more subdued role, often appearing indistinguishable from normal humans. Yet even there they were guardians of righteousness, intervening on humankind's behalf in matters both spiritual and natural, defending and inspiring humanity. Indeed, many humans had entertained angels unaware.

Some of the buildings around him were the mansions of the saints who had more urban inclinations; yet most were public buildings, houses of worship, schools, art galleries, open air theatres, museums, and many libraries. As the two made their way through the joyful streets, it was the numerous libraries that caught Chris's attention. Since the time of Adam and Eve, humans had an intense desire for knowledge, and sometimes that desire had gotten them into trouble. Yet, that quest had also carried them to the depths of the sea, and lifted them to the stars, allowing them to glimpse the glory of creation. God recognized that need.

"And the truth shall make you free," he whispered.

Chris also noticed shops along the avenues. Now that was curious, something he hadn't expected. But that made sense too, didn't it? Some people loved their work on Earth, loved it to the point where it was no longer work, it was a joy. There were also the hobbies of humanity; work turned to pleasure. To some people, their labors in Heaven and their hobby on Earth were one and the same.

Chris and Jennifer visited some of the shops along the way. The handicrafts practiced here were diverse indeed. There were weavers, bakers, cabinetmakers, makers of musical instruments, silversmiths, and carpenters. There were even trades unique to Heaven; crafts and technologies to be found nowhere else. For example, there was a sort of horn that could take music from the mind of whoever held it, and transform the thought into audible notes. Anyone could become a composer.

Chris thought back to the music he had heard within the anteroom of the great judgment hall, music that had sounded so very familiar. Perhaps the same heavenly technology in play here was responsible for that as well.

The wares in Heaven were neither sold nor rented, but given freely, a gift of beauty from one to another. People here weren't working because they had to—only because they wanted to. They took pride in their work, and that sort of pride was not a bad thing. Just as Jennifer loved to cook, these merchants loved to build and create, and there was no point in creating, unless it could be shared with others. Their unifying goal was to spread the beauty of their creations throughout Heaven.

"Within us is the desire to create," Jennifer said as they walked through a shop offering fine crystal figurines not fashioned in a kiln, but fashioned by means of pure thought. "Perhaps the desire to create was a result of man's own creation. God made man in His own image and likeness. It was in God's nature to create beauty. That aspect of God has been passed down to us, much as a father's trade is passed to his children."

"It's just amazing," Chris said as he and his mother left the shop. "Those figurines were so detailed, and they were all created by someone just thinking about them?"

"It isn't as simple as all that," cautioned Jennifer. "Those artisans study for years to develop their talents. They tap a hidden reservoir of power to accomplish what they do. It is the same reservoir of power that allows us to move instantly from one place to another, or allows a crippled child to be miraculously healed on Earth. The source of that power is God Himself, and He allows us to tap into it. Jesus talked about it to His followers. He told them that He had to leave them in order for the power to be brought to Earth for their use. They were waiting for it in the upper room on the Day of Pentecost. There appeared to them as tongues of fire, alighting on every one of them, remember?"

"Sure," Chris said. "Then it's here too?"

"Of course," replied Jennifer. "It was here long before it came to Earth. It was always in the presence of the Father, but throughout most of human history, it was only given out to a few select individuals, and even then, very sparingly. But in Heaven, it has always flowed abundantly."

"I see," Chris said. "How did you learn all of these things, anyway?"

That question made Jennifer laugh. "I didn't figure it out all on my own, if that's what you think. God told me all about it. That's the main reason we came here, to speak to God personally. You need to start developing a personal relationship with the Father. The best way to do that is to talk with Him face to face. He is easier to talk to than you'd ever imagine. You'll see. It is marvelous. But we'll get to that, I wanted you to see a few things along the way first."

Chris shook his head in wonderment. There was so much here to take in. Now he knew why his mother had waited a few days before bringing him to Zion. It wasn't just selfishness, as she had claimed. She wanted him to stay near to his new home for a while, adjust a bit, before introducing him to this city of wonders.

As they continued walking, Chris noted that the city was also replete with rows of trees, parks, and a multitude of elaborate fountains and pools. There was even a river with crystal clear water flowing through it. Along the river's banks were mighty trees bearing many different fruits. Some of the trees bore fruit of tropical varieties, while others trees were those found in more temperate zones. Apples, pears, oranges, grapefruit, figs, and other varieties he didn't recognize lined the great river, all bearing large, ripe fruit.

A great park of green grass extended for several hundred yards on either side of the river, adding to the beauty and tranquility of the scene. Multitudes gathered along the river's banks. Some came to dine on the fruit and drink of the waters, while others came to congregate and fellowship. Some, in their joy, sang of the glory of God, and others joined in. Their heavenly melody rose from the park. God had gone to great lengths to make his children comfortable and content, and they seemed determined to give voice to their happiness, to their love and appreciation.

Chris and his mother walked across one of the many wide bridges of gold that spanned the flowing waters. Below, Chris saw what looked like gems of many colors, sizes, and shapes embedded in the golden sands. They caught the light of the eternal day, shimmering and glistening like so many stars on a clear night.

"You know, in a way, I almost expected Heaven to be some sort of spirit realm," admitted Chris. "I think I prefer this better."

"I agree," said Jennifer. "I think God created Heaven as a place we could relate to. Not a nebulous spiritual realm, but a real, solid block and mortar, gold and silver, flesh and blood place. In lots of ways, it's like Earth, at least the better parts of it. But one day, when we become a little more mature, there is going to be a new Heaven and a new Earth. What they are going to be like, I don't know. Maybe they'll be more spiritual."

The two walked for hours, taking in the incredible beauty of Zion, yet they never grew weary. Jennifer directed her son's attention to a great building that stood nearly 200 feet high, and perhaps a half mile in length. It had great ornate columns of marble on all sides, and beyond were large windows outlined in gold. Some of the windows were clear, while others were various shades of green, blue, and yellow. Chris looked through the window and saw many hallways made of glistening translucent crystal. It was the largest single structure he had seen in Zion.

Its architecture was unique, a fantastic cross between Greek and ultramodern. Even considering man's many advances in construction, Chris wondered if such a structure was practical, or even possible, to build given early 21st century technology.

"The Hall of Records," Jennifer announced. "Within those walls, can be found the record of the deeds of every person who ever drew breath upon Earth. There is a book for everyone."

"Everyone?" asked Chris; amazed that such a thing was possible.

"Everyone, dear. Whether they lived for a hundred and twenty years, or barely were afforded the opportunity to draw breath, the record of their existence is here."

"Can anyone view the records?" asked Chris. "I mean, aren't there any privacy rules here?"

Jennifer giggled slightly, putting her arm around her son. He still had a lot to learn about heavenly matters. "Of course not, why should there be? This isn't Earth, full of dirty little secrets and scandals that can ruin a reputation. We are all family, and we have already been judged by God. If God has judged us pure, if the blood of Jesus has cleansed us, what does it matter if others here know all about us? We are, literally, an open book, no secrets."

The two walked up the 12 marble stairs and passed between the great columns toward one of the many open doorways in the Hall of Records. The inside was brightly lit, illuminated by the sky above. There were stairways leading up to a dozen floors; glistening translucent walkways suspended in midair, and along the walkways, row after row of bookshelves.

"I've been told that there are over thirty billion books here. But before we view any of them, I must caution you that the knowledge you can gain here can be enlightening, but it can also be very disturbing. This is the place Jesus spoke of when he told you that it was possible to fill in the blanks in your life on Earth. Anyone here in Heaven is free to explore the contents of these books. It is all here, and it's not sugarcoated. The question is, whether you are truly ready to fill in those blanks. Most people shy away from this place, especially after they've gotten a taste of it. You might get more than you bargained for—I did."

"I'd still like to see how it works," Chris said. "I'm willing to take the chance."

"But I'm not, at least not yet. Today, let's play it safe. Let's look in on the life of someone special. Now, who would you like to know about?" asked Jennifer, almost rhetorically. "I know, let's find out all about me."

Chris couldn't help but laugh. "I hope you know the cataloguing system."

Jennifer looked at him with a twinkle in her eye. "Actually, I don't have a clue."

"OK," Chris said, looking around. "So, how much time do you figure it's going to take to find your book? Should we ask a librarian to help?"

"Well, I'm not all that sure that there's a librarian, but we don't need one. I can find my book. Follow me."

"Lead on," Chris said.

"Well, let me see," pondered Jennifer, placing her index finger to her chin. "We've got to go up to the ninth level." She pointed to a nearby stairway. "Race you."

Jennifer was off like a flash. She had rounded the first turn of the marble spiral staircase before Chris had a chance to respond. In an instant he took off after her. As they steadily ascended, he pondered if it might be somehow sacrilegious to run up the stairs in the Hall of Records. He recalled Pastor Harris reminding him not to run up and down the stairs in the church when he was a youth. It was a rather noisy practice, and the pastor had been concerned about one of the children falling and getting hurt. Even his mother had reminded him several times about it. It wasn't OK for him to run up and down the stairway in the church, but it was OK for her to run up and down the stairway in Heaven's Hall of Records. He'd have to give her a good talking to later, but right now he'd focus on catching up.

Four, five, and six floors passed by, yet they both continued their pace, laughing all the way. Jennifer hit the ninth floor just four steps ahead of her son.

"Beat you!" she laughed.

Chris laughed. Right now, his mother seemed like a kid again. "It's OK to run up the steps here?"

"Sure," replied Jennifer. "God loves to watch His children playing."

Chris was amazed that he didn't feel the slightest bit winded after the long uphill run. He gazed around at the rows of books that seemed to go on forever. Now that he could get a closer look, he saw that the books were not all the same. About a quarter of the books were bound in the purest white, another quarter were a sort of light gray. A very few of the books were bound in glistening gold, while the remainder appeared to be bound in black.

"Is there some significance to the color of the books?" asked Chris, pointing to a nearby shelf.

"Oh yes," confirmed his mother. "The books bound in white are the records of the saints, those who are already here in Heaven. The gold books are the records of the martyrs, those who lost their lives because of the profession of their faith. They are the most blessed of all of God's children. The gray books are the records of those still living on Earth. Their fates hang in the balance. Even as we speak, those books are being written." Jennifer paused and then smiled broadly. "Once, several years ago, I actually saw a gray book turn white, right before my eyes as another saint came home to glory. It was a wonderful feeling to know that the family of God had grown by one."

"And the black books?" asked Chris.

There was a momentary silence. It was obvious that Jennifer didn't want to speak of those books.

"Those are the books of those who departed life without accepting God's plan of salvation. Without the blood of Christ to cleanse them, their sins have doomed them to eternity in outer darkness...to Hell."

A chill passed through Chris. He knew that Hell existed, but no one in Heaven spoke of it. It was just too sad. No, not sad, tragic.

"My book is over this way," said Jennifer, motioning to her right.

They journeyed down a long corridor lined with shelves of books. There were surprisingly few people here. Apparently, the contents of the books were something that most cared not to view. Yet there was one young woman, obviously of Oriental descent, standing in the corridor ahead of them. In her hands she held open a book, a black book. She seemed to take no notice of the passing pair.

Chris turned to look at the woman more carefully. She seemed to be in a trance-like state as she gazed at the thick volume. Though she uttered not a syllable, Chris could see the grief on her face, the tears in her eyes.

"Chris, come along," urged Jennifer, "don't disturb her. My book is down this way."

Chris hesitated, then followed his mother. As it was with all people in Heaven, he recognized this woman. Her name was Mao Yeng. But to recognize her was not to understand the depths of her sorrow. Chris recalled a Scripture that spoke of weeping in Heaven. Perhaps it was sadness for those who had not made it, those individuals who had not found the narrow way.

Chris followed Jennifer until they stood before a shelf full of books. Jennifer reached for a book bound in white on the third shelf. Chris noted that his mother's name was on the book's cover. "Now wait a minute, Mom, how did you know where your book was? You've been here before, right?"

His mother looked back at him, the slightest of smiles upon her face. "Well, yes, but that's not the way I found it. All I had to do was to think about the book I was looking for, and immediately I knew where it was."

Jennifer paused to allow that concept to sink into her son's thoughts before she opened the book to the first page. Yes, there were words in it, but Chris hardly had time to read them because he immediately saw a vision, not unlike the one he had seen in the Hall of Judgment. His surroundings faded to a deep blue, and in the midst of it all he saw a hospital room and his mother's birth. He saw his grandmother hold his mother in her arms for the first time. It was incredible, and so very real. He could see the adult version of his mother standing by his side, watching the scene unfold before them, but the rest of the library had faded away. This was virtual reality on the ultimate scale.

"Do you remember the Dickens novel, *A Christmas Carol*?" asked Jennifer, turning to her son.

"Yes," confirmed Chris, "the Ebenezer Scrooge story."

"That's right," replied Jennifer. "The ghost of Christmas past took Scrooge by the hand and showed him a vision of the past, his past. The ghost told him that the images he saw were shadows and had no consciousness of him. Well, that's the way it is here. This is a record of the past, like a movie, only more real."

"In three dimensions," noted Chris, turning to view the scene that totally wrapped around them. "It's a hologram, a very big and detailed one."

Jennifer smiled. "I'm not sure I know what a hologram is, exactly. But I suppose so. Why don't we move forward a few years."

The scene changed. Chris saw his mother as a child of nine, playing checkers with her grandfather at the kitchen table. The two laughed and joked around, while her mother prepared lunch for them. Beyond the window behind them, snow was falling. It was a beautiful family moment, full of love and fun. The two told corny jokes while they played the game.

"I can see any point in my life by just turning the pages of my book," explained Jennifer. "That way I can relive all of the happy moments from my youth, laugh at my antics all over again."

Again the scene changed. Chris witnessed his parents getting married. He saw his grandfather giving away the bride in a little country church. His father and mother looked so young. He had seen photographs of that happy day, but this was a special treat. It was almost like being there. It made him smile to witness his own parent's wedding; an event that occurred two years before he was born.

"I look forward to the day when I will see my parents again," said Jennifer. "I've missed them so much these past years."

Again Jennifer flipped the pages. Chris witnessed his own childhood through his mother's eyes, felt a mother's love and pride in her only son. He smiled.

The page turned. Chris became a witness of his own mother's day of judgment. Jesus stood at her side; spoke on her behalf before the Father. Now more than ever before, Chris realized the full magnitude of the love and sacrifice of their Savior. Surely He must have acted as the advocate of everyone who had placed their faith in Him over the ages.

Chris watched as his mother stepped into the mansion for the first time. She was welcomed home by her paternal grandparents, her uncle, and others; who had preceded her on the road of life. They did their best to make her feel at ease in her new surroundings. Apparently, the books even covered that part of life that existed beyond judgment.

The vision faded as Jennifer closed the book and returned it to the shelf from which she had retrieved it. "That's all there is to it," she explained, "very easy to use. You just open the book and turn the pages like any ordinary book. When you are finished, you close it and the vision ends. You can even use it to look in on your friends and family back on Earth. The records are always up-to-date. Just turn to the last page and you see all that they have done today."

"Did you ever use it to look in on Dad and me?" asked Chris, hoping that the question wasn't too personal.

"Many times," admitted Jennifer, turning toward her son, "but not for years. The last time I looked through your book, was to watch you graduate from high school."

"Why did you stop?"

Jennifer paused, considering how best to explain it. "Well, it was nice looking in on you from time to time, and I know a few people here who do this a lot, but I couldn't. There were times when I would see something in your life that was absolutely heartbreaking. Do you remember when you broke your leg playing football?"

Yes," replied Chris. "That was during my senior year, about two years after you…well, came here. I remember that I became quite ill a day or so later and had to be readmitted to the hospital."

"One night, when you were really sick, you were calling for me in your sleep, remember?"

"Yes," Chris said, "I remember."

"You can't imagine what it was like not to be with you at that time, to know that there was nothing I could do to ease your pain. I felt so helpless. It wasn't long after that when I stopped looking in. Can you understand that? It wasn't that I didn't care; it was that I cared too much. After that, I simply asked God to look after you." Tears welled up in Jennifer's eyes.

Chris hugged her. "It's OK, Mom, I understand."

"And there is another danger. Sometimes you can discover things about your life that later you wish you didn't know."

"I'd still like to know," Chris said.

Are you so sure?" asked Jennifer. "You find out about forgotten friends you will never see again because they are in Hell, or at least headed in that direction, and there is nothing you can do about it. You feel helpless." Jennifer hesitated. "It was a mistake to bring you here. What was I thinking of?"

"No, its fine," said Chris, "I think its all pretty cool, really."

Again Jennifer paused. "Chris, tell me about your Uncle Bill. What do you remember about him?"

Chris looked at his mother incredulously. "Nothing. I don't have an Uncle Bill."

"Yes you do, or at least you did. He was my older brother. He used to take you out fishing when you were a kid, remember? You always had such a great time with him. Sometimes you came back with such outlandish fish stories."

Again Chris shook his head. He stepped back. "Mom, you're kidding, right? You don't have an older brother."

"I assure you, dear, I do. He died the year before I did. You went to his funeral. You cried a lot, remember?"

Again Chris shook his head.

"It's OK, I didn't remember him either, not until I opened your book. Only then did I learn of his existence. I looked through my own book to discover still more. I learned plenty, yet it still didn't stir any memories. I guess I should say that I now know about him, not remember him. He was good to you, and me, but he was a real partier and a womanizer. I searched out his book in the library. It had a black cover. I didn't open it. I couldn't bear to. Now, I have to live with the knowledge that my brother is in Hell. When I opened my book for you a moment ago, I carefully selected the parts of my life I showed you, made sure that they were things that wouldn't hurt you. I don't want you to look into your own book, not yet. You're not ready."

Chris could see how hurt, and, yes, afraid, his mother was. Still, he really wanted to explore his book. "OK, Mom, I'll hold off, I promise." He hugged her again and tried to comfort her.

It was several minutes before they were finally ready to depart. They retraced their steps down the long corridor of books.

"I'm sorry, Chris," said Jennifer, managing a slight smile. "I didn't want to make a scene in front of you."

"No, that's all right, really. I understand."

Mao Yeng was gone by the time they reached the place where she had stood in such deep contemplation. Chris would have liked very much to have had a few sympathetic words with her. Perhaps it was best that he didn't. He considered the black book she held in her hands. Had she been mourning the fate of a loved one? He didn't have the answer for that one, but it was a most disturbing thought. To spend eternity here, only to know that someone you cared deeply for was suffering in the pit of Hell was an unimaginable concept. His own mother carried such a burden.

For a moment, he considered the souls in Hell, souls without hope. What was it like? He paused, glanced at a nearby black book. It would be easy enough to find out, wouldn't it? No, it was too horrible, too lurid. He felt ashamed to have even pondered such a thing. He moved on.

Chris walked past the stairway and to the end of the corridor. The clear crystal windows offered a panoramic vista of the city. He figured that he was well over 100 feet above the street. His attention was drawn toward an open plaza about half a mile away. It was a vast expanse of shimmering gold, circular in shape, stretching on for untold miles, and filled with people, perhaps tens of millions. At what appeared to be its center, several miles away, was a great glow, a luminance that Chris had come to associate with the presence of God. Even from this distance, he could hear the sound of song and praise rising from the place.

"The most holy place in Zion," said Jennifer standing by her son's side and placing her arm around him. "That's where we're going. It is the place where the people come to worship God in person, to sing His praises. I often go there. You can feel such unity, such belonging. Many times I've gotten lost in His spirit and His love there, losing all track of time. I wanted you to see it, to experience it." Jennifer's excitement and anticipation was very obvious.

"OK, let's go," Chris said.

A few minutes later Chris and Jennifer were stepping back out into the busy street. Absentmindedly, Chris glanced up at the sun.

There was a region of brightness high in the sky, but it didn't look exactly like the sun. According to Jennifer, it was always daylight in Zion, a city that basked in the light of the eternal love of the Father.

They walked toward the great gathering. As they did, the sound of singing grew louder and the street more crowded.

Chris looked ahead into the swelling crowds, "It sounds like people sing to God as much as they talk to Him."

"Yes, dear, in part," confirmed Jennifer. "You see, when lucifer fell, he took a third of the angels with him. Most of that third were angels under his command. He was a sort of praise leader, Heaven's choir director, and the angels under his direction were the members of his choir. Their very purpose was to sing to God. With them gone, there was little or no song in Heaven—until humans came."

"Oh come on, Mom, how do you figure that?"

"Well, I've been here for a few years longer than you have, but think about it. How many times does the Bible speak of angels singing?"

Chris paused. Right now he wished he knew his Bible as well as his mother did. "I'm not sure. Didn't the angels sing glory to God in the highest and on Earth, peace, good will when Jesus was born?"

"No, they proclaimed it," said Jennifer, her tone definitive. "It's humanity who sings the praises of God. But it is more than praise and song that awaits us. It is worship, communion with God. Like I told you, it is not a monologue, but a dialog when you are speaking with God and He is speaking to you."

Chris gave his mother a look of astonishment. "But there must be millions of people, all worshiping God at the same time. Are you saying that He is holding a conversation with each and every one of them?"

"Exactly," Jennifer said. "He talks personally to every one of them. God heard all of our prayers on Earth, so what makes you think that He can't talk to all of us individually here?"

Chris didn't reply. He'd never been the prayer warrior his mother was. Actually, he had not taken as much time to speak to God as he probably should have. He'd sometimes wondered if God had heard him at all. What did that say about his faith?

"I like to get as close as I can to the throne of God," said Jennifer, "but it takes time and patience. There are just so many people gathered for miles around to be close to God. You have to slowly work your way through the crowd, moving forward when possible."

Jennifer had piqued her son's curiosity. "How close to God have you gotten?"

"You mean, other than at my judgment? Well, not all that close, maybe a hundred yards or so. There are people who spend years in this place, just to be in the presence of God. It took me days to get that close. To get really close might take years.

"There's a lot to see if you can get that close—like the twenty-four elders who are constantly gathered around the Creator, and the four living beings, not human, that surround Him. I actually saw them when I got close that one time. I really don't know how to describe them…they're like nothing I've ever seen before. I'll just put it that way. But at our Creator's right hand is Jesus, right where the Bible said He would be. It's all so wonderful. But understand, you don't have to get that close to speak to Him, to be with Him. You'll see."

It was a few minutes before Chris and Jennifer stepped into the great plaza and worked their way through the crowd. Some of the people were singing, others talking among themselves, others were praising the Lord, their arms outstretched. Here and there, people had gathered with musical instruments, leading songs of all sorts to God. Some played to a country or rock beat, while others led those around them in familiar old hymns. The sheer variety of the music was as vast as the crowd.

Most of the crowd, though, was sitting on the translucent golden surface of the plaza, speaking quietly, perhaps in prayer. They would speak for a time, and then grow silent and attentive. Occasionally some jumped and shouted, praising their Creator. There were even a few who were dancing before the Lord as King David had done.

Chris could see the warm glow in the distance, the place where the Lord of Hosts sat in the midst of His people, but he figured that he was still well over a mile away. Never had he seen a gathering such as this. Jennifer found a place where the two of them could sit and motioned to Chris.

"This will be fine," she said, as her son sat down at her side. "Now just relax." Jennifer paused for a moment before speaking again, but when she did, it was not to her son. "Father, I'm so glad to be here with you again. Oh, I thank you for your mercy in bringing my son to me. I missed him so much. I brought him with me today."

"Welcome, Chris," said a powerful yet kind voice that emanated from everywhere. "I am pleased that you have come into My presence this day."

Despite the fact that his mother had told him about this aspect of his communion with God, Chris was not quite prepared for the reality. "Thank you, Lord, I'm very happy to be here." Chris felt very awkward about his response, and a little bit fearful. He also felt foolish for doubting that this level of communication with God was possible. Just how should he conduct himself in a conversation with the Creator of the entire universe?

"Chris, you need not be afraid," the reassuring voice said. "You are my son, and I love you dearly."

"I love you too," replied Chris, who felt more at ease now.

"I know you do," replied God, "and it makes me very happy." There was a pause before God continued. "Your mother has awaited your coming for a long time. Many times we have spoken of you. We both rejoice now that you are home."

"He's always been a blessing to me, Father God," Jennifer said, looking toward the place where God sat in the midst of His people.

"I think you mean he was a blessing *most* of the time," God said.

Chris was surprised. He was certain that he had detected a trace of amusement in the voice of God.

"Yes, Father, *most* of the time," giggled Jennifer.

"But you taught him well," continued God. "Very well indeed. Even after you departed, his faith and love endured. That was the greatest test of his character."

Jennifer was on her knees now, tears of joy in her eyes. "I praise and thank You, Father God, for bringing my son safely home. We would be lost without Your love."

"I am happy to see a family reunited," replied God. "One day, your reunion will be complete." Again, the Creator's attention turned to Chris. "My son, the days ahead will hold for you many joys and wonders, yet I know your heart. The day will come when your heart will be very troubled, and your mind full of questions. On that day, I do not wish for you to hesitate or fear to come to me. In the natural world, children will often turn to friends for council before they turn to their own parents. Even here, it is often that way. In that day, come to me, Chris, I will have your answers."

"Yes, Lord, I will come to you," promised Chris.

To Chris, God's words seemed strange. He wasn't quite sure that he understood, and yet he somehow knew that the day God spoke of would come. Of course it would, God Himself had plainly said so. Chris could have asked for clarification, but he refrained from pursuing the issue further. Perhaps he would ask later, there was plenty of time.

Chris and his mother remained in the presence of God for many hours, praising, singing, and communing with those around them. When they finally turned for home, Chris was full of joy. To have been in the presence of God, to have actually talked with Him was fantastic. It had left him with a lot to think about, though. The events of the day stirred within him a sense of awe, yet, with a strange undercurrent. Something was wrong. Even as he turned in for the night, he could sense an approaching storm.

chapter twelve

I T was some days after his return from the City of Zion that Chris found himself wandering through the forest several miles from the mansion. On this warm afternoon, he felt very relaxed and in perfect harmony with the world around him. The dreams that had disturbed his sleep had finally relented, allowing the undiluted joy of Heaven to hold sway over his heart.

The forest realm had an almost enchanted character to it. There were no thorns, no tangle of bushes, no snakes, and no dangers, only God's handiwork, perfected beyond anything he had ever seen on Earth. Chris pondered if the Garden of Eden might have been something like this. No, this was probably even better.

The trees were familiar: oak, maple, poplar, and a collection of pines, and each one was a perfect example of the species. Birds sang new songs from the trees, while uniquely colorful butterflies flitted about him.

Chris approached one that sat perched upon a blue flower. Upon close inspection, he discovered that it was unlike any insect he had ever seen on Earth. It had a smooth, tan body that gave it perfect aerodynamic grace. When viewed closely, the bodies of earthly butterflies were dark and segmented, almost mechanical, lacking the beauty they seemed to possess from afar. But these heavenly butterflies were wonderfully different.

The process of inspection drew his attention to another curious fact. On Earth his eyes could focus on an object about 8 inches away, but to draw closer than that left the object a blur. Now his perfect eyesight could view objects a mere inch away, or all the way to infinity, with an absolute clarity that only eagles might know on Earth. It was positively fascinating.

He thought back to stories his mother had read to him as a child, stories of enchanted mystical forests. He had never associated enchanted forests with Heaven. The two topics seemed somehow divergent. But they weren't, were they? How could anything created by the hand of God be anything short of wondrous, enchanted, and yes, mystical. To the simple mind of man, the works of God might be described by any of those terms.

From up ahead, he heard the sound of running water. Heading in that direction, he reached the bank of a stream about 50 feet wide. It flowed down across rocks and boulders, forming clear pools here and there. The pools were teaming with fish. Not far away, he noticed a man standing about midstream, wielding a long fishing pole. He wore a floppy hat to keep the sunlight out of his eyes and the sort of woodsy attire that Chris might associate with a veteran fisherman. Beside him was a tackle box and wicker basket with a lid to hold whatever he might catch. He looked to be in his mid-forties, with graying hair and strong arms.

At his side was a large hound dog that, along with his master, was focused on a large pool of deeper water. Chris smiled thinking that he was not alone in having a special animal friend in Heaven.

As Chris approached, the man looked up and smiled. "Hello, Chris."

"Hi Bill," Chris said, still amazed to recognize a man whom he had never met. "Are they biting?"

Bill shook his head. "Nope, not today. Just because it's Heaven doesn't mean that the fish are biting every day. They were yesterday, all right, but today, that's another matter."

"You out here every day?" Chris asked while sitting down on a boulder at the edge of the stream.

"Most of the time. Ya know, I was afraid that when I ended up in glory, I'd have to give up fishing, that there'd be no good fishing streams in Heaven. Boy, was I wrong; Heaven has the best trout streams around. I live just a couple miles downstream."

"I live over that way," Chris said, pointing toward the woods.

"Yeah, that's what I hear," Bill said, pulling a bit on his line. "You're Jennifer's boy, if I'm not mistaken."

"That's right," confirmed Chris, watching the expert fisherman reel in his line only to cast it out again.

"Fine woman, your mother," said Bill. "I've crossed paths with her many a time in this forest. She loves these here woods as much as I do. She has had the misses and me over many times for dinner. She sure is a fine cook."

"You got that right," said Chris, watching a particularly large trout swim around the hook only to pass it by.

"I'm sure she's in her glory now that you're here with her," continued Bill. "She's spoken of you many times. How are you liking it here so far?"

"It's everything I expected and more," Chris said. "How long have you been here, Bill?"

"Since fifty-nine." Bill chuckled. "If I'd have known this place was so wonderful, I don't think I'd have fancied living to be eighty-seven back on Earth. My wife followed me only a few months after I arrived, so our separation was a brief one. There's no marriage here, you see, but we've still continued on our journey to eternity together. We probably always will. We spent better than sixty years together on Earth, and nearly fifty here. We've kinda grown on each other. Blessed be the name of Jesus for giving us the opportunity."

"Amen," Chris said. "Where would we all be without Him?"

Bill shook his head. "I don't even want to think about that one. Sarah and I often go to the great City of Zion to express our gratitude to our Maker. It's a wonderful experience, it surely is. You been to the city yet?"

"Yes indeed," replied Chris. "My mom took me there about a week ago. It was fantastic, no, better even than that."

"I know," Bill said. He paused for a moment, then turned toward Chris, the fish temporarily forgotten. "Come to think of it, when I first came here, it was my mother who took me to the city. I remember how wonderful it was to be with her again. You see, I hadn't seen her in nearly thirty years. We still get together often. She's not much for fishing, understand, but we always have a good time when we get together."

"What about your father?" asked Chris. "Does he like to fish?"

The long silence, and the expression on Bill's face, told Chris that he had just asked the wrong question.

"I don't remember my father," admitted Bill. "That's odd isn't it? My memories of my life on Earth are a bit hazy here and there, but you'd think that I'd remember my own father. My mother doesn't remember him either."

Chris was certain that he had somehow violated a code of heavenly etiquette in the course of his question. He felt so very awkward. "I'm sorry."

"Oh, don't be," replied Bill, smiling slightly. "This isn't Earth, its Heaven. Those earthly things that would be a stumbling block are, well, forgotten, cast into the sea of forgetfulness, allowing us to move on." Bill reeled in his line and walked toward Chris. "I reckon that the memory of my father would have been a painful one for me. That is why I don't remember him. The fact that he ain't here can mean only one thing."

Bill didn't need to continue; Chris got his meaning clear enough.

"I feel sorry for all those in Hell, truly I do, but they are nameless, faceless people, far removed from us. I know that it must sound terrible, but I'll not be questioning God's wisdom in removing that part of my life from me, for there ain't nothing I can do about it."

"And you've never had the desire to find out about him?"

"Nope," confirmed Bill. "It's for my own good that I don't remember. I mean, would you want to remember a loved one, doomed to the torments of Hell? Would you want to be aware that they were suffering through all eternity and that there was nothing you could do about it? I wouldn't."

"I understand," Chris said. "I guess it's better we don't know."

Their conversation was interrupted by the arrival of a young boy. Chris was so transfixed by Bill's words, that the freckled-face youth caught him by surprise. The grinning boy appeared to be about 11 or 12 years old and he held a fishing pole in his hand. With his old straw hat and suspenders, he looked like a character straight out of a Mark Twain novel, perhaps Tom Sawyer or Huck Finn. He rubbed the large brown hound on the head before turning to the men sitting on the rocks.

"I thought I'd come on out and help you with the fishin'," he said, his smile growing.

"Did you finish with your studies and your chores?" asked Bill, turning his attention to the excited youth.

"An hour ago. Mom said it was OK if I went fishing with you for a while."

"OK, Jerry," replied Bill. "Maybe you'll have more luck than I've had today."

That was all it took, Jerry's hook was bated and in the water in the wink of an eye.

"Oh, Chris, this is my son, Jeremiah," said Bill.

Jerry took a moment to turn from the pool of water where he had just cast his line. "Good afternoon, sir," he said politely.

For a moment Chris was confused. Jerry had to be older than he looked, he just had to. "Hello Jerry. Do you mind if I ask how old you are?"

Jerry just kept on grinning. "Oh, no sir, I don't mind. I turned twelve just last week."

Bill placed a loving arm around his son. "And we had quite a party, didn't we?"

"A swell party," confirmed the youth.

Now Chris really was confused. There was no marriage in Heaven, no births, no deaths, he was certain of it. That being the case, how could one explain the presence of Jerry?

Bill sensed his friend's confusion. "My wife and I never had any children of our own while we were on Earth. It was always one of our greatest regrets. But here, God has blessed us with Jerry, and we praise Him for His love and mercy."

"God has been so good to all of us," confirmed Jerry. "I love Him more than I can say."

Jerry's proclamation of love brought a smile to Bill's face. He rose to his feet and hugged his son.

"Jerry wasn't born here," continued Bill. "He would have been born on Earth twelve years ago, but something happened." Bill hesitated; he still had trouble talking about it. "You see, his earthly mother didn't want him, didn't want him to be born. She had a doctor sweep him from her, kill him while he was still within her womb. She didn't want to be troubled with him."

Again Bill hesitated, and a tear appeared.

"It's all right, Daddy," said Jerry. "I'd rather be here with you than on Earth. From what I hear, it isn't all that great a place anyway."

"But you should have been allowed to live," said Bill. "To grow up on Earth, to have earthly parents, go to school, have a wife, children, and a full life. What was done to you wasn't right; it was a crime against humanity, against God who created you."

Bill looked back toward Chris, to see the concern in his eyes. "Twelve years ago, an angel came to us. In his arms he held a tiny baby, Jeremiah. He told my wife and me that God had chosen us to raise this child in His ways. We were to love him, comfort him, and instruct him. We would become the only parents he would ever know. You see, Chris, no soul goes unaccounted for, even if that soul is still in the womb. Since Jerry wasn't given the opportunity to know God on Earth, to select the road he would follow, that opportunity shall be given to him here. The day will come when he will be brought before God, and given the choice to serve Him or turn from Him."

"And that day is less than a year away, when I turn thirteen," Jerry chimed in. "I can hardly wait."

"My wife and I have done all we could to let Jerry know just how much God loves him," continued Bill. "We've even taken him to talk to God, in Zion."

"And we've had some swell talks," Jerry said. "God is just so wonderful. I always feel so good after I've talked to Him."

"I want him to be able to make the right choice when that day comes," continued Bill.

"I will," Jerry said, hugging his father all the more. "I promise."

"I know you will," Bill said, kissing him on the cheek. "Sometimes, angels are given the responsibility of bringing up children who have died before their time, before they have reached the age of accountability. This is the way of children whose parents shall one day be reunited with them here in Heaven, ones with no other kin here. But for those who shall not be reunited with their earthly parents, heavenly parents are selected. God blessed Sarah and I by allowing us to become heavenly parents. Just like the Sarah of the Old Testament, my Sarah has become a mother in her old age." Bill couldn't help but chuckle at the irony of it all. Still, it was a sweet irony, one that had blessed them both.

"May God's name be praised forever. I can tell you that Sarah and I are more grateful than we can say."

Almost on cue, there was a tug on Jerry's pole. Jerry barely got a hold on it before the battle with a particularly large trout began in earnest. The pole bent toward the water as Jerry pulled upward.

"You've got one!" exclaimed Bill, helping his son steady the pole, as it twisted to the left.

"A big one by the looks of it," said Chris, looking toward the deep pool just in time to see the trout stir the waters.

"Sure looks like it," confirmed Bill, trying to coach his son more than take over the line. "Take your time Jerry, play him. Don't try to reel him in all at once."

"Well, I've had a great time chatting with the two of you, but I think I'll be heading on back home," said Chris, as he stood up. He didn't want to interfere with this moment between a father and son.

"Send my regards to your mother," said Bill, looking up momentarily.

"I surely will," Chris said, turning to leave.

"And don't be a stranger," added Bill, "drop by sometime. I'd really love to continue our conversation. I like hearing the perspectives of other saints."

Chris nodded and headed for home. He heard them laughing as they reeled in the big one together. He smiled, remembering such times with his own father back on Earth. He remembered his father, and all of the great times they had together. That very fact meant that they would be reunited again. It was something to look forward to.

Yet, as Chris continued the trek home, he couldn't help but think of what his mother had said about his uncle Bill and their fishing adventures; adventures he no longer remembered. And he thought of the woman in his dreams. Who was she? Did she really exist? He thought he'd managed to shake the feeling that something was missing in his life here, but he realized that this thought had been in the back of his mind all day, hidden but present. His conversation with Bill merely brought it to the surface.

⊰✲⊱ ⊰✲⊱ ⊰✲⊱

"I'm happy that you had the opportunity to meet Bill Anderson this afternoon," Jennifer said, as she sat down to dinner with her son. "He and Sarah are wonderful people. After I got here, they were two of the first people I met. They've been so happy since Jerry came into their lives. God senses our needs, and like the loving Father He is, He gives us those things that would be beneficial to us."

Chris looked up from his salad. "I was just thinking about Jerry. I suppose that he's aging just like he would on Earth, right?"

"Yes, he seems to be," replied Jennifer. "He'll continue to grow, to become the man he would have become on Earth, if he'd had the opportunity. He won't go through puberty, he'll be spared that, but his body will develop to adulthood." Jennifer paused, then started to laugh.

"What's so funny, Mom?"

It was several seconds before Jennifer was able to respond. "Oh, I was just thinking of you when you were about Jerry's age, when your body started to go through those changes. I was thinking of the Sunday morning that your catechism class graduated. You were all standing up in front of the church. I was so proud of you that morning; you were just thirteen, but you looked so much like a man, like your father. Well, when it came to the part where you introduced yourself to the congregation, you said Christopher Davis. You said Christopher in such a low manly voice, but then, your voiced cracked, and you said Davis in the voice of a child. I'm sure no one thought a thing of it, I mean they didn't laugh. I know you were embarrassed by it, but afterward it seemed so funny." Again Jennifer laughed. "I think that was the last time your voice did that."

Chris managed a chuckle. He remembered the incident all too vividly. It was so embarrassing. The pastor had moved right on with the program and hadn't said a word about it later. As a mater of fact, no one had said a word about it. Nevertheless, that incident had rattled around in his mind for days.

"Cracking voice or not, your father and I were so proud of you."

"So Jerry is in a sort of probationary period." noted Chris, all too eager to change the subject.

"I guess you could call it that," Jennifer said. "People like Jerry aren't exactly like us. Like any human being, he must make the conscious decision to love God, to be a part of His family. He wasn't afforded that opportunity on Earth, so he is being given it here. He has to choose. Jerry is not like one of the angels either. You see, when the angels were created, God gave them all the knowledge they needed to do their tasks. God created them with the desire to do whatever that is."

"Except satan," interrupted Chris.

Jennifer had to think about that one. "I didn't say that angels didn't have a free will, they all do. They also have very human-like emotions. Satan's pride and arrogance became his undoing. He knew God but rejected His love and His authority. Humans like Jerry who are born into Heaven need time to learn, time to experience the presence of God. They are born with a clean-slate mind and need parents, guides, who are given the responsibility to teach them.

It is only natural for them to love their parents and the Creator that loves them so very much. Sure, there will be problems; kids everywhere learn by making mistakes, but Heaven is a whole lot more forgiving than Earth. Nothing they do here will permanently injure them, but they will remember the consequences. You can still burn yourself on a hot stove, and it still hurts. The nice thing is that after a minute, the burn heals completely. As for their personality, it is being molded by loving, caring parents. In the end, the child grows to become a loving adult. Eventually he will have to appear before God and announce his choice."

"What if he elects to serve God?" asked Chris.

"Then he becomes like us, a full-fledged child of God."

"And if he turns his back on God?"

"Well, how could he?" objected Jennifer, just a bit flustered at the thought. "After all he has seen, all he has experienced, why would he?"

"I know Jerry wouldn't, but some people might just do that. What about them?"

"None that I've ever heard of have. Think of the kind of parents they have here, the guidance, the very presence of God." She paused, deciding not to avoid the question. "I suppose they'd be cast into outer darkness, but it's never happened," Jennifer said.

"And if any ever had, would we even remember? How certain can we be of anything here, if we can't be sure of our own memories?" Chris's tone had risen. There was a sense of frustration in it.

"Chris!" scolded Jennifer, "What's gotten into you? You need to listen to yourself for a moment. It's like you were accusing God of manipulating you. He loves you, you know that. He wants you to be happy here."

"I'm sorry, Mom," replied Chris, "There have been a lot of things on my mind. I've had those dreams, the sense that something was wrong. I need to know what's going on. I don't want God to shield me from the truth. I need to face it, no matter how terrible it is."

"Be careful what you wish for, because you just might get it," warned Jennifer.

"Do you remember what God told me in Zion?" asked Chris, his tone somewhat more calm. "It was almost like a warning."

"And He told you to turn to Him when you were troubled," said Jennifer. "You need to remember that. Maybe you need to ask Him to help you find peace. I assure you, He will do it." Jennifer paused, her expression grew somewhat solemn. "I wasn't going to tell you about it, but I've heard stories of other people like you in Heaven, people who had a sense that something, or someone, was missing. I've never actually met anyone who was like that; you see, it's just so rare. I don't know why it happens to a few people and not to the rest of us. It didn't happen to me."

Chris looked at his mother with an expression of incredulity. He leaned forward in his chair. "You mean others have had bad dreams, fragments of memories?"

"So I've been told," confirmed Jennifer. "I was wrong not to tell you, I know that now. By not telling you, I've been a poor witness for God. I'm sorry."

Chris saw the sadness in his mother's eyes, and he felt about an inch tall. He had upset her, him and his attitude. He rose from his chair and walked over to embrace her. "I'm sorry, Mom, really."

"No," Jennifer said, "it's all right, you need to know. I was just hoping you wouldn't have to go through this. I was hoping that it would all blow over, but I can see that it won't. Please, walk with me in the garden."

The two walked out into the cool afternoon air. It was Jennifer who spoke first.

"Do you recall a Scripture about tears in Heaven, about crying, about God wiping the tears from the eyes of those persons?"

Chris had to think about that one. "Sort of, but I don't remember where it is in the Bible."

"The tears are shed for the lost, for things we failed to accomplish on Earth, for people we failed to win to the Kingdom of Heaven. I can't even imagine the burden; I don't want to. But you might end up carrying that burden if you keep going in the direction you're going now. You need to ask God to help you let go of that burden. It is He who can wipe the tears from your eyes and remove the burden from your heart."

The thought of the woman in the Hall of Records rushed into the young man's mind. She remembered a soul in Hell and mourned for him or her. He knew it was a memory that brought her tremendous grief. Most certainly it was the memory of a loved one. Was there an escape from that grief? Chris knew the answer to that question. The escape would be found in the loving arms of his heavenly Father.

"Turn to God," continued Jennifer, "He asked you to. He is the only one who can help you with this. We can go to Zion this very minute, if you wish. I think we should."

"No," replied Chris. "We don't need to. God is everywhere in this place. If I ask Him here and now to have this burden lifted from my heart, I believe it would be done."

"But you haven't asked, have you?"

Chris hesitated to reply. "No, I haven't."

"Oh, honey, why not?" asked Jennifer.

"Well, it's just that…well, suppose it's important that I eventually remember. Suppose that this person who has appeared in my dreams needs me. I have this sense that someone, someone important to me, is crying out to me and needs my help."

"OK, Chris, suppose you're right. That someone can't be here in Heaven, you'd remember them if they were. If they're on Earth, there is nothing you can do for them, don't you see? It's not in your power to interfere in their destiny. That's why I stopped looking in on you. I could never be more than an observer. Even as much as God loves them, He will not force His desires on them." Jennifer hesitated before continuing. "And if they're in Hell, there is even less you can do. There is a huge gulf between us and them; they're already doomed. Oh please, dear, give it up."

"All right," replied Chris, gazing across the green fields toward the setting sun, "I'll ask that this memory or whatever it is be lifted from me; I'll do it tonight."

"It's for the best, really," said Jennifer, obviously relieved by her son's decision. "I really feel that you should go to Zion and make your petition to God, face to face."

"Perhaps later," Chris said.

Chris walked from the garden to the porch and sat down in the old rocking chair, watching the light of another day fade from the sky. His mother sat down in the chair by his side.

Chris did as he promised. Before bedtime, he had presented his petition to God in prayer; yet he still had some reservations. Was this really what he wanted?

"Father God, not my will but your will be done," he said, as his prayer concluded. "You know what's best for me. I leave it in your loving hands."

And so, sleep fell upon him, a sleep without disturbing dreams, a sleep of total peace in the loving arms of the Father. It was the first of many peaceful nights, as the images in his head, the images of the mysterious young woman, faded away into oblivion. At last he could experience the undiminished joys of Heaven, the joy of being in the Father's house forever.

chapter thirteen

MONTHS passed, and a spirit of peace and joy came to dwell in the mansion. The disturbing dreams that had troubled Chris during his first weeks in paradise had faded into the nothingness from which they had arisen, and finally Chris could enjoy the world that the heavenly Father had prepared.

The person, whoever he was, who said that Heaven was the most boring place in the universe, didn't have a clue. How could he have? Life here was an adventure, a journey through a realm of infinite possibilities, and Chris was determined to explore them all.

Heaven's vastness dwarfed the humble Earth. There were great snow-capped mountains, deserts, forests, fresh-water oceans vast and deep, and meadows filled with colorful flowers. To top it all off, Heaven's many different environments were perfected well beyond any so called paradise Earth had to offer.

Now that Chris had mastered the art of physical projection, the process by which he could move instantly and effortlessly from one place to another far away, the ends of Heaven were open to him. His mother had told him that many people had problems making projection work when they first arrived in Heaven. The more intellectual individuals had the greatest problem because their earthly experience told them that such things aren't possible. People didn't simply teleport around on this side of the glass tube or silver screen. Their lack of faith became their stumbling block. They failed to understand that the power was within the Holy Spirit of God. It was a matter of childlike faith; they had to believe that it could be done.

Chris had figured it out quickly, and was swift to reap the benefits. Like a teenager who finally got his fingers on the keys to the family car, he was ready to explore. There was so much to see, and he was anxious to get started.

During the past months, Chris had visited the perfect beach, learned how to surf, and loved every minute of it. He had climbed to the summit of Heaven's highest mountain peaks and explored the depths of a tropical jungle.

Closer to home, Chris spent many a pleasant afternoon fishing with Bill and Jerry. Sometimes, it was the simpler things that brought the most joy to his heart. Even Jennifer occasionally joined in the ongoing quest for the big one that always seems to get away. Apparently even Heaven was replete with traditional fish stories.

Chris was amazed to discover that many earthly sports survived in Heaven. His mother was correct when she had said that God loved to watch His children play. Even Chris's favorite sport, tennis, was here; and there was no shortage of people who loved to play. Much of the equipment was fashioned by artisans in Zion, through the power of physical projection. They envisioned the equipment in their minds and turned that vision into physical reality.

The tennis games were fascinating to watch. With fatigue no longer a factor and the physical limitations of the players stretched, the games took on a new athleticism. Once, Chris actually saw a pair of angels play. Though their wings were somewhat of a hindrance, especially on the backhand, their ability to fly added a new dimension to the game. Truly, there was something here for everyone.

Chris made frequent trips to Zion, sometimes in the company of his mother, sometimes alone. He explored the many libraries, seeking out the wisdom of the ages. He wandered through the parks, mingled with people, and visited the shops of the craftsmen to experience the many faces of the beauty that is Heaven.

More importantly, however, he went there to commune with the Father. To actually hold a two-way conversation with God was the most precious experience of all. Their conversations were not unlike those between a son and his loving earthly father, except, of course, the heavenly Father is infinitely wiser.

This was the God of the Universe, the being who created all things, whose presence pervades everything. He was a personal and loving Creator. He didn't demand the worship of His people; they gave it freely. Chris felt free to take any concern he had to Him and always spoke from the heart. God was never too busy to talk to him, never. Now, Chris understood how someone could remain for hours, even days, in the Father's presence, not wanting to depart. The knowledge and wisdom that God imparted to him was a priceless treasure.

During one conversation, they might discuss the words of the prophets, and God's plans for humanity. During another, the topic might be the physical nature of the universe, from atoms to stars.

Yet, God did not answer all of his questions directly. Sometimes, He would inspire Chris to seek out the answers himself. And the Father asked questions too, not to gather knowledge, but to bring Chris to explore his own heart. The Father spoke of the value of individual experience and personal discovery. Often the joy of discovery was found in the search itself. The Father's guidance led Chris on many a wonderful adventure.

It was on one of those adventures when something most unusual and unexpected happened—at one of Heaven's great libraries. Chris was in a vast central reading room, the size of a football field, amid a thousand other saints. On all sides, towering seven floors high, were great balconies, and beyond the balconies, well-lit corridors filled with books. Some of the books were the work of angels, others found their source amid the saints in Heaven, while still others were the popular classics written throughout the centuries on Earth.

Chris sat in a comfortable leather upholstered chair, engrossed in a large clothbound book that spoke of the early days of the Christian church in Rome. To say that the book spoke of events was very accurate, for upon opening it, he was engulfed in the experience, seeing and hearing the narration and the events of the past as if they were unfolding before him.

The book's narration paused as Chris pondered the dangers and sacrifices the early converts faced every day because of their profession of faith. It made him appreciate how good life had been for him in 21st century America. Yes, there had been the controversy of prayer in the schools, the issues of morality and ethics in government, but these problems paled in comparison to the decadence that was first century Rome.

As Chris closed the book, he placed it on the long oak table before him, and his attention was drawn to a young woman across from him. She too was engrossed in a book, sitting spellbound as its message unfolded.

She was pretty, in her late twenties, with brown hair, and well proportioned. She was attired in a long, frilly white dress, laced up the front, with flowing sleeves. Like many of the people in Heaven, she apparently preferred to dress in the fashion of her time on Earth. From the looks of her, Chris figured that time must have been the late Middle Ages, perhaps the early Renaissance.

On Earth, a man, might have lusted after one such as her. However, that was not the sort of response that a woman elicited here. In a man's eyes, she would be appreciated for her physical beauty, but not lusted after—that sort of thinking had been left far behind.

No, there was something else about this one. Her name was Elizabeth, Chris knew that much. She was familiar as all people in this place were, yet there was more. What was it about her that made her seem closer than everyone else around him? Why couldn't he take his eyes from her? What was it about her?

Just then Elizabeth looked up from her book. Maybe it was just a random pause, but perhaps she had become aware that she was being watched. She glanced toward Chris and smiled. "Hello, Chris."

"Oh, hello," Chris replied awkwardly. "Sorry if it seemed like I was staring."

Elizabeth giggled slightly. "Tis all right, Chris. Is there something on your mind, something you wanted to ask me?"

Chris turned a shade of red. He hadn't offended her, he knew that, still it was embarrassing. "Yes…I mean no…well, you seem so familiar."

Again there was a slight giggle. "Of course I seem familiar to thee, we are both children of God. I am thy sister." Elizabeth paused to reflect. "Yet, I think it is more than that. Perhaps you have seen me here before. I come oft to the library. I come here to learn about the changing world, the Earth that we left behind."

"What are you reading about today?" asked Chris, thinking that it might be best to change the subject.

"I am reading poetry, the poetry of a man by the name of Robert Frost. His work is really quite good."

"I've heard of him," confirmed Chris. "He was an American writer, lived about fifty years ago, I think."

"Yes, that's right," replied Elizabeth, "four and a half centuries after my time on Earth. But, I believe that there was something on thy mind, something other than the poems of Mister Frost."

Chris smiled. "Yes, it was just that there was something familiar about you, something beyond just recognizing you."

Elizabeth smiled broadly, making Chris feel more at ease. "How long have you been here, Chris?"

"Just a few months, I arrived a few days before Christmas 2007."

"My, 2007, so much time. It truly does not seem so long to me. Over five centuries separate our times on Earth, so we could not have met there. There was never a painting made of me during my lifetime, not even one. You see, my parents were poor and could afford neither a portrait nor a dowry for me. I was sent off to the convent when I was but thirteen, there to be schooled, and later, take my vows to serve the Lord and the holy mother church. There I remained for the next forty-one years. So you see, you could not have met me or even seen a painting of me." There was a moment of silence as Elizabeth contemplated. "Perhaps it is that I look like someone you knew at one time or another."

"That must be it," replied Chris, whose embarrassment had returned anew. On Earth he had often had trouble talking to attractive women. That was until…his mind went blank. There had been a train of thought there, he was certain of it, but the tracks that had conveyed it had abruptly vanished. His uneasiness was growing. He was certain that he had just made a total fool of himself. Perhaps it would be best if he simply excused himself at this point.

"Do you know who?" asked Elizabeth.

Chris hesitated before responding. "No, I don't think so."

Elizabeth's smile broadened, "Chris, I think you do."

It took Chris a few seconds to recover from the shock of that one. "What?"

Elizabeth set her book down upon the table and leaned forward. Chris was surprised when she took his hand in hers. "Think back, Chris, who do I remind thee of, and why?"

This encounter was rapidly becoming deeper than Chris had intended. Elizabeth had, apparently, already made a connection that he was just finding now. Her face, her hair, even the clothing she was wearing, was remarkably similar to that of the mystery woman from his dreams. It had been months since that face had appeared in his mind's eye, but he could see it now, more clearly than ever. Elizabeth didn't look exactly like her, but there was a strong resemblance. How could she know? Did she know?

"Look, I need to be going, I've disturbed your reading enough," said Chris, rising to leave.

"You can not walk away from this thing," said Elizabeth, who seemed unwilling to release his hand. "Who is she?"

"I don't know," Chris admitted. "When I first arrived in Heaven, she appeared in my dreams. She was there night after night, like a phantom. Her face was familiar. I knew I should have known her, but I didn't."

"But she appears no longer," deduced Elizabeth.

"No, she doesn't," Chris said. "Maybe it's best that she doesn't. I've found peace since she left."

"Then she evoked bad dreams?" continued Elizabeth. "Bad dreams in Heaven are rare. In very truth, I cannot say that I have ever heard of such a thing."

"No, they weren't bad dreams," Chris said, "not at all. Her appearance was comforting; I had the feeling that she was very important to me. I just couldn't remember who she was."

"Yes, I see," said Elizabeth. Her eyes were deep and under-standing. "Why did she go away?"

"I asked God to free me from those dreams, and that was the last I was bothered by them. That was all there was to it."

"What did God tell thee about the dreams, about this woman of your dreams, that caused you to ask Him to free you from them?" asked Elizabeth, who now rose to her feet as well.

"Well, nothing," was the reply. "I asked Him in prayer from my home. It doesn't matter where I am; I know that the Father hears my every prayer."

"That is true," replied Elizabeth. "But it would seem that you did not want to hear what God had to say about your dream. Do you commune with Him often?"

"Well, yes," replied Chris. How had he allowed this conversa-tion to get this far? "I go to the holiest place to talk to God a lot."

"But not about this. Never about this," deduced Elizabeth. "Why is that?"

This time, Chris didn't reply.

"Had you considered that God himself was communicating something to thee through these dreams?"

"No," objected Chris, who definitely wanted out of this con-versation at this point. "Why would He do that? I think it was a fragment of a memory, one that I shouldn't have had, but did. I was holding on to something, someone, who I shouldn't have been hanging on to. They were a part of my life on Earth, but not here. My mother told me that this happens sometimes. When I was finally willing to let go, I was freed of it. Now, finally, I am at peace."

Elizabeth motioned to Chris to sit once more. He hesitated, then complied.

"My brother, listen to yourself for a moment. What you have said makes no sense. Everything happens for a purpose, both on

Earth and in Heaven. I know that there are memories from our earthly existence that have been lost to us. Believe me when I tell thee that these things have been done for our benefit. God, in His wisdom, spares us the pain of living through eternity with the knowledge of tragedies for which we can not change the outcomes."

"I know," interjected Chris, "like lost ones that we will never see again because they've been sentenced to Hell."

"Among other things," confirmed Elizabeth. "But allow me to continue. We do not serve a God of confusion. If you had a fragment of a memory, it wasn't an oversight on God's part. It is in God's plan that it was so. Your mother was right; such things do happen, but you have not dealt with this thing as you should. You have set it aside rather than deal with it."

If Chris wasn't confused before, he was now. He thought that the entire matter had been solved months ago, but apparently it had not. "OK, so what do I do now?"

"I think you know the answer to that question."

"Ask God?"

Elizabeth nodded. "All things begin and end with Him. God holds thy answers. Perhaps this memory has been left with you to see if you will bring it before the Father. He has been waiting for you to bring it before Him personally."

That possibility had never crossed his mind. "You're saying it's a test?"

"No," was the reply. "I tell thee that it might be a test. I know not the mind of God. Take this problem to Him—His answer, and His answer alone, will be the right one."

"Thank you," said Chris, rising once more and pulling from Elizabeth's grasp. "I know your advice is sound."

Elizabeth smiled. "Gain wisdom from the road that stretches before you, my dear brother."

"Thank you. It's really been nice meeting you…talking with you, but I've gotta be going."

Again Elizabeth nodded, but said no more.

Chris turned and quickly headed for the door. For a time, Elizabeth's eyes followed him; then they returned to the book of poetry.

Chris glanced back as he left the reading gallery of the library. Elizabeth's words had troubled him. He had been doing so well these past three months, and now this. Right now, he wished that he had never had the dreams at all. Perhaps it was better not to know who this woman was. Everyone else in Heaven seemed to have a perfect peace that still eluded him. As he reached the steps of the library, he faced a decision. There were solutions to this problem.

Chris considered returning to the Hall of Records. Yes, the answers to his questions would most assuredly be found in his own book. He hadn't been to the Hall of Records since that first time with his mother. He'd promised her that he would not go in alone, that he would not return there unless she was with him, to guide him. During these past months the desire to go there had evaporated. His life was here, not back on Earth. Now the desire to seek out the truth was stronger than ever.

But there was another solution, wasn't there. Perhaps he should go to the most holy place, go there right now. He should speak to God personally. No, he had already prayed about this matter; there was no point in troubling God with this issue. But if not that, what should he do? He couldn't keep going on like this.

Chris headed down to the river banks where he walked amid the splendid beauty for hours. He looked toward the most holy place, beyond the far bank. Even from here, he could hear the praises of God's children, rising like a beautiful melody, flowing through the city like a cool, refreshing breeze.

He came to a decision. He would head home, speak to his mother first. Then he would return to Zion to speak to God tomorrow. He and his mother would come here together. Yes, that is what he would do. He turned for home, yet his heart was still troubled.

⌁※⌁ ⌁※⌁ ⌁※⌁

It was over dinner when Chris told his mother of the strange events that had happened at the library. She listened without comment as Chris went on about it. After Chris had related the entire story, Jennifer had a lot to think about.

"I don't really know this Elizabeth you met at the library," she began. "You haven't had too much exposure to the saints who have been in Heaven as long as Elizabeth has." Jennifer paused before continuing. "God continues to refine us, and with time we become more and more like His son. Chris, it doesn't surprise me that she could read you so well; think of how well Jesus read people. Remember the story of the woman at the well? Jesus knew all about her questionable past, her many husbands. He saw right into her heart and told her all about what she had done. Then he told her what she needed to know to bring her heart peace and her spirit salvation. Well, saints who have been here for hundreds or even thousands of years get sort of like that. They are not infallible, but sometimes they see right into our hearts."

"Then what should I do, Mom," asked Chris.

"Well, I think her advice was sound, don't you?"

"Well, yes."

"You don't sound very convinced," Jennifer said. "You've been avoiding this subject for months. You haven't even told God about it, have you?"

"In my prayer that night," objected Chris.

"But not face to face," countered Jennifer, "not in the holiest of holy places. You know, God could speak to us anytime, anywhere; nothing is stopping Him. He knows all that we do and think; but for our sake, He chooses to allow us to select the time when we wish to speak to Him. That is why that holiest of holy places exists. Are you afraid of what you might find, what He might say?"

Mom had come right to the point, hadn't she? Chris had never been able to hide anything from her as he was growing up. He might just as well have been as transparent as glass. "I'm very afraid. I have a bad feeling, a real bad feeling about it. I'm afraid that what I find out is going to hurt."

Jennifer saw tears forming in her son's eyes. She rose from her chair and rushed to her son, they embraced. "You're not going to go through this alone. I'll go to Zion with you tomorrow. We can go right now if you like. But I want to be with you when you meet with God."

"Thanks, Mom. I'd really like for you to be with me. We will go tomorrow; my mind is made up."

"Good," Jennifer said, holding her son all the more tightly. "I know it might be rough, dear, but the sooner we find out what's going on, the sooner the healing process can get started. You know God. He would never do anything to hurt you, never. And remember, I'm here for you too, dear. I always will be. We'll get through this, you and I."

After dinner, Chris and Jennifer took a walk around the grounds beneath a myriad of stars. Jennifer didn't speak of it, but she was deeply concerned. She, like her son, had assumed that the problem had been resolved months ago. Apparently, she had been mistaken. Tomorrow would bring some sort of resolution to this issue, of that she was certain. As to what form that resolution would take, remained a mystery. She only hoped that her son would find the peace that he so desperately sought.

⊟※⊟ ⊟※⊟ ⊟※⊟

In the midst of dreams, turbulent and confusing, Chris found himself surrounded by a myriad of shooting stars streaming out of a black sky. No, not shooting stars, snowflakes falling swiftly from the night sky, illuminated by the headlights of a car, his car. He felt an arm on his shoulder. He turned to see the woman from his dreams at his side. She wasn't nameless, not now, her name was Serena. He knew her; she was his wife. His mind was full of images of a courtship, a wedding, a rock house in which they lived, so much happiness.

Then, he felt the car begin to slide on the icy road. He had taken the turn too quickly, hadn't noticed the patch of ice. There were headlights bearing down upon them. He tried to regain control of the car, but his efforts were for naught. There was a violent impact and a terrible scream. The world spun wildly around him, even as the gaps in his memory were swiftly filled with lost images and sensations. He hadn't been wearing his seat belt, and neither had she. They didn't have air bags. The steering wheel had hit him solidly in the chest. Yet, that was only the first impact; there was a second, and then a third. The snowy landscape beyond the windshield spun around, and then upside down. Then it righted itself once more. When the world of his dreams stopped gyrating, when the sound of the grinding of metal against metal had faded away, he was faced with a final earthly reality. He turned to behold his love. A terrible laceration stretched from her forehead to her cheek. It was bleeding profusely. She had hit the windshield and then the ceiling of the passenger compartment during the tumble.

Now she sat in such an unnatural position, her glassy unseeing eyes stared into his. The light of her life had been extinguished.

Chris let out a cry of despair that penetrated the veil of sleep and erupted into waking reality. The image of his lost love vanished. He opened his eyes to see his bedroom in the mansion, illuminated only in starlight. His heart was racing, his face full of tears, and his mind full of new memories. He was crying bitterly. He would never be the same again.

Ebbie was sitting at his side, having been aroused from a sound sleep. She was looking at her best friend with sympathetic yellow eyes that glistened, even in the semidarkness.

"Oh, God! What has happened to me?"

The overhead light came on abruptly as his mother burst into the room, barefoot and still dressed in her nightgown. "Chris, what's wrong? What happened?"

"Mom," Chris gasped, yet said no more; he couldn't.

Jennifer was at her son's bedside now as he struggled to sit up. "I heard you crying from my room. You've had another one of those dreams, haven't you?"

"Mom, I remember," said Chris breathlessly. "I remember everything, every detail. Oh God, it was my fault!"

Jennifer hugged her trembling son. "Chris, calm down, you've had a bad dream. I don't know how that's possible, but that's all it is. You're all right; you're home. It wasn't real."

"No, it wasn't a dream, Mom. It was my memory. Mom, I know who that woman in my dreams is, the one I couldn't remember. Mom, she's my wife, her name is Serena."

"You were married?"

"Yes," Chris said. "She was the love of my life, so beautiful, so wonderful, so loving. I remember it all, now. She worked at a health food store, that's where I met her. I remember our wonderful times together, our marriage in the park, everything."

Chris swung his legs over the bed.

"But why now?" asked Jennifer.

"I don't know. Why didn't I remember her?" Chris paused; he might have the answer to that question. Why would a resident of Heaven not remember a loved one on Earth? To his way of thinking, there was only one reason. But why did he remember her now? This sort of thing didn't happen.

"OK," replied Jennifer, trying to make some sense of what she had just heard. "You said something about it being your fault. What was your fault?"

"The accident. I was driving her back from a Christmas party. I was distracted, not paying attention to my driving. I hit a patch of black ice and slid out of control, right into the path of an eighteen wheeler. I'd sort of remembered the accident before, but without my wife in the picture. Now I remember everything."

Jennifer didn't quite know what to say about this revelation, but she could already see the devastating impact it had on her son. Tears in Heaven were inevitably tears of joy, not tears of grief—until now.

"Mom, you know what this means?" continued Chris, his eyes growing wide, practically wild. "My not remembering her can mean only one thing; she's in Hell! The love of my life is lost to me forever…no, more than that, she's being tortured, and there's nothing I can do about it!"

"Stop it, Chris," said Jennifer, her voice suddenly firm. "You're jumping to conclusions. If that were true, why do you remember her now? No one remembers loved ones in Hell, they just don't." There was a pause as Jennifer did her best to assemble a reasonable explanation for what had just happened. "How do you know that she died in the crash? She might have survived, did you ever think about that?"

"No," Chris said. "She was with me after the crash, I remember that now. Before the tunnel when the light appeared, before God called me home, we were together. I had her hand in mine as we headed for the tunnel; then suddenly she was gone, and so was my memory of her. Don't you see what must have happened? She got sidetracked somehow. She was swept out of my life for her unbelief, I know it."

"No you don't," insisted Jennifer. "Listen to me. You've heard about near death experiences haven't you?"

Chris paused to consider it. "Yes, I've heard of them. I saw a television program about it a long time ago. People who had died, and then were brought back, spoke of a tunnel and a light at the end. It seemed like almost everyone had seen it."

"Yes," confirmed Jennifer. "They didn't reach the light. They weren't allowed to go there. You watched that television documentary with me, remember? Well, suppose your wife was prevented from entering the tunnel, because she wasn't supposed to die yet. God may have had plans for her."

"But she didn't believe," objected Chris. "I tried to win her over, but I don't think she ever believed in her heart."

"And so you didn't remember her," continued Jennifer. "She survived, but because she wasn't born again, wasn't yet a Christian, you didn't remember her. But just a few minutes ago that changed. Now, think about this, months after your death, she accepts Jesus as her personal Lord and Savior. She might have been considering it for a long time, hedging, but she only made up her mind just a few minutes ago. Maybe she took the altar call. Maybe she just knelt down and prayed. So, what happens?"

Abruptly Chris perked up, he hadn't considered that possibility, but it made perfect sense. It explained what had just happened. Now, finally, her name was in the Lamb's Book of Life. She was Heaven bound, and as a result, he knew her once more. "You really think so?"

"I do," said Jennifer. "Admit it, your old mother has figured it all out."

"Yes, of course," said Chris, "it all makes sense."

"I still think we need to take a trip to Zion, just to make sure that we have all of our ducks in a row, but I think you and your wife will one day have a glorious reunion." Jennifer paused, shaking her head. "Dear, I wish I could have been there for your wedding."

"You would have loved it," said Chris, who at last was calm, able to talk about his beloved wife. "You remember my friend from high school, Cliff Morris?"

"Yes, yes I think so, the red-headed boy with the freckles, the one who was in little league with you?"

"Yes, that's the one. Well, he was my best man. He got married just a month after me, and I was the best man at his wedding."

Jennifer nodded. "Dear, I want you to get a few more hours of sleep before we go to Zion. But this time, don't worry…and no more bad dreams, OK?"

"OK, Mom," said Chris, settling back into bed. "Just a couple more hours, but I want us to get an early start."

"We will, dear," promised Jennifer, "but for now, rest."

Jennifer tucked the blankets around her son as she had done when he was just a child; then she walked quietly from the room. As she stepped into the hall and turned out the light, she thought of what she had said. She realized that Chris had been grasping for straws, searching for any trace of hope. She had just given it to him, but as she considered the matter further, she wondered just how sound her own explanation really was.

Yes, it was possible, very possible, but she was beginning to realize that she might just have raised her son's hopes only to see them dashed. There were alternative explanations to what had happened this morning, dark and terrible explanations. Yes, they would travel to Zion and discover the truth. Jennifer hoped that the truth would set her son free.

chapter fourteen

CHRIS and Jennifer joined hands and prepared to step from their front porch into to the gates of the Heavenly City of Zion. Both were dressed totally in long white linen robes for their meeting with the heavenly Father. It wasn't so much that God required a ritual purity, He didn't. No, it was more for their benefit, than for that of the Father. They wanted to feel clean when they stood before Him. It put their minds more at ease, and this was a good thing.

Chris concentrated a moment before the shimmering portal appeared before them. He looked back to see his cat sitting at the edge of the porch watching him intently.

"We'll be back, Ebbie," he promised, looking into her wide yellow eyes. "Now, you be a good kitty while we're gone. Maybe we can play later this afternoon. Does that sound good?" No, she didn't answer, not exactly; but the swishes of her long black tail led Chris to wonder if she hadn't understood him just the same.

Chris and his mother stepped into the shimmering portal, and vanished amid a flurry of sparkling stars. Almost instantly, they stood at the gate of Zion. It was as busy as always, with people coming and going, appearing and vanishing in a swirl of glowing stardust. They entered the gates with little fanfare and made their way in the direction of the most holy place.

"You never had any children?" asked Jennifer, trying to learn as much as possible about her newfound daughter-in-law. "I didn't think to ask that earlier. I guess I was just too flustered."

Chris chuckled. "No, Mom, you aren't a grandmother. Serena and I talked about it, but we just weren't ready. Right now, I don't know if I regret that decision or not. It would have been nice to have left some part of our union behind; but then again, I'd hate to think of her having to raise a child on her own, the world being what it is."

"You realize that she might remarry eventually," Jennifer said, hesitating to bring that matter up at this point. "I just wanted to prepare you for that possibility."

"I'd want her to," Chris said. There was no hesitation in his voice whatsoever. "I don't want her to remain alone for the rest of her years, not on my account. I want her to have a good life. She certainly deserves it." Chris suddenly stopped dead in his tracks, as a frightening thought overtook him. "Suppose she was hurt really bad in the accident?" She might have lost a leg or an arm, she might have been paralyzed. Mom; suppose she's gonna be in a wheelchair for the rest of her life. It's a horrible thought."

Jennifer placed her arm around her son. "Now you're just guessing. Still, suppose you're right. It's still better to enter the Kingdom of Heaven missing a limb, or an eye, or even totally paralyzed, than to spend eternity in Hell. Think about it. Whatever has happened to her since the accident is just for the moment. You know the rewards that lay ahead of her. One day when she comes to be with us, she will be restored."

"But she has had such a rough life already," lamented Chris. "She had such a terrible childhood, did I tell you about that?"

"No," replied Jennifer, seizing an opportunity to focus her son's mind elsewhere. "You need to tell me all about it. I want to know everything you remember about your wife."

Chris perked up immediately. Now that he remembered her, he wanted to tell his mother about the love of his life. He wasted no time giving her the full story. He related to her everything that Serena had told him about her childhood. He was amazed at how detailed his memory was. He could recall their every conversation, practically word for word. It was wonderful.

On through the streets the two traveled practically in a daze, unaware of the multitudes around them. Jennifer learned both the good and the bad in Serena's life. Before her son had entered the scene, most of it had been bad, a true human tragedy. Yet, that had quickly changed. From there on, it was a modern-day fairy tale, with her son playing the part of Serena's knight in shining armor. There was no doubt in her mind that it was he who had planted the seed of salvation in her heart. She was so very proud of him.

There she was, thinking so positively, but how else was she to feel? She had become so very confident in her explanation of why the memory of Serena was once more in her son's thoughts. How could it be otherwise? No one in Heaven could have any remembrance of an individual who had been cast out of the light and into Hell. No, her explanation had to be right; or at least had to be close to being right. She did her best to put her mind at ease. This wasn't Earth; it was Heaven. Tragedy was a thing that simply didn't happen here. Things would work to the good, perhaps not exactly as she thought, but to the good nonetheless.

They had reached the Great Hall of Records when Chris abruptly stopped. He looked toward the grand building as if suddenly inspired. "We can find our answers in there," he announced. "I've gotta know what's happened to Serena. Even if she's found someone else, I don't care. I've just gotta see her." Immediately, Chris turned toward the main entrance of the building. Jennifer never had a chance to object.

This wasn't the way she wanted to find out what had really happened to her son's wife. "Why don't we go to talk with God first," she suggested. "Then we can come back here and pick up on all of the details. I'd rather do it that way."

"I've gotta know now," insisted Chris, as he walked through the front entrance. "I can't wait another minute."

It was in the great hallway, just beyond the entrance, where Chris stopped again. He closed his eyes, sought direction.

He turned to his mother. "Fifth floor, eleventh hall, twenty-second row." Chris wasted no time. He headed straight for the nearest stairway.

"Chris, wait," said Jennifer, but her words fell on deaf ears. He was already at the stairway.

Upward and upward Chris went, nearly running, his mother in close pursuit. It took less than two minutes to reach the fifth floor. Now he was on his way toward the 11th hall. It was almost on the other side of the building, better than 400 yards away; he continued on. The sooner he got there, the sooner he would know.

Again Jennifer asked Chris to stop, but if her words were even heard, they went unheeded. A sense of dread suddenly overwhelmed her. This wasn't the right way to discover the truth; it held great personal and emotional dangers for them both, yet her headstrong son was in no mood to discuss it.

A sharp right turn at row 22 and Chris was nearly at the end of his quest. Another dozen steps brought Chris to a halt. He turned to face the wall of books and began his search. "Serena Farnsworth," he murmured to himself, his fingers passing book after book. "The book is under her maiden name. That's sort of strange."

Jennifer now stood at his side. The rows of books before them were particularly dismal, especially for one who knew what the colors represented. Most of the books were bound in dull black leather, indicative of those who had rejected God's salvation. Some were white, and just a few were gray. Instinctively, her son's attention had turned to a short stretch of gray books, at about eye level. He scanned them and moved on. As the seconds passed, he became increasingly agitated, something was wrong. He wasn't finding the book. Had he somehow misread the instructions? Suddenly, his roaming hand froze in place. It moved forward, caressing the spine of a book before him.

Jennifer drew closer, close enough to read the name embossed in golden letters on the spine, "Serena Farnsworth." The book was black—jet black. "Oh, Lord God!" she gasped. "Oh, Lord, no!"

Chris said nothing. The tips of his fingers continued to caress the volume before him, almost as though it was Serena's hand and not her book. His eyes were in a wide disbelieving stare. Then without warning, he collapsed to his knees. He buried his face in his hands. His mother wrapped her arms around her shaking son.

"It doesn't make any sense," he murmured. "Why has God done this to me?"

Jennifer didn't know what to say. She had somehow convinced herself that this quest would end differently. There was only one recourse. "Chris, we must go on to the most holy place and ask God. We've gotta do it right now, this very minute. Only God can help us now."

Chris turned abruptly to his mother, tears in his eyes. Yet, there was far more than just tears; there was anger. "Why should we go to talk to God now? He did this to her. He sentenced her to Hell."

Jennifer's face lit up with alarm. "No, Serena made her own choice. I'm sorry, Chris, but you know I'm right. You can't blame this on God. You told her the way to salvation; she was surrounded by the love of God's people at our church. God didn't reject her, Chris, she rejected Him. Everyone makes their own choices.

There has to be healing now. God's love will see us through this. You know that. We've got to go see Him, and we've got to do it now."

"No we don't," said Chris, rising to his feet. "You know what will happen if we go to God now. No one gets out of Hell, no one; that's what He will tell us. We could beg and plead for the rest of eternity, and it wouldn't do any good."

"I'm not talking about pleading for her release," Jennifer said. "She made her choice. I'm talking about our healing, Chris."

"Oh, I see," said Chris, tears streaming from his angry eyes. "Maybe He will wipe our memories clean, take away our pain. That would solve our problems, wouldn't it, Mother? Then Serena could suffer on, and no one would care because she'd be a non-entity, forgotten, discarded. No, she deserves more than that. No one will ever take her memory from me. She may be tormented in Hell for eternity, but there will be someone who still loves her, someone who will grieve for her. She deserves to be remembered.

"You're right, Mom, Serena didn't accept Jesus as her personal Lord and Savior, but look at how life had treated her. She was abused and tormented. It hardened her heart, hardened it to the point where she couldn't believe in anything she couldn't see. Maybe if she'd had more time. She didn't have more time because of me. It was my fault!"

Jennifer looked to her son with horrified eyes. "*Your* fault?"

"Yes, my fault," cried Chris. "I was at the wheel of the car that night. I wasn't paying attention to the road. I was driving way too fast. Now Serena is paying for my mistake, *my* mistake! It wasn't her fault, but she has to pay for it anyway. Tell me about God's love, Mother."

Jennifer was crying as she watched her son storm away. "Chris, where are you going? Chris!"

There was no answer. He turned the corner and vanished behind a wall of books. What could be done now? Should she run after him? No, he wouldn't listen to her, not in his current state of mind. She hesitated, uncertain as to what she should do. Was there anything she could do that would matter? Again, she turned to the ominous black book. Slowly she was drawn to it. Who was this woman, this Serena Farnsworth? She was her daughter-in-law. Regardless of whether she knew her or not, this was the woman who had brought joy into her son's heart, the woman whose fate now so distressed him. Perhaps Chris was right. Perhaps God would, in the end, wipe the memory of this woman from her mind, but for now, she wanted to know more about her. She had to understand what it was about Serena, a non-believer, that had captivated her son's heart.

Jennifer pulled the book from its place on the shelf. She felt a wave of sadness hit her, as if the very materials from which this volume was fabricated contained the essence of Serena's soul. She had never felt such a sensation. Slowly, she opened the book to its first page and was inundated by the first life experiences of this young woman. She was tempted to close the volume, to spare herself the pain that it most certainly contained, but she couldn't. She had to know this woman, and this was the only way.

⁂

How long the book's vision went on, Jennifer couldn't say, but she came to know well the daughter-in-law she had never met. She saw the darkness and the light, the depths of her depravity and summit of her sweet love, the love Serena and Chris had shared. She had changed. The Spirit of God had been working with her. During the last years of her life, she was in the process of being remade. Jennifer was sure of it. Serena had become so caring, so giving to all those around her. Her life was a mirror of the Christian experience. She had walked the walk, but deep within her battered heart, she had been unable to accept God's free gift of eternal life. The words of the song, "Almost Persuaded," swept into her mind, as if they had been written for Serena Farnsworth. If only there had been more time. This story, this life, was a tragedy in every sense of the word. If only she had realized what little time remained. Would knowing this have helped her?

Jesus had told so many parables of those who would be unprepared for His coming. For them, the Lord had returned at a time when they least expected it. The story before her, that she now witnessed unfolding all around her, was every bit as tragic as any within the Bible.

Jennifer continued to page through the book, which carried her from Serena's life into her afterlife. She saw Serena standing before the judgment seat of God, felt her despair as her sentence was brought forth and she was carried into outer darkness. But what amazed Jennifer most was the kindness, the compassion she had shown to others, even in Hell. Though damned, she would not bow before satan nor do him homage, even when faced with the dire consequences of her disobedience.

Jennifer could bear it no longer and closed the book as she saw Serena tumble toward the sea of fire. The vision faded, and she found herself in the quiet of the Hall of Records once more. She had to see God, had to council with her Creator. Only He could become her refuge, as He had always promised. He would have her answers. But would they be the answers that she wanted to hear?

Could she possibly hope to convince him to change his verdict regarding Serena? She had grave doubts about that, but she would try. After all, hadn't Moses once convinced God to change His mind when He had decided to destroy the disobedient children of

Israel while they were in the wilderness? With all of her heart, she would try.

⊰※⊱ ⊰※⊱ ⊰※⊱

Jennifer made her way through the busy streets of Zion toward the most holy of holy places. She took no notice of those around her. She was desperate, and speaking to the Father became her only focus.

The great plaza was as crowded as usual as Jennifer entered. She was determined to get as close to God as she possibly could. It wasn't that it really mattered, even from a mile away she could hold the same intimate conversation with the heavenly Father. But this time she had to be close. She moved forward through the swelling crowds, searching for any avenue that would bring her just a bit nearer to the thrown of God. Today, she seemed to be finding those avenues, moving among the singing and praising people, drawing ever closer. One gap in the crowd would open before her, and then another. Humans and angels seemed to actually be moving out of her way, making room before her.

She was reminded of the parting of the Red Sea before the Israelites, but instead of a sea of water, it was a sea of people making way for her. An avenue seemed to be opening up before her, an avenue leading straight to the Father. Her eyes were affixed upon Him all the while as she drew ever closer. All the while, she was aware that she was being watched by those around her, the gaze of loving and concerned eyes. Time seemed to blur; she knew not how long she had walked into the growing radiance of the Father. A final parting of the people around her brought her almost to the great platform upon which God, the four beasts, and the 24 elders abided.

Jennifer was so close. Never had she dreamed of being so close to God. She could discern the features of the 24 elders robed in white who sat atop the great platform of white marble, upon golden thrones in a great circle about the Father. Their hair was long and white and each wore a crown of glistening gold. She sensed that they were very old, yet their faces did not display the telltale traces of that age. Every one of them turned toward her as she approached. Amid the great throng that surrounded her, she was convinced that they were looking directly at her. She could see the look of deep concern, of compassion upon their faces. She could even see the color and depth of their eyes. Within them, she could discern wisdom, as great a wisdom as could be contained within a human frame.

Within the circle formed by the elders, the surface of the great platform took on a very different aspect, no longer that of white marble, but rather like that of shimmering green glass, which reflected the rainbow-like aura which surrounded the Father. Seven flaming pillars of light, looking very much like flaming torches, surrounded God, creating a zone of demarcation, forming the threshold of the most holy place in all of creation.

Still closer to the Creator she beheld the four beasts. They stood around the throne of God in a perfect square. For the first time, she could see them clearly. She recalled the apostle John's description of the beasts. He spoke of one appearing as a lion, another as an ox, while still another had a human face. The last was like an eagle in flight. She wondered if he had gotten so close a look at them as she now did.

They looked so very strange. Indeed, they looked unreal. They had an eerie luminescence and appeared translucent. Their visage seemed to change from second to second. At times, they seemed to take on the forms that John had ascribed to them, yet those forms were transitory. What were they? What purpose did they serve? Those were the sorts of questions that her son might have asked, if only he were here. They sang praises unto the Father, just as John had said, praises that Jennifer only partially comprehended. She continued forward, but more slowly.

There was so much happening here, flashes of lightning, peals of thunder, swirling light, it was almost too much for her to take in. It was only then that Jennifer's gaze turned back.

To her amazement, she discovered that all of the multitudes in attendance were some distance behind her. She stood alone between the great throng of people and God Himself. The power and majesty of this place was beyond description. Here was more than just an incredible scene; it was in the air, radiating out from the Being who sat upon the throne. The Wellspring of creation, the Author of time and space, sat before her. How had she arrived in this place? One might remain in this assembly for months, perhaps years, and never be able to draw as close as she had in but a few minutes. It could only be that God Himself had willed it so, that He felt so much for her grief that He had brought her right to His throne. Jennifer was shivering. Instinctively, she dropped to her knees before the Creator of the universe.

Jennifer was there for a few seconds, when she felt a warm hand on her shoulder. She looked up to see the kind face of Jesus, kneeling down before her. She fell into His arms. "Oh, Lord," she wept, "something horrible has happened."

"Peace, Jennifer," He said in a soft reassuring tone while placing His arm around her. "It's going to be all right, I promise." Jesus rose to His feet, drawing Jennifer with Him. "Come."

Slowly they walked up the 12 steps, toward the luminous being who sat in the midst of the four beasts. Jennifer was shaking as she looked up to see God. Never had she stood so close to the Creator, not even during her judgment. Back then, she had been aware of His brilliance and grandeur, but now she could see so much more.

He was beautiful beyond description, His proportions absolutely perfect. Surely, God was Spirit, yet He took on a form with which His people could relate. After all, He had made man in His image and likeness. Therefore, He was the template of human creation, the perfect example of the human form, without wrinkle or blemish. No, it was not He who had taken a form with which humanity could relate. Perhaps it was the other way around.

His hair appeared white, or perhaps the lightest shade of blond, and his eyes were an azure blue. Yet, any attempt to ascribe some color to his skin, his hair, or his eyes was, at best, highly subjective. Unlike human beings who were seen by reflected light, God's body was actually radiant. He was the source of the light by which He was viewed.

Although God was watching Jennifer with kind, understanding eyes, there was fear within her. How would she present her petition? Did she even have to? Yet, her greatest fear and concern was for her son. She wondered if he was somehow in trouble, perhaps very grave trouble. Within a minute she stood closer to God than she had ever seen anyone stand, so close that she might well have reached out and touched Him.

Slowly the crowd around her faded from view, to be replaced by white billowing clouds. The four beasts and the elders all vanished, leaving only God, His son, and herself, standing on the great glistening stage of onyx. Beyond the stage and below the clouds, Jennifer saw the green Earth, many thousands of feet beneath them; it was a spectacular vista.

"Beloved and faithful daughter, don't be afraid," said God, in a very human voice. "I know that you are very troubled by the events of the past days, especially those that have transpired today.

You don't understand why these things have come to pass, why your son has experienced troubling dreams since his arrival."

"But I gave him hope when there was none," cried Jennifer, weeping openly. "Father, I started guessing about the meaning of his dreams, just making up stories, telling Chris what I thought he wanted to hear. Then I took pride in it all. I'm so ashamed."

"Daughter, you have done nothing to be ashamed of," said the Father, leaning toward the distraught woman, His voice gentle and understanding. "There was no sin in what you did; none at all. You interpreted his dreams to the best of your ability. You did it out of love and concern for your son. You didn't want to see him suffer."

"I just don't understand what's going on," replied Jennifer, weeping.

"I know," replied the Father, rising from His throne. He walked the two steps toward Jennifer.

Jennifer had been unprepared for this. She didn't know whether to fall to her knees or look her Creator straight in the face. She chose the latter, gazing into the Father's eternally deep eyes.

Now that God stood beside her, she could gain a true measure of His stature. He was well over 6 feet in height. He reached out to her, His luminous hand caressed her chin gently. His hand was soft and warm, yet the sensation of His touch went far beyond that. She could sense His pure power, His divine nature as He took her hand in His.

"Jennifer, what has happened this day will try your son, measure the quality of his heart." God's expression turned somewhat more solemn. "The road he travels is not an easy one, but what has happened is necessary. His faith and conviction must be put to the test. He must come to realize his limits and his capabilities. If he is to become greater in the Kingdom of Heaven, he must go through this trial. What he does in the coming days shall shape his destiny and that of many others."

Jennifer was still confused. Her mind was an avalanche of so many emotions. "But, Lord, why did this all have to happen to him?

"Daughter, you assume that Heaven offers no trials for the saints, but now you know otherwise. We have not spoken of these things before. There was no need to. Your sweet loving spirit has allowed you to overcome the minor challenges you have met here with ease. So much so, that you hardly realized that they were there at all. When Chris was a child, you once told him that into every life a little rain must fall. Do you recall that?"

"Yes, Father, I remember," Jennifer said, thinking back to another life. In her mind's eye, she envisioned the incident clearly. "I also remember my own mother telling that to me when I was a child."

"It is as true in Heaven as it was on Earth," continued the Father. "The saying does not only mean that the rain of adversity is likely to enter your life, it also means that it is essential that it enter your life. Do you know why?"

Jennifer hesitated. "I think so. Is it because problems that we face and overcome make us stronger people?"

A broad smile appeared upon the Father's face. "Yes, beloved daughter, that is exactly what it means. Without this rain, how would you grow? Such things as these strengthen the spirit. I want all of my children to grow, to become the image of my first born. If Heaven were a place devoid of such trials, how would that be possible?"

"OK," said Jennifer. "I understand that what my son is going through is a trial, a test that will, I hope, make him a better person. But why this? Why did he have to remember this woman sentenced to Hell, a woman he loved so much?"

"Daughter, that was his choice," was the response. "Often, man creates his own trials and tribulations. His love for Serena was deep; he would not let go of her memory, even here. He needed to remember. For this reason, I allowed him to keep a portion of the memory of her; that he might decide for himself if he truly wished to let go of her."

"I looked at her life in her book in the Hall of Records," continued Jennifer, who seemed determined to act as an advocate for her son and perhaps even his wife. "I know she wasn't a Christian. I know that she died in her sins; but Father, isn't there something you can do for her?"

The compassion in the eyes of the heavenly Father didn't dim, not in the least. "I already have. Her grandmother imparted my message of love to her. At first, she accepted it joyfully, yet the circumstances of her life eventually hardened her heart. Chris knew these things, yet despite that knowledge, he chose to marry her, to yoke himself unevenly with one who would not believe. That choice has brought him great pain, and it will bring him more anguish still."

"So, what's going to happen now?" asked Jennifer. "How is this trial going to make him stronger?"

"Only Chris can decide that. His love for Serena is great. It is a pure and noble love, and that love will give genesis to a desperate plan. There will be no dissuading him from it when he finally arrives at it."

"But, Father, can't you stop him from doing something foolish? I mean, he's suffered enough."

God shook his head. "Beloved daughter, I will not stand in his way. All of my children have a free will, and I have very rarely prevented them from exercising it. He feared that I would erase the memory of Serena from his mind. I would never do that. If he chooses to continue to mourn her condition, that is his decision.

But listen carefully, Jennifer, an important decision lies ahead for him, the most important decision that he will ever make. You cannot make that decision for him; however, your desire to council him will be fulfilled. Eventually, he will come to you."

"But what should I tell him?" asked Jennifer, her frustration only too obvious.

"You already know the answer to that question," was the reply. "You will tell him to have faith, to seek Me. You will plead with him; but understand, he may not listen to you. Nonetheless, you must try, for in doing so you will plant a seed that might later germinate." The Father released Jennifer's hand and turned to His first born. He said nothing that Jennifer heard; yet clearly there had been communication.

"Come, Jennifer," said Jesus. "I will take you home."

Jennifer wanted to know more, but she realized that the mind of the Father was made up. She went with Jesus.

Jennifer turned once more to her Creator, whose sympathetic eyes were focused on her. "Thank you, Father. Thank you for hearing me."

God smiled, but said nothing. Jennifer was lead away into the mists. She felt comforted in the presence of Jesus, but she still feared for her son. Suppose he would not listen to reason? Could a human be kicked out of Heaven? She wasn't sure.

The mists parted before them and the two travelers walked onto the lawn in front of her mansion. It was pleasantly cool, and a gentle breeze blew in from the forests beyond the rolling field of grass, carrying with it the odor of honeysuckle and pine needles.

Ebbie still sat on the porch, exactly where she had been when Jennifer and Chris had left this morning. Normally, she would have come right out into the yard and welcomed them home; yet today she held her ground. She seemed confused that Chris hadn't returned.

"I will stay with you for a time," said Jesus, placing His arm around the distraught woman. "I understand how you feel. Just remember; all things work to the good for those who love God. It is as true here as it was upon the Earth."

They sat on the steps of the porch looking out across the lawn toward the forest. Ebbie walked slowly forward, sat down beside Jesus, and began to purr as if she knew who He was. He reached over and stroked her soft fur, causing her to purr even louder.

"If I only knew that everything was going to be all right, with Chris," Jennifer said. "Lord, what's going to happen? You know—I know you do."

"I do not know," said Jesus, "but I have faith in the Father. There are some things that only the Father knows. The Son cannot know all that is on the Father's mind, especially when that mind is so vast."

"Lord, maybe you could go to my son and speak to him," said Jennifer. "He would listen to you; I know he would."

"I'm sorry, I cannot," replied Jesus. "You see, it isn't the proper time yet. It is the Father's will that your son should go through the trial before him, and he is going to have to do it on his own. When I walked the Earth, I had a dear friend by the name of Lazarus."

"The brother of Mary and Martha," said Jennifer.

"Yes," confirmed Jesus. "I was by the Jordan River, near the place where John had baptized so many, when word reached me that he had fallen ill. His sisters urged me to come at once. You see, they feared for his life and were convinced that I could save him from death."

"But you didn't go immediately," chimed in Jennifer.

Jesus smiled. "No, I didn't. Two days passed before I set off for Bethany. When I arrived there, Lazarus had already been in the tomb for four days. I believe that you know the rest of the story."

"Yes," replied Jennifer. "You had the stone to his tomb rolled away, and told him to come forth. You raised him from the dead."

"And many people witnessed it," replied Jesus. "A multitude came to believe in my message because of that one event." Jesus paused to allow Jennifer to consider that miracle anew. "Now, suppose I had gone immediately, the moment Martha's message had reached me. I would have found my friend on his death bed, very ill, with only Mary and Martha there to see to his needs. I might have laid my hand upon him and seen to his recovery. It would have been a thing done in secret, as many of my earlier miracles were. But it was the Father's plan that this not be the case. Do you understand why?"

Jennifer considered the words of Jesus before she replied. "I think so. God wanted there to be a grander miracle, one that a whole lot of people would see, not just Mary and Martha."

"Yes, in part. It was a matter of timing, God's timing. The day that I would enter Jerusalem for the Passover was not far off. In your time, you might say that God was setting the stage for the final conflict, setting the stage for my own personal trial. It is the same here. The time is not right for me to speak to Chris, perhaps later it will be."

"I think I'm going through a trial too," Jennifer said.

"Of course you are," confirmed Jesus. "By going directly to the Father, you have taken the first step to placing this trial behind you."

"But I'm seeing eternity in a whole new light now," said Jennifer. Her head turned away from Jesus. "Nothing will ever be the same again. I guess, before, I was only seeing what I wanted to see here in Heaven. I felt good. I mean, everyone around me felt good. There didn't seem to be a problem in all creation, but there is, isn't there?"

For a moment there was only silence. "Go on," urged Jesus.

"I saw Hell," said Jennifer, who found it difficult to continue. "I looked into one of the black books. I know that I shouldn't have, but I did. What I saw, it was awful. I saw a black sea of fire and people being horribly tortured everywhere. How can the Father let this go on? Why did He create such a horrible place?"

"You might also ask why the Father allows so many terrible things to happen on Earth," answered Jesus. "He told you. He said that He rarely interferes in the free will of man. Humanity creates most of their own problems. Wars, famines, even what you might call natural disasters, are mostly man's doing, though satan has had a hand in it as well. Understand, outer darkness, where Hell exists, is a realm beyond God's creation. It is a cold and harsh realm to absolute nothingness. Yet, at the center of this nothingness, is a world called Hell. God made the light that shown warmly upon it, and the winds that blew across it, but He did not create the horrors that transpire there. That was satan's doing. It was he and his angels who have defiled that place. Though it was his prison, satan was determined to rule it. He vowed to rule that domain through fear and pain. That is the source of his power. He has harbored a jealous hatred for humanity in his heart since the Father created Adam and Eve. In bringing pain and grief to humanity, especially those condemned to outer darkness as he is, he is striking out at the Father in the only way that he can. Only so long as he could control them, would his lust for power and domination be partially placated."

"And once someone is condemned to satan's kingdom, they're stuck there," deduced Jennifer. "No one has ever gotten out."

"That is not exactly true," said Jesus. "Long ago, I traveled to that domain. For a full day I preached to the lost in that place, as I had on Earth. I preached to all who would listen. I offered them a way back to God, offering them the same opportunity that I offered to all those living on Earth. When I departed, I took all who would accept my sacrifice with me. They dwell with us in Heaven, even unto this day."

"But there is nothing that Chris could do for Serena, is there?"

"Nothing," confirmed Jesus. "God's decision on this matter is final. We both grieve that Serena made the choice not to walk with the Father, but that was her decision."

"And now, because Chris loved this woman, he's in pain. Why did he ever have to marry her? My son would have been happy here if only…," Jennifer was too upset to continue.

"Jennifer," Jesus said, "don't blame this woman for whom Chris has such deep love. Don't blame her for what has happened to him. You must not harbor resentment in your heart for her, not even now. For I tell you, she is already reaping the terrible reward for her disobedience to the Father. Though she rejected my sacrifice, I feel no ill will toward her, only sorrow for her loss. Remember, I loved you long before you even knew me. If I still love Serena, even now, can you, who were bought with a price, do any less?"

Jennifer lowered her head, ashamed to have even considered the thoughts she had just given voice to. Through Serena's book, she had been given a glimpse of the suffering of those in Hell. Surely, Serena's fate was horrible beyond imagining. Now more than ever before, she understood why God, in His wisdom, had veiled the minds of the saints to the suffering of those who had not found the narrow path. "I'm sorry."

"I know," said Jesus. "Let us speak no more of it."

"But in trying to help her, Chris couldn't get kicked out of Heaven, could he? I mean, could his name be removed from the Book of Life?"

Jesus' response was unexpected. He stood up and extended His hand to Jennifer. "Sister, grasp my wrist, grasp it firmly."

Jennifer obeyed, and as she did so, Jesus took her wrist in his hand. His grasp was gentle but firm.

"Now, Jennifer, try to let go."

Jennifer opened her hand, releasing the wrist of Jesus, yet He did not reciprocate, His grasp remained firm. "You see, you might let go of God, but He will not let go of you. Such is the depth of His love for you and your son. The Father will not allow you to fall from His Kingdom. You love your son very deeply; but I tell you that the Father loves him even more. Do you truly think He would condemn one of His beloved children to outer darkness because that child made a mistake in judgment?"

"I understand now," Jennifer said, rising to her feet as well.

A smile appeared on the face of Jesus as He released Jennifer's wrist. "Be at peace. Let this situation be in God's hands. All things work to the good for those who love God. It is as true here as it was on Earth. Trust Him, Jennifer; place this crisis in His hands."

Nothing more was said about the trial ahead. There was nothing more to say. Jesus was right; it was all in God's hands now.

chapter fifteen

EXCRUCIATING pain; it had become the center point of her existence, dominating her entire being, as surely as the flaming black sea dominated her world from horizon to horizon. Its cruel currents had swept Serena far from the barren brown cliffs of the shore and into the endless, heaving nightmare beyond. Eventually, those currents had carried her from the land of eternal daylight into the sea of eternal night. Serena remembered her final sunset, as the bloated red orb sank below the horizon never to rise again.

The sky overhead faded, first to a pale gray then to black, until only a narrow band of amber stretched across the lonely horizon, giving evidence to a red sun far beyond. Yet, that bow of light was fading as she was carried deeper into eternal night. Only the flames illuminated her surroundings now. Not that there was anything to see beyond the black boiling ooze, heaving and churning in an endless dance of suffering.

Her once beautiful skin had become a reddish brown hide, covered with boils and sores that erupted and healed in a never-ending cycle of destruction and regeneration, as her body's incredible healing power fought an eternal battle with the scalding black oil that engulfed her. Beneath her burnt flesh, her blood boiled within her veins, giving rise to its own unique pain, a pain which penetrated to the depths of her being.

The portions of her body above the roiling black liquid fared no better, for they were scorched, and occasionally charred by the terrible flames that swept randomly across its surface. Her long, beautiful hair had been totally burned away; leaving only inflamed and scarred flesh covering her head. She had no eyebrows or eyelashes, for the parts of her body that could be burned away had been.

She thrashed about in crazed pain. There was no respite and no rest, only the continuing torment that ripped her humanity from her, leaving only her base animal instincts. Those instincts told her to do anything to escape, yet escape was impossible. Yes, therein was the source of her escalating desperation, a desperation that would lead inevitably to madness.

How long had she been here? Only an instant compared to the eternity that stretched before her, and that realization alone was driving her toward insanity. If only the heat would increase, consume her utterly, destroying both body and soul. Nothingness would be infinitely preferable to this. But that nothingness would never come, for her existence would stretch into infinity. The human spirit was eternal and, thus, so would be her suffering.

She tried to think of Chris, to dwell on the love that they shared in life, but love had been drained from her. There was no room for love in her heart. It had been replaced by fear, regret, and grief, the emotions which dominated this place. Those emotions seemed like tangible entities. The sulfurous air, the boiling sea, the flames, they were all infused with it, and their abundance penetrated everything, even to the depths of her soul. She couldn't even picture his face in her mind's eye. No matter how she tried, her efforts met with failure. His face was hidden beyond her terrible veil of agony. What she wouldn't give for just a few minutes without pain.

She spun around as her ravaged body rode over a mighty swell. There was nothing to see but the black sea and the orange flames. She was absolutely alone. Was there still light on the horizon behind her? She wasn't sure.

The sea wasn't always a realm of solitude and isolation. Occasionally she encountered others, fellow souls being swept along on their eternal journey by the currents. She had learned the hard way to do her best to avoid them, for in their pain-generated madness, they might very well attack her. They were like rabid animals, no, worse. Rabies plagued its victim with its maddening pain for only a matter of days or weeks. The torment of this place was on a wholly different scale.

Ten years, a hundred, a thousand—what could that much pain do to the human soul? It created a being who would lash out at any living creature with frightening ferocity, hoping that in doing so, their pain might in some way be eased. Worse still, she realized that eventually, she would be just like them, a vicious animal with no trace of reason, conscience, or compassion that made her a human being. It was a ghastly thought. Yes, it was best to avoid others here.

Twice Serena had seen a most curious sight, an angel robed in white, traveling on powerful wings high overhead. What were they doing here, in the most unholy of places? She couldn't say. Would that she could have gone with them, yet they paid no attention to her.

Then there were the dark demons. From time to time, one would cross the sky, borne on black leathery wings, riding the ever-present thermals. They were a kind of patrol, sentinels whose task it was to insure that none cheated their fate. They had been sent here for good reason, for here and there, the waves of the boiling sea crashed upon isolated islands of black volcanic rock. She had seen several of them in the course of her involuntary journey. They were little more than jagged treacherous spires that protruded from the waves; yet to the human souls doomed to this sea of agony, they were a place of sanctuary. If you could swim hard enough through the ooze, time the crashing of the waves upon the rocks just right, the waves might throw you onto the craggy flanks of one of these pillars. If you could get a handhold and climb, you might escape the grip of this dreadful sea, if only for a few minutes.

It would be difficult to accomplish because the swift currents of this sea carried its victims along on an endless voyage. If she missed the opportunity, it would be unlikely that she would have a second chance. Still, it was a hope, the only hope she had of even a momentary escape from the sea.

It could be done, Serena had seen it. Perhaps a month ago, in the fading daylight, she had watched a ragtag man clinging from a craggy rock that rose a dozen feet above the crashing waves. His fingers were dug into holes in the nearly vertical rock face. His refuge held no level ground upon which he could rest, not even a ledge upon which he might sit, yet she had envied him nonetheless. He was free of the terrible hot embrace of the sea, perched above the swirling flames. For a time he had found some measure of relief.

Yet his victory was short lived, for even as she watched, a large black demon swept down upon him. He had barely avoided the demon's claws by casting himself back into the turbulent fiery sea and hiding in its dark depths. The demon had sought him out for several minutes, eventually being joined by others. They played a dreadful game of cat and mouse with their terrified victim. The pitiful soul would duck beneath the waves to avoid his tormenters, only to pop up somewhere else. Then, he was once more compelled to seek refuge in the merciless depths as the demons made for him again. In the end, they grew weary of the game and went off in search of other sources of amusement.

Serena was catapulted back to the present, as her attention was drawn by a bolt of lightning that illuminated the dark skies before her. There was a storm up ahead, and the current was carrying her toward it. Serena shuddered, for with the storm would come rain. Not a rain of water, but a burning rain of powerful acid and flaming sulfur, driven by hot gale-force winds. It would make the ordeal all the worse.

Again the lightning flashed, just as she was carried across the crest of another wave. She could see the torrential rains mixed with blue fire on the horizon. This one looked particularly bad. But wait, there was something else. Amid the torrential rains ahead, she beheld a shadowy form jutting up from the flaming sea. It was an island, and she was being carried straight toward it. In the absence of the storm, it might have gone unnoticed. Here was her chance, slim as that chance might be. How far away was it? How big was it? She couldn't tell. She did the only thing she knew to do; she began to swim toward it.

Swimming through this sea was far worse than just floating in it, but she was being driven by desperation. She tried to force the pain into the back of her mind, focus upon the task ahead. Only another prisoner of the sea of fire could begin to understand her motivations. Even if she did make it, which seemed unlikely, her victory would likely be short lived. Even in the dark, a demon would most certainly spot her within minutes; throw her back into the heaving maelstrom, or worse. But she had to do it. She had to get out of this stuff, even if it were only a momentary reprieve.

She focused her attention on the dark silhouette, occasionally illuminated by the distant flashes of lightning. As the minutes passed, she began to realize the true scale of the landmass before her. This was no mere rock jutting up from the depths, but a full blown island, the largest she had seen. If only she could reach it. With all of her strength, she pulled herself through the oily sea, through the cruel flames. Her tired muscles pained her almost as much as the searing sea, yet she refused to give in.

"No!" she gasped, "I won't give up. I am going to make it. Oh, God in Heaven give me strength; help me to keep going, please God!"

It seemed so strange that a damned soul should call upon the Lord. She had done it so often during the past months, more than all of the years before, when it might have done her some good. Whether God really heard her now, she couldn't say.

She did her best to judge the distance to the island and the direction of the current. There was so little margin for error. If only she could be free of the pain, she might be able to think clearly, put her full concentration on the problem. These were the worst conditions imaginable.

Slowly, inexorably, the island grew larger, yet even as it did, she began to realize that the current was not carrying her directly toward it, she was drifting to the left. Unless she worked harder, she might well be carried past it, unable to return. She struggled all the more.

The dark island loomed before her. The flashes of lightning had showed only its silhouette from afar, but now that she was closer, she could see the island itself. The flames of the sea illuminated its flanks in an eerie amber glow, adding a third dimension to the landmass before her. The island was large, perhaps a mile across, dominated by a mighty peak that towered above the evil sea. To the left of the peak, the slopes plunged steeply into the fiery surf, but to the right the slopes were far more gentle. That would be the best place to try for. From the looks of it, there was a rocky beach there. She could practically step from the sea and onto dry land, if she could only reach it.

It seemed almost too good to be true; perhaps it was. Though she was fighting as hard as she could, the current was just too strong. The easier slopes couldn't have been more than a few hundred yards away, yet they might as well have been on the other side of the world. There was no way that she could reach them. Her heart was plunged into despair.

She turned her attention to the left side of the island, the only shores that she had a chance of reaching. Here the cliffs were high, steep, and treacherous, but wait, there was something. Near the very tip of the island, was what appeared to be a tiny cove, little more than an indentation in the rock face, really. The black sea was exceedingly rough here, swirling and heaving, pounding high upon the cliffs. If she could reach it, she might be held there for a time by the swirling ooze, and eventually thrown against the cliff by a large wave. It might be her best chance to get a handhold, to pull herself from this huge deep-fryer. It was also a place where she would most certainly be hammered mercilessly against the rocks, but that didn't matter now. She had to try.

The oily sea became rougher and more turbulent as she drew nearer to the base of the cliff. Here the current was even swifter, as if trying to yank her away from the sanctuary she sought. She wasn't going to make it.

"No!" she gasped, struggling all the more. To come so close, only to be denied, it was too cruel.

She reached out, but the cliff was just too far away. The current swept her past the cove; then pulled her down into the swirling mire. She quickly closed her eyes, protecting them as best she could. She couldn't have them splitting wide open in the intense heat. She might need them very soon. She was spun around, slammed into sharp submerged rocks time and time again, before being catapulted upward unto the crest of a mighty wave.

She opened her eyes to see the towering cliff face rushing toward her. Instinctively, her arms moved forward to meet the rocks. Her body hit them with tremendous force, twisting and crushing her left arm in the process. She was dazed, confused, and so very heavy. Then the realization dawned upon her; she was clinging to the cliff face several feet above the roaring turbulent blackness. She had made it! The cliff was very steep here, but not vertical. Her right hand had a firm grasp on the rocks, as did her left foot. A few seconds later, her right foot found a toe hold, but the movement of her left arm was accompanied by shooting pain. She looked at it to find it shattered and twisted, broken in no less than three places. She looked up; she knew that she had to climb. The next large wave might sweep her away, as surely as the last one had deposited her here. Time was short.

Serena's bloody right foot lifted from the rocks, searching for another toehold. There had to be one! She felt along the cliff face, searching blindly for something she couldn't even be certain existed. A few seconds later she found it, about a foot higher on the craggy rock wall. She swallowed hard and pushed, her bare belly scraped against the jagged hot rocks. She looked up once more, identifying a potential handhold. Her right arm swept toward it. She grasped it. It crumbled, even as she began to sense a failing balance.

"Oh God, no!" she whimpered. "Please, give me strength!"

She considered reaching back for the handhold she had found when she first reached the rocks, she quickly decided against it. She had to climb and do so quickly. Her hand moved to the left and up, searching for, then finding another shallow handhold at the very limit of her reach. She grasped it with all of her strength, her fingers curling into the small jagged hole. It held; her balance returned.

Again, she pulled upward, this time seeking a toehold with her left foot. It took several seconds of searching before her foot found a small cleft in the rocks. Again she pulled upward. All the while, the terrible sea roared beneath her, threatening, urging her upward.

Then there was a loud thundering that shook the cliff as another mighty wave pounded the rocks below her. The black ooze swept upward, engulfing her feet, then her legs, up to her thighs. She felt the terrible burning grasp of her nemesis, as it swept violently around her. She cried as an old familiar pain engulfed her to her waist. Her grip on the rocks tightened. She felt the scalding liquid trying to dislodge her, trying to return her to the place to which she had been sentenced. Surely, if she lost her footholds, her right arm alone could not hold her weight.

In Serena's mind, the black oily sea had become a living breathing entity, a sort of cruel and greedy child that had been denied one of its favorite play things. It had many toys, scattered carelessly and randomly about, yet it was mindful of them all. No, it would not part with a single one of them and certainly not this one. It would have this toy back; playtime wasn't over yet. It demanded that she abandon this refuge that she had found, and allow herself to fall back into its waiting arms so that the game might continue.

Serena struggled to clear her head. No, she couldn't think this way, and she couldn't give up now. She gasped, cringed, but held firm. This had to end. She would see the end of it. After a few seconds, the sea receded once more. She regained her wits and resumed her climb.

If only she could have used her left arm, yet it hung uselessly at her side. Still she pushed upward, finding a new toehold, finding a new handhold, pulling her ravaged body toward the black skies overhead. She was discovering strength and determination that she never realized she possessed.

Behind her she heard the roar of yet another mighty wave, but this one barely caressed her feet with its scalding touch. Again she pulled upward, making slow but steady progress, one new foothold, one new handhold at a time.

Serena had never been an accomplished climber, had never had a single lesson in this fine art, but desperation and necessity made excellent teachers. To fail now was unthinkable; therefore, she could not fail. Though the pain that racked her body made it difficult for her to think, she struggled to focus her full attention upon the rugged rock wall before her and the task ahead. The climbing process had become practically mechanical.

When she at last looked down, she was shocked to see how far she had progressed. She was far beyond the reach of the fiery sea. Another flash of lightning caught her attention, this time it was accompanied by a distant rumble of thunder. In the desperation of the moment, she had forgotten about this second complication. The terrible storm with its rain of vitriol was drawing closer.

Serena had been lucky so far, she had accomplished the unthinkable, escape from the scalding sea. Better still, she had not attracted the attention of any demon. "Lord, thank you for Your mercy," she whispered.

Serena was not so certain that God even heard her prayer of thanks, yet it had been offered nevertheless. She looked upward to see yet another blessing. Only 10 feet above her, was a narrow ledge slashed into the steep rocky slope. She wasn't sure if it was natural or made by the hands of something else, but right now she didn't care. She pressed on.

Less than a minute found her crawling onto the 4-foot-wide ledge. She rolled over unto her back and gazed into the dark sky.

No demon wings reflected the light of the sea below, and only the distant crashing of the breakers on the rocks broke the silence. So far so good. She should move on, search for cover, yet she lay there motionless.

Her left arm pained her terribly as its bones realigned themselves and fused together once more. She felt a terrible itching from head to toe as her flesh swiftly healed, reversing months of abuse in minutes. Within the depths of her body, her blood slowly cooled, and with it, the awful pain within her heart and lungs subsided.

"Lord, just another minute. Please, give me just one more minute of peace," she pleaded, in a voice no louder than a whisper. "How wonderful it would be to become a whole woman once again, just for a little while."

Her wish was granted; the dark sky remained empty, free of menacing demons. Even the terrible itching, that always accompanied healing in Hell, began to subside. She slowly raised her right arm in front of her. By the light of the fires below, she beheld her flesh. She was surprised to discover that most of the dark viscous oil had dripped away. Her flesh was soft and whole again, free of the dreadful scars, gashes, and boils that had covered it for so long.

Strength was returning to her left arm as well, and the pain that had radiated from deep within was nearly gone. How difficult it would be to return to the great sea of fire, to continue her eternal sentence, and surely she must return. Satan could not be cheated, not here. His hatred, his vengeance upon humanity, had to be quenched in pain and suffering. Yet, the silence remained unbroken, and Serena's peace undisturbed. It was inconceivable; her pain was gone. In this blessed moment, she had found the peace that had eluded her for months. On Earth, she had taken this simple sensation—the ability to rest free of pain—for granted. Now it was the most precious gift she could imagine, greater than any earthly riches. In the absence of pain, she drifted toward sleep.

As she faded away, she could hear a distant voice, a voice calling her name.

"Get up, get up, Serena," it cried. "Please, Serena, you've got to get up." It sounded like Chris. It had been so long since she had heard his sweet voice. Yet it was him, she was sure of it.

It was the loud thunder that finally stirred her to action—a sound she knew all too well. It heralded the coming of the storm that would very soon strike the island with pouring sheets of burning acid rain. She quickly rose to a sitting position. She was dizzy and confused, as she did her best to push back the veil of sleep. How long had she been asleep? She had no idea, but it couldn't have been too long.

As she turned, her long hair swept across her face, it felt wonderful. She took a strand of it in her hand, caressing it. It was as it had always been, restored to its natural state. But there was no time to savor this sensation; time was running short, she had to find refuge, any cover she could find from the encroaching storm. She swiftly surveyed the ledge and was surprised to discover that this place of rest wasn't just an isolated shelf along the mountainside, but a full blown trail cut into the flanks of the island. Cut by whom? She wasn't so sure that she wanted to know the answer to that one.

The trail sloped gently downward, perhaps leading to the low lands she had seen on the far end of the island. Should she head off in that direction? Would she find shelter? If only there was more time.

She turned in the other direction. Beyond the cliffs, faintly illuminated by the burning sea, she saw the towering clouds, swiftly sweeping toward the craggy island. It was a frightening apparition, a billowing maelstrom aglow from the pure power that pulsed within, with ragged bolts of lightning coursing around it. The storm was almost upon her. Its gale force winds might sweep her back into the sea.

But something caught her eye—a cleft in the rocks less than a dozen feet away. She crawled toward it. Perhaps it was deep enough to offer her some cover from the torrents of acid that would soon drop from the angry sky. As she got closer she saw it wasn't just a cleft, but a cave—large enough to walk in without stooping and nearly as wide as it was high. It extended far into the darkness.

Serena hesitated at its mouth. She could feel the cool breeze that emanated from within, a breeze free of the pungent odor of sulfur. Could it possibly be? Did she detect just the trace of moisture in this cool air? It was a wonderful smell. This cave would not only offer her shelter from the approaching acid rain, but was also a hiding place from the demons. It was almost too good to be true. She drew back, considering her circumstances. "No, too convenient, too easy," she whispered.

A trap? Might there be something in the depths of this cave that would make the agony of the sea of fire and the sting of the acid rains pale by comparison? No, nothing could be so terrible.

The rising wind, filled with the acrid aroma of acid, reached her nostrils. She turned to see the horrible rain, the encroaching gray veil illuminated by the lightning in the clouds beyond. Her time was running out. What choice did she really have? Without further hesitation, she ventured into the darkness, feeling her way along the smooth cavern wall. She traveled on her hands and knees, unable to find the strength, or stability, to rise to her feet. No, that would come later. For now, it was best to crawl before she walked.

The cave walls were dry and surprisingly cool, sharply contrasting the torrid environment beyond. The sound of the crashing waves, the wind, the thunder, slowly faded, as she crawled deeper into the darkness. She was now 20 feet or more into the passageway, and though her eyes had become somewhat accustomed to the darkness, she could discern little of the passageway around her.

As she moved on, the narrow tunnel seemed to open up into a sizable chamber. Finally, her hand met a cool wall in front of her, and she sat down facing the entrance of the cave, illuminated by the almost continual lightning. She figured that she was 30 or 40 feet in. The slight upward slope of the passage would keep the acid rain from streaming into the tunnel. She was safe for the moment.

Then it began; the terrible rain. Slowly at first, the drops making a slight hissing sound as they struck the black rocks. Quickly it escalated into a torrential downpour. The winds howled, making a strange whistling sound, as they swept over the pitted rocks and around the mouth of the cave. Then came the hot burning sulfur. Marble-sized pellets surrounded in a halo of blue flame pelted the ground unmercifully. Serena offered up a prayer, for others caught on that awful sea during this eternal night, as she watched the terrible pyrotechnics from the safety of the cave. She even thought of her mother, trapped in that horrible underground furnace. She had not thought of her in a long time. Her own agony had left little room in her mind for anything else. Now her mind, released from its dreadful bonds, wandered into unexplored territories.

What now? In her wildest imaginings, she had not expected to get this far. Not only had she escaped the terrible sea, but she had found shelter as well. It would be a rough life here, the life of a cave dweller, but it was infinitely preferable to the alternative. Here, she had found refuge from fear and pain. She thought of the odor of moisture within the cave. Perhaps, somewhere in its depths, she might even discover water. It just kept getting better and better.

No, now she was thinking too optimistically. She had found shelter and safety for a time, but only for a time. Her mind wandered back to the woman in the geyser. She had carefully planned her escape too, hadn't she? Serena shuddered to contemplate the sacrifices she had endured along the way, cutting off her own foot with a makeshift knife, to rid herself of her shackles. It was unimaginable. But, in the end, the demons had thwarted her efforts. Perhaps they'd known what she'd been up to all along. Afterward, she was all the worse off for her efforts.

Serena wondered if she would face a similar fate. Had she been allowed to escape the sea of fire, only to set the stage for an even grizzlier means by which to face eternity? That trail beyond the cave had most certainly been cut from the rock by someone or something. That entity, whoever it was, might return, perhaps soon.

No, this kind of thinking was getting her nowhere. She would set such thoughts aside for the moment.

Serena curled up on the bare floor of the cave, watching the tempest beyond. She thought of all of the times she had experienced it before, experienced it more intimately. Still those meetings were in a state of half-crazed pain. From the safety of the cave, she could view it more objectively, yet it was none the less frightening. She watched all the while as the infernal storm raged, a horror that only Hell could offer; yet she did not witness its end, for the nearly forgotten blessing of sleep overcame her. It was a blissful sleep that offered her the escape she had so often prayed for, yet had hardly thought she would ever experience again. She dreamed of home and her lost love as she lay there in the darkness.

chapter sixteen

THE sound of flapping wings, then light, awakened her. At first she was confused, not sure where she was. This wasn't her bedroom in the rock house; it was a cave, a temporary sanctuary in the very heart of Hell—and she had been found. She focused her eyes on a large crystal imbedded in the black rock ceiling. It was glowing with a sallow yellow light, illuminating the cavern room around her. Then she heard a voice like the sound of thunder.

"You are a trespasser! Your place is in the sea of fire, human, not here in my domain."

Serena turned quickly—ten feet away, a crouching dark form with folded wings was watching her. He was a strange being, a demon of a sort she hadn't seen before. His wings were not like those of a bat but like those of a gigantic crow, black and feathery. His long dark cloak nearly covered his body, and his flesh was light brown, like a man who had spent much of his life in the open sun. He was large and muscular, and his face was that of a middle-aged human man, a rough burley face, handsome in a way, but the face of one who had seen his share of trouble. His dark eyes were deep and penetrating, seeming to stare into Serena's very soul. The scowl on that face was far from encouraging.

Serena quaked in fear. Yes, she had expected this, but she had expected it to happen on the cliff face or on the ledge, not here and now. Now more than ever she wanted to stay. To be cast back into the sea, now that she was whole once more, was an even more ghastly thought. She sat up; her eyes met and locked with those of the terrifying being. She was surprised when his countenance transformed from one of anger into one of amazement.

"It's you," he said in a quieter tone. "I know you, Serena Farnsworth. I was at your sentencing, though I hardly expected to see you again."

Serena held her peace, unsure what to say to this terrible being. She would do everything possible to delay her return to the sea of fire.

"Yes," continued the dark being. "Satan was rather impressed with you, as I recall. Most humans cry and grovel in his presence, but not you. No, you stood boldly before him, riding the thin line between evoking his anger and titillating his curiosity. It was amusing." The demon paused, reflecting on some thought. "And you've been in the sea of fire all of this time?"

Right now, Serena was too terrified to respond verbally, all she managed to do was nod her head.

The demon scratched his short, dark beard, apparently still deep in contemplation. "Yes, I wonder how so much time in the sea, so much pain, has adjusted your attitude. Would you grovel before him now?"

Still Serena held her peace, sizing up this strange being as best she could. She hadn't expected him to engage her in conversation, far from it. She had expected to be mauled, torn to shreds, and then thrown unceremoniously back into the sea below.

"But what strange twist of fate has brought you to me, here and now?" It was then that a scowl swept across his face as his mood abruptly changed course. "Who sent you here, Serena? Speak, or you will be all the sorrier for your silence!"

The question caught her by surprise. "Sent me here? No one sent me."

"Liar!" yelled the demon, growing vastly more agitated. In his rage, he struck the cavern wall with his huge fist. Serena was surprised to see a shower of sparks, as shards of rock scattered about the room. As he withdrew his hand, a visible indentation was left upon the wall.

He growled like an animal; then roared in a loud unearthly tone. He lunged forward, grabbing Serena by her right wrist and drawing her abruptly to her feet. The action nearly pulled her arm from its socket. She cried out in pain.

"How did you get here?" he demanded, shaking Serena like a child's doll. "Tell me!"

"The waves threw me up against the cliff," she replied, her voice soft and trembling. "I climbed from there."

The dark being stared at her. "Do you take me for a fool, woman? It could not be as simple as that. My island is well to the north of the mighty current that ushers your kind along on their eternal journey through the vast realm that is the great sea of fire. Even if one of your kind were carried here by some rogue tide, the currents that sweep around this island are far too violent, too cruel to have been as accommodating as you claim. The undertows, the riptides, and the razor sharp rocks, would act as a barrier against unwary souls so foolish as to approach it. In the end, the currents would carry them far away, beaten and battered, all the sorrier for the experience. The currents alone could not have brought you here."

Serena didn't respond. She looked up at the demon, dazed and confused. What was happening here just didn't make sense. What was he talking about?

"So, you expect me to believe that, after months of pain and abuse in that terrible sea, after being violently thrown against the scalding hot rocks of that cliff, your weakened and desecrated body was actually capable of scaling its craggy flanks. It is nearly vertical, with few handholds, yet you climbed it barefoot. Tell me, have I left anything out? Its location and these dire perils have kept your kind off my island, safeguarded my solitude, until now, until you."

The demon hesitated, staring intently at his uninvited guest. "I do not know what pains satan threatened you with before sending you here. I'm sure that he did not attempt to entice you with rewards, no, that's not his way. But whatever he threatened you with, I assure you, I am capable of doing far worse to you, if you do not answer me truthfully. If you tell me all, I might be merciful. Now, I will ask you again, what did satan tell you?"

"Satan didn't tell me anything, I swear. He didn't send me," objected Serena, her voice pleading. "I don't even know who you are. Please, you've gotta believe me! I haven't seen him since the day I was cast into the sea of fire."

"Liar!" screamed the demon, grabbing Serena by the throat and lifting her off her feet. He held her in midair with one hand, his long fingers tightening around her neck. She gasped, unable to breathe, unable to dislodge his powerful hand. Then he threw her violently at the wall. She struck the rocks with a force that most surely would have killed her, if she were still mortal. She heard the terrible crack within her body and felt the sickening pain shoot through her spine. She cried in agony as she hit the ground. She crumpled to the floor gasping for breath. There was blood oozing from a wide gash in the side of her head, and pain shooting through her dislocated left shoulder.

The demon took two steps toward Serena, rage in his eyes. "Death can't release you from me and what I can do to you. There are no limits. Now, you will answer me. Spy on Abaddon, yes, that's what he told you, but what else? What else did he say? I will know it all! What did he say?"

"This doesn't make any sense!" cried Serena, trying to rise from her prone position, yet without success. She quickly realized that her back was broken. She could still move her right arm, but she was paralyzed from the waist down, and overcome with a terrible nausea. She stared up helplessly at her advancing adversary. It was only then that Serena's fear turned into a rage, a rage to match that of this physical titan.

"I wasn't sent to spy on you!" she cried. "Why would satan be spying on you? It's me you both hate! You know what I think? I think you know damned well that he didn't send me; no, you just want an excuse to knock me around. The big bad demon beating up on a helpless woman! Oh, you're the brave one, you are. Your kind, you're all the same! Does it make you feel good; does it make you feel powerful?"

For a moment Abaddon was taken by surprise. Never had a human spoken to him in such a tone. Humans usually begged and groveled in his presence, but not this one. This woman was full of surprises. "That will be quite enough!" he roared.

"No it won't. I'm not finished!" Serena said, not backing down in the least. "I wouldn't help satan! I'd never help him, no matter what that megalomaniac threatens me with! And if you don't believe me, you can just go to...." Serena stopped dead in her tracks, growing suddenly silent.

"Go ahead, finish your sentence. Just in case you haven't kept up with current events, we're both in Hell," Abaddon said. Amazingly, despite this human's challenge, his anger had ebbed a bit.

He continued to move forward, but amazingly, stopped about 4 feet short of the prone woman. He abruptly dropped to his knees. His piercing dark eyes met Serena's; their eyes locked in a tight embrace.

Nearly a minute passed between them, an incredible minute of total silence. There was no movement from either of them. Their mutual stare was unflinching, unrelenting. Yet even as the seconds passed, the anger drained from both of them. In the end, it was Abaddon who spoke.

"You are telling me the truth; I can see it in your soul. In all of my existence, I have never seen a human soul such as yours. Even after so many months in the sea of fire, it is so lucid, so pure. Yes, now I truly see what satan saw in you. You would have been a considerable adversary, had you taken sides with the Creator. Yes, satan was interested in you, but he didn't send you."

"No, he didn't send me," replied Serena, wiping away the blood from the side of her head. She was surprised to find that the gash on her forehead was nearly healed. Sensation was even returning to her legs. Unfortunately, that sensation mainly took the form of sharp shooting pain.

"Then tell me," continued Abaddon, his tone of voice now calm, "tell me how you came to be here."

"I already did," Serena said while trying to move, though without success.

"Humor me," replied the demon, his tone patient but insistent. He sat down upon the floor but a few feet away, facing his uninvited guest.

Serena wasn't sure where to begin. Should she give this dark being the long version, or would that try his patience? In the end, she told the whole story, in all the detail she could remember. Abaddon didn't seem impatient during the telling at all; in fact, he listened intently to every word. He wanted to hear it all, every detail. From her journey across the barren plains, to her mountaintop encounter with satan, to her encounter with her mother and her plunge into the great sea of fire, she unfolded her journey through Hell to the dark being. He seemed particularly interested in her struggle to ascend the cliff to the cave. When the story was at an end, Abaddon didn't immediately respond; he seemed deep in thought.

"You are the clever one," he noted, smiling slightly. "But not cleaver enough, I think. You were thrown with such force against the rocks, and then climbed so very far, suffered so very much, and for what? Certainly you must have realized that you would inevitably be caught, and then matters would be all the worse. Was it really worth it?"

That was not a difficult question. "Yes, to be free of that horrible boiling sea for just a few hours, it was worth it. Do you have any idea what it's like to be in there, day after day, till eternity? Can you even imagine the pain that your kind puts us through?"

It was an impertinent question, one that might arouse a demon's anger. Serena knew it, but right now she didn't care. What could this being do to her that would be more horrible than what she had already been through? She was surprised to see a trace of sympathy in Abaddon's eyes.

"No, I suppose I don't."

"So why do you do it?" continued Serena, pushing the point on home.

That comment ruffled Abaddon's feathers, figuratively speaking. It was met with a scowl. "Me? You speak as if you think all of my kind are the same, of one mind and body. We are not. Anyway, it was *your* decision to reject the Creator's plan of salvation and place yourself in satan's path. That was most foolish, for it cast you into the most terrible region in all of creation. The fire of satan's hatred for your kind has never dimmed, no, not one bit over the countless thousands of years he has been here. If anything, it has grown greater. He has lost any trace of mercy; his vengeance knows no limits. At this point in time, I believe that he is mad."

"Yet you still follow him." Serena regretted the words almost the instant they parted her lips. Why would she say something as foolish as that? Surely, she had just rekindled his rage. She was amazed to find him unaffected by her comment.

"I don't have much choice, do I?" he replied. There was no emotion in his voice whatsoever. "I am trapped, as are you. Here, there are two destinies—to be a part of his plan, or an object of his wrath. I do not wish to be an object of his wrath. This aspect of his being you understand all too well. However, I am not over-joyed to be a part of his plan either. That is the reason that I dwell here in solitude, as far out of his way as possible."

"But his plan doesn't make any sense," objected Serena, her tone of voice betraying a growing agitation.

"Yes, you said that at your sentencing," Abaddon said. "You said that demons and the humans damned to Hell should work together, to make the best of their lot. You are such a foolish ide-alist."

"What's wrong with that?" objected Serena, trying once more to get up. A sickening pain radiating from her shattered spine rewarded her efforts. She landed once more on her side.

"You ask too many questions," retorted Abaddon. "Surely you realize that this coalition you speak of is not going to happen. So long as satan rules this realm, your kind will be subjugated, tor-tured, offered not so much as a moment's peace."

"Because of his hate for humanity?" asked Serena.

"In part," said Abaddon, who leaned forward, as if to examine her more closely. "However, as I see it, there are other considera-tions."

Serena was surprised when the demon grasped her dislocated arm, and swiftly thrust it back into its joint. She gasped in agony, yet she didn't scream. Perhaps, so many months in the sea of fire had made her more accustomed to the touch of pain.

"There, that should help somewhat," said Abaddon, still showing no sign of emotion.

"Thank you," said Serena, struggling to conquer her pain. "What other considerations?"

The demon cocked his head to the side in a swift and unnatural manner. "I'm actually surprised you don't know that. When I perused your mind, I saw it. You almost had it figured out at one point. Have your months in the sea of fire dulled your senses that much?"

Then it came to Serena. Yes, she had pondered that thought months ago. "Our ever growing numbers."

"Exactly," confirmed Abaddon. "There are only so many of us. Yes, we are powerful, but we are not all powerful, we have our limitations. It was not long after the creation of humankind that the first humans arrived in this place, condemned by God. I am confident in the belief that it was God's intention to merely cast them out, to exile them from His presence, as he had satan and his minions, not to sentence them to eternal pain and torment. Such cruelty is not in the Father's nature. Still, satan had other plans. Satan and his minions were in their glory. They tormented your kind unmercifully for their own pleasure and amusement. They tormented them out of their hatred for humanity and out of hatred of the Creator.

In the form of spirits, they traveled to your world, to deceive even more of you. Thanks in part to their efforts, your numbers in this place swelled. So many crafty and devious humans now dwell among us, and among them were the natural leaders, those that might inspire revolution. For this reason, humans must be kept in check by their bonds, the nature of their confinement, and most important of all, the constant agony they endure. This gives them little opportunity to think rationally, no less scheme of rebellion. Thus satan retained control of his realm."

Serena was dumbfounded. She had been right all along.

"But, it's a reckless game he is playing. Just how many of you can he and his minions control? It's an interesting question, isn't it? He wouldn't admit it, no, not that megalomaniac, as you call him, but one way or another he will be our undoing. His kingdom will fall. Perhaps, one day, his interfering in the affairs of men will cross the line, and God Himself will move against him. Perhaps it shall be the very humans he tortures, who will rise up and topple him. I don't know, but I for one look forward to that day, forward to the end of the torture and cruelty he has turned into an art during these many millennia."

Wow! That comment caught the young woman by surprise. Time and time again, she had watched the demons swarming over humans whose only crime was trying to escape the source of their agony. Those demons seemed to perform their duty with such efficiency, such pleasure. It was nearly inconceivable that even one of them should have the slightest bit of sympathy.

Abaddon shook his head, as he rose and walked across the small room and leaned with one hand upon the far wall. Again there was a silence, a silence that Serena felt it best not to interrupt. It was over a minute before Abaddon turned toward his guest. His eyes were tired and sad. Any trace of anger had long since evaporated. "How satan rules his minions, I will never understand. Over the course of a hundred centuries, he has gained their absolute obedience. They are mindless followers; they obey him without question. So, you see, he has deceived his own people, as well as yours."

"But not you," observed Serena, who had finally managed to rise to a sitting position with her back to the rock wall.

"No, not me," confirmed Abaddon. "I am not as they. I am not blinded by his bold rhetoric, by his threats, or his little bag of tricks. I see him for what he is, a liar, he who beguiled a third of all of the angels in Heaven to follow him to their own destruction." Abaddon shook his head. "Raising up arms against God Himself. Now that is stupidity."

Serena did her best to word her next question as carefully as possible. "How are you different from the other demons?"

"Demon?" objected Abaddon. "I prefer the term fallen angel, if you don't mind."

"Fallen angel, then," Serena said. "Why are you able to see through satan's deception, while the others don't? There is a kindness deep within you, I can sense it. I don't see it in the others."

"A kindness?" replied Abaddon, smiling slightly. "After what I just did to you, you still say that you can sense kindness within me?"

Serena nodded. She wasn't just trying to placate this titan. The aura of evil that she sensed around all of the others was conspicuously absent in Abaddon. She prayed that it wasn't simply wishful thinking.

"Thank you," he finally said.

Serena didn't reply; she was still awaiting the answer to her original question.

"Yes, child, I am different. I didn't side with satan in the battle in Heaven. In fact, I fought against him in that day. I fought at the side of Michael. However, I do not feel disposed to speak of those times right now."

Serena was still confused. "But how did you end up here?"

Abaddon shook his head. "Woman, you do not listen very well, do you? I do not wish to discuss such matters at this time." Abaddon hesitated for a moment. He seemed deep in thought. "I will tell you this; I am not the only one of my kind here. There are others similar to myself, and there is no love lost between any of us and satan. Still, we are but a few against satan's multitude. We all exist together here in a sort of uneasy truce. We are the uninvited guests, loose cannons, as your people might say. Satan doesn't trust me or my kind, and we don't trust him. Let us leave it at that."

"So that's why you thought I might be sent here by satan," Serena asked while trying her best to rise to her feet.

Abaddon took Serena's hand and led her to a squared off boulder upon which she might more comfortably sit. Again there was a brief pause. "But tell me, child, your world was so full of the handiwork of the Creator, so full of His greatness. Surely, it must have been overwhelming. Knowing God, why did you refuse to honor Him?"

That question cut right to Serena's heart. From where she stood, or sat, right now, her life on Earth seemed so futile, so foolish and irresponsible. But it hadn't at the time. "I really didn't believe in God."

Abaddon raised an eyebrow in dull surprise. "Surely, you didn't think that the universe around you was some sort of cosmic coincidence."

"I don't know what I thought," admitted Serena.

Abaddon leaned against the rock wall and crossed his arms. "I suppose it doesn't matter now. The past is the past, for both of us."

Again, a long moment of silence passed between them. "So, what do we do now?" asked Serena.

"What can we do?" posed Abaddon. "We both have our destinies, and yours is in the sea of fire." Again there was silence, as Abaddon's eyes acquired a momentary blank stare. "Strange that satan should have sentenced you to the sea of fire. He usually reserves the sea for far more despicable individuals than you. I wonder what he was thinking. You seem a gentile creature, misguided, perhaps, but hardly evil, hardly deserving of such a fate as this. What did he see that I do not? The sea is the worst fate in all of Hell. It generates the greatest amount of pain, by keeping your body essentially intact. It is the eternal dwelling place of so many of the fiends of your history, great and small. Such ignoble personages as Nero, the one they called Jack the Ripper, Adolph Hitler, and Osama bin Laden. But why did he sentence you here? This is what I don't understand."

Serena did not have an answer. How could she be compared with the likes of Hitler or bin Laden? Perhaps, it was the way in which she had conducted herself before satan. Perhaps, she had brought this fate upon herself. Maybe she should have kept her big mouth shut.

"Nonetheless, a power greater than you or I has decreed our destiny," continued Abaddon. "It is He who placed you in satan's hands. It matters not whether we agree with that power or His judgments. Our opinions are irrelevant. You and I both are damned, cut off from God for all eternity by our own sins against Him. We both feel the pain of that separation. We cannot escape our destinies, child; we must face them for all eternity. It is by our own hands that they have been created. We sowed the seeds of our own destruction."

"That's easy for you to say," Serena said. "I'm the one who feels the burning agony of that horrible sea day after day, not you. I'm sure that you suffer in your own way. You speak of the pain of being separated from God. Well, I feel it too, believe me. But I feel far more than just that."

Abaddon heaved a deep sigh. "I will not argue that point with you."

"It wasn't God's decision that I spend eternity in that horrible sea, that was satan's idea. If you toss me back in there, you're doing satan a favor, you're serving him."

Abaddon shook his head in disapproval, but said nothing.

But you're still going to throw me back into the sea of fire, aren't you?"

"What choice do I have?" continued Abaddon. "However, I have a plan. There is a place, a place at the very tip of the island, from there, you could be thrown back into the sea of fire and swept swiftly away. You would not be dashed against the cliff or sliced to pieces by any rocks below. Better still, I could carry you out over the sea myself, swooping down to give you a shorter and gentler fall. It would be the most merciful way. I hope that meets with your approval."

Serena was horrified by Abaddon's proposal. "Merciful!" she exclaimed, her sudden boldness surprising even herself. "Throwing me into that boiling black sea is merciful? If it was my total destruction, the ending of my very existence we were talking about, that might be merciful. But it isn't, is it? I'll go on living and feeling and suffering for all eternity. You get rid of me and I go on suffering. I don't need that kind of mercy."

Serena's voice faded away to be replaced by complete silence. Abaddon stared at her incredulously. The silence held sway over that cavern room for what appeared to Serena to be a very long time. Slowly, ever so slowly, a smile began to materialize upon the dark being's countenance. There was nothing evil or malicious about the smile, if any words could describe it, they were stunned amusement. Then he chuckled.

"I take it that was a no," replied Abaddon, who now laughed openly.

Serena looked at the fallen angel with amazement. Never had she considered the sight of one of these beings in such mirth.

Finally the laughter died down. Abaddon took Serena gently by the wrist and drew her to her feet. She was surprised that she was able to stand.

"Come child." His voice was calm but insistent, and considering his strength, Serena had no choice but to follow wherever he would lead.

A chill shot up Serena's still mending spine as Abaddon led her back out through the tunnel, into the outside world. A moment later they stepped onto the ledge at the mouth of the cave. The hot breeze and the odor of sulfur once again assaulted her senses. The rocks beneath her bare feet had a wet gritty feel, no doubt a result of the flood of acid that had recently inundated them. Fortunately, the acid itself had either been absorbed or neutralized, thus saving the soles of her feet from further harm.

For a moment Abaddon paused, allowing Serena to take in the terrible vista. The sea of fire swelled and ebbed far below, pounding the rocks with its terrible fury. Serena looked down. She had not realized just how far she had climbed. It must have been nearly 100 feet. To have accomplished such a feat was nothing short of a miracle. She now understood Abaddon's amazement. She herself could hardly believe that she had managed such a climb. The details of the ascent were a blur to her now, an exercise in agony that her mind had managed to cloud from her as a self-defense mechanism.

She looked outward. As far as her eye could see there was fire, fire leaping from a turbulent oily sea. It spread out in all directions, lending its harsh amber illumination to the only solid object that could reflect it insidious evil glow, the dark craggy island. All around her it created bizarre inverted shadows. For here, the only light came from below, not from above. The sky overhead was inky black, free of clouds, yet with not so much as a single star to lighten the somber realm.

On the distant horizon was a bow of deepest blue, that gave witness to a red sun far beyond. Now that she was in no pain and could concentrate on such matters, Serena could more clearly understand the dynamics of this world. She recalled her astronomy professor in college, speaking of worlds which kept one face perpetually to the planet or star they circled. If a planet circled too close to its star, its rotation would slow until it rotated only once in each orbit. When that happened, one half of the world lived in perpetual daylight, while the other half dwelled in eternal night. Apparently, Hell was just such a world. Were it not for this boiling black sea, this environment might be unimaginably cold. Why should she recall this obscure fact right now? Perhaps, it was the realization that pain would soon monopolize her entire world, leaving no room for anything else.

As she had slept in the cave, her mind had focused upon Chris, taking her to those beautiful years in the rock house, years she would never see again. Now her mind wandered, spanning the length and breadth of her earthly experience, even to a college classroom eight years ago.

"Behold my world," declared Abaddon, stretching forth one hand while maintaining a grip on Serena's wrist with the other. "It is always the same. There are no changes of the seasons, no day and night, not even a star to guide the way. Only an occasional acid rain breaks the monotony." Abaddon paused for a moment. "It wasn't always this way. Satan told you that he had created this world, but that was a lie. This world and the sun it circles were here long before satan was cast into outer darkness. Perhaps, it was a final act of divine kindness on the part of God, to provide to us the solid ground and light of this world, even in our exile. It was a far kinder world then, but satan and his minions devastated it, remaking it into an image more to their liking and purpose. I despise their kind. They exist only to destroy."

Abaddon turned Serena to view the narrow ledge that snaked its way along the steeply sloping cliff face. He pointed to the left. "Go this way, and the trail takes you down to the flats, to the bubbling acid mud pits on the other side of the island, a thoroughly nasty place. I rarely go there myself. It is my understanding that, in a former time, it was a spring of fresh water, but no longer."

Again he turned his comely companion around. "Ah, but if you follow the trail in this direction you climb to the very pinnacle of my humble archipelago. From there you can see for miles around, an exceptional vista of true desolation. From there, you can behold this terrible sea, stretching to the horizon in every direction. Regrettably, we will not be traveling there this day; you have somewhere else to go."

Serena swallowed hard; she wasn't ready for this, not now. She looked down at the swirling black mass of burning fury far below. It pounded the cliff relentlessly, it wanted her back. This cruel entity, the great sea, wanted what belonged to it; it wanted her. Serena's knees began to quiver uncontrollably. She was certain that she was on the very threshold of going mad. It had taken the events of the past several hours to bring her to this point. They had done a more effective job at bringing her to the edge of insanity than all of her months in the sea of fire.

Abaddon apparently noticed that Serena had become suddenly very shaky and took steps to steady her. "Easy, Serena, we can't have you tumbling back into the great sea of fire, especially after you worked so hard to escape from it. Come, child, let us go back inside; I have the perfect place for you, far from the heaving sea."

Serena was confused. Had she heard this fallen angel correctly? "Back inside?"

"Yes," confirmed Abaddon, "it is not safe for you out here, though few of satan's minions travel this region. That is, no doubt, why you managed to scale the flanks of my island undetected and unchallenged. As I mentioned before, the currents of the sea rarely carry your kind into this remote corner of Hell. It was an errant tide indeed that brought you to me. That is why I was particularly surprised to discover you at my doorstep. Nevertheless, I can ill afford to have a wandering demon discover you, here, on my island. It would raise questions that I would prefer not to have to answer."

"Then you're not going to throw me back into the sea of fire?"

Abaddon smiled, though slightly. "No, not at this time; perhaps I shall later. Right now, I need time to think, time to decide exactly what I shall do with you."

Abaddon escorted the quivering woman back into the cave. They proceeded deeper into the roughly hewn tunnel, and as they did, one after another, the great crystals imbedded within the ceiling above their heads, ignited into cool white illumination. The air grew cooler and damper as they went.

"There are severe penalties for a fallen angel who would offer aid and assistance to one of your kind," Abaddon said. "For this reason, I can hardly afford for you to be discovered here on my island."

"Where are you taking me? What do you plan to do to me now?"

"So many questions," Abaddon said. "Let's just say that I'm taking you to a hiding place and leave it at that."

The narrow twisting tunnel abruptly opened into a vast dark cavern room. Serena could not estimate the size of the room nor ascertain its contents, for most of it was bathed in deep shadows. Only a single crystal in the rocky ceiling illuminated her way. She proceeded along the wall; then she was directed into yet another corridor. This one was somewhat wider than the first, with a series of branching tunnels on either side. She was led into the second tunnel on the left. The tunnel led 5 feet to a partially open door composed of heavy metal bars. It was a cell door, not unlike the many she had beheld on her first day in Hell. It brought back the memories of that terrible day, the first day of her eternity. The room beyond the door brightened, illuminated by a crystal within the ceiling. A few seconds later, Serena stepped in and the cell door closed and locked behind her.

"Make yourself at home," said Abaddon. "You may be here for some time, so you might as well become comfortable; enjoy this chamber's limited amenities. I must apologize; you see, I was not expecting a guest so I haven't had a chance to clean up the place. It is small and somewhat Spartan, but I think you shall find it preferable to the vastness of the sea of fire."

Serena looked around—it was a prison cell all right but not the sort she was expecting. This cell was at least three times the size of the cell she had been imprisoned within on that first day. It has surprisingly smooth rock walls, not unlike the textured interior walls of a contemporary American home on Earth. Yet, most of its walls were hidden from sight.

From the left wall, a colorful tapestry ran from the floor to the ceiling. It bore the image of an oak tree with green leaves and twisting branches. Upon the back wall, a second brightly colored tapestry depicting a sunlit meadow, lightened the otherwise somber atmosphere of this place. Both tapestries were exceptionally intricate and were obviously the result of hundreds of hours of hard work.

Then Serena's eyes settled on a circular stone table near the center of the room. On the table she was surprised to see a small earthen pot and within the brown earth that nearly filled the pot, sprouted a small green plant with a single yellow flower. It was alive. Tears came to Serena's eyes at the sight of it.

"Please, sit," bid Abaddon, pointing toward a stone bed, overlaid with some sort of thin mattress. "You look as if you need it."

Serena sat down, surprised at how soft its surface was. She was still in somewhat of a daze.

"Yes, much better," Abaddon said standing with his arms folded, just beyond the cell door. He motioned to a sort of stone basin, carved out of the wall, at the far corner of the cell. Abruptly, a spring of water erupted from its center, quickly filling the basin. Serena's eyes grew wide with both surprise and joy. She stumbled to the basin, dipping her hands into the cool nectar. For over a minute, she did nothing but drink the delicious liquid, a blessed substance that she was certain she would never partake of again. She had become so accustomed to her thirst that she had forgotten how wonderful taking a sip of water really was. She shed tears of joy, as she took one handful of water after another to her mouth.

"There is a cup in the cabinet to your right," Abaddon said, mildly amused by his guest's actions. "In the closet beside it are some clothes left here by the former occupant of this place. They might fit you, they might not. However, I believe that you will find them preferable to that ragged garb that satan provided you. That garb is infinitely durable, capable of withstanding the worst abuse that Hell can offer. However, I suspect that you will be more than happy to part with it." Abaddon pointed to a set of dusty blue drapes on Serena's side of the cell door. "Pulling those across the door shall offer you a degree of privacy, should you require it."

Serena really did not know what to say. She had so many questions, but she realized that now was not the time. She did not want to push her luck. "Thank you. Thank you for your kindness."

Abaddon nodded, but did not directly respond to her comment. "It might be some time before I make my decision, and it might not be in your favor. So, even if the clothing within the closet does fit you, I advise you not to discard that gray tattered garment you've been wearing. You might need it again." There was a pause before Abaddon continued. "I suggest that you get some rest." With those words, Abaddon departed.

For a moment, Serena just stood there in silence. She was overwhelmed with emotion, yet she managed to keep it in. Even if Abaddon kept her locked up in this small cell forever, it would be a far kinder fate than what awaited her beyond his island realm.

Serena set about exploring the room in greater detail. She found the crude metal cup as well as a small enclave cut into the rock, covered by a pair of drapes. Within it hung several plain white dresses made from material not unlike cotton. On the floor was a pair of sandals that might have been worn in antiquity. She also found undergarments and several pieces of simple jewelry on a small shelf within this peculiar closet. Like everything else in this room, they were quite dusty; they hadn't been worn or even moved in a very long time.

The presence of these items raised more questions than answers. Who was the woman who had occupied this room and what had become of her? Why had Abaddon imprisoned her here and for how long? Serena would not trouble herself with such issues at this moment. The clothes were here, and whoever had worn them was about Serena's size.

Serena went to the bars of her cell and gazed out. The corridor beyond was dark, and Abaddon was nowhere in sight. Nevertheless, she pulled the drapes shut for privacy.

A horrible thought crossed her mind. She had worn these awful rags for months. They had endured fire, burning oil, and more than their share of abuse without ripping or burning. The currents of the sea had not ripped them from her. They had clung to her body through it all, appearing no different than they had on that first day. She had never tried to remove them. Suppose they wouldn't come off. Suppose they had become a permanent part of her body. What then? It was an absurd thought; or was it? She drew a deep breath.

They slipped off with minimal effort, and she placed them on an empty shelf in the closet. She prayed that she would never have to wear them again. The other clothing within the closet turned out to be a very good fit for her. After putting on one of the long white dresses, she felt much better, less exposed. A portion of her human dignity had been restored.

Then her eyes settled on a series of scrolls that were on another shelf in the closet. She took one and carefully opened it. It was not as fragile as she had at first thought. The writing on it was totally unfamiliar. It was not Greek or Chinese, of that she was certain. Perhaps, it was not an earthly language at all. She carefully returned it to its place on the shelf—another piece to the cryptic puzzle.

There was little more to explore within her 10-by-16-foot cell. Serena brushed the dust from the bed as best she could, and spread the single brown blanket over it. She stretched out and tried to get comfortable. It wasn't difficult. Even as she thought of how nice it would be if she could dim the crystal light over her head, its glow faded as if in response to her command. No, an eternity of imprisonment in this place would not be all that bad, especially when she considered the alternatives.

Before Serena started to slip off to sleep, she took a moment to thank God for His mercy. All that had happened today could not have been by chance. She hoped that a higher power might have been involved. Perhaps God was watching after all.

The word *hope* had become a part of her language and experience once more. With no pain to burden her, Serena faded off into a peaceful sleep.

chapter seventeen

INDESCRIBABLE beauty surrounded Chris as he wandered aimlessly through the busy thoroughfares of Zion. Anyone else would have been filled with wonder at the sights and sounds of this holiest of realms. Yet to Chris it had become empty, an exercise in exotic architecture. He needed to walk, to occupy his mind with some task, any task. For in its absence, he was consumed with dwelling upon the fate of his lovely Serena.

No, he couldn't do that. He would travel the width and breadth of the mighty city in search of a solution that he knew didn't exist. Without hunger, thirst, or the need for sleep, there was nothing to bring an end to his sojourn through paradise. Time became a blur, a highway that extended to the horizon of eternity, and he was very capable of traveling the full length of that highway.

His mind wandered back to his existence on Earth, to a life that he now remembered with crystal clarity. Around him a million people passed by; people with only a vague recollection of their time of trial and tribulation upon the world of their first birth. To them, it was only the second birth that mattered, the birth that had granted them entrance into a better world, one without the troubles and sorrows of the first. To them, the events before that second birth were largely inconsequential. He knew not whether to envy their state of bliss or feel pity for their ignorance. For a time those around him were kindred spirits on the road to eternity, yet now, amid the multitudes, Chris felt very much alone.

Perhaps he should retreat to some secluded spot where he could find solitude, where he could sort things out. Maybe he could find some measure of peace, learn to live in this new world. But how could he go on, knowing what he now knew? Maybe he should go home, to his mother. Perhaps together they could figure out a way through this crisis.

Then again, he might take his petition to the very throne of God. He had spoken to Him many times before. If he appealed to God Himself, got down on his knees before the heavenly Father, perhaps something could be worked out. Surely the heavenly Father's mercy knew no bounds. Maybe He could give Serena a second chance. She was a good woman, really she was. She simply hadn't understood his message of salvation. Perhaps, that was why he had come to remember her. Maybe this was a test, to determine if he would turn to the Father in his moment of need.

Chris stopped in his tracks and looked toward the center of the city. Amid his wanderings, he still knew exactly where he was. It would not take long to reach the place where he could speak to God personally. What other solution was there? Yet a moment later he abandoned the thought. God would listen to him, of that much he was certain. He would comfort him. But how could He release Serena from the pit? She had her chance to accept Him, and she had chosen to reject His plan of salvation. She had rejected His son and His sacrifice. There could be no second chance, not now, not ever.

What was more likely to happen was that God would wipe his memory clean, remove the pain he now experienced. That would be an act of divine mercy toward him, but what about Serena? She would be forever forgotten. He could not allow that to happen to her, he just couldn't. Someone had to remember her; someone had to grieve for her. To be suffering, yet forgotten, was too cruel a fate to contemplate. Serena was worth more than that, at least to him.

If only he could change what had happened. If only he could alter the chain of events that had separated him from the one he loved more than life itself. To live without Serena was terrible enough, but to live knowing of the dreadful place in which she would spend eternity was unbearable. If only he could be with his love one more time, see her as she appeared on Earth, before that terrible evening.

Chris moved on, prepared to continue his sojourn. A moment later he stopped dead in his tracks. Yes, he could do it, he knew how. His aimless wandering became a focused quest as he turned back toward the great Hall of Records. He would return to her book. It wasn't just any book, was it? It was a doorway to the past. He could behold his love once more, be with her in the rock house, he could relive their best moments as often as he wanted. Heaven could offer him escape, offer it for all eternity if he so desired. It was a journey into fantasy, into the now dead past. Yet, fantasy was preferable to a world without her.

He walked quickly toward the place that would offer him escape. He had wandered a long way from the hall, but that was all right. So what if it took hours or even days to reach it. Did it really matter? After all, he had all eternity to spend there with the image of his beloved wife.

It was many hours before the great hall came into view. He quickened his pace and practically ran through the crystalline doorway, bounding up the stairway with a speed and agility that the best earthly athlete could not have matched. He was gripped by a sort of madness, born of the anticipation of seeing his love once again. What would it be like? Might he be able to interact with her in some way? His mother had spoken of the images in the book as shadows, but what if she was wrong? Perhaps the book was some kind of doorway into the past. Perhaps he could intervene. Could he possibly alter the past? And if he did, would that change the present? He would soon know.

He reached her book's floor, then the proper shelf, scanning for the only part of her that remained. His eyes came to focus on the large black book with the golden letters on the spine. To him, it was the only book in the hall, the only book in all of creation. He reached out, caressing the name of his love. Then he looked around and saw there were no others nearby. He pulled the book from its resting place, and sat down on the floor. Slowly he opened the volume to the first page.

In the beginning, all he saw were letters and words, sentences and paragraphs describing the beginning of a new life. Then the words quickly dissolved into a vivid vision of a world long past, a vision of a young mother with a newborn baby girl in her arms. That baby was his Serena.

Chris was unprepared for the full reality of what he saw. Yes, he had witnessed it all before, when he and his mother had opened her book, yet this was somehow different, even more real. Perhaps it was because he held the book and turned the pages without assistance from another. Direct contact produced an even richer experience. Yet, another thought occurred to him. He had never done this before, not by himself. He had perused many of the books in the libraries of Heaven, and they worked in much the same way, but was it exactly the same?

Would he be able to control the process? Hadn't his mother cautioned him about this? He hesitated. Perhaps he should pull out, ask for instructions before proceeding. No, there wasn't time, and he didn't want to answer any probing questions that might be raised. After all, who would want to explore the contents of one of the black books? In a realm of joy, who would knowingly seek out tragedy? He had to press on. He would accept the risk. He turned the page.

This experience was unlike viewing a motion picture on the silver screen in a darkened theater. No, this vision had the depth and even the smells and sensations of reality. Quite accidentally, he discovered that he had the ability to move through the vision, to view it from many different angles. He hadn't tried that the last time he was here, and the books in the library didn't allow the viewer that degree of freedom. He simply thought of where he wished to move, and in which direction he wished to look, and it was so.

His ability to move through the vision was not limited to three dimensions, but also included the dimension of time. He willed his hands to page forward. The vision faded to a soft blur, only to reshape itself once more. He saw Serena taken home from the hospital, saw her take her first step, speak her first words, it was incredible. He paged ever forward. A brightly-lit scene crystallized around him. He found himself on a playground, on a summer day, watching five-year-old Serena running and playing with her friends. She was so happy, vibrant, and alive. How could such a wonderful human being have been sentenced to outer darkness? It just didn't make any sense. After watching their merriment for some time, he moved on in search of the adult Serena, the Serena that he so dearly loved.

Along the way, he stopped many times to gaze upon the beautiful growing child. In doing so, he witnessed the forces that would shape her destiny, the tragedies that brought the element of darkness and pain into her life. Chris had never met Serena's mother. She had died of cancer two years before he and Serena had met. Yet he came to realize that she was at the very heart of the darkness that had engulfed Serena's soul.

She was unpredictable, very unpredictable. She was fully capable of love and compassion one minute, only to become domineering and unyielding in the next. She made life in the Farnsworth family a continuing crisis. She was supposedly a counselor, one whose job it was to help people work through their personal problems, yet she seemed inept at dealing with her own mental issues. Chris recalled that Serena had spoken of those dark days, yet he was unprepared for the full reality, the totally dysfunctional family from which his love had emerged.

Serena's stepfather, though a good and kind man, lacked the strength to control the ranting and raving of his domineering wife. Serena's paternal grandmother had been the only truly stabilizing force within her life. She had been the lone guiding light to the impressionable youth. Irene Farnsworth had been a prayer warrior for her church, a woman of unwavering faith. Through her love, she did her best to lead the young and impressionable Serena in the ways of righteousness. But time worked against her as her health deteriorated. With her untimely passing, Serena's life was heading for disaster. Serena's strong will and stubbornness were carrying her and her mother into even greater conflict.

Again and again the two squared off, sometimes over the most trivial of issues. Just a few items out of place in Serena's bedroom were enough to send her mother on a ballistic trajectory. At first Serena had tried to please her mother, yet there seemed to be no way to placate her anger. More than a few times, Bedillia Farnsworth had backhanded her young daughter in the midst of her ravings. She called Serena all manners of things, and as she did, Serena's defiance grew.

Then came that fateful day—the day Serena responded to her years of mistreatment. In an argument over whom she could or could not associate with, she blocked her mother's abusive arm with her hand. And before she knew what was happening, Bedillia found herself on the floor looking up. The 14-year-old Serena had thrown her mother forcefully to the ground.

Chris was amazed when he saw Serena apologizing and helping her mother to her feet. He was even more surprised when Bedillia accepted Serena's help, and walked away rather than continue the altercation. Yet, no amount of reconciliation on Serena's part could alter the course of events that followed—Bedillia's mind was set on revenge, cold and calculated.

The extent of her revenge, and the means by which it was measured out, horrified Chris. Although he knew what was to come, because Serena had told him, he was not prepared to see it played out before him. The turn of a page brought an image of Serena and her mother traveling in the family car. It was to have been a trip to the mall to go shopping for some new clothes for Serena, a sort of peace offering between Bedillia and her daughter. They were going to stop on the way to see an old friend Bedillia knew from college. It was the perfect ploy to get Serena to the hospital—the perfect dumping ground where her rebellious daughter would be dealt with harshly.

Serena never realized what was happening, what sort of place it was. How could she? She believed that her mother wanted to iron things out between the two of them. Only now, as they stood in the admissions room, did it dawn on Serena what her mother had done. She had been betrayed. The only "new clothes" she was going to get that day was a hospital gown.

"Mom, you lied to me!" she screamed, as her mother signed the commitment papers.

"I fear that she is going to turn violent again," replied her mother, looking to the doctor and a pair of male orderlies standing by a double door at the far side of the admission's room. "She has done this before, countless times, and when she does, she is practically uncontrollable."

She turned to Serena, who had suddenly turned very pale. "Honey, you're going to need to stay here for a while. These people are going to help you to get better. And when you're well again, you will be able to come home. I'm sorry, but that's the way it has to be for now."

"What did you tell them?" gasped Serena. "You told them I'm crazy didn't you?" Serena turned to the young doctor. She did her best to keep her cool. "Hey, I'm not crazy. Really, I'm not. My mother just wants to get rid of me, don't you see that?"

"Serena, no one is saying that you're crazy," assured the doctor, placing a gentle hand on her shoulder. "But there is something wrong. We're just going to see if we can find out what it is. I promise; no one here is going to hurt you."

"You don't believe me," replied Serena, her tone somewhat more agitated. She pointed to her mother. "She's the one who's crazy!"

"You don't mean that," said the doctor, glancing toward the orderlies who were already approaching the distraught girl.

Serena hadn't noticed until one grasped her by the arm.

"Keep your hands off me, I haven't done anything wrong," she said, trying to squirm from the powerful man's grasp.

But it was far too late as the two orderlies restrained the distraught youth. The series of events set into motion were already unalterable.

"Mommy, please," she cried, "don't let them take me! I wanna go home! I'll be good, I promise! Please!"

The reality of the vision overwhelmed Chris. "Leave her alone!" he cried, as he moved toward one of the orderlies—his hand passed through the large man like a phantasm. Despite the seeming reality of this scene, it was but an image of the past and there would be no altering the course of time.

Chris could bear to watch this tragedy no longer. He moved further into the future, beyond Serena's months in the mental hospital, only to see a quiet and depressed young woman, the product of her mother's vengeance, sitting alone in her room, typing on her computer. He could sense the vast loneliness that she felt, the loneliness that had led her to desperate acts.

"It wasn't her fault," he said with tears in his eyes. "So much pain, oh God, so much hurt. How could You have expected her to become anything other than what she became?"

He drew closer to the screen to read the confusing and jumbled verse that she was composing. It spoke of sweet death and suicide. He could read no more. Further ahead, yes, further. He had to find that woman he loved. He did his best to bypass the ugliest era of her life, her first marriage, the affairs, the drugs. He had to find the Serena he had come to love. He paged further ahead. At long last he found that special moment. He saw her working in that health food store, just as he entered the door for the first time. He felt as if he were seeing himself through her eyes—loving, kind eyes. It was not a busy day, and they ended up talking for over 20 minutes about vitamins. Vitamins, what an odd topic, yet it had led to so much more.

Another page turned, and he witnessed their first date, so quiet and innocent. He saw their first kiss, their growing love. For the first time, he came to realize that it was he himself and the love of God within him, that had pulled her from the pit of despair. She had arrived. The Serena he loved was here before him.

Time swept him forward as he turned more pages. He relived that wonderful afternoon when he proposed to her by the lake. The unexpected shower had given him the opportunity that he might not otherwise have found the nerve to take.

He became a guest at his own wedding, watching himself and his bride taking their vows. It was so wonderful. He could have passed this way a thousand times and not become bored with the moment. Then he experienced anew the days, weeks, and months that followed. It was such a wonderful time.

Yet amid it all he began to question himself. Might he have done a better job of trying to win his wife into the Kingdom of Heaven? Sure, he had spoken of Jesus and His sacrifice, but had he put his all into it? Did he realize the full gravity of the situation? No, rather than offend his wife, he had tiptoed around the issue. Oh, if only he had known what lay ahead.

Time passed as he gazed unceasingly at the woman he loved— he was lost in his obsession, watching bits and pieces of the last five years of his life. He was unsure how long he tarried here. Certainly it had been days, yet all too soon the last night approached. He could not bear to see the end. The time had come to either withdraw from the book or turn the page back to an earlier era, to relive still more of the good times.

Try as he might, he could do neither. He was inexperienced in this mode of travel through the lifetime of another. He had become so caught up in the experience that he had lost contact with reality, and the ability to close the book or reposition his hand to turn the pages back. Yes, this was what he had sought, an escape from reality; but he hadn't anticipated this turn of events.

"Oh, no!" He cried, as he watched the car approach the icy curve on that dark night. The car began its fateful slide. He looked in horror as the truck careened toward them. There would be no changing the inevitable. The crash, the terrible scream, the end of Serena's earthly existence, all passed before Chris. Surely the book would end, fade to black. But it didn't. The images kept coming, and why not? Death was not the end of existence.

Chris witnessed the moments right after the crash when he realized that he and Serena were dead and they were preparing to begin their personal eternal destiny journeys. He saw himself leading Serena to the portal, toward the light. At that moment he truly believed that they were about to spend eternity together. Surely she would make the journey with him.

Yet at the very threshold of the tunnel his hand slipped through hers. Why hadn't he noticed? Why hadn't he returned for her? The answer was all too simple. He had lost all recollection of her. He was about to become a citizen of Heaven, separated from all of the memories that might get in the way of his happiness. In doing so, he had left her to make the journey through the tunnel alone, and that journey was a turbulent and frightening experience.

From the tunnel to the trial, he followed Serena as she knelt alone before the judgment seat of God. Without Christ as her advocate, the trial that followed could have only one conclusion. To hear his beloved condemned by God was the cruelest blow of all. His heavenly Father had condemned her to an eternity of pain and horror.

Then came Serena's journey into outer darkness, her incarceration within that dreadful cell, and the terrible waiting. He was grateful that the man in the cell across from her had done his best to lend some comfort. He listened to their conversation closely. All he knew of the man across the hall was what he told Serena. He did not seem the sort of person one would associate with a one-way journey to Hell.

When Serena at last curled up on the floor in the corner of her cell, Chris remained. "I'm here, my love," he said, walking over to Serena. He reached out to her but as with the hospital orderly, his hand passed through her like a phantasm.

Chris lingered for the longest time, even after his wife had fallen asleep. He felt so helpless, so useless. Eventually he turned the page forward by willing time to pass more quickly, moving in the only direction he could.

Exactly how much time had passed, he couldn't judge, but he found Serena on her knees clothed in gray rags, her wrists chained behind her back before old slew foot himself.

The devil's appearance surprised Chris at first. Yet thinking back on the Scriptures, he realized that it shouldn't have. After all, satan had the ability to assume a pleasing form. Chris watched in stunned amazement as his brave wife defended herself before the slyest one of them all. She was calm and so very clever. Chris was proud of her. Maybe she could negotiate some sort of truce with this monster. She might find a way to turn his own sin of pride against him; but in the end she only managed to delay her sentence.

With Serena, Chris saw the horrors of Hell on the road to the sea of fire. He was moved by her tenderness and compassion as she encountered one tormented soul after another along the way. Who else would have tried to alleviate some measure of their suffering?

He beheld her moment of temptation, and her small victory, as she refused to pay the devil homage upon the mountaintop. Though satan used all of his charm and cunning, she would not yield. His mind wandered back to Christ's temptation in the wilderness. It too had been a mountaintop experience. Like the Savior, Serena had denied the devil a victory and damaged his pride. How many others would have resisted the devil as she had? Yet all of her courage, all of her compassion, was for naught, for all too soon she reached the frightening precipice, overlooking the vast sea of fire.

There would be no salvation, no mercy, and no second chance for the woman who had captured his heart. Yet even now, Chris noticed, Serena showed courage. In the face of the ultimate terror, she remained in control of herself. Yes she cried, but in that last moment, she refused to give the devil the satisfaction of breaking her spirit. Chris wept as his love stepped silently to the precipice of terror. For a moment she stood like a statue. Then she leaned forward, allowing herself to fall.

Chris looked on in pure horror as his love plunged into the swirling black caldron. He watched as she flailed futilely about in the turbulent oily sea, as her body underwent a ghastly transformation. Her soft skin became brown and scaly as the heat of the scalding sea assaulted it. Within a minute her skin was ravaged with boils, and her long beautiful hair was burned to blackened stubble. Only her screams spoke of the pure agony she was enduring.

"No!" cried Chris, who could bear no more. "Make it stop!"

But it didn't stop, it went on and on, as his love's blood steamed and boiled within her, as flames swept over her again and again. How could she possibly remain alive and conscious through all of that? Why couldn't she just die? How could a merciful God condone such a thing?

In desperation, Chris advanced the page only to encounter the same horror again and again. Of course it would be this way. Serena's torment would be for all eternity. Chris turned the page a hundred times, yet the only thing that changed was the growing darkness of the sky, as the currents swept Serena into the realm of eternal night.

At times, demons flew overhead, taunting the tormented soul below. At other times great storms swept in, bringing rains of fire, brimstone, and acid, as if the scalding sea and the flames that swept across its surface were not enough.

How long had Serena endured this living, feeling nightmare? Chris had no way of knowing. Did time in Hell even pass at the same rate as it did in Heaven? Or did it drag, one minute becoming a millennium? For this question there would be no answer. Yet for now, Chris suffered with her. His was not a physical suffering, but one of mind and spirit. It gnawed at his sanity to see Serena in such absolute torment while he was powerless to prevent it. Within her black book, he had found his own version of Hell.

Suddenly, with the turn of one page there was an unexpected change. Serena was no longer being swept along by the rolling sea, but was climbing the face of a blackened cliff, the waves pounding beneath her. With determination born of desperation, she pulled her desecrated body up the precipitous slopes. Blood oozed from her fingers as she struggled for a handhold, any handhold, amid the sharp rocks. One of her arms appeared to be broken in several places, and yet she continued to climb.

Chris gasped in astonishment. Serena had somehow escaped the sea. Was he just imagining it, inserting his own hopes into this horrible vision, or was this real? He could not be sure of anything he saw at this point. He looked around, searching the blackness for any demons that might end his love's bid for freedom; there were none. Yet, the infernal firmament held another peril. The sky was filled with lightning and the air with the report of thunder; a terrible sulfurous storm was approaching.

"Climb, Serena!" cried Chris, his voice choked with emotion. "You can do it, I know you can."

And she did, pulling herself farther above the heaving sea, but toward what? At this point Chris couldn't tell either, but it appeared to be a very long climb; and at the top of the sharp pinnacle, there could be no respite. Then he saw that Serena found a narrow shelf cut into the rock face, a sanctuary in which she could finally rest. She rolled into it.

She lay there on her back, gasping for breath. She had done it; she had actually done it! Again Chris looked around searching the sky for wandering demons, but there was only darkness. Serena appeared to be safe, at least for the moment. Slowly her body cooled and her incredible recuperative powers reversed a seeming eternity of damage wroth by the flaming sea. The desecrated mass of boils and scars was slowly becoming the beautiful woman Chris adored.

Through it all, Chris was with her, standing on that narrow ledge. If there were only something he could do. What he was witnessing, how long ago did it happen? If only he knew. Time was running out. The winds were rising, as the terrible storm drew ever closer, and with it a new source of agony. He could actually feel the wind, sense the terrible odor of sulfur. "Get up! Get up, Serena," he cried, though he knew in vain. She could not hear him.

The hellish tempest was nearly upon her, when Serena finally rose to her knees, whole once more. She perceived the danger and frantically searched for shelter. To her amazement, she saw a deep cave in the rocks of the cliff.

Chris was hardly able to believe that his beloved had been so fortunate. In the midst of the turmoil, he hadn't noticed the cave.

Through the howling winds and crashing thunder of the vision, Chris heard a new sound—a voice calling his name. He felt a warm hand on his shoulder, as he saw Serena scurry into the cave and safety.

Then the vision of Serena dissolved around him and the sounds faded to silence. He was in the Hall of Records once more and a man robed in white had taken the book from his hand and returned it to its place on the shelf. Chris tried to move, yet was unable. He was surrounded by a cloud of confusion. The robed man leaned over him.

"Easy, my son," he said, slowly lifting Chris to his feet. "You're going to be all right, I promise you. It will only take a short time."

"But I've got to save her," muttered Chris. "Don't you see? She needs my help."

"That may be," came the gentle response, "but for now, you are the one in need of help."

Like everyone in Heaven, Chris knew this man. There were, after all, no strangers here. Yet there was something more to his face. Somehow, he was doubly familiar. Had Chris known him on Earth? He gazed into the kind, brown eyes that met his. This man's face was thin and his forehead a bit large. His hair was jet black, as was his short, pointed beard. Amid his confusion, Chris could discern that this man's name was Johann. No, he couldn't have known him on Earth. He had never known a Johann, of that he was quite certain.

"Come," said Johann, placing his arm around the still reeling young man, "I will take you to my home. There you can regain your strength and composure. Then you can tell me of your quandary."

Chris drew strength from Johann as he was led down the stairway and into the street. He was aware of the brightness, of the multitude around him, yet his mind was still in a fog that would not lift. Though he seemed to be able to walk well enough, reality whirled around him refusing to stand still. From time to time his mind drifted back to that terrible oily sea. The street around him would fade and he would again find himself in that dark realm. Yet, he knew he was walking, walking under his own power. His mysterious benefactor was directing his movements, but he was able to provide the locomotion. Despite Johann's assurances, he wondered if he would ever be whole again.

Time was a blur as the crowded city became a forest of solitude, and then a soft bed. There was comfort, darkness, then the bliss of sleep.

chapter eighteen

CHRIS awoke quite abruptly from his dreamless sleep to a myriad of ticking sounds coming from every quarter. At first he was confused, unsure where he was.

Chris sat up slowly. The window shades behind him were drawn, lending a sort of shadowy atmosphere to the room. He was in a large bedroom with a glossy hardwood floor, reflecting a single shaft of light streaming in from the partially open door far to his right. The beige walls were covered with maps—maps not of terrestrial landforms, but of those forms celestial, of the stars. And then, there were the clocks, clocks of all sizes and descriptions, perfectly synchronized. There was a grandfather clock on the floor along the far wall of the room. Three smaller clocks, with swinging and whirling pendulums beneath bold faces, sat upon a fireplace mantle not far away. There were at least two or three clocks on every wall. The throng of timepieces even included a late 20th century digital clock with red glowing numbers sitting on a small table by the bed, beside an old style oil lamp that burned with a remarkably steady flame.

Chris pondered why one would possess so many timepieces in a place where time was an almost meaningless concept. It was as incongruous as the room itself, which was generally furnished in a style that was most certainly many centuries old.

"Are you feeling better now?" said a voice from near the door.

Chris turned to see a dark form silhouetted against the now wide-open entryway that led to a flower garden. "Yes, I'm better now."

The dark figure moved toward Chris and stepped into the light of the oil lamp by the bed. Chris recognized him as the man from the Hall of Records, Johann. He was dressed in a black, loose-fitting cloak, of a fashion that Chris imagined was centuries old.

"I wanted to thank you for saving me," said Chris, feeling very awkward. "I don't know what would have happened to me if you hadn't come along."

"I assure you, you were never in any real danger. There are few real dangers here. Eventually, you would have contrived a means of escaping the pages of the book by yourself, though it might have taken you some time. I just saved you from additional grief." Johann walked to the bedside and helped the young man to his feet.

"How long was I out," asked Chris, who was surprised that he could stand at all.

"Not long, a few hours, no more," replied Johann, walking back toward the door. He rested his hand upon the wall and gazed out into the flower garden, deep in thought. He turned quite abruptly. His countenance had taken on a quite stern visage.

"What would ever possess you to do such a foolhardy thing as you did? Do you really desire to know what transpires in Hell, to see the fate that our Lord Jesus spared us from? Do you have a passion for tragedy? That is all you will find in a black book—tragedy. There is no happy ending, no moral, just the futility of a life lived in vain."

There was just a trace of anger in his voice. It was the sort of anger a father might express when his son had done something that might well have caused him serious harm. It was an anger ignited from love and concern.

"She didn't live in vain," objected Chris, his voice full of emotion. "She was a kind and gentile woman in life, the kindest and most gentle woman I ever knew."

That comment produced raised eyebrows from Johann. For a moment, he said nothing. He appeared to be intellectually digesting what he had just heard. When he spoke again, his voice held the trace of surprise. "Are you trying to tell me that you knew this woman, this Serena Farnsworth?"

"She was my wife," Chris said in a voice barely above a whisper, "of course I knew her."

"Surely you jest. You could not remember her. She is one of the lost. You've perused the books of the Hall of Records only to discover that you did indeed have a wife during your days upon the Earth. That is how you know of her."

"No," objected Chris. "I told you, I remember her. I remember everything about her, everything. I don't need some image conjured up by a book in the Hall of Records to tell me about my own wife."

Quite abruptly Johann's expression softened to one of deep sympathy. "You are serious, aren't you?"

Chris nodded.

"Oh, I am deeply sorry, my friend. Truly I am. I should not have spoken to you in anger. I had no right. I am still prone to losing my temper from time to time. After three and a half centuries, God is still perfecting me."

It was only now that Chris recognized this man. He was dumbfounded that he hadn't put it all together before this. His thinking patterns were still far too earthly. "I know you!" he gasped. "I've seen your picture in science books. I saw a documentary about you on television a few years ago. You're Professor Johann Kepler, aren't you?"

Johann nodded.

"You're famous! You're the father of modern astronomy!"

Johann couldn't help but chuckle. "Me, an astronomer? The father of modern astronomy? That title should more rightly go to Copernicus, Galileo, or perhaps my dear friend Tycho Brahe. Tycho, now there was an astronomer, an observer without equal. I actually consider myself more of a physicist or mathematician than an astronomer."

"Incredible, that it should be you, of all people that came to my rescue," Chris said, his mind swimming once more.

"Why is it incredible?" asked Johann.

Chris did his best to compose himself. "Well, it's just that you were one of my favorite people out of history. I first heard about your work from watching a TV documentary when I was a kid. It was called "Cosmos." There was an entire episode about you and your contribution to astronomy. I thought at the time how wonderful it would have been to have met you in person. That it was you who came to my rescue is…well, incredible."

Johann smiled slightly. "I just happened to be there, that is all there is to it. History might have been kind to me, recognized me for my accomplishments in life, but there is nothing special about me. I'm just another one of God's loving children. The Father is no respecter of persons. We are all equal in His eyes. I assure you, being Johann Kepler does not give me favored status in the eyes of our gracious heavenly Father. Let us speak no more of this.

"What I am interested in is your experience. You must tell me more. Tell me how it is that you remember your lost wife, while all of those around you are spared the knowledge of those whose names were not written in the Lamb's Book of Life. Come with me into my study, sit with me; tell me all that you remember. There is something of great importance here, I am certain of it. You must tell me every detail."

Every detail? Chris wasn't all that certain that Johann would want to sit through that. Nevertheless, they retreated to the study which was more like a meeting room than a private study room, with its high ceiling, fine crystal chandelier, and large comfortable chairs. On the far wall was a large, old-style chalkboard upon which was scrolled a very complex series of mathematical equations that Chris couldn't even begin to fathom.

"I often entertain friends in this room," said Johann, seeming to read his guest's thoughts. "We talk for hours about the nature of the universe and the greatness of the Creator. We are all of one mind, you see, intent upon understanding the template of creation. It is a daunting task, but we are slowly coming into the light."

Chris gazed once more at the extensive equations upon the board, then back at his host. "Who are these friends?"

"Persons with a desire to understand the handiwork of God," was the reply. "But we can discuss that at a later date; right now I want to hear what you have to say."

For nearly two hours they sat there, Chris doing most of the talking. Chris told Johann a mountain of information, yet Johann kept probing for even greater detail. Some of his inquiries seemed absolutely trivial, yet Chris did not question his motives in asking them. Perhaps, just perhaps, there was some light that this genius from the past could shed on the situation. When the inquiry came to an end, Johann sat back in his chair, his hands folded, deep in thought. It was more than a minute before he spoke.

"I am mystified by your refusal to go to the Father with this enigma," he admitted. "Nothing happens in Heaven, or the universe, for that matter, without His knowledge. He has allowed this thing to transpire for some purpose. Surely, the most reasonable starting point in solving this mystery would be to go to Him."

"I can't," insisted Chris.

"Because you're afraid of what He might say," deduced Johann. "You fear that you would not like His solution. That is not very logical."

"His solution might be for me to forget her, to go blindly on, unaware. Well, I don't want to forget her again," said Chris, growing emotion in his voice. "She doesn't deserve to be forgotten. Someone has to mourn for her."

"Yes, and I suppose that someone has to be you," Johann said.

"Yes, it has to be me," confirmed Chris, tears welling up in his eyes.

"And if you spend your eternity in a perpetual state of mourning…this will accomplish something? Do you think that your wife would want you to do this thing? I find that most unlikely. From what you have told me of her, I think that she would want you to move on, to be happy. Chris, you spoke of your admiration for me; if so, then heed my words now; take council in them. I do not wish to appear cruel or callous, but you must let go of her, for your grief will avail nothing."

Chris didn't respond.

"Or does it go deeper than that?" asked Johann, leaning toward his young protégé. "Do you harbor in your heart some hope of rescuing her?"

Johann's query bordered on an accusation. Again, it was met with complete silence.

"I pray that this is not the case," he continued, "for know that those in Hell are doomed to an eternity of suffering. There is no respite from their agony, no peace, and no hope of rescue. Hell is a prison like none other, rescue is not a possibility."

"Are you so sure?" retorted Chris.

"Yes, I am sure," Johann said, without so much as an instant of hesitation. "Did you ever read Dante's *Divine Comedy*? I speak specifically of the canticle known as the Inferno?"

"Yes, I think I know what you're talking about," replied Chris. "It's the story of a journey through Hell, but I don't see what that has to do with my Serena."

"It has everything to do with her," Johann said. "Do you recall the inscription at the very gates of Hell?"

"Not exactly," replied Chris.

"It said: abandon all hope, ye that enter here."

"You're treating Dante's story like it was Scripture," objected Chris, "it's just a work of fiction."

"In part," Johann said. "Understand this. Dante's vision of Hell is flawed. But I truly believe that he received a divine revelation. Prophetic visions from God didn't end with the Book of Revelation; they continue to this very day. They will continue as long as God's Holy Spirit dwells in the presence of humans. However, like so many who have been granted a glimpse of the dark realm, Dante allowed his own intellect to stand in the way of his understanding. In the end, his vision became a surreal mixture of the mythical Greek underworld, and the real Hell—but that inscription perfectly describes the condition of those sentenced there."

Chris shook his head sadly. "You know, in the short time I've been here, I really haven't thought very much about Hell."

"And that is as it should be," replied Johann. "Most of the inhabitants of Heaven know practically nothing about Hell, nor do they have any desire to learn about it."

"You know, I don't even know where Hell is," admitted Chris, leaning forward. "Some people say that it is in the center of the Earth."

"Indeed they do," confirmed Johann. "Those people have made the mistake of confusing the biblical Hell with the Greek underworld. I suppose that confusion arose from the fact that so many of the Christians of the early church were of Greek heritage. It was only natural for them to relate the biblical concept of Hell with their traditional underworld, the realm of the dead. Eventually that tradition became dogma, and the meaning of the divine Scripture became distorted by humankind's own earthly traditions. They read the Scriptures but chose their own interpretation. It was so during my time, and it remains true even in your era. There are some scriptural references to lucifer falling down into the Earth, but I feel that they are open to interpretation. Indeed, it might be the foretelling of events yet to come."

"OK, so where is Hell?" asked Chris. "What makes it so inescapable? Is it on the far end of the universe or something?"

Johann leaned toward Chris, trying to decide how best to describe so complicated a concept to the uninitiated. "No, Chris, Hell is not at the far end of the universe. I suppose you could say it is beyond the bounds of the universe as you understand space and time. You see, there are no ends of the universe. The natural universe is a closed system. You can't escape it by simply traveling on and on in normal space, for no matter how far or in which direction you travel, you are still within its bounds, you never reach its end."

Chris wasn't so sure he was following Johann's logic. "You're not saying that the universe goes on forever, are you?"

"No, it is finite, but I am telling you that it has no end as you know it. Escape from it is, for all intents and purposes, impossible."

Chris had to think about that one. His mind went back to what little he actually knew about physics and astronomy. His wife had been the family authority in that field of study. "Then are you saying that it's like traveling around the Earth? That it's curved, and if you go far enough, you end up back where you started from?"

"That is essentially correct," replied Johann.

"So, where is Hell?" Chris asked again.

"It is not within the universe at all," said Johann, rising to his feet. He walked to an empty area of the room before turning toward Chris. "Listen and understand; in life, you experienced four dimensions. Three of them were directions, up and down, left and right, backward and forward. The fourth dimension is a temporal one; you call it time. It brought order to your existence on Earth, allowing your experiences of life to occur in a set order. Yet, there are more dimensions than these; and with them, more realities."

He waved his hand through the air before him. Immediately, a three dimensional image took shape, a myriad of colorful spheres floating in midair. One of the spheres was far larger than its neighbors. He pointed toward the large sphere, upon whose black face was imprinted an image of what appeared to be stars.

"The entire physical universe is curved into a sphere along a fifth dimension that you can not perceive. It is the curving along this fifth dimension that closes the universe in upon itself, and gives rise to the phenomenon we all refer to as gravity. Here I portray the entire universe as what appears to be a simple sphere, with stars and galaxies floating upon its surface. From this vantage point, you cannot see all of the dimensions of our universe, at least not at first glance. In life, we humans are not so sophisticated as to perceive so many aspects of the cosmos. For centuries this deficiency kept humanity from discerning the true nature of creation, but I hope you are getting the general picture."

Chris rose to his feet but didn't respond. He was awestruck by the cosmic display before him. He approached it cautiously.

"Yet in your time, physicists are beginning to understand that there are many additional dimensions that they cannot detect directly. Many believe, incorrectly, that these are micro-dimensions, too small to be detected. Yet I tell you that these dimensions are vast, forming entirely different realities beyond the universe you knew. They are the underpinnings of the cosmos."

Johann directed Chris's attention to one of the smaller, brighter spheres. "Heaven, for example, lies upon a set of dimensions beyond the five that bind the natural universe together. It is not physically connected to the universe you knew at all; it is entirely beyond it, but is just as real—as you and I can attest. However, the laws that govern it are somewhat different, something I believe you are coming to realize."

Chris stopped just beyond the cosmic display, scanning the vast collection of spheres carefully. At first the large sphere representing the natural universe looked like a darkened glass globe with what appeared to be faintly glowing white dots engraved on its surface. Yet as he looked still closer, the surface of the sphere took on an additional dimension. The entire vista seemed to grow, becoming a vast three dimensional expanse of galaxies, and within those galaxies, a myriad of stars. Never had he seen such a spectacle. He wasn't just seeing in three dimensions, but four. The vista totally engulfed him. The experience stretched his mind's capability of comprehension. He drew back, and the sphere took on its original appearance.

"Wow!"

Johann smiled slightly, "I thought you might be impressed. You have just set foot into a new realm of consciousness; you've viewed more dimensions of space than you ever could have with your natural senses. God's perspective of the universe is grander still. He sees the entire universe in its true perspective, something we could never do. That is why I wish you would take your problem to Him."

"And Hell, where is it in the scheme of things?" asked Chris, who apparently had not heard or had refused to hear Johann's suggestion.

Johann shook his head in disapproval and pointed toward a small dark sphere, vastly smaller than the star-studded sphere he had previously investigated. "Yes, this is it."

Again, Chris focused his attention on the sphere. It seemed to grow larger as he gazed at it. At first it appeared void, but after a few seconds, a single faint luminary appeared within. It grew larger and brighter, until he could perceive it for what it was, a dim red star, and circling it, a small lonely world—the realm of Hell.

He focused his attention toward the ruddy orb that appeared barren and lifeless, a vast desert frequently interrupted by glowing red seas. In fact, the night hemisphere appeared dominated by a great sea of fire. A chill ran up his spine as, in his mind, he pictured Serena thrashing about amid the terrible ocean of pain. A moment later he turned away. "It's a whole universe unto itself," he gasped. "It's dreadful."

"I believe you are beginning to understand," said Johann. "Do you recall the parable of Lazarus and the rich man?"

Chris nodded. "Yes, I think so. Jesus told that parable. Lazarus was a leper, a poor man who begged for food, just beyond the door of the rich man's house. In life, the rich man hardly noticed him. Yet when they died, Lazarus was made clean and went to Heaven, while the rich man was sentenced to the fires of Hell."

"Basically," Johann said. "Actually, Lazarus was with Father Abraham in Abraham's Bosom, the forerunner of the Heaven you've come to know and love."

"Abraham's Bosom?" queried Chris.

Johann paused, searching for the words to explain the differ-ence. "The people of your century might refer to Abraham's Bosom as Heaven's waiting room. Before the coming of the Lamb of God, man could not step into the presence of the Father as we can today. Man was still unclean. Still, there were those humans who sought to follow God's commands as best they could. They made sacrifices in the temple, gave to the poor, held God in rev-erence. For their sake, God spared them from the wrath of satan and the agonies of Hell. He created a resting place for them, beyond the glory of His presence, beyond the veil of the holy of holies. There they would await the coming of the Messiah, who would, through His perfect sacrifice, grant them entrance into the presence of the Father, into Heaven. This waiting place has long since faded from existence, for it no longer serves a purpose."

Chris nodded. At this point, he wished that he had studied the Bible more thoroughly during his lifetime. There had been so many opportunities. But he never seemed to have the time. He should have made time. If he had, he might not have found him-self in the situation he was in now.

"But allow me to return to the original topic," said Johann. "The parable of Lazarus and the rich man unfolds great wisdom about what is important and not important in life. But that is not my point in bringing it to your attention. I wanted to focus on a single issue of the parable. Not so much its moral but an aspect of Abraham's Bosom and Hell that Jesus brings to light.

"In the parable, the rich man who was sentenced to Hell could see Lazarus afar off. He begged for a favor from Father Abraham. If Lazarus could but put a drop of water upon his tongue, he would be grateful. Yet Abraham told him about a wide gulf that separated them, a gulf that none could cross. To cross the entire length of the known universe would be by far a simpler task, for then you would only be dealing with distance. The gulf between

Abraham's Bosom and Hell or Heaven and Hell, for that matter, is not one only of distance but of totally different dimensions that do not so much as intersect."

Johann directed Chris's attention to the bright sphere that was Heaven. "Here in Heaven, we come and go as we please, covering vast distances in an instant of time. Yet, it is this same barrier spoken of in the parable that prevents us from visiting Earth or traveling to Hell."

"But there's something I don't get," replied Chris. "If Hell and Abraham's Bosom were on two different dimensions of existence, how could the rich man have even seen Lazarus if he was in Hell and Lazarus was in Abraham's Bosom?"

"Good question," Johann said. "I can only assume that it was because these planes of existence were so close to one another. Close in one respect, yet a universe apart in another. Jesus preached to the children of Abraham in the Bosom, allowed those who would follow Him to cross over into Heaven. Then He bridged the narrow gap into Hell itself to preach there. Satan tried to entrap Him as he had all other humans who entered into his realm.

"You see, he was not about to surrender the souls he had held captive for so very long. Indeed he felt confident that he could hold captive the most precious human soul of them all, but he was sadly mistaken. The Bible tells us that Jesus took from satan the keys to Hell and set the captives free, and that is exactly what happened. Within two days, he had emptied Hell of nearly a third of its tormented souls."

"A third," gasped Chris, "why not all of them?"

"It certainly was not a lack of effort or ability on the part of our Lord. Some just wouldn't accept Him. Despite their suffering, they could not comprehend His message. In your century, you have a saying, 'Hell didn't frighten them, and Heaven didn't appeal to them.' Understand, my brother, Heaven is not for every-one, though everyone is free to enter in."

"And they just decided to remain there, in torment?"

"Essentially," Johann said. "Of course, satan tried to sway them too. He promised that if they would stay that he would turn over a new leaf. He promised them that their days of torment were over. He promised that Hell would become a great bastion of sin, where they could practice any manner of vice that pleased them."

"For many, it was an offer too good to pass up, yet it was a lie. The moment that Jesus departed with those who would follow Him, the gates slammed shut once more. Much to their horror, those who remained behind were once more thrown into their chains to resume their eternal torment. They had missed their only opportunity of escape. Since then, the gates of Hell have been closed. Once you are there; there you remain. You are separated from the rest of creation by a dimensional barrier."

"But an angel took my wife there," objected Chris. "I saw it in the book. You can get there from here; this dimensional thing doesn't have to be a problem."

"Yes, but now you're talking about angels, not us. An angel, with a far greater knowledge of celestial and interdimensional mechanics than we humans, might accomplish such a feat. I, how-ever, am probably many centuries from realizing such a level of sophistication. Angels travel back and forth from Heaven to Hell and from Heaven to Earth on a regular basis. That is why the Bible speaks of humans entertaining angels unaware. But where does it speak of men and women on Earth entertaining loved ones who have passed on to their reward in Heaven? It does not because it does not happen."

"Fine," Chris said, "but I'm more concerned with my wife, not the coming and going of angels. There has to be a way out of Hell for her."

Johann stared at Chris incredulously. "You haven't been listening. You hear and comprehend only that which you want to hear. There is no way out of Hell for those sentenced there. Even if you could reach her, snatch her away from that horrible realm, you could not bring her back here."

"Why not?" Chris asked.

"Because the space time that governs that place is tenuous. If you took her beyond that realm, her reality would fade. Her physical form would vanish, and she would dissolve to become nothing more than a disembodied spirit. It is this fact that confines the physical form of satan and his minions to their eternal prison. As it confines them, it confines your wife. You might be able to see what is happening to her, be a witness to her suffering, but, as in the parable, you will be unable to reach out to her."

"I will never accept that, Professor Kepler," said Chris. His voice and expression no longer held that sense of desperation, but of determination. "Look, how many of the souls sentenced to Hell ever manage to escape their torment, even for a short time?"

"None that I have seen," replied Johann, "Their sufferings go on endlessly. There is not so much as a moment's respite." It was only then that he realized he had said too much.

"None that you have seen?" queried Chris, who immediately caught the slip. "This vision you've produced, the one that shows the nature of the whole universe, can give us that close of a view?"

"No, not nearly," came the hesitating reply.

"Then you've looked into the black books too, haven't you?"

The celestial image before them vanished as Johann abruptly turned away. "Yes, I have."

Chris advanced through the now empty space where the image of creation had existed a few seconds earlier. "Why, professor? Was it scientific curiosity, or just a desire to witness tragedy?"

Johann turned around slowly. The tables had been turned on him. Chris almost expected to have kindled Johann's anger with his bold remark. In life, this man had been known to have a temper. Instead, the man's eyes were full of sadness. "You judge me too harshly, young man. That was not my motivation at all. My motivation was to learn all that I could about God's universe. I wished to continue the quest that I had begun in life.

"At first, I consulted God himself. He told me something of His creation, but He did not reveal everything, far from it. He gave me the intellectual tools; the mathematical foundations I needed to uncover most of the universal secrets myself. In doing so, He gave me what I desired—a scientific challenge."

"I first utilized the resources of the Hall of Records to gain insight into my own life and times. You see, like everyone here in Heaven, the memory of my earthly existence was a blur. I had to bring that existence into sharp focus, so I carefully scanned the record of my own life. In doing so, I came to many of the same realizations that you have come to. But what I saw didn't awaken dormant memories; it simply filled in the gaps; and yes, some of them were painful. Yet, this did not deter me. I was convinced that the truth would set me free. That is what the Bible tells us; though I fear I have taken that verse somewhat out of context."

Chris was not about to let the issue come to rest there. "But you didn't stop there, did you? You opened other books in the hall, not just your own."

"Yes," confirmed Johann. "The next book I opened was that of Tycho Brahe. Through Tycho's book, I managed to view myself through someone else's eyes, thereby gaining a new perspective of myself and of him. My search led me to others on Earth, those who were continuing the work that I had started, men such as Isaac Newton and Christian Huygens. I beheld a changing world through the eyes of others. Yet, my interests led me to look at other aspects of creation. I wanted to see and understand more. I scanned the books of significant figures from the Bible....people like King David, Solomon, and Moses. I even beheld the life of our Savior through the eyes of several of the disciples. It was a marvelous experience. I spent more and more of my time within the books of the Hall of Records. It became an all-consuming passion."

Chris nodded. "I can see how it could become almost addicting. In my time, millions of people sit for hours in front of the television. They become 'couch potatoes,' wasting their lives away, preferring soap operas and game shows to the reality of the world around them. They just can't cope."

"Couch potatoes?" asked Johann. "I'm not familiar with that species of potato."

"Never mind," Chris said, "please, go on."

"But still my view of the universe was incomplete. I had to place creation in perspective; I had to view all aspects of it. Up to that point, I had confined my studies to the books of the saints, those who dwelt in Heaven. I had to view the contents of the black books. In doing so, I became a witness to the acts of a monster—satan, the beast of Hell. He is a sadist on the grandest of scales. He revels in the eternal suffering of others. I became quite familiar with his realm."

"And no one ever escapes their fate?" asked Chris.

"No one," confirmed Johann.

"But that's just the thing; before you rescued me, I saw Serena escape the sea of fire and the rain of fire and brimstone. I saw her take shelter in some sort of cave. I know she's safe."

"You don't know that," objected Johann. "She might have found shelter for a season, but eventually, her hiding place would be found." Again there was a pause of total silence. "Though, I do admit that this is curious. Then again, who can say what might have awaited her within that cave? Have you considered that?"

"I don't want to," admitted Chris. "Still, I need to go back to the hall. I have to know what happened to Serena."

"Very well," replied Johann, "but you shall not go there alone, I will accompany you."

"You really don't have to."

"I disagree," Johann said. "If you insist upon delving into the darkness, someone is going to have to teach you how to find your way around. Anyway, I don't think you should go into that book alone."

Chris hesitated before continuing. "Yes, I'd appreciate your help."

"Understand, I think that you are far too hopeful, but I want to see this thing for myself. Perhaps…well, let us see what transpires."

chapter nineteen

"COME out, Serena, I wish to speak to you."

The deep and powerful voice aroused Serena from a light sleep. She knew that voice; it was Abaddon. No doubt he had arrived at some solution to his new dilemma. Perhaps he would throw her back into the fiery black sea in order to be rid of her. After a day without pain, the thought seemed all the more ghastly. Still, what could she do? She rose to her feet and walked to the bars of her cell. She drew back the drapes and saw Abaddon. He scanned his guest's dress with a look of approval.

"Yes, that is much better. I am glad to see that you got out of those rags."

"I was very glad to be rid of them," Serena said. "They were a bit tight, but they came off easy enough. This dress is so much better, thank you."

Abaddon nodded. "I did not mention it when you first arrived. I did not wish to alarm you needlessly, but I was not so certain that you would be able to remove the garb that satan had provided you with."

The comment caught Serena by surprise because that fear had actually visited her momentarily on the previous day. "Why do you say that, sir?"

"It is just another one of satan's tricks from his cruel bag of evil," Abaddon said. "It has been my observation that, as time passes, the tattered garbs satan has you wear become almost a part of you. Eventually it becomes impossible to tell where they end and you humans begin. I once heard satan speak of it. He said that it was a bit like sin; the more you dwell within it, the more it becomes a part of you, the more difficult it becomes to separate yourself from it. In the end, you become one with it, eternally trapped. It is an analogy that satan revels in, that is why he created this garb. He thinks that he is clever."

Serena nodded. "I've noticed that about him."

"Yes, but I also see that Ariadne's clothes fit you rather well; this is good. In a way, you remind me of her. You have the same nose, the same eyes. Perhaps, that is why I showed some measure of mercy to you, why I gave you her cell." There was a long pause and the slight smile dissolved from Abaddon's face. It made Serena nervous. "I truly miss her, even after so many centuries."

Many questions crossed Serena's mind, yet she resisted giving them utterance. She could ill afford to offend her host.

"I've come to a decision," announced Abaddon, unlocking Serena's cell with a wave of his hand, "one that will best serve all concerned. I've decided to spare you, for the time being at least."

Spare her? What did that mean? Serena was apprehensive, yet hopeful.

"The sea of fire will have to surge along its course without you," he continued. "I have been alone here for centuries, totally without companionship. I long for someone to talk to, someone to share my fate, and you intrigue me. Let us share each other's company on a trial basis. If it does not work out; well, there is always the sea of fire. Do we have an agreement?"

It all sounded too good to be true. Serena's immortal heart skipped a beat. "Oh yes, thank you. I agree."

Abaddon's countenance took on a momentary sternness. "Understand this, I am the master of this domain, I make the rules. If you do not understand this from the start, our days together will be indeed brief. You stand to gain much from our relationship; freedom from pain, the gift of knowledge, and the benefit of my charming personality."

That last comment brought a slight smile to Serena's face. It was returned by Abaddon.

"Good," he replied. "Then we do understand each other. Come with me. I will show you your new world."

The two walked out into the corridor. It was more brightly lit now. Serena realized that it was lined with cells, not unlike hers. But the other cells were not as well maintained as hers had been. They were dark and dingy with bare walls, and the floors were littered with rubble. Their presence raised still more questions.

Abaddon and Serena walked down the corridor and into the large room that had been engulfed in shadows the day before. Now, it was brightly illuminated by more than 20 brightly glowing crystals.

The room was nearly square, about 50 feet on a side. The walls were amazingly smooth for an underground chamber hewn from the rock, and 12 white stone columns, evenly spaced around the room, added support to the lofty ceiling. The large columns were like those that would support some ancient Greek temple, finely cut and engraved with symbols that Serena could not decipher.

A large and ornate throne of stone and gold was in the center of the chamber, sitting atop a glistening platform of garnet; while around it, a ring of smaller stone chairs faced the throne. Judging from the layer of dust that covered them, Serena assumed that they had not been used in some time. Around the room were other chairs and couches that were made from some sort of dark wood and covered with red cloth. Near the far corner of the room was a white stone basin about 3 feet across. At its center, four black obsidian figurines in the form of winged angels with trumpets in their hands spouted small streams of clear water that splashed into the basin. Serena slowly turned, taking in the fantastic scene.

"Your new home," Abaddon said. There was the slightest smile on his face, a smile that spoke of his pride in this place. "This is, without a doubt, the very best accommodations Hell has to offer. You will have the freedom of my realm."

"It's wonderful," gasped Serena. "Thank you."

Abaddon nodded. "I assume you can sew."

"Yes," confirmed Serena.

"Then, I shall see about providing you with the materials to make still more clothing for yourself, perhaps, attire more to your liking."

"That would be wonderful," Serena said. "I can't even begin to thank you for your kindness."

"It is quite all right," replied Abaddon, whose smile grew even larger. "You will add an air of beauty to my humble home."

"You shall continue to sleep within your cell. Your cell door will be left unlocked most of the time. You will be able to come and go as you please. You are not a prisoner here, I assure you. However, when I am gone, it will be necessary to lock you within your cell. It is for your own protection. I do not wish for you to travel beyond this place unescorted, it would be unsafe. I am taking a risk in keeping you here at all, a very large risk. As I told you before, it is forbidden for any of us to offer comfort or assistance to your kind in escaping their place of eternal torment."

"But you've done it before," Serena said. "Who were they, these people who lived with you?"

Abaddon scowled. "For a guest, you ask many personal questions." A moment later his countenance softened. "No, you have the right to know. There shall be no secrets between us. Yes, once that hallway was filled with your kind, though it was many centuries ago. Those humans that shared this home with me were not servants, slaves, or even pets, they were my family."

That comment caught Serena by surprise. "Your family? I don't understand."

"You will. Come," said Abaddon, leading Serena toward a pair of large cushioned chairs near the corner. Serena was surprised to feel how soft the dark blue chair was. Abaddon's wings folded around the other chair as he sat down by her side.

"When you first came here, you asked me why there might be animosity between satan and myself. I declined to answer your question at that time. I will answer it now. You were right; satan and I are not on the friendliest of terms, far from it. A most uneasy truce indeed exists between us. I listened well to what satan told you on the day you were dragged before him; he never changes. He is a liar, but he is very cleaver about how he does it. How could he be anything else? He has had so many centuries of practice.

"He mixes lies with the truth in order to mask them, but they are nonetheless lies. In very fact, I believe that many of his followers, though they were there in the beginning and should know better, have actually come to believe this prince of lies. Thus is his influence over them. They have lost any semblance of a will of their own. They once had one, yet now they do his bidding, blind followers of a blind guide."

Serena worded her next comment as carefully as possible. "Yesterday you told me that you didn't fall with lucifer and his angels; that you fought against them, but you wouldn't tell me more. I'd like to know all about you. As far as I'm concerned, you're a knight in shining armor."

That comment elicited a hearty good-natured laugh from Abaddon. "A knight in shining armor, am I? If you knew me better, I wonder if you would still feel that way. But let me start from the beginning, that you might better understand what angels truly are. We are sons of God, created in a form much like His. We were the first born, created tens of thousands of years before He brought man into being. When God created the angels, He created most of them to serve one of three tasks. Some were messengers, others warriors, while others were singers, ministering directly unto God.

"The messengers were what you and your society might term data gatherers. In addition to delivering messages to the far ends of the cosmos, they were agents that transferred, processed, and disseminated the information necessary to keep the hierarchy of Heaven functioning. They were created to be fast and efficient, with an almost uncanny ability of recall. Their leader was the archangel Gabriel."

Serena was surprised. "Are you saying that God needed them to spy for Him? I thought that God knew everything about everyone."

Abaddon smiled at Serena's reply. "That is an interesting question, young one, a question for which I do not have an answer. Even after all of these centuries, God is still an enigma to me. I have spoken to Him countless times; I've marveled at His wisdom, yet been perplexed by His actions. God is ancient beyond all reckoning. His universe existed long before He created the first angel, and He existed long before the dawn of creation. For that matter, I am not even certain why He created us. The universe seemed to have functioned for an eternity without our intervention. Some say that God created us out of His own need for companionship. Others say we were created to help guide and safeguard the human race. Perhaps both are true, perhaps neither. I am just not certain. There are certain things that God would not speak of. Who can truly know the mind of God?"

Serena couldn't argue with that. "But what class of angel were you?"

"I was a warrior," Abaddon said, then paused, sensing the next question in this young human's mind. "I know, I know; if God is all powerful, why would He need warriors? Again, I am uncertain. Nonetheless, He created us, and I was one of the best. I was set in charge of an entire legion of angels. I answered directly to Michael himself and had twelve lieutenants under my command."

"But allow me to speak of the third class of angels, for herein lay the seeds of disunity. They were those who surrounded the thrown of God, singing praises unto the Father of the universe. Lucifer, who now calls himself satan, led them. No other angels had closer access to God than these. They formed an administrative council of sorts, directing the activities of the other angelic classes. Yet, as time passed, they began to think of themselves as being better than the rest of us. As your people might say, they were becoming legends in their own minds, and none of them thought more highly of himself than lucifer."

"He told you at your sentencing that he rebelled against God over the issue of God's love for man, but I tell you, that is only partially true. Lucifer used man as an excuse, as a rallying point; he had delusions of grandeur long before God proclaimed that He would create your kind. Lucifer actually thought that he could lead a successful revolt against the Father, as he stirred up discontent among the angels under his command. He convinced them that Michael's and Gabriel's angels would follow them if only he made the first move, so he did."

"But they didn't follow him," deduced Serena.

"No, they didn't," confirmed Abaddon. "They remained faithful to their heavenly Father and took up arms against lucifer and his followers. Strange, isn't it? Lucifer's cast was supposed to have possessed the most highly developed minds of all of the angels, yet it was they who perpetrated the most irrational act in the history of the cosmos. Supposedly, they had their revolt planned perfectly, the ultimate coup d'état. I was among those who battled against lucifer and his angels on that day. Lucifer and his angels had the element of surprise and careful preparation on their side. We were totally unprepared for such an eventuality."

"What kind of a battle was it?" asked Serena. "Was it a battle of swords?"

That comment brought Abaddon to outright laughter. "No, child, it was not a battle with swords, at least not the kind of swords that you are familiar with. All too often, you humans picture warring angels with shields in hand, broad sword raised high, but it is not like that at all. Our weapons may take the appearance of classical human weapons, but they are far more than a sharp implement of hardened steel. I doubt that you could comprehend the nature of the weapons used in the battles we fight."

"To put it simply, the war against satan and his minions was a battle of angelic wills, wills that commanded vast forces. It was a battle that was raged on the ground, in the air, and into realms that you could not even comprehend. It was a battle like none other, utilizing forces that make the nuclear weapons of your age look like toys. Amid the sound of thunder, the blinding brilliance of the lightning, it raged on for days, trying all of us that fought it. None could be slain in the battle, for we are immortal. Yet our immortality did not mean that the battle would go on indefinitely. We are capable of feeling heat, pain, and exhaustion. What gave the victory to us was our endurance, our numbers, and I would like to think, the blessings of the Father."

"Then God didn't take part in the battle personally?"

"Not in the battle itself," confirmed Abaddon. "At some level, I'm certain that He was involved, but not in the way you might think. Understand; God manifests Himself as a physical and a spiritual presence. You saw His physical presence at your sentencing, but you can also feel His spiritual presence. During the days of the battle, His physical presence vanished from our midst. In very fact, it is my understanding that lucifer and his allies were convinced that they could hold the physical presence of God captive, perhaps use it as a bargaining chip. Imagine, trying to hold God hostage. Such was their pride and their foolishness."

Serena seemed most puzzled. "But couldn't God have simply waved His hand and defeated satan and his angels?"

Abaddon leaned back as if to ponder Serena's question. "Perhaps, but I now believe that this battle was part of His divine plan. I have become convinced that God intended to test His angels, to see who would be faithful to Him in the time of crisis. God's thinking is so far above ours. He seemed so close when I talked to Him, so understanding, so loving. It is hard to fathom just how powerful He really is. I loved Him too, I guess I still do. I was not going to betray the Father on that day. I would fight for Him, for however long it would take to defeat His enemies, and I know He gave us strength in those trying times."

"I encouraged the legion under my command to be true to the Father, to fight for His cause to the end of their endurance and beyond. I can tell you that during the battle there were times when my strength and those around me was tried to nearly its limits. There were times when I was very uncertain of the battle's outcome, yet I and hundreds of millions of other angels endured. I earned a name during that struggle. I became known as the Destroyer."

Serena shuddered slightly at the name given this strange fallen angel. Would the Destroyer continue to show mercy upon her, or would he eventually discard her into the sea of fire?

"In the end, lucifer and his minions were exhausted, unable to continue the fight. We pushed them back, confined them, and in the end, brought them to their knees. Then we awaited God's judgment. I was convinced that God would bring an end to the very existence of the rebellious angels, yet His love and compassion held sway over the moment. Rather than destroy them, He exiled them to this place, a realm beyond His creation, never to return. Their punishment was to dwell beyond His presence. Here they would spend eternity."

"But look at this place," Serena said. "It is its own punishment. To be sentenced to a barren, burned out cinder such as this one might be worse than blinking out of existence."

"Perhaps, but it is my understanding that this place was never a paradise; but in the beginning it was not the world you see today. God was not so unmerciful. Satan and his followers could have molded this world into something better; but instead, they reduced it to a savage wasteland. He created the Hell you have experienced out of his own insane hatred for humanity, to exact some vengeance on God's most prized creation."

He knew one day that there would be humans who, in their ignorance, would rebel against the Father as he had. He prepared this place for that day. It became his single passion, his very reason for existence, and he convinced his followers to labor with him. With so many capable and willing hands and hearts at his disposal, it was accomplished in a relatively short span of years. Indeed, he continues to make certain improvements. Now he views himself as the lord of this realm, the architect of this twisted creation, master of all that he surveys; yet he is mistaken. He is just another prisoner in this accursed place. He retains the illusion of power by commanding his legions, by subjecting the humans of Hell to constant agony. He is a pathetic creature."

Serena leaned forward slightly, still not knowing what to make of this strange being. Was he an ally, a friend, or just a disgruntled demon in need of sympathy? "But how did you end up here?"

Abaddon continued, his tone still calm and deliberate. "It was many centuries, indeed, over a thousand years after the fall of satan and his minions that I made my fatal mistake. I had, on occasion, made my way to Earth to see God's most prized creation, and I liked what I saw. Humans, especially human females, were fascinating to watch. To see them learn and develop, to discover the world around them, was a unique experience. I was delighted when the Father asked me and others to journey to Earth to safeguard humanity. I took a form not unlike that of a human male, that I might observe these fascinating beings more readily, and as situations dictated, guide them. Indeed, angels of God do it to this day."

"Guardian angels? They actually exist?" Serena asked.

"Of course they do," was the reply. "There are more of us in your world than you could possibly imagine. There are millions. Unfortunately, I grew too close to the problem, and I was not alone. Many angels in that day erred as I did. We interfered in ways that had been forbidden by the Father. We rendered unto humankind certain knowledge. Knowledge of how to forge certain metals, of creating more effective plows and weapons, and of utilizing natural herbs to create simple potions to treat illness; all of these things we did."

"But that doesn't sound so bad," objected Serena. "So you saw suffering and ignorance and tried to alleviate it. Certainly God didn't object to that."

"But it didn't end there," Abaddon said. "In taking on a human form, we also became subject to human passions. The daughters of man were fine indeed, objects of beauty crafted by the Father, and we decided to take them unto ourselves, to become even more human. Need I elaborate?"

Serena was stunned by this revelation. "You mean you had sex with them?"

"More than that, we gave them children, children who were more than human. Your society might say that they were genetically engineered. We sought to hurry along the development of humankind, introduce into their primitive culture a number of truly superior specimens, men of valor who would grow to lead the human race into a golden age. The legends of ancient history echo their names—Hercules, Imhotep, and Perseus still stir the imagination. However, in doing this thing, we exceeded our mandate from God."

Serena sat in stunned amazement. Why wasn't this story in the Bible? Then she realized that it was, but briefly. Didn't the Book of Genesis mention the sons of God becoming involved with the daughters of men? Strange that she should recall that vague reference now.

"We weren't prepared for the full consequences of our actions," continued Abaddon. "We thought that we had the art of creation mastered, that we could engineer a superior human. How foolish, how arrogant we were. We failed to realize that our essence was not truly compatible with that of humankind. In trying to create a superior human, we created a race of inhuman monsters bent upon conquest. Some were of titanic proportions. Now, matters were worse. Still, God might have forgiven us for such an error in judgment. After all, in some respects, our hearts were in the right place; but we didn't stop there."

When things started to go badly, when the children we had fathered started to go astray, we took desperate measures. Some of us revealed ourselves to humanity, not as servants of the Father, but as deities in our own right. We proclaimed ourselves to be gods or sons of God, hoping to strike fear and reverence in the hearts of our wayward children. The stories of Zeus, Amon Ra, and Marduk are all based upon the exploits of angels among humanity. But this made matters even worse. We reveled in the role we had created for ourselves, accepting the adoration of humanity. We quickly became lost in the fantasy, becoming false gods, and this is what the Father would not permit. In our own way, we had subverted God. Not as openly as lucifer and his angels, but just as deliberately."

"Oh my god," gasped Serena, before she was able to stop herself. She was surprised to find that her hasty comment had not affected Abaddon in the least.

"Like lucifer and his followers before us, we too were sentenced to outer darkness. Needless to say, there was no love lost between satan and his followers and ourselves. We lived in a state of uneasy peace with these original inhabitants of Hell. There were those among them who felt that they had a score to settle with me and the others. We were always on the move, attempting to avoid confrontations with satan's minions, beings that we had helped condemn to this place."

"I tried to place as much distance between myself and satan as I could. You might say that he and I go way back. The divisions between us are deep. I eventually made my home in this remote region, far from satan's infernal palace. At the time, satan and his minions hadn't quite transformed Hell into the obscenity that it is today. I roamed far and wide across this globe, managed to rescue some of the last plant and animal life that still struggled for survival on this barren rock. The small flower in your room is one of its descendants. You see, I loved your green Earth. I wanted to preserve something that might remind me of its beauty." Abaddon rose to his feet and extended his hand to Serena. "Come, walk with me."

Serena accepted his hand and walked with the dark angel toward another hewn passageway along the far wall. The passageway followed a twisting course through the depths of the island. There was an increasing odor of moisture, and more than that, an air of life. Ahead Serena witnessed a growing illumination until they emerged into another cavern room, a room whose size staggered the imagination. Its ceiling was covered with brightly glowing crystals, giving the vast chamber an illumination that rivaled true daylight. What Serena saw made her gasp.

The cavern was alive with greenery—grass, flowers, even small trees. Vines with large glossy emerald leaves grew up the cavern walls and along natural rock pillars that supported the lofty, crystaled ceiling, their source of life. At the center of the cavern, a pool of water, green with algae and lily pads glistened in the glow of the crystalline light. Never had she imagined seeing such a display of life again. Tears of joy came to her eyes as she scanned the green vastness.

Abaddon stretched out his hand to the microcosm of life. "So little remained of the chain of life of this world by the time I arrived. I searched far and wide, salvaged what I could, nurtured it, preserved it in this place. I saved many species from certain extinction. And I had help in this task, the help of human hands. Come."

The two continued through the subterranean oasis of life. Here and there, Serena caught a glimpse of animal life that Abaddon had managed to preserve—a caterpillar scurried along a leaf, a small lizard watched from the shadows, even a yellow-winged butterfly flittered between orange and gold flowers. How precious each one seemed now.

"This was a natural cavern when I first found it," said Abaddon. "It is the very reason I settled here. It was lifeless, and yet it offered protection from the elements that were growing ever more hostile to life. It was isolated, foreboding, and far from the center of satan's power. It was the perfect place to establish this preserve, as the rains were growing more acidic, extinguishing the last traces of life upon this rock. It is so much easier to destroy than to create, wouldn't you agree?"

Serena nodded her head. Her heart was too full of emotion to allow utterance. What was welling up within her? Did she recall it from her days on the green Earth? Yes, it was joy, an emotion all but forgotten in the dark pits of Hell. It was the joy she had felt witnessing the rising of the sun and strolling through a cool dew-laden forest. It all came back to her in this place. She understood why Abaddon had sought to preserve it.

"Life is the most precious thing that the universe has to offer," continued the dark angel, gazing at his small green world. "It is only in this age that humankind is beginning to understand just how rare life is in the cosmos. For that reason, I brought the fading spark of life in here, where it could be preserved and nurtured."

"It's a miracle!" Serena said joyfully.

Abaddon shook his head sadly, and placed a gentle arm around her. "A miracle? Perhaps it is. It is the last good deed of a proud fallen angel. Oh, Serena, if only I had a second chance, an opportunity to undo some of the crimes I have committed against God and humans; but it is far too late now. Both of us have missed our last opportunity at redemption. Yet, we still dream of it, don't we? The hearts of all of satan's minions are cold and dead. And yet ours still beat. That makes us a threat."

They moved on. Near the center of the oasis was a small vegetable garden, its green flora in neat orderly rows. Serena scanned the array of plant life carefully. Some of the species looked familiar.

Abaddon directed Serena's attention to other parts of the garden. "My own version of the earthly tomato, carrot, lettuce, and onion. It took a long time for me to develop them. After all, I lack the skills of the Father in such matters. But I am getting better at it. I developed them from the local flora. However, I think that you will find their taste remarkably similar to the real thing. They are yours to eat and cultivate. It will give you something meaningful to do here. It will take your mind away from the loss of the Father's Kingdom, at least for a time. To till the soil in the depths of a cave, to be the caretaker of the last bastion of life on this forgotten world, this shall be your fate. Perhaps, it is not such a terrible fate. It is certainly preferable to the one you were facing a few days ago."

Serena was overwhelmed by a revelation. What had happened to her in the past day could be nothing less than divine providence. Perhaps God was still watching over her, even here. Somehow she had been given a new life. Among the billions of suffering souls, she had found rest.

"At one time, this garden was considerably larger, tilled by five of your kind. They were my family."

"I'm afraid I still don't understand," admitted Serena.

"It is not so complicated," Abaddon said. "I thought you would have figured it out by now. After I arrived here and established this place, I vowed to find the humans I had seduced and misled, at least some of them. I wanted to save them from satan's wrath. It was a daunting task, and it took a very long time, but I eventually found five of them, even the one with whom I shared an intimate relationship on Earth, my wife.

Now she knew me for what I truly was, a deceiver; a false god who had relegated her to the most terrible fate imaginable. I had much to answer for—much to ask for forgiveness for. She forgave me. Imagine that, even after all that I had done. Within her lived a spark of the Father's love. I took her and the others away from their torments, tried to shield them from the horrors of this place, and for a time, many years, I did just that. They lived with me here. I was a guardian angel once again. I believe that I did it for myself as much as I did it for them, to ease my own guilt. We became a self-sufficient community, caring for one another, a family."

Abaddon turned away quite abruptly. He leaned against a small tree nearby and said nothing for more than a minute.

"Abaddon?" said Serena, walking toward the distraught angel. She was shocked when he turned with tears in his eyes.

"We lived here for many years. Then satan discovered what I had done. He was enraged. With a score of his minions he burst into my domain, my oasis. He vowed to take my family away, sentence them to an even more awful fate than before. I stood in his way. I could do nothing less. I was created to be a warrior, far stronger than one of his kind—even stronger than he. I fought to defend my family, fought with all of my strength. My human family fought by my side, fought for their very eternity. For a brief time we held them at bay. But there were too many of them."

"In the end, his minions took them away. Then they turned to me. Satan spoke of exacting his revenge upon the destroyer. I will not go into the details of what they put me through in the months that followed. Suffice it to say that I can, in some measure, understand the suffering of humans in this place. When it was done, I was warned to never again cheat satan, to never again rescue one of the lost, and I didn't—until now. That is why I was so suspicious of you when you arrived here. I thought that satan had sent you to bait me into a trap he had prepared for me. I realize now that is not the case."

Serena placed her hand on the dark angel's shoulder, "I can't believe that all that has happened to us is an accident...can you?"

Abaddon looked into Serena's eyes. "I cannot be certain. Perhaps my heart has become too hardened to sense the presence of the Father's hand. Nonetheless, my mind is made up; you shall dwell with me. If we are discovered, understand, I will say that you are but a play thing to me, the subject of my amusement. Your life free of pain will be at an end."

"I understand," Serena said. "I'll do everything I can to make your story believable if that ever happens." Serena paused for a moment. "How often do you have visitors? I mean, how often does satan check up on you?"

"Not often anymore," Abaddon said. "It has been over a hundred years. I leave him alone, he leaves me alone."

"Then we might be OK."

"Perhaps, but satan took an interest in you during your sentencing," continued Abaddon. "The day might arrive when you come to his remembrance once more. He might seek you out to see how poorly you have fared. I shall endeavor to shield you from his sight, yet if he does search for you, he will surely come here. I hope that day never comes."

Serena nodded. She was, after all, not out of the woods yet. She was still in satan's domain, and this might well be only a temporary reprieve.

The two walked back to the main chamber where they sat in each other's company and talked. Serena spoke of her life on Earth for hours, of her hopes and dreams. Abaddon was interested in all that she had to say. For the first time in centuries, he had someone to talk with; he couldn't have been happier. Yet more importantly, he had someone to protect, someone who depended on him. No, he wouldn't allow satan to take her back, regardless of what he had told Serena openly, he would be her guardian angel from this day forward.

chapter twenty

CHRIS and Johann stepped from the front door of his mansion and into a small meadow of yellow flowers mixed between large blue-gray boulders. The meadow was surrounded by a tall and imposing forest of large, stately conifers. It was late in the day, and the sun had already dropped below the boughs of the great stand of trees to their left. A cool breeze blew from the forest, carrying with it the wonderful and very unmistakable odor of pine.

"I've always enjoyed my seclusion," Johann said. "It's not that I don't like people, but I like my space. It gives me time to think, to contemplate creation."

Chris nodded, gazing at the sylvan setting. He looked back at Johann's house. He really hadn't noticed anything about it when they had arrived. Actually, he hadn't recalled the arrival at all. Kepler's house reminded him of the sort of quaint architecture he had seen in travel shows about central Europe and the Alps. The home was of stout wooden construction, painted white, with a very steep roof and a stone chimney. The large ornate windows had wooden shutters that could be closed against the winds of winter or opened to the summer breezes. Chris wondered if this region of Heaven had four definite seasons.

"We had best be on our way," Johann said. "We have much to accomplish today."

The portal appeared rather abruptly before them and Chris followed Johann into it. They emerged at the very gates of Zion. Here, of course, it wasn't early evening, but midday, as it always was.

"The city that never sleeps," Chris thought, as the two hurried through the tall gates and into the city itself. He was both nervous and in a hurry. Would that they might have materialized directly in front of the Hall of Records itself, but that was not possible. Everyone had to enter the city on foot.

Under normal conditions, the journey through the city might have passed quickly, but not on this occasion. Time seemed to drag, and the journey to the Hall of Records seemed a very long one indeed. Johann wasn't one for chit chat along the way either. He seemed deep in thought, and nothing around him seemed to disturb his quiet contemplation.

Chris was hesitant to interrupt him. Perhaps his mind was already working on a plan that could save the day. Yet Chris's mind was still awash in emotion. He had so many more questions.

"How could Serena survive in the terrible heat of the sea of fire? I don't understand. I was a health professional on Earth and have a pretty good understanding of the chemical and biological processes of life. Her blood must have been boiling in that horrible sea."

Johann glanced briefly at his companion. "That sea of fire would elevate her blood somewhat beyond the boiling point of water, I'd expect."

"OK, Then how could the hemoglobin in her blood carry oxygen at that temperature? Why wouldn't her cells simply explode? She should be at least unconscious. Why does she just go on suffering?"

"You have much to learn about Heaven and Hell, my young friend," Johann said, his gaze focused on the road ahead. "Your perception of reality is jaded by your lifetime of experiences on Earth and your own preconceived notion of reality. So it was in my time. In your era, the work of physicists like Einstein, Bohr, and Schroedinger have expanded those horizons somewhat; but the people of your time are still very shortsighted. The physical laws that govern Heaven and Hell are very different from those that hold sway in your world." Johann paused for a moment. He really hadn't wanted to become involved in this discussion right now. "I suppose you have seen the artisans that dwell here in the city, those who create physical works of art by simply envisioning them within their mind."

"Yes," Chris said.

"Surely, no such thing could be accomplished on Earth, would you not agree? It would violate several laws of physics or require vast amounts of focused energy to accomplish. Yet, with practice, these artisans make it look easy—how?"

Chris was stumped. He had seen these things done often. It had become almost commonplace to his heavenly experience. He'd come to accept it as a gift from God. "Are they using God's own power to somehow manipulate matter, transmute it into new forms?"

"You are thinking in far too complex terms," replied Johann. "Suppose I were to tell you that the reality you perceive here is shaped by God Himself. Both Heaven and Hell are spiritual realms, quite unlike the universe with which you are familiar."

Chris looked around, felt the gentle breeze, saw the bright reflections from polished stone and glass, heard the sounds of Zion. "Spiritual realms? But it all seems so real. Are you telling me that all this around us isn't real…that it's some sort of mass hallucination?"

"No, of course not," Johann said. "But it's not the sort of reality you knew on Earth either. Understand, matter on Earth seemed solid. You could touch it, taste it, and feel comforted by its presence. Yet surely you realize that what you perceived as solid objects were mostly composed of empty space. Only one hundredth of one percent of anything was truly solid, the overall solidity of matter was an illusion, created by the fields of electrical force that surrounded protons and electrons.

"Yet to us it was no phantasm, no illusion, it was real because we all perceived it to be real. That is the true test of reality—perception. We are all spiritual beings here in Heaven. The Spirit of God gives us form and substance. God fashioned Heaven to take on a form similar to the Earth we left behind. He did this because He cares for us. Things may seem in many ways to be as they were on Earth. Yet I assure you, they are not. This in no way makes them less real, only different.

"This world is just as real as the one you left behind. Unlike Earth, real eternities exist in this place, bringing with them blessings and tragedies we couldn't have imagined in life. Satan understands this well. He uses this very fact to subject those humans in his realm to indescribable torment, even as God uses it to bless His children.

"In this environment, we shall grow and mature. In time, we shall evolve beyond those earthly needs we still cling to, to become more like the angels. In fact, we shall far exceed them. Indeed, many of the saints here in Heaven are already well along the path to becoming true spiritual beings, leaving the things of Earth behind."

"Then all that is happening to Serena is in her mind?" deduced Chris.

"In her *perception*," corrected Johann. "There is a difference. It is a part of her current reality. Even if she did realize that her world is a spiritual one, not like the reality of the physical universe, it would do her no good. Chris, as I told you, Hell is a reality, not an illusion. I have much to teach you about spiritual realities, but right now is not the time."

Chris spent several minutes in silence trying to digest this incredible epiphany that Kepler had related to him; it was shocking, challenging his very perception of reality. He wasn't all that certain that he understood it. Indeed, he wasn't all that certain that he wanted to. In the end, his thoughts were interrupted by a new source.

"Professor Kepler?" came a voice from behind them.

Chris and Johann stopped in midstride and turned to see a young man, perhaps 16 or 17 years of age, wearing a white robe. His deep blue eyes sparkled and his smile brimmed from ear to ear.

"Hello, David," said Johann, "I didn't see you."

"I figured you hadn't," said the youth, walking up to the two. "I was going to drop over to see you tomorrow, but now I guess I won't have to. What brings you to Zion, sir? Is it research?"

Johann smiled slightly. "Yes, David, it is. We will be exploring a book in search of information." Johann turned to Chris. "Oh yes, Chris Davis, this is David Bonner, one of my students."

"Pleased to meet you, sir," said David, shaking Chris's hand.

Chris wondered if he had just shaken David's hand or if he only thought that he had. He readjusted his thinking. He turned to Johann. "Students? You teach students here in Heaven?"

"A few," replied Johann. "David sought me out on his own about four years ago. Like you, he had read about me in his science book back on Earth."

"I wanted to learn about the universe," said David, still smiling. "I wanted to understand the miracle of creation, quantum theory, hyper-dimensional physics, that sort of thing."

"Hyper-dimensional physics?" Chris repeated, not quite certain of the meaning.

"Yes, that's right, a variation on super-string theory," confirmed the youth. "I went straight to the Father and talked to Him about it. He told me quite a lot, but then instructed me to seek out Professor Kepler."

"Wow," said Chris, turning to Johann, "that must be the ultimate compliment…God Himself referring a student to you. You can't get a better reference than that."

"Actually, the Father has directed quite a number of students to me over the years. I told you about the group that meets regularly with me to discuss the nature of the universe. Quite a number of them came to me by this same route. I was confused at first. Why would God send these young aspiring physicists to me? Then I understood. It was my love for teaching and my desire to search for the truth that the Father saw. He sent them to me as much for my benefit as theirs. Together we seek the truth, the ultimate truth."

"Professor Kepler is the best science teacher I ever had," said David. "I've learned so much from him, things I'd never have learned at the academy."

"What was it you wanted to see me about, David?" asked Johann. His voice was patient, but he clearly wanted to continue this new quest.

"Well, sir, I'm sort of stuck. It has to do with that partial differential equation you showed me how to solve. It was the one used in solving the shape of the intersection point of two separate hypothetical five dimensional constructs, assuming both are perfectly hyper-spherical. I know the intersection point should come out as a four dimensional hyper-sphere, but I can't make the math work. I'm setting something up wrong."

"Intersection region," corrected Johann, "only lines and segments have intersection points."

"Oh yes, intersection region," replied David, whose face flushed slightly. He hesitated. "I get the feeling that this isn't such a good time to discuss this topic, is it?"

"Well, not the best," replied Johann.

"You're involved in something really important right now—something incredible."

"Yes, we are," Johann said.

"You're going the Hall of Records?" asked David.

"Yes."

"Please, I'd like to come along, if it would be OK. Maybe I can help."

By now, Chris was well past the point of being amazed. Perhaps he was imagining it all, but this young man seemed perceptive almost beyond the point of all reason. "Why do you think you can help?"

"I'm not sure," admitted David. "Sometimes I just have feelings about things."

Chris wasn't all that certain that he wanted someone else involved in his quest, especially one as young as David. How could he help?

Johann looked at David, then toward Chris, then back at David again. "David, this is a rather personal matter that Chris and I are attending to. It is research, true, but there is a bit more to it than that. You might find it very disturbing."

"I'd still like to come along," repeated David.

"It's OK, Johann, as far as I'm concerned, David can come along with us. Maybe he can help." Chris wasn't certain as to why he had said that—a hunch?

"Great!" David said.

Without further delay the three continued on.

"How old are you, David?" asked Chris.

"I'll be eighteen next month," he replied.

Chris tried to word his next question carefully, "You were kind of young when you…well…came here, weren't you?"

"You mean when I died," David said. "It's OK. I don't mind using that word. I died back on September eleventh of 2001."

A chill ran up Chris's spine. "Nine, one, one?"

"That's right," confirmed David. "I understand that's what people came to call it. I was only twelve at the time. I was attending an academy for gifted students in New York City. I was involved in what they called a shadow program. You see, my mom worked as a stockbroker for a brokerage firm on the eighty-ninth floor of the World Trade Center Building, Tower One. On that morning, I went to work with her. My assignment was to watch what she did during the course of a day and then do a report on it for my social studies class."

"Oh no!" Chris said.

"Yea. Terrorists crashed a plane into the tower. Both my mom and I were killed pretty quickly. Next thing I knew, we were walking hand in hand through this tunnel toward the brightest light I had ever seen. Or was it floating or flying? …I don't know how to describe it, exactly. We were together.

"Anyway, when we got here, we realized that the light was Jesus. He was more wonderful than I could ever have imagined. We were going to our judgment. God was going to judge us. Both my mom and I had already placed our lives in the hand of Jesus years before. I had when I was seven, and she had nearly twenty years before that. Jesus said that we would stand before God together. That wasn't usually the way it was done, but I got the feeling that He didn't want to separate us.

"He told us that we had nothing to be afraid of, that we were going to meet our Father, our Creator. It was all kind of exciting.

As we stood before God, we both saw a vision of our lives, minus the bad parts, of course. Jesus had already removed those from the record. Well, I guess you know the rest."

Chris smiled. "Yes, I think so."

"My mom and I have a mansion together, right here in the city itself. It is so very cool. Much better than the condo we had in Manhattan. It has hot and cold running water, electric lights, and a totally awesome hot tub. God knew that we liked living in the city. But I'm interested in you, tell me about you. It's something about you that this whole trip, this whole research expedition, is about, right?"

Like so many young people, David didn't mince words. Chris would do the same. He gave David the short version of the story he had told Johann, but he did his best to present all the facts, even the ones that hurt. David seemed very sympathetic, but at the same time, Chris could tell that the young man looked at this journey as an adventure. He couldn't really blame him for that.

They had almost reached the great hall when Johann finally spoke again.

"You said that satan sentenced her to the sea of fire."

"Yes," replied Chris, surprised after nearly an hour of complete silence.

"You are sure that it was the sea of fire."

"I'm absolutely sure. I saw it in the vision."

"Curious," Johann said. "And you said that Serena was a kind and thoughtful woman."

"The kindest," confirmed Chris.

"Yes, now that is quite odd," said Johann. "Satan is, if anything, methodical and consistent in his methods. To place your Serena, whose sins were relatively innocuous, within the sea of fire is very unusual. He tends to reserve that terrible sea for vile and unrepentant sinners. Yes, this is strange."

"Sounds like you've studied him a lot," Chris said.

"I have," confirmed Johann. "He is a key element in the flow of cosmic time. I have viewed him through the eyes of many poor souls who have crossed his path. Chris, I like to think of myself as a positive thinking person, an optimist. I can usually find some good qualities in almost anyone, but satan has absolutely no redeeming qualities whatsoever. Nonetheless, what he has done to your wife is inconsistent with his nature, unless there is something that I am not seeing."

"Maybe he sees her as a threat," suggested David.

"Yes, yes, that's right," said Chris, his voice rising in volume and tension. "That's what satan told her. I heard it. It was something about what she might have done to him if she had only lived."

"But she didn't live," observed Johann. "Why would he punish her so severely for something that she might have done but didn't?"

"A temporal paradox?" suggested David.

This young man sure threw around a lot of strange terms. "A what?" asked Chris.

"An oddity in the flow of time," replied Johann, "An event that doesn't make sense from our view of time. It is a sort of event that shouldn't be able to happen."

"Like going back a couple minutes in time and warning yourself not to make a stupid mistake," noted David. "If you had done it, you might prevent yourself from making the mistake. But if you didn't make the mistake, why did you go back and warn yourself about something that you didn't do in the first place. Satan is punishing Serena for something that she would have done if she had lived, something against his kingdom."

"That doesn't make any sense," objected Chris. "That can't happen. Satan was talking about what she *might* have done, not what she *would* have done."

"But suppose that they are the same thing," said David. "Suppose that she is actually going to do these things, and satan wants to punish her for them?"

That comment even perplexed David's teacher. "Supposition," he objected. "David, you're talking about an event that has never occurred."

"Are we so sure?" asked David. There was a trace of amusement in his voice.

Chris wondered as to whether he should have invited this youth along or not, as the three walked up the steps of the Hall of Records and through the main entryway. Despite his obvious high intelligence, he was rather brash and somewhat immature. He was certain that David didn't realize what he was getting into.

As usual, the Hall of Records was not a very busy place. Not many people pried into the records of others, or even their own.

"I'll handle the book," said Johann, as they made their way up the spiral staircase. "It is better if the one in control is a bit more removed from the situation. It was your emotional state that got you in trouble before, Chris. You lost touch with what was reality and what was not. That is why you became lost. You can't allow that to happen here."

"OK," agreed Chris, "do what you think is best.

Within minutes the three stood before Serena's book. It was Johann who withdrew it from its shelf. He turned to David. "You have never examined the content of a black book, have you?"

"No, sir," confirmed David.

"I feel that I should warn you that what you are about to see is likely to be very disturbing. My chief concern is that you are not prepared for what you are about to witness. We're talking about the terrors of Hell. You are going to witness them firsthand. What you are about to see could well have a tremendous impact upon you. If you have any doubts at all, I'd advise you to withdraw."

"I can handle it," said David, his tone full of confidence. "It will be an adventure. It is a part of God's creation that I must experience, disturbing or not."

Johann nodded. "Very well, then. Let us keep talking to a minimum during this exercise. David, I know that you become easily excited; however, I must ask you to refrain from making any unnecessary comments until we have concluded our work here. Do you understand?"

"Yes, professor," confirmed David, bowing his head slightly.

"Then, we shall begin," said Johann, opening the book.

The shelves of books dissolved around them, replaced with the images of Serena's past. Johann paced through Serena's early life rather quickly. He paused only briefly to observe the many crises that transpired between Serena and her mother. These were contributing elements of his research, but not the primary topic. He could always come back to them if conditions dictated.

Chris watched without comment as the years sped by. He could see his two companions standing in the midst of the flowing images, one to his left, and the other to his right. They looked somehow less real than the vision itself. He tried not to show his emotions as he witnessed Serena's death once more. He glanced toward David in time to see him cringe at the moment of the crash.

Johann seemed particularly interested by the circumstances of Serena's trial, yet he said nothing to Chris or David. He moved on to Serena's experience with the angel Aaron, and her fellow lost soul, Benny, then on to her audience with the prince of darkness himself and her journey through Hell.

Chris turned to David as they watched Serena walk amid the black altars, amid the myriad of helpless men and women being horribly desecrated by the ravenous birds of prey. David's expression was one of wide-eyed terror, yet he couldn't seem to turn away from it. Chris was very much afraid that he was beginning to lose it.

"It's horrible," whispered David, trying to stifle his emotions. "This can't be real, it's a nightmare."

Chris leaned toward David, placing his hand on the youth's shoulder. "Do you want out? We can stop and then go on without you."

"No," he replied. "I'm cool. I'll be OK."

Chris wasn't certain that David could cope with what was to come. He was from an age of televised violence, yet he had turned out to be more sensitive to this sort of thing than Chris had figured. He'd keep a close eye on him.

Johann too turned occasionally toward the youth, though he said nothing. Johann did his best to view the horrors before him with a dispassionate eye. His fears about David's involvement had been confirmed. He really should have left the youth behind; he was not emotionally up to the rigors of this expedition.

Eventually Serena plummeted from the cliff and into the heaving fiery sea. From there, Johann mercifully initiated a fast forward. What must have been months passed in far less than a minute. Then Serena was climbing up the cliff, the waves of the fiery sea crashing ever farther below. Johann stepped forward, watched her every move carefully. He followed her progress to the ledge and then, as the terrible sulfurous storm bore down upon her, into the cave.

"Way to go, Serena," David whispered, totally caught up in the drama.

They were in unknown territory now. Chris watched cautiously as Serena curled up in the darkness to watch the storm beyond the cave. He could barely discern her or her surroundings, yet there seemed to be no immediate dangers. She was safe, for the moment. He dreaded to think of her becoming some sort of primitive cave dweller, yet it was infinitely preferable to the alternative.

Johann paged forward, accelerating the march of time. There was a flash of light and Serena was pulled to her feet by a large demon with feathery wings. The suddenness of the attack startled all of them. Here it was; the end of Serena's short-lived peace. Johann had been right; one could not long evade the devil within his own domain. Yet none of the observers could have predicted the outcome of the brief altercation between this fallen angel and the brave Serena. Though cast across the cavern room like a toy and in great pain, Serena courageously defied her assailant, questioning his motives, and somewhere along the line, hit a cord. The tension within the cave eased, and soon she was actually negotiating with the titan.

"Abaddon!" David said. He could keep his silence no longer, and looked to his mentor, realizing that he had just broken one of the ground rules. "Do you realize who this guy is?"

"Quiet, please!" scolded Johann, drawing closer to the two negotiating parties in the vision.

David still seemed agitated; nonetheless, he held his peace.

All that Chris could do was to pray, pray that his beloved Serena might be able to work her charm on this being; that seemed so much a walking contradiction. How might one negotiate with a demon? He figured that he was getting his first lesson.

They watched the story unfold for hours, from the confrontation in Abaddon's cavern, to the precipice overlooking the flaming sea, to the small cell in which the fallen angel had imprisoned Serena. Then they witnessed the making of a covenant between the two unlikely partners. By this time, Chris was on top of the world. Tears of joy flowed from his eyes; and he was not alone; the experience had touched his young compatriot as well.

"Way to go," whispered Chris, words that brought a broad smile to David's face.

She was safe! Serena had found a safe harbor in the most tumultuous of all storms. Chris watched in wonder as his wife tended the subterranean garden and explored Abaddon's small domain. She had found some measure of peace at last.

Johann turned to Chris as the vision vanished, giving way to the Hall of Records once more. Johann's expression was one of total disbelief. "That is where your wife has been these past forty-three days, in the realm of Abaddon. That is where she is now. I have scanned the width and breadth of Hell in my expeditions within this hall; but I never dreamed that there were such beings as Abaddon in satan's realm."

"He had to be somewhere," David said.

Johann shook his head. "David, what do you mean?"

"Well don't you see? He *has* to be the Abaddon, the one mentioned in the Book of Revelation. John talks about a dark angel, the destroyer, who brings great destruction into the beast's camp in the last of the last days. This is the guy, the destroyer, the bringer of the first curse. It is his destiny to rain on the beast's parade. He leaves the saints of God in peace, leaves nature untouched, but torments the followers of the beast."

"I don't like to admit it," Johann said, "but I'm not that familiar with this element of John's Revelation."

David was eager to enlighten his companions. "Well, he is only mentioned in the Bible once by name, and then only in a couple of verses. He's one of those obscure characters that most people just dismiss. Some say Abaddon is just another name for satan, but I never thought so. It doesn't fit at all. When I read Revelation, I remember wondering who he might be.

"He's kind of like the Lone Ranger of angels, you know? He's a dark knight, a loose cannon. He leads a hoard of...well, something or others, that plague the followers of the beast. This hoard makes them long for death but doesn't kill them. Look, you've seen his love for nature, how he saved the ecosystem that once existed in Hell. In the Book of Revelation it says that he does no harm to nature or the saints. He's one of the good guys, sort of. Now we know who he is, don't we? We've unlocked a small piece of the mystery. This is just so cool!"

"You're making an assumption that he is that same Abaddon," Johann said. "I for one am not that certain."

"But, who else could he be? It all fits," insisted David.

Chris nodded. "Yes, it makes sense to me. So, where do we go from here?"

"Who said that there was anywhere to go from here," objected Johann. "By a miracle, you now know that your wife is safe, at least for a season; surely this is more than you had dared hope for."

"We make contact," announced David, his voice full of youthful confidence. He turned to Chris, who was more than willing to hear what he had to say. "We contact this angel who took your wife into outer darkness...this Aaron. He made a promise to Serena, didn't he?"

"Yes," replied Chris with the slightest of a hopeful smile materializing.

"Well, we confront him," continued David. "We ask him about Serena. Now, no one here is supposed to remember the damned in Hell, right?"

Chris nodded. He could see where David was taking this, and he liked it.

"We'll blow his mind," said David, a brief but devious smile sweeping across his face. "Now, he has to be one of a select group of angels that make the trip back and forth between Heaven and outer darkness on a regular basis, and once in a while he is going to have a few free minutes.

"Why couldn't you write your wife a letter? Aaron could deliver it. It wouldn't take us too long to figure out where Abaddon's island is. We could determine the exact location. All we have to do is to pass that information on to Aaron. It's not like being able to be with her again, but at least it's something."

Chris turned to Johann. He was certain that he would object to this reckless plan. He was surprised to see Johann nodding.

"Yes," he said. "It just might be possible. Angels have a mandate to serve humankind, so long as it doesn't interfere with their mandates from God. I can see nothing about this plan that might be viewed as an act of disobedience to God. Yes, I will support you in this thing."

Quite abruptly the smile vanished from Chris's face. "Yeah, but how do we locate one specific angel out of millions."

"Oh, that's not so hard," assured David, "and we're already in the right place."

That one raised Chris's eyebrows. "You mean to say that there are books here for the angels as well?"

"Of course there are," assured David.

"There is a section here especially for them," interjected Johann. "It contains information about every angel who was ever created. Not just the ones here in Heaven, but those who have fallen as well. There are nearly four hundred million volumes, one for each angel. Not so many, when you consider that there are nearly thirty billion volumes for humanity."

"You mean *all* of them, even satan himself?" asked Chris.

"Even satan himself," confirmed Johann.

"I suppose you could keep him under surveillance if you had a mind to," said David.

"I don't think you would want to do that," said Johann, just a little annoyed at his young apprentice's attitude. "He is vile beyond description, David. I don't know that you could walk away from his book unaffected. You had trouble with what you saw today."

David nodded.

"When can we begin?" asked Chris.

"Immediately," assured Johann. "We can proceed to the angel's section of the hall and locate Aaron's book. We've seen him, we know who he is. That is sufficient information to locate his book. I already know where it is."

"Same here," replied Chris, who had suddenly found the information within his own mind as well.

The three walked to the lower level, below street level, where the angel's section was located. Here, rather than being made of the clearest crystal, the walkways and shelves were composed of the finest white-cultured marble. The books were about the same size as those designed for their human counterparts.

"The ivory-colored books are the records of the angels still in Heaven," explained Johann. "I think you can deduce the meaning of the black covers on about a third of the books."

Chris nodded.

It was not long before they stood before one particular shelf. There they found an ivory- colored book with the name of Aaron on the cover. They also noted a blue and a brown band along its upper binding.

"The blue band indicates that Aaron is a messenger," noted Johann. "The brown band tells us his rank. He is not a high-ranking angel; he is a member of the seventh tier."

"Seventh tier?" asked Chris.

"Yes," replied Johann. "There are seven tiers in the community of angels. The highest tier now has only two members; Gabriel and Michael, the archangels. The second tier has forty-eight, the third has 1,152, and so on."

Johann scanned the pages of the book for about five minutes, concentrating on the last pages of the volume. Strangely, Chris sensed no visual sensation whatsoever. Perhaps it was Johann's intention to keep the contents of this book to himself. He closed the volume and returned it to its shelf. "We should be able to meet with Aaron tomorrow. I've noted a pattern to his travels."

"Don't angels have a home?" asked Chris, who suddenly realized how very little he actually knew about these sons of God.

"Yes, they do," replied Johann, "but their homes are not like ours. Most of them live a sort of communal existence. They're not so much like you or I. In your era, people might say that they were 'programmed.' They were created with all of the knowledge and skills they would ever need. They were created with the desire to perform a specific task, whatever that might be. Their emotions and personalities are subtle, not as complex as ours. They have amazingly few real needs, only the desire to serve. Perhaps that is why lucifer found it so easy to enlist the assistance and establish the undying loyalty of those angels in his charge."

"So, they're like robots?"

"No, nothing so two dimensional," Johann said. "They have emotions and a soul. They can reason for themselves, and as time has passed, they have become so much more than they were at their beginnings. But they would seem to have no pastimes, no hobbies. They live for their work, engines of creation, as God intended. This Aaron that we seek spends some of his time in the Hall of Angels, a magnificent marble structure about two miles on a side and over two hundred feet high, near the heart of Zion. His actual living space is very small, an unfurnished white cubical about seven or eight feet square. Angels sleep on their feet, resting upon their wings. They don't require much space."

"It doesn't sound like much of a life," noted Chris.

"From our perspective, no, but you have to understand how angels think. To them it is totally adequate."

"So, where do we meet him? At the Hall of Angels?" asked David, who had heard all of this before and was anxious to move on.

Johann shook his head as he turned toward his student. "No, we wouldn't want to do that. For one thing, he doesn't need to rest that often, and he doesn't always rest in the same place. I can't be certain as to when he will return there. Second, human beings really aren't that welcome in the hall; it is a place intended for the angelic beings of Heaven. It would be considered impolite to invade their space. We need to respect their privacy, what little they have. Anyway, it has no entrance from the street, only from the sky."

"So, where?" repeated David.

"I've located a forest glade, far to the north. Aaron visits it with uncanny regularity, although I'm not certain why. It is not uncommon for angels to, as you might put it, 'hang out' at one location."

Chris laughed. This physicist from the past just didn't seem the type to use modern slang.

Johann ignored Chris's little outburst. "We will try to intercept him tomorrow evening. Let us all meet at my home at the noon hour tomorrow. There we can make our final plans and prepare to contact the angel."

"What should I do until then?" Chris asked, very unhappy with having to wait another day.

"Well, for one thing, you had best compose your letter," said Johann, smiling slightly. "But, go home, Chris. I am sure, from what you have told me, that your mother is most concerned by now. Get some rest, whether you think you need it or not." Johann turned to David. "The same goes for you."

David nodded. He would be at Professor Kepler's home especially early tomorrow. This whole affair promised to be interesting. David parted company with Johann and Chris on the Hall of Records stairway. The two men walked on toward the city gate.

"He's an interesting student," Chris said as he and Johann continued on down the busy avenue.

"One of my most gifted," replied Johann. "It is hard indeed to say what he might have accomplished in the world of mortal men. He is remarkably perceptive, both mentally and spiritually."

"Doesn't it seem strange to you that we ran into him this morning? And the way he seemed to know what we were doing and where we were going. Well...it's just too weird."

"That is David's way," was the reply. "His mother once told me that he had a gift for uncanny timing during his lifetime as well. What he did this morning is far from unusual for him. I will indeed contemplate what he said about a temporal paradox. Perhaps the student does have something to teach his mentor."

Johann paused before changing the topic. "You understand that what has happened today is a most unique event, but I must caution you that this fortuitous situation in which your wife finds herself cannot last. She has found but a temporary reprieve from her torments, you must realize that. In the end, she will be discovered and matters are likely to be worse."

"I can't think that way," objected Chris. "Don't you see? My remembering my lost wife, Serena's escape from the sea, David's appearance today, it's all part of a plan—it has to be."

"There is one way to know for certain," replied Johann. "But you won't go to Him, will you?"

"I can't," Chris said.

"I thought as much," said Johann. "Very well; we shall do it your way, for now. But when I say it's over, it is over."

"I understand."

"Do you?" asked Johann. "I wonder."

There was not much more to say. At the gates of Zion, the two men went their separate ways. Already Chris was thinking of what he might include in his letter to Serena. Certainly it would be the most remarkable letter of all times.

chapter twentyone

AMID a white fog and a shower of glimmering stars, Chris stepped onto the lawn in front of the mansion. Ebbie was sitting on the porch waiting for him. An unusually loud meow greeted Chris, as Ebbie scampered down the three steps and to her master's feet. Chris leaned over and scratched her gently on the head.

"I'm sorry I'm so late," he said.

A few seconds later his mother opened the front door. Her face lit up with surprise and relief. "Oh Chris, I've been so worried." She rushed to hug him. "You've been gone four days, where have you been?"

Chris shook his head. "Has it been that long? I'm sorry I worried you, Mom. I've been a real heel. But where I've been…that's going to be a bit of a long story. I think you'd better be sitting down when I tell it."

They sat on the porch swing and Chris told his mother all of the details of his adventure. This story had twists and turns that Jennifer had been completely unprepared for. Perhaps she should have read more of Serena's book. The gruesome details of Serena's journey through Hell and her tragic plunge into the sea of fire was a bit too much for Jennifer. She had assumed that Serena's story was all but over. A letter from Heaven to Hell? Was such a thing really possible? Apparently Chris and his new friends seemed to think so.

With her son's story told, Jennifer, in turn, told Chris of her incredible personal encounter with God. Even Moses on Mount Sinai had not experienced such a thing. To have actually touched the hand of God, to be granted such a personal audience with the Creator of the universe, was nothing short of miraculous. She told her son everything that God had related to her. She did her best to try and convince Chris to speak to Him personally.

Chris nodded, though reluctantly. "Maybe you're right. I guess I really need to go to God with this, but I want to get this letter off first. Mom, I have to do this. I don't have much time to pull it together. We're going to meet with this angel tomorrow afternoon, and the letter needs to be ready to go by then."

Jennifer wasn't quite prepared for that response. She smiled slightly. "All right, dear, I understand. I don't see that God would mind your doing this thing. I'm sure your letter will lift Serena's spirits. But promise me that you will go to God once you get this thing done. Do it for me."

"OK, Mom, I promise."

The stories told, Chris wasted no time composing his letter. He sat at his desk for hours into the night writing.

"How's it coming?" asked Jennifer.

"Fine," he said, glancing over momentarily. "I'm almost done."

Jennifer handed her son two handwritten pages and a small package. "I decided to write to her too. I wanted to get to know her better. She was…no, she *is* my daughter-in-law. I wanted her to know that she's in my prayers. "

Chris rose to his feet and hugged his mother. "Thanks, Mom. I'm sure Serena will appreciate it."

"You'll be sending your letter off tomorrow, with this angel, Aaron?"

"If we can find him," replied Chris. "Johann has a pretty good idea where he might be, but it could take a few days before we track him down."

Jennifer hesitated before continuing. "Chris, just be careful, OK?"

Chris moved back slightly to see a tear in his mother's eye. "What's this now?"

"I don't know," admitted his mother. "I don't know if they're tears of joy or of fear. I'm so thankful that Serena has found a safe haven; but I have a bad feeling, like something terrible is about to happen. I don't want to lose you. Please, just be careful."

Chris was speechless. All he could do was nod.

Jennifer quickly wiped away her tears. "Look, you get that letter finished and get to bed, OK? You have a big day tomorrow."

There was nothing more to say. Jennifer retired to her room for the night and Chris got back to his letter. Amid the joy of the moment, he hadn't given much thought to the future. He most certainly had one, but what about Serena? She had been very fortunate, had found a comfortable hiding place, but it wouldn't last, it couldn't. In the end, satan or one of his minions would discover her. It might be many years, but what were ten, even a hundred years compared to eternity? He needed to come up with a more permanent solution to Serena's dilemma. He wondered if one existed.

⊰✳⊱ ⊰✳⊱ ⊰✳⊱

Jennifer and Ebbie watched from the front porch as Chris stepped into the starry mist, his small care package for Serena in his hand. It took only a few seconds to transcend the distance between the mansion and the forest home of Johann Kepler, yet Chris suspected that the actual physical distance was vast.

Though it had been morning at his point of departure, it felt much later at his destination.

It was quiet at Johann's modest home. The air was completely still, and only the faintest songs of birds echoed from the mighty forest. Chris had almost expected to find Johann and David awaiting his arrival. Walking toward the house, he noticed that many of the window shutters were closed. Yesterday they had all been open. It seemed strange that they should be drawn on such a crystal-clear day.

He walked to the front door, still not a sound. He knocked; nothing. After a moment, he cautiously ventured in. It was strangely dark in the hallway that led to Johann's study, yet the study itself was aglow in harsh amber light. Chris saw Johann and David standing transfixed before a glistening orange luminary, which hovered near the center of the room, several faintly glowing spheres gathered about it. It was very unlike the three-dimensional image of creation that had been displayed in this very spot yesterday.

"A hidden corner of creation," said Johann, obviously sensing Chris's arrival, "a world hitherto unseen by anyone, save God."

"What is it?" asked Chris, drawing closer.

"It's a star," replied Johann, who still had not turned toward his guest. "About two-thirds as luminous as the sun. Yet it is no ordinary star, not one of a hundred quadrillion in the universe of our birth. No, this one is in outer darkness."

"The star that Hell circles?" deduced Chris.

"Oh no, not this baby," said David, turning to Chris, his eyes full of wonder. "Professor Kepler has found another star in outer darkness."

"Wait a minute, I thought that there were no other stars in outer darkness," Chris said, drawing still closer.

"And so has everyone else for millennia," said Johann. "We were all wrong. In the past I've conducted extensive searches of outer darkness, utilizing every resource at my disposal, yet all I ever found was cold, endless nothingness."

"Until now," Chris said.

Johann rubbed his eyes. "Until now. Last night I decided to take another look. I don't know why, really. You might call it a hunch, intuition perhaps; I really don't know. I just started scanning; there was no rhyme or reason to it. It took less than ten minutes to locate this thing you see before you."

"How far is it from Hell?" asked Chris.

"About 780 parsecs," replied Johann, who stepped closer to the phantasmal luminary. "My records show that I'd scanned this region before, but with negative results…now this."

Chris wasn't at all certain of the implications of Johann's discovery. He wasn't sure just how far 780 parsecs was either. From his perspective, it was all a waste of time. They had other more important things to concentrate on.

Johann turned toward Chris. "Perhaps it was the Spirit of God that led me to it. Perhaps the Father wanted me to find it." Johann hesitated. "Or maybe I just got lucky. Throughout history, many of the great scientific discoveries were made by chance. Perhaps this was one of them."

"Show Chris the planets," said David excitedly.

"Oh yes," replied Johann. He pointed toward the tiny objects, almost lost in the glare of the star. "These are planets, two of them, as far as I can tell."

Then quite abruptly the entire scene whirled about. They seemed to be traveling; though there was no actual sense of motion beyond a visual one. They were zooming in on the inner planet of this mysterious sun. It loomed larger, becoming a glistening red ball of fury.

"It is a primordial world of molten rock," Johann said. "It is not the heat of its sun that makes it so. The condition of its surface and its primitive atmosphere indicate it is a world that is still cooling down from the heat of its own formation. But if that is the case, if this system is so young, then there should be fantastic quantities of dust and rock tumbling around the star, the afterbirth of creation. So, where is it?"

Again the view changed, and within a few seconds their focus had shifted to the second planet. It was a world of blue oceans, predominantly green continents, and swirling white clouds. It was beautiful almost beyond imagining.

"Planets such as this are exceptionally rare in the cosmos. They require many billions of years to evolve. This system is a paradox. Based upon the condition of the inner planet, it is very young, but based upon the condition of the second planet and the empty space between them, this system is about the age of our solar system. These planets do not belong in the same system."

Perhaps one of them was captured from another system," suggested David. His words were faltering and uncertain, as if he himself didn't believe his own explanation.

"What other system?" Johann asked. "The only other system in outer darkness is Hell. That's too far away. And what mechanism ejected it from there or captured it here? No, this system is a true mystery."

"Maybe God just created it this way for some reason," suggested Chris.

"Perhaps," replied Johann. "God could have created this system as you see it in a single day. But my experience indicates that He generally doesn't do that sort of thing." There was a momentary pause. "But this isn't the most mysterious aspect of this system…this is." The blue planet swung out of view to be replaced by a third world of misty white. It shimmered and glistened like nothing Chris had ever seen.

"I thought you said there were only two planets," said Chris, stepping forward for a closer look.

"I did," confirmed Johann. "I'm not quite sure what this is. It doesn't seem to be shining by reflected light from its sun. It is in itself luminous. In fact, it is not circling this sun like the other two planets. It is standing motionless in space, unaffected by any of the natural forces around it."

Chris looked perplexed. "But that's impossible, isn't it?"

"I would say so," Johann said. "But I'm not so certain that it is a planet at all."

"It almost doesn't look real," said Chris, as the image rippled and swirled, like a mirage viewed from across a torrid desert wasteland.

"It's like this whole star system—a paradox," Johann said.

"Maybe it's not truly in outer darkness," suggested David. "It acts like something that is out of phase with this space-time. Maybe it's a part of another universe. It shares a couple dimensions with outer darkness, but not all of them. Maybe all of the planets in this system are like that."

Johann shook his head. "That's purely theoretical, David. To my knowledge there are no examples of such a phenomenon in the known universe, at least none that I have personally encountered."

Chris had heard enough of this science lesson for one day. It seemed to him that Johann and David were far too easily distracted, and he was becoming quickly frustrated. "Look, I'm sure that all of this is quite interesting to you guys, but we have something else to do today, don't we?"

The image vanished from their midst. Johann walked to the window and opened the shutters allowing the daylight to flood the room. "Of course, but I am convinced that what we have just seen is related to what we seek to do this day."

Chris shook his head. "Oh, how do you figure?"

"I don't know yet, but allow me to submit this for your consideration. I searched the realm of outer darkness many times over the past few hundred years and found it to be a complete void, until last night. Why now?"

The question went unanswered. Even David had nothing to say.

Johann looked at the small package in Chris's hand. "I see you've put together your letter."

Chris nodded.

"Very well, let us adjourn to the out-of-doors and begin our journey. I suspect that we might find the angel we seek this very day."

The three walked outside into the cool afternoon air. The misty portal immediately opened before them and they entered. In a few seconds they were by a small lake, surrounded on all sides by tall golden grass and a scattering of pine trees. It was distinctly chilly, and before them a range of tall, snow-capped peaks towered toward the deep blue sky, their images mirrored by the calm waters of the lake. The area reminded Chris a little of Glacier National Park. He and Serena had visited that majestic region two summers ago. No, this was even grander than that.

"How certain are you that this angel is even going to be here? I don't see anyone."

"I am not that certain," Johann said, looking around the peaceful meadow. "I can only tell you that he comes here often. Angels are not as complex as you or I. They tend to be creatures of habit. We might find him today. Then again, it might require several days for our paths to cross. However, he does frequent this place, he has for centuries. Eventually we will encounter him."

To Chris, it sounded like visiting the mall in hopes of running into a specific individual. Sure, that individual might love shopping at the mall, but what were the odds of finding him there on any given afternoon? There had to be a better way.

The three scanned the area with their keen, other-worldly vision, looking for an angel. Along the shoreline, several hundred yards away, a winged being robed in white sat on a large boulder, looking out at the serene waters. The three visitors wasted no time moving in his direction.

"Congratulations, professor," said David. "You were right on!"

Johann nodded. "Now, allow me to do the talking. This is a very delicate subject we mean to discuss with him, and there are protocols that need to be followed. It might be better if the two of you spoke only if spoken to."

Chris had never heard anything about protocols for talking to angels. In actual fact, he had few opportunities to talk with angels since he had been in Heaven. That seemed sort of strange in retrospect. He had seen them often enough, issued forth many a friendly greeting that was always reciprocated, but the relationship had not been more than that. They weren't the sort to strike up a conversation with you. Angels didn't have much in common with their human counterparts beyond a common master and creator. They traveled in different circles, and Chris had accepted that.

The magnificent being noted their approach when they were still a hundred or so feet away. He rose to his feet; then stood as if a statue.

"I bid you welcome," he said as the three drew closer.

"Peace be onto you, Aaron, messenger of God," said Johann, by way of a greeting.

The angel scanned his three visitors. Chris was certain that there was a look of subdued surprise when the angel looked at him.

"We have come to discuss a matter of some importance with you," continued Johann. "We are very much in need of an angelic messenger."

Aaron nodded. "You have found one."

"It is our understanding that you travel between Heaven and outer darkness on our Father's business on a regular basis."

"That is correct," Aaron said. "It is my duty to ferry those human beings found unworthy in the sight of God to that place where they shall spend their eternity, the realm of wailing and gnashing of teeth. It is a task that demands much of my time. But why do you seek me, Johann Kepler? Certainly you do not wish me to deliver a message to Hell."

Chris felt chilled as the angel turned to look at him rather than he who addressed him. Chris felt as if the angel was looking down on him, looking down upon the lowly human. He could hold his silence no more—this was the being that had delivered his love to her torment. "Sir, it's about my wife, Serena Davis. I believe you know her. Or perhaps you knew her as Serena Farnsworth."

Aaron gazed at Chris with calm, cool eyes. It might have been there, somewhere beneath the serene surface of his countenance, yet Chris's comment had not elicited any sort of emotional response, at least not yet.

"You did ferry her into outer darkness, into Hell. I believe that's the way you described it. You locked her in a cell to await satan's pleasure, put her right where his agents could locate her. But before you left her, she gave you a message to pass on to me, her husband. You did tell her that you would convey that message to me if I should ever ask you about her. Well, I'm asking."

Aaron turned away from the group, walking several steps before coming to a stop. He bowed his head as if in a state of contemplation and became totally still.

Johann turned to Chris. There was a sense quite close to anger upon his countenance. Johann had not anticipated this emotional outburst. He decided to say nothing, at least not right now.

After half a minute, Aaron turned toward the group. Johann had fully intended to offer an apology for his companion's outburst. He was amazed at what he saw. Over the course of centuries, Johann had seen countless angels, yet never had he seen one with such a look of stunned amazement.

"Yes," said Aaron, "I remember her. But how is it that you do? No man or woman in Heaven truly remembers those condemned to outer darkness. It is an act of kindness that the Father has extended to all of you."

"I remember her, every detail," replied Chris, who now struggled to remain in control. It was not easy under the circumstances. "Despite what you told her, she was and shall always be my wife."

"Yes, of course," replied Aaron, who seemed genuinely confused by this state of affairs. "I gave her my word that I would tell you all that she related to me, yet I suspect that you already know what she told me. Do you still wish me to relay to you what she said?"

"That won't be necessary," interrupted Johann. "Chris has already reviewed her book in the Hall of Records at least twice. Yet, that is not how he found out about her. I believe that his memories are genuine."

Aaron looked deep into Chris's eyes. "Do you believe that I find any pleasure, any joy, in delivering the condemned into outer darkness? Is this why you are angry with me Christopher Davis?"

Chris didn't reply. His mind was far too awash in emotions.

"Are you then angry with God as well? It was He who passed judgment upon her, a judgment dictated by her own lack of faith in Him. It was my duty to see that His will was carried out. Where do you stand? What is it that you wish of me?"

He'd just blown it, of that Chris was certain. He had failed to anticipate his reaction to meeting this angel. Seconds passed, but no one spoke.

"What would you have me do, Christopher Davis?" repeated Aaron. His tone of voice was softer, more understanding this time.

It was not Chris, but David who finally spoke up. "Chris prepared a letter, a letter for his wife. He was hoping that you might deliver it. That is, if you're allowed to do something like that."

"I could deliver this message for you, if that is what you wish." The angel's words were slow and deliberate. He had obviously chosen them carefully. "It might be difficult to find her, but I shall make the attempt. Such an act would not be counter to the will of the Father. Still, I must tell you this; even if I did locate her, your efforts would probably be to no avail. I know not what torments satan has subjected her to, but it is most unlikely that she will be in any position to read the words you have set forth for her in this testament. Even if I were to read them to her, it is not at all certain that she would even comprehend their meaning in the midst of her pain."

"She is in no torment," said Chris, who had finally brought his emotions into some measure of control. "She was in the sea of fire, but not anymore; she escaped. She's being hidden from satan, protected by a fallen angel."

Aaron looked at Chris incredulously. "Protected by a fallen angel? None of satan's minions would protect a human, not one. They are all totally loyal to their master. You must be mistaken."

"I have seen it myself," confirmed Johann. "What Chris tells you is true."

"And this fallen angel, who is he?"

"His name is Abaddon," said Chris.

That name brought yet another stare of amazement to Aaron's countenance. "Abaddon?"

"Yes," confirmed Chris, "do you know him?"

"We were close friends, long ago…though we have not spoken in many centuries."

Young David was enjoying the conversation. He was certain that he was witnessing something most remarkable. Between Chris and Johann, the series of events that had brought them here were carefully unfolded to Aaron. It was when they attempted to describe the location of Serena's haven that Aaron stopped them.

"I know of the dwelling place of the destroyer," he replied. "He is one of the very few within the realm of Hell that would so much as consider giving assistance to a human. He is one of the very few who would even dare. He is indeed powerful, he might be able to shield Serena from satan's vengeance for a season, hide her from his sight; but in the end, she will be discovered and matters will be worse. Still, that Serena should encounter Abaddon, that you should remember her, is no accident; of that I am certain."

He took a step toward Chris, placed his hand on his shoulder. "It is important that you have this time to share your hopes and dreams with Serena. I know not why you have been given this opportunity, yet it is a fleeting and precious time, measured against the backdrop of eternity. Yes, Christopher Davis, I will help you. I will do it gladly. Give me that which you wish placed into her hands."

There were tears in Chris's eyes as he handed the package over to the angel. "Thank you. I'm sorry for what I said. I shouldn't have blamed you."

"I understand," Aaron said. "Let us speak no more of it. Yet heed my words, let there be no feelings of bitterness or resentment between you and the Father. For I tell you, the fault is not His."

Chris nodded.

There was no fanfare in Aaron's departure. He took a few steps away from the three men before spreading his powerful wings and bolting into the sky. A powerful swirling wind engulfed the men as the great angel's wings propelled him upward. It took less than half a minute for him to vanish from sight.

"What now?" asked Chris, turning to Johann.

"We wait patiently." There was anger and frustration in Johann's voice. "This is something that you will, no doubt, have difficulty with. Why can't you follow my instructions? Why can't you control yourself? Why do you have to act so impulsively, so emotionally?"

"It's my wife we're talking about," retorted Chris. "How do you expect me to act?"

"I expect for you to act in a manner that will benefit her cause." Johann paused, allowing his anger and frustration to ebb. "Your unstable emotional state isn't helping us; in fact, it is a hindrance. Chris, I want you to go home. Stay there for a few days. If I'm right, Aaron will come to you there. You and he can work out the details as to how to conduct your business. I am assuming that you will want to continue writing to Serena."

Chris nodded.

"And so you should. In the meantime, I have other matters to attend to and would appreciate your respecting my privacy. You have what you wanted and more. I need time to contemplate and follow other avenues of interest. Do you understand?"

Again Chris nodded. Johann was trying to get rid of him. He supposed that he couldn't blame the professor. He figured that he had been a thorn in his side during the last couple of days, especially after today's outburst. He very much doubted that he would be very welcome in the Kepler household for a very long time.

David was unusually quiet as Chris prepared to open the gateway that would take him home. It seemed odd that this excitable young man should, for once, be at a loss for words. Chris figured that David had read the frustration in his mentor's countenance and thought that any flippant comments at this time would be ill advised. The three parted company, allowing peace to return once more to the alpine valley.

chapter twentytwo

THE ragtag man wept bitterly as satan stood to pronounce his sentence upon him. The man looked up at he who had sentenced him, his lips quivering. "Oh please, don't hurt me. I'll do anything, anything."

There was a glimmer in satan's eyes at those words. "Anything?"

The man was quick to respond. "Oh yes, anything you want."

"Very well, then worship me, worship me as your only god."

The man immediately fell on his face. "Oh god and master, I worship you, I love you. I'll do anything you ask. You are my one and only god. I'll live only for you!"

For over a minute the man raved on, heaping all kinds of praise on his new master. Satan watched him in amusement. "But for much of your life on Earth you had worshiped someone else other than me. When you were not worshiping money, you paid a sort of homage to another. What of him, how do I know that you will give your allegiance only to me?"

"I was wrong," he replied, looking to his new lord and master. "I didn't know."

"So, will you renounce him?"

"Yes," replied the man. "I renounce Allah, I renounce Mohammed, and all of his teachings. You are my only god. Please, you must believe me."

There was a long pause. Satan took several steps forward, gazing intently at the pathetic human before him. "Very well, I believe you."

The man once more fell on his face. "Oh thank you, lord, you won't regret this, I promise. I'll serve you with all of my strength."

"I'm sure you will," satan said, turning to two demonic guards standing at the man's side. "Take him to the sea of fire where he may begin his eternal service to me. Be certain that you cast him into a particularly hot and turbulent region."

"No!" screamed the man as he was swiftly led away and into the glowing portal, through which he could already see the fiery, tossing sea. He and his escorts passed quickly through, flying over the maelstrom and fading into the distance.

Satan turned from the portal. He paced back and forth across the floor of his audience hall like a caged lion. He was bored, in need of some different amusement. This encounter had made him mindful of something, something that needed closure.

The audience hall was unusually empty. Only a few dozen demons were in attendance to view the proceedings on this day. The prince of darkness turned to one of his advisors who stood at the edge of the platform.

"Moloch, I have need of a diversion. There is unfinished business that requires our attention."

The slightest of smiles appeared on the arch demon's face. "I am intrigued, my lord. What might that business be?"

"It has to do with a human wench I sentenced to the sea of fire some months ago, Serena Farnsworth."

The demon's smile broadened. "Yes, my lord, I remember her well. She provided us with considerable amusement. May I say, you were most clever in your dealings with her."

"Yes, you may," chuckled satan. "I wish to have her brought before me again. I wish to see if her experience in the sea of fire has softened her, made her more pliable. I wish to see her kneeling at my feet, worshiping me, begging for my favor."

"Yes," confirmed Moloch, "that would be most amusing. I will see that she is located and brought to you at once. It should not take long. The currents within the sea that have carried her are most predictable."

Satan nodded as Moloch bowed and departed. He returned to his throne to continue with the business at hand. Yes, this would be the perfect diversion. He was confident that he would not be disappointed.

⊰✳⊱ ⊰✳⊱ ⊰✳⊱

The days turned to weeks, and what might best be described as a routine settled into Serena's life. She spent a lot of time in the green cavern, tending to the small garden and the plants and trees around it. She had become the caretaker of this world's only remaining ecosystem. It was an awesome responsibility, and she gave it her full attention. She pruned trees and pulled weeds from the garden and transplanted them elsewhere. No, even the life of a weed was too precious to destroy.

Occasionally, she even caught sight of what she thought might be a bird, flittering quickly among the tall grasses near the cavern walls, though Abaddon assured her that no such species had been saved. It became one of the wonderful mysteries of this strange new world.

In life, she had lovingly tended to the garden behind the rock house. She had grown many of her own herbs, tomatoes, carrots, onions, practically anything that would flourish in a garden in the Northwest. She'd learned a lot about horticulture—the garden had been a labor of love for her and Chris. No, she wouldn't let her mind wander back there. She would try not to dwell on the past and what she had lost forever.

Living here with Abaddon offered so many blessings. Not dealing with the terrible pain of eternal torment from moment to moment was the most precious of them all. But in its absence, she had time to think, time to remember the past. Now she knew something of Abaddon's torment, not a physical torment, but one of the mind. She did her best to escape it; immersing herself in her work in the garden, anything to keep her mind occupied.

When she was not tending the garden, she sat and talked with Abaddon, learning of his existence here, a cycle of never-ending boredom and regret—all that Hell had to offer its occupants. He spoke of the loss of Heaven, of the comings and goings of angels, and of his experiences with God. She could sit here for a human lifetime and not learn a tenth of what he had to teach.

He taught her the rudimentary aspects of his own language, the language spoken by all angels, either here or in Heaven. She even learned to read and write in this strange alien tongue. It was another distraction.

Abaddon took Serena on a tour of his island, yet he took no chances when she was out in the open. So she would more readily blend into the surroundings, he prepared a long hooded cloak and a pair of high boots of the darkest black. It rendered her virtually invisible from the air, where the minions of satan traveled on their appointed rounds. He took her down the mountain trail to see the acid swamps that simmered and bubbled on the low, pockmarked plains on the far side of the island. Here the aroma of sulfur was almost stifling.

He took her to the summit of the mountain that dominated this side of the small archipelago. It was not as steep as she might have imagined, rather taking the form of a gentle knoll, nearly level at its summit, becoming gradually steeper as one moved away. From here, over 500 feet above the heaving sea, Serena was presented with a grand vista of pain and desolation. The fiery black oil extended in all directions to the very horizon, uninterrupted by any other land.

It was cooler than she imagined, and the odor of sulfur was more subdued. Farther from the fires below, the bow of blue that stretched across the horizon seemed brighter, somehow closer.

"The wind blows perpetually here," explained Abaddon, his cloak flapping at its insistence. "It blows always from the west, always from the land of sunlight into the realm of eternal night. I suppose that a seer of things climatic would have an explanation for such a phenomenon, but to me it holds no interest."

Serena scanned the strange realm around her. Far to the east, amid the darkness, she could see the lightning of a powerful storm, a source of torment to those trapped within the cruel sea. It brought a terrible heaviness to her soul.

"Long ago, or so I am told, this was a land of gently rolling hills," Abaddon said, stretching his hand out over the infernal vista, "In those days, there was still a day and night in this place. There wasn't much life here even then, but it was not as you see it today. Where we now stand was the highest mountain in the region; that is why I chose it as my home."

"But the sea of fire," asked Serena. "Where did it come from?"

"From below. Satan and his minions went to a lot of effort to bring its foulness to the surface, to nurture it, to make it what it is today. You see, it was all part of the plan, all part of his reshaping of this now accursed world. When I first arrived, the shoreline of the then young sea of fire was still some miles away from these highlands. Over the years it slowly rose to its present height, spreading out like a plague over much of the globe, accommodating an ever-growing number of tormented inhabitants, and still it rises."

"How fast?" asked Serena.

"It has slowed somewhat in recent centuries, as it has become so vast; but still it rises about a quarter of an inch a year. It continues to eat away at my shrinking oasis, assaulting it from all sides, pounding its flanks, inundating the lower regions during times of storms. One day it may destroy all that I have fought to preserve." He looked out at the horizons. "I come here often to think and contemplate. I wonder if my human family is still out there, afloat upon this accursed sea. Were it not for my arrogance, they might not have tasted of this horrible realm at all."

Serena looked into Abaddon's eyes. "You can't continue to torment yourself like this."

"I can do no less," he replied, only momentarily returning her gaze. "I am the cause of their grief. You said on that first day that I had no concept of the suffering of your people."

"I didn't understand then, I'm sorry."

"But I do understand their suffering," Abaddon said, looking at his comely protégé. "I had a brief taste of it when satan vented upon me his wrath. I spent days in that maelstrom before I managed to free myself. After that, I did my best to push the experience out of my mind. I never wanted to partake of it again. Therefore, I've turned my back upon what goes on here, afraid to arouse satan's wrath again. I decided to hide, and here I found my hiding place, that is until now."

"Until now?" asked Serena.

"Yes," confirmed Abaddon. "I know what I told you on that first day. I told you that there may come a time when I have to abandon you, denounce you, rather than face satan's wrath. I tell you now that I will never do that."

Abaddon took Serena's hand in his. "I have enjoyed your company, more than I can say. From this day forth, I will be your guardian angel. I will pledge myself to protect you from satan and his minions, and believe me when I tell you that I am a considerable adversary. One of his minions, even satan himself, would be ill advised to challenge the destroyer. It is my sincerest hope that you do not mind having a guardian angel the likes of me."

Serena's face lit up with joy, as she drew her arms around the mighty angel. "I cannot think of a single angel in all of Heaven that I would rather have as a guardian. You are more than my knight in shining armor, much more."

Abaddon smiled broadly. Before meeting Serena, he had almost forgotten how to smile. He had more than a companion to talk to, he had someone to protect, someone who was family. "Then that is how it shall be."

⊰※⊱ ⊰※⊱ ⊰※⊱

Moloch walked up the shimmering obsidian stairway to confer with his master. He was nervous because he had news that would make satan unhappy. Glancing up at the prince of darkness, evaluating his demeanor, he was certain that he had chosen a particularly bad time to bring such tidings.

The master watched him from his throne, watched his lieutenant bow in humble subjection before him. "What is it that you have for me this day?"

Moloch was squirming inside of his own skin. "Lord satan, I have come to you regarding your request to bring Serena Farnsworth into your presence."

"And?"

"We have encountered a problem."

Satan's impatience grew, as did his volume. "What is the nature of the problem?"

"Sir, our scouts have scanned the sea of fire for three days but have been unable to locate her."

"Unable to locate her?!" said satan. His fist came down hard on the arm of his throne. "How could that be? How many did you send in search of her?"

"Twelve. They have searched everywhere that the currents could have taken her. She was not to be found."

"So, she just crawled out of the sea of fire, is that what you're telling me?" Again the master's fist came down on the arm of his throne, more forcefully this time. "I will not tolerate this kind of incompetence. I placed you in charge of all of our human guests writhing within the sea of fire, did I not?"

"Yes, lord."

"And those under you have patrolled it, kept a regular vigil upon it?"

"Yes, lord, but there are now so many souls to be accounted for. It is not possible to keep a record of all of them on a daily basis. We do our best."

Satan leaned forward. "Then tell me Moloch, when was the last time Serena Farnsworth was accounted for?"

"My lord, she was last sighted fifty-eight Earth days ago, just exactly where she should have been. She was reported being carried along by a strong current, ever deeper into the realm of darkness. She was in exquisite agony. All was as it should have been."

"Fifty-eight days!" roared satan, jumping to his feet. "Is it your policy to lose track of a damned soul for fifty-eight days at a time?"

"Well, no, that's a bit long, but not that unusual. My sentries usually report their sightings of an individual guest every five or six days. We do keep an accurate accounting of those souls consigned to us."

Satan paced away from his lieutenant, then turned toward him abruptly. "Then what are you telling me, Moloch? Are you saying that she is simply misplaced and that you will soon locate her—or that she is gone?"

There was a pause as Moloch searched for the words. "My lord, I'm saying that in my opinion she is no longer within the sea of fire. She has somehow escaped. This sort of thing doesn't happen often, and we always locate them eventually."

"Very well," replied satan, his anger barely contained. "Then, this is what you shall do. You will conduct a search for this little wench, and you will find her. I am holding you personally responsible for the success of this mission. When you have found her, bring her into my presence at once. Don't disappoint me."

"Yes, Lord," confirmed Moloch, bowing low as he walked backward from the master's presence. He retreated from the audience chamber and into the wide corridor beyond. He was in deep trouble. How could the master possibly expect him to keep track of so many souls? Their numbers grew by the day and the resources at his disposal were actually diminishing.

He had been placed in charge of nearly a third of all of Hell. It was a vast domain to govern; encompassing some of the most grizzly torments this place had to offer, from the sea of fire, to the fire pits of the plains, to the graves of torment. It was almost too much, and now this.

How could she simply vanish? He, like any demon under his charge, could sense the presence of a human, even one hiding within the depths of the sea or within the darkest recesses of a cave. How had she eluded them? It didn't matter; he wouldn't rest until he found her, and when he did, she would pay dearly. He would expand his search beyond the sea if need be. He would not be denied.

⚜ ⚜ ⚜

It had been a long day of planting and transplanting in the green cavern. At its end, Abaddon and Serena sat across from one another in the great room, having one of their talks. The dark angel waved his hand before him, and immediately a large disk appeared before them, the image of a planet floating in midair. One side of the planet lay in perpetual daylight, the other in eternal darkness.

Abaddon smiled at the astonishment on his companion's face. "Far superior to a common map, wouldn't you agree? Behold the world you know as Hell, the world desecrated by satan and his angels, transformed into this abomination you see before you. Once a world rich in life, he has transformed it into a world of death. Everything he touches is destroyed. I still cannot comprehend the workings of a mind so foul."

Serena moved closer to the barren globe. The daylight side was an endless expanse of windswept desert, no oceans of water, no green whatsoever, only vast desolation. Even the cruel sun-baked expanses of the Sahara were more gentle than the world she saw here.

"The sunlit regions of this world bake at over 250 of your degrees Fahrenheit," said Abaddon. "Many and terrible are the torments of the souls imprisoned in the midst of its brutal midday radiance."

Serena's attention turned to the darkened hemisphere, a realm of glowing fire, the sea of fire. Yet there was something else, a peculiar shaped region of darkness. It was some sort of continent, a large one, surrounded by the flaming sea. Its shape reminded her of a prone human figure lying across the fiery sea. Well, maybe not a human figure, not exactly. It was more like a gingerbread man with short arms and legs. Then again, the continent of Australia had always reminded her of the head of a Scotty dog.

"The Continent of Darkness, curious, is it not? Is the shape a coincidence or is it by design?"

Serena shrugged. "I wouldn't know."

Abaddon pointed toward the short stubby arms of the continent. "This feature is formed by a long mountain range, as high and imposing as the Rocky Mountains of your Earth. The central regions of the continent are a vast windswept plateau over a mile high."

Serena noticed a few small regions of the dark continent that glowed a dull red, like a dying ember in the coal black darkness. There was even a blotch of white luminescence not far from the glowing sea. She felt a chill, a terrible sense of dread deep within.

Abaddon allowed Serena a moment to study this gloomy land. "To this place we shall soon make a pilgrimage. It is necessary, I assure you. If you are to ever truly appreciate the mind of the greatest enemy of all humankind, we must do this thing. I want you to understand."

Serena wasn't all that certain that she wanted to understand the mind of satan. Right now she was only too happy to hide within this great cavern. Any curiosity about the nature of satan had been burned away amid the flames of the sea. "When?"

"Soon."

The phantasmal globe vanished as Serena returned to her chair. The topic of their conversation shifted to lighter subjects; yet, what she had seen remained in the back of her mind, even as she retreated to her room for some well-deserved rest.

⚜ ⚜ ⚜

It was several days later when Abaddon and Serena climbed once more to the very highest peak of the island. It was a special day. Though Hell kept one face perpetually toward its sun, that axial lock was not absolute. Once every 71 days, the island moved closer to the daylight side than at any other time. It was a time to go up top and soak in the twilight.

Upon reaching the summit, Serena saw the band of blue across the western horizon, far brighter than she had ever seen it before. Its glow extended twice as high as it had the last time she had been up here, and the horizon itself took on an aspect of near daylight. It was an awesome sight. She might nearly have read a book by its glow. For a time they both admired its beauty, then Abaddon turned away. He walked from her, apparently in deep contemplation. Then he turned toward her.

"Serena, the time has come. I wish to broaden your horizons, to give unto you a better understanding of this place into which you have been set adrift. You should know all, know the hidden things that satan would have no humans understand. I wish, this day, to take you on that journey of discovery of which we had spoken, not so much to see the suffering of humankind in this place, but to understand all the more those who inflict it. In knowing your enemy, you can be all the better fortified against him."

"You mean we'll be traveling away from the island?"

"Yes," confirmed Abaddon, motioning toward the darkened eastern sky, illuminated occasionally by the lightning flashes of a distant storm.

The thought of traveling from this sanctuary brought a momentary shudder to Serena. "Across the sea of fire?"

"Very high above it," assured Abaddon. "From such heights you will scarcely feel its heat. I will protect you."

Serena wasn't so sure that she liked this idea. Right now she would have been more than satisfied to dwell in the cavern forever. The sea of fire had burned from her any curiosity she might have once had about this place. "What if we meet demons along the way?"

"They wouldn't see you," assured Abaddon. "The cloak you wear will obscure you from their view. Furthermore, it is within my power to cloud their minds, even as they have clouded the minds of so many of your kind. To them you would appear as I wish you to appear, as one of them if I so desired. Trust me in this; it is important."

"We're going to the Continent of Darkness, aren't we?"

Abaddon nodded.

Serena hesitated, then relented. "OK, Abaddon, I'll go with you. When do we leave?"

"Right now." Abaddon reached out to her. "Take my hand."

She wasn't quite prepared for that. Nonetheless, Serena moved toward her guardian, offering him her hand. His fingers wrapped around it as he drew her close. Serena closed her eyes as he entwined his arms about her, partially covering her in his cloak.

"Have courage," he said, spreading his dark wings. "The time has come for us to take flight."

With a few strokes of his wings, Abaddon bounded into the dark, featureless sky. Serena was surprised at how little motion she actually felt. This journey reminded her of her first journey beneath angel's wings, although there was less fear this time. Still, it was over a minute before she had the courage to open her eyes.

She was thousands of feet above the fiery sea and still climbing, flying eastward into the darkness. She could hear the rushing wind around her; sense the growing coolness of the air. She was unsure as to how fast they were traveling, for Abaddon seemed to be shielding her from the howling gale, yet she suspected that they were moving very fast indeed.

"We will be traveling well above those places frequented by the demons that patrol these skies," explained Abaddon. "There will be none to interfere with our sojourn this day."

"What are we going to see," asked Serena, gazing at the infernal seascape below.

"The City of Sheol, a congregating place for satan's minions as they try to seduce the whole of humankind. It is over a thousand miles distance, it will take us some time to arrive there. I will do my best to keep you comfortable until then."

Again Serena looked at the fiery sea directly below. So high were they that Serena saw the fires as a blur of pulsing, amber luminance stretching from horizon to horizon. Yet even from this lofty vantage, it brought back terrible memories. How many still suffered in its broiling vastness? She looked forward and to the left to see towering clouds, aglow from the tremendous electrical forces at work within their turbulent depths. It was an acid storm, viewed from a perspective that she had never imagined.

The storm was alive with blue white bolts of lightning coursing through, below, and around the yellowish white clouds. Below the cloudy mass, rains of acid and glowing blue sulfur fire fell in thick sheets to the sea. The thunder grew in volume and the lightning in brightness as their journey carried them closer, uncomfortably close, to the roiling maelstrom far below and toward the black, featureless firmament far above. Serena was certain that she could smell the acrid sulphurous stench as they flew past the storm's outer fringe and toward the blackness beyond.

Beyond the storm, the seascape was an expanse of amber beneath a black velvet sky. There was no turbulence, only the steady stream of air around wings that beat with a slow rhythm. Serena's initial fears faded. She was in the arms of someone who cared for her, someone she trusted. She finally relaxed. For a while she scanned the vista below her, then the beat of Abaddon's wings and the rushing of the air lulled her into a dreamless sleep.

When she opened her eyes, she sensed a change. Abaddon's wings were still; they were gliding. Far below, she saw what appeared to be an abrupt end to the glowing sea, as if they had reached the end of this world and were about to fly over the edge. But no, there was light some distance beyond the sea's edge. She had flown by night on a jet plane several times during her life. This looked like the lights of a great city, viewed from far off. Yet, there was more to this place than a pattern of lights on the ground; she could see the traces of glowing vapors rising from it, swirling above it, stretching high into the sky like some other-worldly aurora.

"Did you have a pleasant rest?" asked Abaddon, glancing down toward her.

"Yes," Serena said, still a bit groggy. "I guess I haven't been very good company for you. How long have I been asleep?"

"Not long, less than an hour. We are almost at our destination. It lies straight ahead, beyond the sea of fire, on the Continent of Darkness. It is the most unholy place in all of Hell."

"Is it a city, a city where demons live?"

"Not exactly, though many spend most of their existence here. It is a city, though not the kind you are familiar with. The City of Sheol is a bridgehead in the spiritual war for the souls of humankind. It is the place where demons gather to begin their ghostly journey to Earth, there to tempt and torment humans."

"But I thought everyone in outer darkness was stuck here."

"Their bodies are, but their spirits, their essence; that is another matter. Long ago, satan realized that he had to find a way to reach out of this realm to Earth. He couldn't allow himself to be confined, to leave humanity in peace; no, that was unthinkable. He knew that he and his angels were physically chained to this place, but they could still reach out with their minds. All they had to do was to find a means of focusing the power of their thoughts, projecting their minds into the living universe. What you see before you, this city, if you will, is that means. It lies at a point where the barrier between this world and your Earth is the weakest. It draws upon the hidden energies trapped within this world, and that radiated by the fiery luminary it circles."

The network of lights that Serena had seen from a distance was growing closer. It was vast, many miles across. She could see tiny dark figures swirling around its many luminaries, coming and going like moths around a light bulb on a sultry summer night. No, not moths, but demons, countless thousands of them.

"At any given time, there are tens or even hundreds of millions demons in this place, seeking to travel to Earth to undermine all that is good and noble about humans, to pit your kind against one another, to place enmity between you and God. It is a campaign orchestrated by satan himself, to his precise specifications. In so doing he brings even more of your kind to this place, subjecting them to whatever horrors he sees fit to bestow upon them."

Abaddon flew to one side, toward the very edge of the city of light. As he drew closer, Serena could see this place for what it truly was. It was not a city of houses, streets, and shops, but an intricate network of crystal pillars, supporting glassy lintels that spanned the distance between them. Here and there tall shimmering archways and lofty towers of black obsidian broke the checkerboard pattern of glistening glass. In the midst of it all were countless demons, standing and kneeling, supported by their black bat-like wings. They were motionless, like so many vulgar gargoyles.

Abaddon pirouetted, sweeping away from this gathering place of evil and the swirling demons above it, moving across the dark rocky plains beyond. He turned once more, and touched down on solid ground. He unfolded his arms to allow Serena to take her first steps upon this dark domain. It was actually cool here, unlike the torrid realm of eternal daylight or even Abaddon's island. The only light radiated from the city. Gone was the bow of blue across the horizon, so far were they into the realm of eternal night.

"We will travel on foot from here," explained Abaddon.

"But won't they recognize me?" asked Serena. "After all, I'm human, they'll be able to tell, even if I am wearing this cloak."

"No they won't," replied Abaddon, leading her forward. "As I mentioned before, it is within my power to cloud their minds. In you they will see another fallen angel, not like themselves, but like me. They will not challenge us so long as we do not interfere with the tasks set before them by their master. We shall not wander into their city of power but view it from the outside. To wander within would be to expose ourselves to satan's minions. There, I could not guarantee you that I could shield you from them."

It was difficult for Serena to see where she was going. The only light around her, the glow of the crystal city, cast long harsh shadows on the rocky ground. Yet if not for its luminance, she would have been in total darkness.

"The Continent of Darkness is a land of perpetual night, as the name implies," Abaddon said as he helped Serena cross the rugged landscape. "You saw it on the globe I revealed to you several days past. It is a vast land, bordered on all sides by the sea of fire. Here, a few miles from its turbulent shoreline, the conditions are warm enough. In this region, the sea of fire lends some measure of warmth to the vast dark realm.

"The farther into the depths of this vast continent one goes, over its high rugged mountains, and across its barren valleys, the more severe the climate becomes. In its deep interior, its frigid breezes rival those of deepest Antarctica. There, amid the unimaginable cold, satan has doomed countless numbers of your people to a cruel and sadistic fate. I shall not speak of the specifics, for they are all too gruesome to imagine. Hell is a realm of vast contrasts, and satan uses them to his advantage." Abaddon motioned toward the city of light. "It all starts here. From this place satan dispatches his hordes to confuse and mislead humanity."

Within a few minutes, they stood at the very threshold of the metropolis. Here the black porous volcanic rock gave way to a floor of shimmering obsidian, from which the crystal columns towered. They rose some 20 feet into the dark sky, flooding the landscape with eerie pulsing luminance. Abaddon pointed to several demons kneeling just beyond the columns.

"These soldiers of satan might remain motionless for months or even years at a time. Without their inner essence, their spirits to guide them, they are empty shells."

Serena watched them carefully. Even in their helpless state, they had a ghastly aura about them. "What can their spirits do on Earth? Can they actually possess a person, take control of them?"

"In some cases, it all depends on the individual. There are those who say that satan and his minions may not enter a body uninvited. That is not as true in the natural sense as it is in the spiritual sense. The spirit of a demon must first surround an individual. From there he can influence their thoughts, sow the seeds of ideas into their minds. If those seeds take root, they might not need to bother further with that person, for he is already beginning to travel the road to perdition on his own. It is like a weed planted among the grain; it will grow and multiply on its own, choking out all that is good about a man or woman. In the end, only the weeds survive, and that individual is ripe for satan's harvest."

"But stories of demonic possession, are they true? Is there such a thing?"

"Yes," Abaddon said. "Though it is easier for a demon to enter into the body of an animal, some demons trick the possessed human to open up to them. They promise them all manners of things. If the house of their soul is empty, unfilled by God's Holy Spirit, they might indeed come to reside there for a time, usually just long enough to bring destruction upon their human host and those around him."

"In other cases, they might linger, dominate that body, using it as their own. They might use that individual to do unspeakable things, perhaps to lure whole nations to their doom. Still, such things are relatively rare. A demon does not have the time to dedicate himself to one person for an extended period. He must be about the destruction of others."

Abaddon pointed toward a winged demon descending into the great metropolis not far away. "Watch carefully and learn."

The demon landed just within the outer ring of columns that formed the boundary of the city, folded his wings, and proceeded to a place prepared for him, an open cubical surrounded by four towering crystals topped with square transparent lintels. The entire structure glowed with a green pulsing light.

The demon knelt in a peculiar fashion, leaning forward, supporting himself on his large leathery wings. He lowered his head and his arms went limp at his side. The crystals around him grew in brightness, even as glowing, swirling vapors emanated from all parts of his body. The vapors gathered about him, then shot sky-ward and out of sight. The form of the demon became motionless, apparently lifeless, like the others around him.

"His essence is on its way to Earth," announced Abaddon. "It will not wander randomly, but has a specific mission. It will attempt to destroy the eternal life of someone upon your green world. It will try to wreak as much damage as possible before returning here for another assignment. Such is the eternity of a demon, to forever seek to destroy. What a pointless existence."

For a time the two stood there quietly, watching the greatest tragedy in the universe unfold. Then they heard footsteps. Both Abaddon and Serena turned to see a demon approaching them, walking just beyond the threshold of the city.

Serena gasped quietly at his countenance. He was robed all in black, with a hood drawn over his head. What she could see of his face was ghastly. Though his facial features were somewhat human, his eyes were like those of an insect—large, amber, and segmented. From his narrow lips, a pair of long menacing fangs protruded. He was the very essence of nightmares.

"Most unusual," Abaddon said. "Rarely does satan post sen-tries around this place."

"Who are you, what are you doing here?" demanded the demon, in a thundering voice. Though this creature spoke in a dialect of the tongue of angels, Serena had learned enough of it to understand his meaning.

"Say nothing," whispered Abaddon stepping toward the being before them.

"I am waiting," roared the demon.

"And you can go on waiting, for all I care," responded Abaddon, showing not the least trace of fear. "We are not here to cause trouble, unless that is what you desire."

"You speak bravely," retorted the demon in a taunting tone. He turned to Serena, who struggled to retain some measure of calm. "And who is your silent companion?"

"That is none of your concern," Abaddon said. "Why don't you dispense with the charade, we are unimpressed."

Quite abruptly the demon's form changed to the aspects with which Serena was more familiar, a dark human-like face replaced that which had preceded it. "I will ask again; what is your business here?"

"We have no business here. We are, as you might say, just passing through, taking but a moment to rest our wings. We thought to observe this game of yours more closely."

"Game? You think this is a game? Your kind disgusts me," said the demon. "God has discarded you. You dwell within the master's domain now, yet you refuse to pay him homage. Satan is the rightful ruler of creation, and one day he shall take his place of honor upon Heaven's throne. When that day comes, we shall be at his side."

"I'm not surprised, a blind guide leading the blind," retorted Abaddon.

"So you say now, but in the end, where shall you and your kind be?"

"One can never know," Abaddon said. "Yet it is clear to me that we are not welcome here. We are sufficiently rested. Furthermore, we have promised your master that we shall not interfere in your affairs. Therefore, we shall take our leave and trouble you no more."

"No you won't," retorted the demon. "You are not telling me the truth. There is something wrong here, you are hiding something. Or is it that you are hiding someone?" The demon turned toward Serena. "You are the mystery. There is something about you, about your aura. I will know what that thing is. You will come with me into the sanctum, there to be interrogated."

"Not likely," replied Abaddon, stepping into the demon's path. His face displayed no emotion.

The demon spun about and cried out in a shrill tone. Then he turned to Serena once more. "There is a strange odor to this one. Yes, you will come with me." He moved toward her, yet barely completed a step before being apprehended by her guardian.

In an instant Abaddon had hold of his throat, rendering the demon unable to speak above a whisper. He lifted him from the ground with one arm. "Now, where are your manners? You do not seem to comprehend the nature of your predicament. Don't make threats that you cannot possibly see to fruition. You were not created to be a warrior. On the other hand, I was. Shall I demonstrate the difference?"

Abaddon paused; he had sensed something. He turned to his left to see several dark figures in the distance, the figures of demon sentries, just beyond the threshold of the city. He had been here many times, yet he had never received such an unpleasant reception. Already two of them had taken flight, and were moving swiftly in his direction. He had erred, and in doing so placed Serena in grave jeopardy.

"No, it is you who are in a predicament. You won't escape us," squeaked the demon, still struggling to free himself from the powerful warrior's grasp.

Serena had now caught sight of the approaching band of demons as well. She was absolutely terrified. She could not see how many there were, yet she feared it was a number greater than Abaddon could handle.

Abaddon cast the demon away like a child's toy. He hurtled over 20 feet through the air, crashing into one of the crystal pillars at the city's edge. Then Abaddon turned to Serena. "We must flee at once, there is great danger here."

He drew her close, picked her from her feet, and began to run. Within seconds, that run had turned to flight. The wind whipped through his cloak, as they soared ever higher; yet, their demon pursuers were closing in on them. With all of his might, Abaddon struggled for speed and altitude. He might have out flown them easily, were it not for the extra weight he carried in his arms, a weight that was far too precious to shed. He pushed himself harder. He swept downward, in an attempt to pick up some additional speed. He turned inland, away from the illumination of the infernal city, toward the realm of profound darkness.

This was a dangerous game. Although his pursuers would be hard pressed to see him in the fading light, he was running the risk of slamming into a rocky ridge in the increasingly rough country before them. He would have to depend on his intuition, upon his memory of the landforms.

The gravity of their situation was not lost on Serena. She knew all too well what it was that Abaddon was attempting to do and the dangers inherent in that undertaking. She kept her silence so he might accomplish the difficult task. She offered a silent prayer.

A dark silhouette hurtled past them on the right, then another on the left. The dark rugged terrain seemed to rush up at them from beneath. They were going to crash! Serena felt the force of the acceleration as Abaddon's wings tilted back, beating to an increasing rhythm. They soared over the ridge top with only a few feet to spare. They pulled steeply up, swung hard to the left, then plunged into the steep walled canyon beyond.

There was a moment of total silence as the angel's wings went still; then came a sudden deceleration as they swung around a barely seen pillar of rock not an arms length away. Abaddon swung upward for a second; then there was a jolt as his feet planted themselves firmly on the ground. They had landed safely in the near total darkness of the canyon.

"Quiet," he whispered, as he gently placed Serena on the ground.

Abaddon wrapped Serena's black cloak around her and pushed her tightly against the rock face.

There was a distant sound of confusion, it was cursing in the language of angels, and a tumbling of rocks to the canyon floor. Apparently one or more of their pursuers had not cleared the ridge above the canyon rim. A second later, Serena could just barely discern the forms of several flying demons against the dark sky, faintly illuminated by the distant lights of the infernal city and the glowing sea beyond. They swung toward them, paying no mind to their companions left behind on the ridge and continued the pursuit at full speed, passing nearly overhead. A moment later, they vanished into the gloom.

"In just a moment, they will realize that we have evaded them," whispered Abaddon, so softly as to barely be heard. "They will probably double back, but by then we shall be gone."

"Do these demons usually treat you like this?" Serena asked, still disoriented from the wild ride.

"No, and this troubles me greatly. Something is going on in the ranks of satan's minions today. They appear to be on a high state of alert. I have been very foolish; I have placed you in great peril."

"It's OK," said Serena, trying to comfort her troubled companion. "Tomorrow we'll probably look back and laugh about this whole affair."

"I only wish that I shared your optimistic appraisal of our situation. Our trip home is going to be most difficult. We would be easily spotted over the sea of fire. We will need to move inland

and try to swing back later, perhaps several hundred of your miles up the coast. It might be sometime before we see home again. We cannot risk our being followed back to our lair."

Abaddon scooped Serena up in his arms and took to the skies. He flew low and with little speed so as to make a minimum of noise. Serena couldn't imagine how Abaddon was navigating this treacherous canyon. She could see the rim on one side and occasionally she could make out the rocky floor below, but not well enough to navigate the labyrinth of towering pillars and sinuous ridges. All the while Abaddon's speed and altitude grew, until they climbed above the canyon rim.

Serena turned her head to see the city far behind them and only darkness ahead. She could feel the growing chill as they penetrated ever deeper into this land of profound gloom.

"I'm afraid it's going to become a little uncomfortable for a while," warned Abaddon, swinging out of the canyon and flying across the barren landscape beyond. "I am going to try to circle back to the sea, and from there on home, but we might have a few very cold hours along the way. I'm sorry to put you through this."

"I'll hold up fine," assured Serena, wrapping herself all the tighter in her black cloak. "You just concentrate on the flying."

Abaddon didn't reply; he was already focusing on his task. His endurance wasn't limitless. He had been flying for hours with only a short break, and he was beginning to tire.

They flew higher, above a towering range of mountains barely seen in the fading light of the sea of fire behind them and the dim glow of an aurora that danced in the sky overhead like a ghostly apparition.

"Those happen quite often in these parts," Abaddon said, sensing the concern of his companion. "It's a completely natural phenomenon, nothing to be concerned about. Actually it may be helpful in lighting our way, making it less likely for us to fly into a mountain. That sort of thing could ruin our entire trip."

Abaddon's attempt at humor didn't dispel her fears, yet she appreciated the thought.

They soared over a sharp mountaintop and down into a vast interior valley. All the while it grew colder. Her cloak helped somewhat, but Serena could not remember when she had felt so cold. Beyond the next ridge of mountains she saw a towering peak, and above it, a red plume of fire and smoke—a volcano.

"Fire and ice," Abaddon said, "the extremes of the senses, both capable of delivering great pain. Your poet, Dante, wrote of fire and ice in Hell. Well, there it is. Satan has devised a whole range of cruel and painful ordeals based around those themes; and there, beyond the next ridge in the Valley of Sheol, one can experience both. The fire comes from the scorching depths of Hell, the ice from the unimaginable cold of outer darkness. We shall avoid that region."

"Are there a lot of demons there?" asked Serena.

Abaddon laughed slightly. "No, not too many at all. Actually, demons try to avoid these regions. The conditions here are even too severe for them. Only the delivering of a soul to his or her eternal torment will bring them to this dark realm."

For over an hour, Abaddon and Serena cruised the black, frigid province before turning back toward the distant sea. The journey seemed to be taking a toll on the mighty angel. His wings beat irregularly and his course through the air wavered. Inevitably, he descended toward the dark, wide valley below.

"I have to rest," he said in a breathless tone. "I can't afford to reach the point of exhaustion over the sea of fire. Such would have dire consequences for us both."

The ground grew closer as the angel battled for control amid the strong, icy breezes. To Serena it looked like a good landing site below, flat with few rocks; yet Abaddon seemed to be struggling. She held her breath.

Abaddon touched down on a vast level expanse of rock and ice. Almost immediately, he dropped to his knees. "Stay close...I must rest for a few hours. Then we can travel home."

Abaddon released Serena as his wings drew tightly about him. Within seconds, he went still, resting upon his large, folded wings and his knees.

"Abaddon?" asked Serena. There was no response. "Abaddon?" Still nothing.

She quickly realized that he had dropped away into some sort of trance-like sleep. She had seen him like this before in the cavern. There would be no waking him until he was ready. All that she could do was to wait. She could definitely think of more pleasant places to do that. It had to be well below zero here, and the constant merciless winds, made it seem all the colder. Right now, she was grateful to be wearing the thick boots and the incredibly resilient cloak. Even still, the wind cut into her like a knife. It produced such a mournful sound as it whined and howled across the barren landscape.

She took a moment to scan her surroundings, seen only by virtue of the auroral lights overhead. The ground was frozen solid, a mixture of dark sand and ice interspersed with flat gray rocks that reminded her of flagstone. There were mountains to either side of the valley; she had seen them from the air, though she couldn't see them from here through the haze of blowing sand and ice. She was by no means inclined to wander away from Abaddon in this place. She would try to rest as well. She settled down beside her guardian angel, allowing his wings to partially shield her from the gale. She pulled her cloak around her, and did her best to catch some sleep.

chapter twentythree

SERENA awoke quite suddenly to the biting cold that had even managed to penetrate the black cloak that Abaddon had made for her. She rose to her knees and looked around. Abaddon hadn't moved a muscle. Apparently he was still in a deep almost comatose sleep. She wondered just how long it might be before he was ready to resume the journey. Whenever, it wouldn't be too soon for her.

The winds had died down to little more than a gentle breeze and the blowing dust and snow had settled, leaving the air crystal clear. Overhead, the aurora coursed in colorful waves of light through the starless heavens. It was far brighter now, allowing her to view her surroundings more vividly than before. It was a haunting and unearthly sight, as ice glistened in the shimmering waves of light from above. To either side she could see distant craggy mountains of dark rock, dusted here and there with snow and ice.

Again she glanced over at her sleeping companion. She considered waking him, but no, she'd best allow him to come around on his own.

Perhaps a short walk would help her warm up a bit. She set off down the valley, mindful not to place too much distance between herself and her guardian. If the winds would rise again, there might be enough snow and ice to produce a whiteout that would make it difficult to find her way back. She would not take any chances.

As she walked, she often scanned the skies, searching for any sign of flying demons, yet the firmament remained clear. What self-respecting demon would travel on a night like this anyway?

She was only about a hundred or so yards from her guardian, and was about to turn back, when a mournful cry emanated from somewhere nearby. To say that it startled her would have been an understatement—she was terrified. She turned in the direction of the cry, yet nothing immediately caught her eye.

"Hello?" she asked, reaching into her cloak and coming up with one of the glowing gems that Abaddon had provided her with. The shape of this one allowed it to create a beam, like a flashlight. She directed it toward the icy ground, scanning in the direction of the commotion. Then she saw it, perhaps 40 or 50 feet away. At first it looked like a rounded rock. She might have passed over it completely had it not moved slightly when the beam hit it. She hesitated before moving cautiously toward it. It wasn't until she was about a dozen feet away that she realized that it was a head, a man's head and a little bit of his neck, protruding up from the icy ground. He was facing in nearly the opposite direction, and ice and snow clung to his frozen hair and bluish skin.

"Who's there?" asked the man, in a trembling voice. He tried to turn his head, but with little success.

"A friend," answered Serena, drawing still closer.

"A friend?" gasped the man, "I don't think I have any friends anymore. Not anymore, not here."

Serena stepped around to see the man's face, one blue with the cold and covered with crystals of ice. She knelt down before him.

"You're not a demon?"

Serena shook her head. "No, of course not, I'm human just like you." She reached out to touch his face; it was as cold as ice."

"Yes," was the response, "I can see that, but how?"

"It's a long story," said Serena. "I was just passing through. I'd stopped to rest, only to find you here."

"Just passing through? Oh, that's rich," said the man, in a tone of voice that was either a laugh or a cry. Serena wasn't quite sure which, yet there was a trace of madness in it. "You, you're on the run, aren't you?"

"Yes, I'm on the run."

"I know what it's like to be on the run," gasped the man, apparently having trouble breathing. "I'd much rather be on the run, than be stuck here in this frozen hole."

For a moment he seemed to be struggling, fighting to move his body; totally encased in the ice. It was an exercise in futility.

Serena was confused. She should have steered clear of this guy. She really didn't want to be having this conversation. It reminded her of that half day traveling through Hell, traveling to her own demise. "Why…"

"Why did the devil send me here? Is that what you want to know, girly?" The man seemed agitated. "I was set up. I've always been set up. I was dealt a pretty lousy hand in life, not that anyone ever cared." He tried to look Serena in the eyes. It was so difficult for him to move his head amid the dirty ice that surrounded him. "They said that I murdered them, that I murdered them all, they said it at my trial, and at my judgment. The state sentenced me to the gas chamber, and then God did the state one better, He sentenced me to Hell."

"Are you trying to tell me that you're innocent?"

"Hell, no," the man said. "I don't think you'd believe that. The jury didn't, and neither did God; and He is supposed to know everything, right? I'm just saying that they had it coming, the ones I killed. They weren't no angels, that's for sure. The world was a whole lot better off without them."

"You took a human life; but you have no remorse, do you?"

"Only that I got caught, that satan sentenced me to this place. He didn't even have the nerve to do it to me himself, he had a couple of his flunkies bring me out here, almost naked, shackled hand and foot.

"They used some sort of crazy firebomb to melt this permafrost, or whatever you call it. It turned it into warm quicksand. Then they just threw me in and left. I thought I might have been able to get out of this stuff, but I couldn't, not with my hands cuffed to this heavy belt around my waist, and my ankles shackled tight together. I had to really struggle just to keep my head above this stuff, to keep from drowning."

"But you can't drown here," objected Serena.

The man chuckled in a way that made a chill course up Serena's back. "Yeah, girly, I sort of figured that one out. I figured it out, even as this stuff started to freeze around me. If you don't put up a fight you freeze in solid with your head beneath the ice. You suffocate as well as freeze. That's even worse. Yeah, I just kept fighting, kept my head above water, even still, the pain was like a hundred knives being driven right through me, but it didn't kill me…no, it just kept getting colder, hurting more."

The man paused. "Soon I was frozen in solid, and the cold just kept going into me, deeper and deeper. You know, you get use to it eventually, you become sort of numb. Oh, it still hurts, but you learn to deal with it. At least some people do. You know, there are people out here in the ice that scream their heads off for hours at a time. Others don't make a sound, cuz their totally buried in the ice."

"There are others around here?"

"A whole bunch," confirmed the man, "scattered out all over. Maybe the demons will catch you and plant you here with the rest of us. I wonder if you'll just stand there like a rock or if you'll scream like a stuck pig." The man lifted his head as high into the air as he could. "Hey demons, I've got a live one for ya, fresh meat. Hey, don't you hear me? Don't you want her?"

Serena stepped back.

"You can plant her here right beside me," he continued. "Even better, plant her right in front of me, facing this way. I'd just love to watch the look on her face for the rest of eternity." Quite abruptly he grew silent and a broad smile came over his face. "Well, well," he mumbled.

Serena was startled when she felt the hand on her shoulder. She spun around to see Abaddon standing right behind her.

"I asked you not to wander," he said, in a patient tone.

"Hey, big fellow," said the man in the ice, looking toward the dark angel, "why not plant this one right here beside me."

Abaddon didn't so much as acknowledge him. He looked to his companion. "Ready to go, Serena?"

"Yes, if you are," she replied, drawing her dark cloak more tightly about her.

The man in the ice seemed confused. "Hey, I thought you guys were supposed hate humans. Well, torment her; plant her in the ice with the rest of us. During my life, I sent you guys a whole lot of girls, just like her. I sent 'em on the highway to Hell. The least you could do is give me a special girlfriend. Let me gaze into her eyes for the rest of eternity."

Abaddon simply shook his head.

The man's agitation grew as Abaddon drew Serena close to him. "Hey, who are you anyway?"

"I'm her ride," replied the dark angel, bounding into the air with a single stroke of his wings, leaving the man in a cloud of dust and ice crystals. He continued to rave on wildly, yet neither Abaddon nor Serena could understand him, for they had already left him far behind.

"If we are going to survive as a team, you need to follow instructions," said Abaddon. There was no anger in his voice at all. If anything, Serena detected a note of concern.

"I'm sorry," she replied.

"Yes, I know you are," confirmed Abaddon. "Did you learn anything useful from that man back there?"

"No, not really," replied Serena. "There was something very disturbing about him. There was no repentance at all in his heart. I could feel it. Even the pains of Hell haven't changed him. If he were to be released right now, I believe he would go back to his old ways. He would go on killing. Why do people have to be that way? It just doesn't make any sense."

"Yes, I know. Many, if not most, of the souls here are just that way."

"There is just no peace in this place, not anywhere," lamented Serena, who was nearly in tears now. "Even out here in the dark, in the ice and snow. Satan's victims are everywhere. How can he keep hurting people? He's just like that man back there, but with the power to hurt so many. Why doesn't someone stop him? I don't want to leave the island again, never again. I don't even want to step outside the cavern."

"Easy, Serena," said Abaddon. "We're flying home now. It is a long flight, but I am well rested. I do not believe that we will have any more trouble."

Serena remained quiet as she watched the cold, hostile landscape slip farther below them. It grew even colder.

"This flight will be a difficult one," continued Abaddon. "We will be flying very high to find a river of wind that sweeps forever westward around the globe of Hell. It will take us far above the realm of demons and shorten our sojourn, but the air will be thin and very cold. I know you will be uncomfortable, but I do not wish for any demons to follow us home. I shall endeavor to make this as fast a flight as possible."

Ever higher the two ascended, toward the glowing auroral curtain above. Though Abaddon did everything within his power to make his companion comfortable, the cold and rare air made the trip, to say the least, miserable. Serena took deep breaths, yet they yielded little reward.

It was a few minutes before the great sea of fire appeared on the horizon, and as they crossed above it, the air seemed a little warmer. Serena tried to sleep but she couldn't, it was just too cold.

Slowly the horizon before them brightened, becoming the familiar bow of blue, yet it took the form of a majestic arch, so great was their altitude. It became brighter and brighter, until Serena could almost imagine the location of the sun at its center, somewhere just beyond the glowing horizon.

"It is beautiful, is it not?" said Abaddon. "We are about twelve of your miles above the great sea. I doubt that any of your kind has ever seen what you are witnessing now."

Yes, it was beautiful, but Serena's discomfort made it very difficult to appreciate it. All she could think about was the cavern and being warm again. Then she saw it, a dark silhouette against the fiery sea below, it was their island home, they had made it.

Their descent was swift; so much so as to leave Serena's ears in considerable pain. The air warmed as they swung in over the tiny archipelago, spiraling ever downward. They were beginning their final descent when a white figure standing at the very summit of the islands lone peak caught Serena's eye. A demon? No it didn't look like one. Even from here she could feel a spiritual radiance from this being. It was an angel! But what had brought an angel to this place? She heard a groan emanate from Abaddon.

"Well, well, who do we have here?" he said, scanning their visitor from above. He swept low over the peak to get a better look at their unexpected guest. "It appears to be one of Gabriel's brood, a messenger. I suppose we shall have to see what business he has with us this day."

Abaddon pirouetted in midair and touched down 20 feet from their visitor in white. He released Serena and stood there like a statue, his wings folded.

Serena stepped forward eyeing their visitor, then she recognized him. Yes, this was the same angel! Before she could speak, Abaddon addressed their unexpected guest. "Welcome to my home, Aaron. I hadn't thought to see you again."

The angel nodded. "Peace be with you, Abaddon, and with you, Serena Davis."

Serena Davis, not Serena Farnsworth, what had happened? Serena was full of questions, yet before even a single one of them could be asked, Aaron produced from his cloak a large envelope. By now Aaron couldn't help but smile slightly. "Serena Davis; this communication is addressed to you."

"For me?" she gasped, taking the letter in hand. She looked at it carefully. Like all proper letters of her time, this one had a return address; Christopher Davis, Heaven. She fell to her knees, tears of joy pouring from her eyes. "It's a miracle!"

"Yes," confirmed Aaron, placing a kind hand upon the weeping woman. "Your husband approached me this very day, handed this letter to me. He instructed me to deliver it here to you, a task I more than gladly fulfill. He remembers you, Serena. He told me that he remembers everything. It is a thing for which I have no explanation."

"Let us retreat to the safety of the caverns," suggested Abaddon. "Something is indeed wrong. Satan's minions are on high alert, for reasons I cannot understand."

Both Abaddon and Aaron assisted Serena to her feet and the three descended down the treacherous path to the cavern entrance. Serena held on tightly to the envelope, caressing it with her hand. She would open it after they were safely inside.

"I have been awaiting your return for several hours," said Aaron. "I was about to depart."

"Thank God you didn't," said Serena, walking between the two angels. "This is the most precious gift I have ever received."

Serena considered their situation for a moment. "I take it that the two of you already know each other. Is that true with all angels?"

There was a pause. "Yes, Serena, that is indeed true, but our relationship is somewhat deeper than that, isn't it, Aaron?" There was something about Abaddon's tone of voice. Serena could sense an air of thinly veiled hostility about it.

"Yes," replied Aaron. "We have worked together before, a very long time ago."

Again silence, a silence that Serena seemed unable to dispel. They walked into the cavern entrance and toward the great room. Serena wasted no time opening the envelope and sitting down in her favorite chair to read it. The two angels watched. The animosity that existed between them seemed temporarily dispelled by their mutual concern for Serena as she read the wonderful letter:

My Lovely Serena,

I miss you terribly. I am so sorry I left you behind. Please find it in your heart to forgive me. From the instant I entered the tunnel of light, until just a few days ago, the memory of you had been almost wiped from my mind. Yet, so strong was our love, that it bridged the great void between Heaven and Hell. You came to me in my dreams, stirring my memory, until I came to my senses, remembering all that I had lost. I came to realize that Heaven without you was somehow empty, eternity without you was empty. A letter is a poor substitute for being with you, yet it is all we have, for now. No one here in Heaven remembers their loved ones lost in Hell. I think that it is in God's plan that I have remembered you. I still believe that there is some hope for us.

Chris's letter went on to speak of his life in Heaven with his mother. It described the wondrous world that surrounded him. He spoke of meeting Jesus. It all sounded so wonderful. And it proclaimed his love for her, over and over again.

When she came to the end of it, she read the letter from her mother-in-law. She seemed so wonderful. How Serena would have loved meeting her. At last she came to the mysterious package. Her eyes grew large at the sight of its contents.

"Abaddon, come look! Seeds, all sorts of seeds. Seeds for flowers, vegetables, vines, even trees. It's a miracle. There are so many things here for the garden."

"Garden?" queried Aaron.

"Yes, I have preserved some of the native vegetation of this world in a large cavern below," noted Abaddon, in an attempt to break the tenseness. "Under the crystal lights, they have survived quite well. Serena has been caring for it. Perhaps you would like to see it."

Aaron nodded. "It surprises me not that you would embark on such a mission. You always held the green Earth in such reverence. Yes, I would like to see this thing you have done."

Abaddon turned to Serena. "We will be adjourning to the garden. I will show Aaron that which you have worked so hard to preserve. Remain here if you wish, read your letter again. I know how important it is to you."

Serena nodded as the angels walked toward the tunnel that led to Hell's only garden. After a minute, she looked up from her reading; then set it aside. She rose to her feet.

Aaron scanned the wondrous realm of green before him. Never had he expected to see such a thing here. He turned to Abaddon. "It is truly a miracle, truly it is."

"It is all that I have left," replied Abaddon, "this and Serena."

"I understand," confirmed Aaron.

"Do you?" said Abaddon, a flash of anger in his eyes. "It is not like that. It is not like it was. She is my companion, my friend, no more."

"I didn't mean to offend," assured Aaron, attempting to be consoling. "We have all suffered as a result of what we did."

"Excuse me if I don't mourn your fate," retorted Abaddon, turning from Aaron and walking deeper into the garden. "I have been sentenced here for all eternity, here among the fallen. I am a true outcast, abandoned by God, rejected by my fellow angels, even scorned and mistrusted by satan and his brood. Not that I would want it to be any other way in their case, but I am truly alone here—until Serena came into my life."

"And do you think I get pleasure in what I do?" said Aaron with a trace of anger in his voice. "Do you think I find joy in delivering the lost directly into satan's hands? I do not. I was brought low over what we did all those years ago, demoted to the lowest level in the ranks of my fellows. I am shunned for what I did. I have suffered too, Abaddon; do not think otherwise."

"Yes, my heart truly bleeds for you," growled Abaddon, turning once more toward Aaron. "I would give anything; become the lowest of the low, if I could be in the Father's presence once more. I long to be with Him. I made a mistake, a terrible mistake. I would do anything if I could take it back, but I can't. That thought torments me constantly, and it will do so eternally."

Aaron's anger dissolved into nothingness, his expression held the deepest sympathy for his former angelic brother. "I'm sorry. You're right; I cannot imagine how it has been for you and the others here. I was fortunate that the Father showed me some measure of leniency. I have been feeling sorry for myself, rather than being grateful for God's mercy. I deserve no better than you."

Abaddon's anger too ebbed. He placed his hand on Aaron's shoulder. "No, your sin was not as great as mine. I fear the pain of my loss has festered within my soul for a very long time. Forgive me, my brother. I should not have felt anger toward you. God's judgment was just."

Abaddon pondered if he should reveal his greatest secret to Aaron. "There is something I have to show you. Yes, I will show it to you," he looked back toward the cavern entrance, "and to you too, Serena."

Serena stepped from the shadows and into the brightness of the green cavern. She was embarrassed that she had been caught listening to their conversation.

"Yes, I knew that you were there," said Abaddon, a slight smile on his face. "You have not offended me. Come, join us."

Abaddon turned and stretched his hand toward the green leafy realm. "It goes beyond this. The thing that has kept me alive all of these years, the work of my hands, my creation. It is the thing that shall one day strike a blow against satan and his minions, strike a blow for the saints against the adversary, against the very kingdom of darkness." He turned to Serena. "It has been here all the while, but you have never seen it. It has remained hidden from you, hidden by design."

Serena was confused. "What has remained hidden?"

"You shall see." Abaddon stepped into some tall bushes nearby and searched for something for more than a minute. Then he emerged with some sort of creature in his hand. Serena cringed at the sight of it. Apparently it had been here all along, but she had never seen it.

Abaddon walked back toward his compatriots, creature in hand. "This is genetic manipulation on the highest level. I created it through selective breading and genetic engineering over the period of some twenty centuries. It is not of the quality that the

Father might bring forth, still it is a noble attempt for an angel. I doubt that any of our kind has ever accomplished this. Come close and meet my friend, one of my children."

Serena cautiously approached his creature. It was the size of a very large insect, four or five inches long. At first she assumed that it was just that, but she was wrong. Its body did have six legs, though two of them were directed forward, more like arms. They even had primitive hands with long sharp nails with which to grab things. Yet, unlike insects, this creature was not covered by some sort of dark exoskeleton, but rather, with tan-colored skin, which in turn, was covered in some areas by brown fur. At its hind end was a large barbed stinger, like a scorpion, but larger and more ominous. It could be retracted partially into its tail. Its legs were covered with fur, with claw-like feet that were used for grasping. It had large almost leathery, translucent wings.

Its large head was far from insect-like. Its eyes were small and black, and had eyelids like those of a human being. Its nose also had human qualities. It had long hair that swept back from its head, and when its mouth opened, a set of sharp white teeth were clearly visible. It cocked its head and gazed toward Serena.

"There are currently about thirty of these things flying around in here," noted Abaddon. Mostly, they live in the small side tunnels, only occasionally venturing into the garden itself. You see, they are mostly meat eaters, feeding on cave worms, small insects in the garden, and ground slugs—keeping their populations under control. They are not immortal, but they are incredibly resilient, very difficult to kill, fast, and highly intelligent. They sense my thoughts and obey them." Abaddon stretched his hand toward Serena. "Here, take her, she won't hurt you. I promise."

Serena stretched out a trembling hand and the creature immediately stepped from Abaddon's hand to hers. Amazingly, the creature started to stroke the fur of her belly and sides against

Serena's skin, rubbing back and forth, walking in a circle, almost like a cat. It sort of tickled. The creature glanced up at Serena. Serena was certain that it had smiled at her.

"She likes you," announced Abaddon, "I knew she would. I'm not making her do that, she is doing it of her own volition."

"So, you use these things for pest control?" Serena asked.

"For now," said Abaddon, "but they one day will be called to a higher purpose. You see, they have their own set of unique instincts, and they are capable of thinking for themselves. They will do no harm to any sort of plant life. Yet, they have the instincts of a predator, a very selective predator. They prey upon demons and all those who follow them. They can sense the contents of the heart, the purity of the soul, the aura. They would never harm you, for that very reason. They hid their presence from you until now. Yet I tell you this; one day, when the time is right, I will release them and their progeny, and I will have my revenge upon satan and his minions. I will make them feel the pain that they have made others feel. My children will feed upon their blood and in doing so multiply. I will make satan and his minions beg for the mercy of oblivion, but they will not find it."

Serena looked at Abaddon incredulously. This was a side of her guardian angel that she hadn't seen until now. Quite abruptly, the creature on her hand flew away.

"It sensed your fear," Abaddon said. "It will not trouble you again."

Serena looked toward Aaron. There was a sense of deep concern in his troubled eyes.

"Have you nothing to say about what you have just seen?" asked Abaddon, looking toward Aaron.

"I don't know what to say about what I have just seen," admitted Aaron. "Does not vengeance belong to the Father and the Father alone?"

"I couldn't say. I am no longer in contact with the Father, remember? When the Father has called upon me, it was to destroy. Long ago, he called me from this place with instructions to kill the first born in Egypt. I obeyed him without question. He has, from time to time, given me other missions as well, any mission that requires my special talents. After all, I am the destroyer. Still, he has not called upon me for twenty-six centuries. In the absence of his guidance, I have busied my hands with a new project. I will decide the best time to release my children." There was a pause. "Let us speak no more of it. I will show you the rest of my realm."

Abaddon led the angel on a tour of the green realm, yet what Aaron had already seen was apparently very troubling to him. Abaddon's isolation had changed him, and not for the better.

After a few minutes, Serena prepared to depart their company. The call of Chris's letter was too strong to resist any longer. She would allow these two angels to visit with one another in private, while she soaked in every word of the love she had found anew.

"I will wait for a time," announced Aaron. "I will give you the opportunity, however long it takes, to write a response to your beloved husband. Rest assured that he will be most glad to hear from you."

"I'm more grateful than you could possibly know," said Serena. "Thank you."

"A remarkable human," Aaron said as Serena departed. "Her soul is so pure." He looked over his shoulder to see her vanish into the tunnel leading back to the main chamber. "It is strange, her experience in Hell has, if anything, refined it. How can that be possible?"

"I don't know," admitted Abaddon, "but she is unique. I recognized it the first time I set eyes upon her, there in satan's infernal chambers. I don't even know why I was there that day. Perhaps it was chance, but perhaps it was something else. I saw it again when she arrived here at my island home. I just couldn't cast her back into the fiery sea, though I knew the dangers of offering her comfort. Aaron, she has reawakened something within me, something that I thought I had surely lost, an angel's love and concern for others. That love which dwells within her is contagious."

Aaron nodded. "Strange that she should find her way here to you."

Abaddon nodded. "It is a circumstance for which I have no answer. It is pleasant to be in her company, so I shall not complain of it. Yet this purity within her may be her undoing. I may have seen it from that first day, but satan saw it too; and I fear that he will one day come looking for her."

"Yes," confirmed Aaron, "I fear that her days of peace are numbered. It is best that we make those days as pleasant as possible."

Abaddon's countenance changed, becoming angry and determined. "Aaron, I won't let satan take her, not without a fight. He will have to destroy me in order to get to her, I swear it."

That comment caught Aaron by surprise, an amazement that was reflected upon his face. "And you think you can stop him, my brother?"

"No, I don't. I can only make it difficult for him. It is the task of a guardian angel to protect humanity. I shall fulfill that responsibility to the best of my ability. If necessary, I shall fall in the performance of my duty."

"Then you have contemplated the unthinkable?"

"Yes," confirmed Abaddon. "Yet there is more, much more. In the event that Serena and I would fall to satan and his minions, my small friends in the cavern have instructions to escape into the vast realm beyond. They are not as ready or as numerous as I would have liked, but I have taught them much. Perhaps enough to survive and multiply, to bide their time until they are ready. In time, they could make things difficult for the prince of Hell. They might even manage to rescue Serena and me from our tormentors."

Aaron considered the situation before he responded. "I would very much like to help you. It might be that I could keep you apprised of the situation, warn you of any impending problems. There are resources in Heaven, resources at my disposal. I shall consult them and inform you of what I discover."

"That is very thoughtful of you," Abaddon said.

"It is the least I can do for an old friend."

※ ※ ※

It was several hours later when Serena put the finishing touch on her letter to Chris. She was very excited as she placed it in Aaron's hand.

"In a very short time this letter will be in your husband's hands," promised Aaron, a smile on his face. "I will endeavor to bring new correspondence to you as often as I am able, or at least as often as my schedule of duties permits. I am certain that your husband will write to you often, such is his love for you."

There was a pause as Aaron gathered his thoughts. "The task of bringing the condemned into this place is a very unpleasant one for me. It might seem hard to believe, but bringing you here was one of the most difficult things I ever had to do. I am indeed thankful that your path has crossed that of Abaddon, my friend. I know not what the future holds for you, but I pray that you shall find some measure of peace."

"Thank you," replied Serena. "Thank you for bringing me such a precious gift."

Aaron smiled but slightly. "Would that I could have done more."

Abaddon and Serena saw Aaron to the cave's entrance. Before them the bow of blue glimmered brightly along the horizon. Aaron bid his friends a last goodbye and bolted into the dark sky. He was momentarily a diminishing silhouette against the blue along the horizon; then he vanished from sight.

"I envy him his freedom," said Abaddon as they made their way back into the deep recesses of the island. "Yet for us, I fear that the dream of escape from this realm is just that, a dream, a vision without substance."

Serena nodded. They had almost reached the great room when she spoke up. "I know that the two of you were speaking of the old days when I walked into the cavern below. I got the feeling that there was something between you, something that was separating you. May I ask what it was?"

"You may," said Abaddon, motioning to their favorite chairs. "You might find it strange, but Aaron and I were the best of friends many centuries ago. As you know, I had been directed by God to watch over a primitive tribe in the land that you now call Greece. Aaron and several others were there with me. We were to protect them, even inspire them from time to time, but under no circumstances were we to interfere with their lives, with their free will.

"From time to time, we even took on a human form in order to mingle with them. I told you of it before, how I erred and took a woman, my wife, onto myself. Aaron also did as I did. He became the father of several human angel hybrids. Yet it turned out that he did not share our vision of a greater humanity. To him it was a carnal game—a fling. Yet he became fearful when our sin passed into a new phase and we proclaimed ourselves to be the sons of God, even gods in our own right. It was then when he left our presence. When God finally intervened and we were brought before His throne to be judged for our crimes, Aaron stood with us."

"But he wasn't sentenced here," deduced Serena.

"No, he wasn't. I remember that day quite vividly. He knelt before the Father, weeping and pleading, seeking His mercy. In the end, he was granted some measure of it, but he did not escape judgment altogether. He was demoted to become the least in the Kingdom of Heaven. He was sentenced to conduct the souls of the damned to Hell, the most terrible task that an angel may be given. While you labored on your letter, he told me much of his ordeal. It is not as terrible as ours, yet it is not so much better. For many years there was great enmity between us, but no more. We have been reconciled at last."

"I'm really glad to hear that," replied Serena. "Aaron is important to me. What he did for Chris and I, uniting us, is a precious gift, as precious as the gift you have offered me here." Serena hesitated, searching for the words to express a thought that had been on her mind for some time. "Abaddon, I really believe that we have all been drawn together for a purpose."

"By whom?"

"By God," Serena said.

Abaddon looked at Serena. It was a ridiculous concept. Surely God had abandoned them long ago. Yet he said nothing to his young companion. Perhaps it was the knowledge that this thought, no matter how misguided, brought her some measure of peace. Or did it go deeper than that? Perhaps, in the deep recesses of his soul, he too wanted to believe as she did.

⊰❊⊱ ⊰❊⊱ ⊰❊⊱

Three demonic sentries gazed upward at lord Moloch, as he descended from the pitch black sky toward the threshold of the great demonic city fortress of Sheol, accompanied by his customary escort. They bowed low before him as he alighted upon the ground just beyond the outer columns and folded his powerful wings.

"Hail, lord Moloch!" cried the three in perfect unison.

Moloch didn't immediately respond. He carefully scanned the dark and dismal surroundings before turning toward his eager followers. "This is where it happened?"

"Yes, my lord," said the demon in the middle, stepping forward. "One of the sentries under my command encountered two dark warrior angels in this very spot. They seemed to be spying on us, so he went to investigate."

Moloch nodded slowly. "This was three days ago?"

"Yes, my lord."

Again Moloch scanned the surroundings. "So, what was their business here? Did your sentry determine their identities?"

"No, my lord, but he said that there was something strange about one of them. He didn't speak, and his spirit was strange, not at all like one of the dark angels. Then there was the smell."

That comment caught Moloch by surprise. "The smell?"

"Yes, sir, the sentry had served for many years as a task master, before being assigned here. He said that one of the two had the smell of a human, a female human. He was certain of it."

"Why didn't he detain them?" roared Moloch.

"He was but one," replied the demon, "he was no match for two warriors. By the time he could summon reinforcements, he had been cast to the ground and the two had taken flight. Yet here is another odd thing; the one angel carried the other, as if he were the only one capable of flight. We took up pursuit, but lost them in a dark canyon. They vanished somewhere into the interior. We are still searching for them, and we will not give up the hunt until we find them."

"Don't bother, they are long gone by now," replied Moloch, turning from the sentry. One of his escorts turned with him.

"My lord Moloch, I am convinced that this silent dark angel was none other than Serena Farnsworth. It could have been none other. In all of Hell, there are no other female humans unaccounted for. Then, there are the footprints." He turned to the muted footprints before them. "This one, so much smaller than the other, was made by no dark angel; it was made by one slight of form and weight. The sentries were deceived by a dark angel skilled in the art of illusion. He might have clouded the mind of the sentry, so as to make him believe that he saw an angel, but no illusion could alter this human's footprint."

"Continue Rathspith; you have my complete attention," said Moloch, who was impressed by this one's perceptiveness.

"My lord, this can mean but one thing, Serena Farnsworth has been befriended by one of the dark angels. After all, they have no allegiance to the master. This dark angel is shielding her, protecting her, for reasons that only he understands."

Moloch nodded. "Yes, Rathspith, I am fully in agreement." He turned to his perceptive lieutenant. "So, what would you do now?"

There was not a moment of hesitation in Rathspith's response. "We must go forth, seek out all of the dark warrior angels. In all of Hell, there are but a few hundred. We must question them. We must determine who has done this thing. When the guilty one is found, we must present him, and this human female, to lord satan, to await his pleasure."

A slight smile appeared upon the face of Moloch. "I like you, Rathspith. With you, the solution is always so simple, so direct."

Rathspith returned the master's smile. "I did not imply that the execution of the plan would be simple, but I believe that you will be pleased with the results."

"Very well," replied Moloch. "Take what forces and resources you require. Find her, Rathspith. I shall reward your service well if you are successful, but do not fail me."

Rathspith was all too quick to pick up the thinly veiled threat. He realized the personal risks that this task carried, but his eye was more upon the potential personal benefits his success would bring. He'd bring this missing wench back to the master and have some fun along the way. He was looking forward to the hunt.

chapter twentyfour

IT was a joyous morning when Aaron arrived at the front door of the mansion with his precious cargo, a letter from the heart of outer darkness. Chris and Jennifer sat side by side at the dining room table as Chris read what might have been the first letter to have made the trip between these two realms of alternate reality. All the while, Aaron stood by, his soul reveling in the joy he had brought into two heavenly hearts. When the reading was finished, it was Jennifer who spoke up first.

"Aaron, I want to thank you from the bottom of my heart for what you have done for my son. Believe me, it is no small thing. I only wish there was something I could do to repay your kindness. Perhaps you could stay and have lunch with us?" Jennifer smiled. "You know, its funny, I don't even know if angels eat. I'm sorry that I've never gotten to know angels like I should have."

Aaron smiled and bowed slightly. "To answer your question, yes, we do eat. Like you, we don't have to, but we can. However, I regret that I will not be able to join you this day. Perhaps I shall another time. At present, I have other duties that require my attention. As for repaying my kindness, you already have. For many centuries I have brought terrible pain and sorrow to human hearts. It has been a burden that weighed greatly upon me. Seeing the joy that this correspondence has brought to you and Serena has lightened my spirit. It is a sort of joy that I had almost forgotten. I shall return in another four days, if you wish, to carry still more correspondence to Serena."

"That would be wonderful!" Chris said.

"It is my hope that I will be able to call upon you on a regular basis, ferrying still more correspondence to your wife. It is a thing that I do, not just for you, but for myself. You see, I have as much reason to thank you as you have to thank me." Aaron paused. "But I must be about my other duties. I bid the two of you a pleasant day."

Jennifer and Chris saw Aaron to the front door, and after a last goodbye, watched as he bolted skyward, vanishing into the sky a moment later. Jennifer paused to reflect; everything had worked to the good, as incredible as it all seemed. There was but one thing left to do.

"Now, Chris, will you finally go to Zion and speak to the Father?" she asked, turning toward her son. The expression she was greeted with was not encouraging.

"I'm going to do it…really I am, but not just yet."

That response was quite near Jennifer's worst nightmare. "Chris, you promised, remember?"

"Mom, I'll keep my promise, but not just yet. I need some time."

Jennifer's growing frustration was obvious. "Time to do what? What are you afraid of, Chris?"

For a moment, Chris looked away. "Mom, I'm not afraid of anything, it just isn't the time. Please, Mom, just let it go for now."

Chris walked back into the mansion, leaving Jennifer alone on the porch with her thoughts, and a black cat. "I guess I shouldn't have expected him to listen; God told me that he wouldn't. I just didn't expect things to work out quite this way. I don't know what to do, Ebbie."

Ebbie sat quietly and attentively. Just the trace of a smile appeared on Jennifer's face as she gazed at her endearing furry friend. It was usually her son who talked to the cat. Now she too had picked up the habit. She walked into the mansion and Ebbie tagged along close behind.

Jennifer had come to a decision. There would be no point in continuing to convince her son to go to the Father. He wasn't going to do it until he was ready, and nothing she would say could change that. God himself had told her that much. She would have to bide her time, be there when her son was finally ready to listen. Until then, she would be as supportive as she possibly could. Right now her son was happy, and she didn't want to change that. Still, she sensed trouble on the horizon, trouble he didn't see. She would need to remain vigilant.

❈ ❈ ❈

It was four days before Chris saw Aaron again. He arrived early in the morning as promised, taking an even bigger package with him on the journey to outer darkness. This one contained an 11-page letter, more vegetable seeds, and a large pan of fudge brownies that Jennifer had prepared for her daughter-in-law.

That evening, Aaron returned with a letter penned by Serena, describing her daily routine within the cavern. There was even a brief note of greetings from her benefactor, Abaddon, who assured her loving family that he would do his best to keep her safe from harm.

The regular mail run had begun. Every fourth day Aaron embarked upon the long and perilous round trip, delivering words of encouragement and hope, leaving happiness in his wake. Never had he been so happy with his lot. Yes, he still delivered the condemned to their terrible fate, yet he had also become a deliverer of hope.

It was on his 12th mail run that he was compelled to be the bearer of disturbing news. As usual, his arrival was anxiously anticipated, and he found both Abaddon and Serena on the cliffside trail at the mouth of the cavern, waiting for him.

It was during the dark season and the bow of blue that usually graced the horizon had nearly faded from sight. There were storm clouds to the south and a hot sulfurous breeze blew along the cliffs, as if to leave no doubt as to where they truly were. The news that Aaron carried this day was as troubling, as dark as the environment into which it was delivered.

"Peace be with you," said Aaron, as he folded his wings behind him.

"And to you," replied Abaddon.

Serena gave Aaron a hug that brought an immediate smile to his face. He reciprocated by handing to her the largest care package to date.

"There is a sweet substance within. It is called angel food cake, curious name. Your mother-in-law baked it. I am no expert on the subject of what constitutes a culinary delicacy; however, I found it to have a most pleasing taste."

Aaron's peculiar comment elicited a good natured laugh from Serena. "I'm sure that it's wonderful."

Aaron turned toward Abaddon. "There is a matter of some gravity that I need to discuss with you and Serena. I believe that it would be best if we discussed it inside."

"Of course," replied Abaddon, motioning toward the cavern entrance.

Aaron and Serena retreated into the depths, followed by Abaddon.

Aaron glanced over his shoulder. "I think that it would be best if you dimmed or even extinguished the light at the cavern entrance. In very fact, if you had a way to block the entrance entirely it might be helpful."

Serena didn't like the sounds of that. Something was very wrong. They had nearly reached the great chamber before Aaron continued.

"I have utilized the resources of the Great Hall of Records in Heaven to observe the activities of the great adversary and his minions. In doing so, I have discovered a disturbing turn of events that I fear will eventually impact your life here. Satan's interest in Serena has been rekindled. It is his desire to have her returned to his audience chamber, to determine if her months of agony in the sea of fire have broken her spirit. He requires her worship. He must know that his will has defeated hers. Rarely has he been so obsessed with the capture of a single human soul."

Serena was beside herself with grief, though she did her best to be strong. "I knew this was going to happen, but I didn't think it would happen so soon."

"But his search for you has been in vain," interjected Aaron. "He assigned the arch demon Moloch to lead the hunt. He in turn assigned a demon lieutenant, a tracker by the name of Rathspith, to see to your recapture. That was quite nearly two months ago. It is his belief that a fallen angelic warrior has given you refuge. Apparently this belief was fueled by your ill-fated trip to the demonic Gate City of Sheol."

"Rathspith has endeavored to find all of the angels that have been cast into outer darkness since the Great War in Heaven, those not loyal to his master. Yet, it has turned out to be a more difficult task than he had anticipated. Those he seeks do not wish to be found. So far he has not found a tenth part of those he wishes to question. Those he has found were stubborn and defiant. And so it goes on and on, even as the trail grows ever colder."

Abaddon paced across the cavern floor. He too had become convinced that this moment would not come so soon. "We have seen no increases in the number of demons patrolling the skies over the island. This Rathspith, of whom you speak, is searching in the wrong place."

"Exactly," replied Aaron. "He assumes that Serena could not have been carried so far north by the currents, so he has focused his attention farther south. However, I fear that he shall eventually broaden the scope of his search to include this island. He is becoming desperate. He made promises to Moloch that he has been unable to keep."

Serena felt ill to her stomach. "Do you think that they might eventually give up the search? I mean, if they don't find me after a while?" Serena sat in her favorite chair, trying to get her wits about her.

"I fear not," replied Aaron. "Satan is single-minded. He will not abandon the search until you have been found, even if a million demons are needed to take up the search."

"Then this is it," lamented Serena, tears in her eyes. She turned to her protector. "I have a plan. It is the only chance for you. I still have those gray rags satan's minions forced me to wear when I first arrived. I will put them back on. Then you will need to carry me back to the flaming sea, dropping me in far from here, in a place where satan might eventually find me. Perhaps, I can convince them that they simply overlooked me, that I have been floating in that awful sea all along. Then I will submit to him. I don't want anything happening to you because of me. After satan is done with me, he might throw me back into the sea. Perhaps you could find me all over again. It's the only way."

"I will not tolerate this!" roared Abaddon. "You have always been the one who held forth so much hope for the future. I will not have you speaking this way in my domain. Satan is not going to have you again. You are not going to appear in his audience hall, you are not going back to the sea of fire, and you are not going to give up hope. Do I make myself understood?"

"Yes."

"Very well then," said the fallen angel, his tone milder. "Understand, you are in my care, and it shall be so until I release you." Serena felt the gentle hand of her guardian angel on her shoulder. "Satan will not have you because I will not permit it."

There was a brief moment before the silence was broken.

"And neither will I." Serena turned to see Aaron standing at Abaddon's side. She could scarcely believe what she was hearing or seeing. There were tears in the angel's eyes.

"You and your husband have given my existence a new meaning. I cannot bear to see you in the hands of satan again. No, I will not see you suffer. We shall come up with a plan."

Abaddon looked at Aaron with astonishment. "The last plan we were involved in resulted in your being demoted to the lowest place in Heaven and placed me into outer darkness."

Aaron shook his head. "No, it is not like that at all. What we choose this day is not against the Kingdom of the Father, it is an act of love. Abaddon, if we as angels do not stand for love, than what shall we stand for?"

Serena was overwhelmed. Two great angels had come to her defense, two knights in shining armor, yet she could not escape reality. "Do you have a plan, Aaron?"

Aaron shook his head. "Not yet, but I shall have one. We shall have one."

"Have you told my husband about this?"

"Not as yet."

"But you've got to," insisted Serena.

"I will do so upon my return to Heaven. And I will tell others. This thing satan intends must not be allowed to happen."

"But I've been condemned to this place by God, remember?"

"That does not mean that we can't take up arms in your defense," said Aaron. "It simply means that we should expect no help from the Father."

"Then so be it," proclaimed Abaddon. "The time has come to deny satan that which he desires. For too long satan has reigned supreme in this realm. No one has dared oppose him. The last time he knew defeat here was nearly two thousand years ago."

"When Jesus set the captives free," deduced Serena.

Abaddon nodded. "Yes, it was Jesus. He stood before satan and his court, stood before him in the very judgment hall in which you stood. He stood there not in rags but in glowing white garments, and though satan and his minions tried to have their way with Him, they could not so much as touch Him."

"He had come to preach to any man or woman who would hear His voice," said Aaron. "From the fire pits to the continent of darkness, all heard what He had to say. Satan and his demons tried to silence Him, but couldn't. When He had finished, all who had been truly touched by His words, all who believed in His message of hope, cried out to Him and He heard them. Shackles fell open and the yoke of oppression was lifted. They stepped from their places of torment and their demonic taskmasters were powerless to stop them.

"Then they rose out of this place in a great throng following Jesus—their redeemer. For He now held the key to the pit, and the lock that held them here had been broken. He set them free."

Abaddon shook his head. "Would that I could have gone with them."

"At least our children went with them," Aaron said. "On that day a heavy burden was lifted from my heart."

Abaddon was puzzled. "Aaron, what are you saying?"

"Brother, I thought that you knew."

Abaddon shook his head.

"Those on Earth whom we had deceived…they all rose from this place on that day. Jesus took them from this place; I can account for every one of them."

Abaddon was shaking. "Even my wife?"

"Of course," confirmed Aaron. "They dwell in Heaven to this day. Your hands are clean, Abaddon."

"I thought that they would be denied salvation," gasped Abaddon. "I thought that their sins were too great."

"No, of course not," Aaron said. "All that believed in the message of the Son of God went with Him. There were no exceptions."

Serena looked to her guardian, despite their grim situation, there was a new spark of joy in her eyes. "That's wonderful. You have no reason to feel guilty, not any more. They're all with God."

"But they suffered so long," Abaddon said.

"As have you, my brother," said Aaron. "But let us focus upon the real villain here. It is not you, but satan. He is the one who tormented them."

"He considers himself practically invincible here in Hell," Abaddon said. "Since the day Jesus freed the multitudes, satan has reigned supreme. I can think of nothing that would please me more than to see him lose yet again." There was a pause. "Except Serena's happiness."

"Then we shall accomplish both," vowed Aaron.

Serena smiled—there was hope; she had to go on believing.

For several hours the three sat together reviewing their options. One thing became clear; they would need more help. Just where that help might come from was by no means certain, but the three of them could not stand against satan in the midst of his own domain.

They agreed to meet again in two days time. That would allow Aaron time to investigate their options, perhaps seek additional help.

Still, neither Serena nor Abaddon were particularly hopeful. They had no illusions that they stood a chance against the prince of darkness. Yes, Abaddon was a warrior and his strength was more than a match for any three of satan's flunkies; even that of satan himself. But he was hopelessly outnumbered. Nevertheless, they would play this game out to its conclusion.

⊰✳⊱ ⊰✳⊱ ⊰✳⊱

Chris's heart sank as Aaron revealed to him his grim discovery. He'd known that Serena's current sanctuary represented only a fleeting reprieve from an eternity of agony, but he'd hoped to see that reprieve continue, for a few years at least. He had become accustomed to the mail call twice a week—to communicating with his beloved wife. His mother took his hand as the three of them sat about the dining room table.

"And you and Abaddon plan to defend her?" asked Jennifer, looking toward the angel in amazement.

The angel looked down at his hands folded on the tabletop. "To say that we plan to stand with her might be more accurate. I doubt that we will prevail."

"But you're going to do it anyway?" Jennifer asked.

"I can do nothing less."

"I'll stand with you," announced Chris. "I've got to."

"It would avail nothing. To take you on such a journey would be to place you in grave jeopardy. You are a child of God. It would be an inexcusable act on my part. Your place is here."

"My place is at my wife's side," objected Chris, his tone of voice more forceful.

"I cannot take you," insisted Aaron, "and there is no one else who can. The issue is closed. I will continue to carry messages between you to your wife for as long as possible, I promise. After that, well, I will probably not be here to deliver them. I will return again in two days. I will take to her whatever you wish at that time."

Aaron did not remain to argue the issue. He left Chris and his mother to their grief.

"This isn't over," said Chris, rising to his feet.

The look of alarm on Jennifer's face was clear. "Where are you going?"

"To see Johann." Chris hurried into his bedroom.

Jennifer followed closely behind him. "Honey, what can he possibly do?"

"I don't know. That's why I'm going."

Jennifer knew she could not reason with her son when he was in this mood; she wouldn't even try. She was watching the Father's words becoming reality, of that she had no doubt. Things weren't unfolding in the manner she had envisioned, yet she could almost hear His words. This was the future He had spoken of.

A moment later, wearing travel clothing, Chris stepped from the mansion and onto the porch, and then into the yard beyond. He glanced up at the sun, trying to determine what time of day it might be at Kepler's home. It mattered not. He looked back toward his mother. "I'll be back as soon as I can."

Jennifer quickly considered what words of wisdom she should say to him that would help him on his way. She knew not. She had already said it all. There was no point in saying it again. She only nodded.

Chris vanished into a swirling mist of stars. She was certain that her son's moment of truth was at hand.

As Chris stepped from the misty portal and into the tall grass surrounding Johann's home, he noticed it was late afternoon. He heard voices, several distinctly different ones. They seemed to be coming from the rear of the home. As Chris walked around the house to see what was happening, he heard a soft eerie whine growing in pitch and intensity. It sounded like some sort of mechanical device, an engine, perhaps. But how could that be, here in Heaven?

Then he saw a large sphere of glass, perhaps 16 feet in diameter, glistening in the sunlight and hovering 10 or so feet above the ground. The upper hemisphere of the mystical sphere appeared to be some sort of crew compartment; a series of high-backed, cushioned chairs formed a circle on an inner floor, while another chair, higher than the rest, sat near the center behind a control panel. There was a man sitting in the center chair, but Chris couldn't identify him.

Within the lower hemisphere, Chris could see a complex array of machinery; protruding from it were four metallic legs extending downward. He recalled photographs of the old NASA lunar lander, and in some respects, this vehicle resembled it. Yet it lacked anything that looked like a rocket engine; indeed, not so much as a blade of grass below was disturbed by its presence.

Johann and David stood on the ground looking up at the vehicle, apparently not mindful that they had a visitor. A moment later the vehicle descended, landing gently on its four metal legs. The soft whine died away, allowing the natural sounds of the forest to once again dominate the strange scene.

Johann turned to see Chris, "I was wondering when you would arrive."

Chris was thoroughly confused. "What do you mean?"

"The crisis in Hell," replied Johann. "It's been brewing for a while, I fear. I don't want you to think that it was your letter that created the problem; it wasn't. I suppose that this was destined to happen. I suppose this proves that satan keeps a close eye on those under his rule. I was hoping that wasn't the case. Your wife's peace is about to be interrupted. I'm sorry."

"How long have you known?" asked Chris who had been totally unprepared for Johann's response.

Johann walked in Chris's direction, David at his side. "We've had our suspicions for quite a while." Johann looked toward his young protégé. "At David's insistence, we traveled to the Hall of Records several times, looked into your wife's book. It was the incident at the Gateway City of Sheol that first concerned us. It was not so much that she was almost discovered; it was the fact that the city was guarded at all. Why should it have been? After all, who is there to threaten it? Over the past centuries I have viewed Hell through the eyes of hundreds of people, mostly those so unfortunate as to find themselves separated from God. But I have also viewed that place through the eyes of demons."

That comment brought a look of surprise from Chris. Johann had looked more deeply into the pit than he had at first thought.

"Yes, I have been so foolish," confirmed Johann. "I know their habits, their ways, and their responsibilities from firsthand knowledge. That has made this situation all the more vexing. Know this; satan's legions are fanatically loyal to him. They would never knowingly betray their master. The humans are all restrained or trapped in one manner or another. They are powerless to interfere in the comings and goings of demons. The fact that there was opposition at the city told me that something was amiss. The fact that so many demons took up the pursuit was even more surprising."

"But we didn't immediately associate that fact with your wife," noted David. "I mean, it would be absurd for satan to put so much effort into finding one lost soul."

Johann shook his head. "No, you don't know satan as I do. He has a single-mindedness of purpose. He will never give up, never admit defeat. He will not rest until he finds her, the task will consume him, as it has these last sixty-seven days."

"Sixty-seven days?" gasped Chris.

"Yes," confirmed Johann. "He first became aware of her absence sixty-seven days ago. He has turned Hell up-side-down in search of her; yet so far, he has searched in vain. Unfortunately, Serena will not be able to elude him indefinitely. It has greatly complicated matters, pushed up our timetable. The problem is that we're just not ready."

Now Chris was really confused. "Not ready for what? Johann, please tell me what's going on."

Johann motioned toward the glassy sphere. A doorway had opened in its side, and a small middle-aged man was standing there watching them.

"The capacitor is still not retaining the charge the way I'd hoped," said the man, sticking his head out of the door. "In the total absence of the field, it would depolarize even more rapidly."

"As it is, how long would we have?" Johann asked the mysterious man.

"I can't be sure, fifteen minutes, perhaps less."

Johann shook his head. "That's not good enough. We'll need at least eight times that much time."

The man jumped to the ground and walked in their direction. "This problem is solvable, we just need time. You should surely understand that. You required nearly twenty years to formulate your three laws of planetary motion. This problem is not so different from that. There are other things to be tried. We will arrive at a solution."

Chris repeated his request, his frustration growing. "Please tell me what's going on."

"Yes, of course." Johann turned to the man from the sphere. "This is my good friend Nichola Tesla. Nichola, meet Chris Davis."

Chris was dumbfounded. He knew this man too, or at least he knew him by his earthly reputation. "The inventor of the AC generator?"

"The same," replied Nichola, bowing slightly, yet not extending his hand. "But please, call me Nick; all of my friends do."

Chris felt honored to be considered among the friends of yet another of humanity's great scientists. "Thank you, Nick, it is truly an honor to meet you."

"Shall we withdraw to my study?" suggested Johann, motioning to the back door.

The group made their way into the house, then through the main hall and into the large study. They gathered around the large oval table near the center of the room.

Johann looked to Chris, who sat directly across the dark, hardwood table from him. "In the nearly seven weeks since we last talked, David and I have examined your problem quite carefully. There are certain techniques that are learned with time when using the books of the Hall of Records. We start with the book of the person of primary interest, and then cross-reference the books of those persons with whom the individual encounters. It can be a slow and painstaking process; but in doing this, we gathered detailed knowledge of the current crisis."

From the original summons for Serena, issued forth by satan to Moloch, all the way down to the ill-fated exploits of Rathspith and his search for disloyal fallen angels, Johann unfolded the story to Chris. It became abundantly clear that Rathspith was getting nowhere fast.

"We're keeping almost daily tabs on Rathspith," noted David. "This dude is in serious trouble. He made promises to Moloch, promises that he can't keep. Now, instead of promises, all he can make are excuses. At the rate he's going, he'll be the one who ends up in satan's audience chamber."

Chris turned to Johann. "Why didn't you tell me about this sooner?"

"There was no point in it. There was nothing that you could do, only worry your wife needlessly. We were going to let you know if Rathspith started getting close, and he hasn't, not yet."

"But the stuff we've learned during the past weeks is just so cool!" David said in his usual youthful excitement. "We've been trying to find out why you remember so much more about your life on Earth than other people here. We were trying to figure out why you're the only one who remembered a loved one in Hell. What we found is that you aren't the only one. There are others, or at least there were."

"Like who?" asked Chris.

David smiled. "You should know; you met one of them."

Chris pondered David's comment. No, it was more like a riddle. He'd never much cared for riddles. He wasn't very good at them. Then it came to him in a wave of remembrance. "Wait a minute, the Hall of Records, the oriental woman with the black book in her hand. She was crying, I remember. It was when I'd looked into my mother's book. By the time we'd finished she was gone. What was her name? I should remember."

"Mao Yeng," said David.

"How'd you know that?" asked Chris. Then he answered his own question. "You opened my book, didn't you?"

"Exactly," said Johann. "You'd mentioned her in this very study on the day we first met, the day I brought you here. She only appeared briefly in your book, but upon close examination, we concluded that her situation might be similar to yours. We decided to look at her book as well, and then interview Mao Yeng herself."

"And?" asked Chris, hanging on every word.

"That's where it becomes confusing," continued Johann. "We located her book, but it wasn't white, it was gray. She wasn't here at all, she was still on Earth. We thought that we might have made a mistake, so we opened her book. It was the same woman all right, but according to her book, she was not here that day, Mao Yeng Wong was in Enola, China. And the man whose book she was reading, her husband, was with her, still alive. They were preaching the gospel in a secret underground church, out of sight of the Chinese government. Further examination showed that his book too was gray, not black. I am certain that they will be here one day, but not yet."

"That doesn't make sense," objected Chris, "I saw her, just as clearly as I see you now."

"And your book confirms it," replied Johann. "We haven't quite figured that one out yet. The records conflict, and they shouldn't. They never have before."

"Unless we're dealing with a temporal paradox," chimed in David. "You see, they really do exist."

Johann hesitated. "Perhaps, but we have more important issues to deal with right now."

Chris hoped with all of his heart that he wasn't jumping to a wrong conclusion. "To rescue Serena?"

Johann leaned back in his chair. "Yes. We've been planning it for over a month."

"And that vehicle out back, it will take you there?"

"Not as it is," Nick said.

"Nick and I built that craft years ago," continued Johann. "We both had a desire to explore the cosmos firsthand, to actually get out there and touch it, but that meant crossing the barriers that separated the different spheres of reality. I had the knowledge of celestial mechanics, and Nick had the knowledge of engineering and force field theory that made the vehicle a reality."

"During my time on Earth, I sought a source of nearly infinite power," noted Nick. "I sought it for the betterment of humankind. Yet those who held the reigns of financial power in my day saw my research as a threat to their growing empires. They determined that I should never reach my goal. Only late in my life did I discover that power. It was there all the time, right in front of me, yet I had not seen it. I finally harnessed it here, where it is least diluted."

"I'm sorry, I don't understand," admitted Chris.

"How did you come to Professor Kepler's home today?"

Then Chris understood. "You harnessed the power of God?"

That brought a smile to Nick's face. "Of course. God placed it there for us to use; it's clearly stated in the Gospels. The Holy Spirit is the source of the power of the great miracles. It is mainly a hidden reservoir of pure energy that pervades the known universe. Its source is right here in Heaven, and it is here where it is least diluted. It is a far more potent power source than can be found in the chemical bonds between atoms or even within the atomic nucleus itself. It is clean and, as far as I can tell, inexhaustible.

"We utilize it to create what I like to refer to as temporal corridors, though I think the physicists of your time call them wormholes. Through these corridors, we can journey from Heaven to the far reaches of the known universe, just as the angels do, unhindered by either physical or temporal distance."

Chris turned once more to Johann. "You said that this was impossible for humans, that it might take you years to figure it out."

Johann smiled. "I'm sorry I misled you, but I couldn't let you know about this. Furthermore, it wasn't me but Nick who figured out how to harness this power. We went to God many times about this very issue, expressing a desire to explore the universe. He agreed to allow us to do just that, so long as we didn't visit Earth and make our presence known to the world of men and women. He even helped us over some of the more difficult concepts in the construction of this vehicle, but it was we who had to design and build it."

"Have you ever flown it?"

"Oh yes," confirmed Johann, "many times. We've visited the great nebula in Orion, the globular cluster of Hercules, and thousands of star systems—all powered by the power of God's Holy Spirit. In very fact, we named our craft the Spirit. It provides us transportation and climatic control. These bodies of ours can tolerate the extreme conditions of space, but it is a far from comfortable experience. In fact, it is downright painful. The Spirit makes it so much easier."

"Then you could fly it into outer darkness," exclaimed Chris. "You could rescue Serena anytime you liked?"

"No, we couldn't," said Nick. "The Holy Spirit of God does not extend into outer darkness. We could fly there, but we would have no power to create the temporal corridor that would allow us to return. It would be a one-way trip.

"We've been trying to perfect a sort of high-energy capacitor that would store the power needed for a return trip. In effect, we would be taking a little bit of God's Spirit with us. The field coils would absorb the energy, but the capacitor itself won't retain sufficient power. When charged beyond a certain point, the containment field fails, the plates depolarize, and we lose power altogether. We will eventually solve the problem; I am sure of it, but it will take time."

"That is the first problem," Johann said. "The second is that we can't bring Serena or Abaddon out of outer darkness. God exiled them from His universe, to return them to it would not be allowed. Anyway, they would decorporialize here. That is to say, they would become nothing more than a spirit."

Johann paused. "So, we've come up with an alternate destination. Outer darkness is vast; we could remove Serena and Abaddon to a place where they would be safe, hidden from satan and his minions."

This time Chris followed Johann's train of thought perfectly. "The other star, the new world you discovered."

"Exactly," confirmed Johann. "I've taken a much closer look at it since we last spoke. It is even more lovely than Earth. It is the perfect refuge."

"If we can get the capacitor to work," said Nick, rising from his seat. "If you will excuse me, gentlemen, I have something else I want to try before darkness falls. You're right, Johann, time is running out." Nick walked from the room, and David followed close behind him.

"We are very fortunate indeed to have Nick with us on this endeavor," noted Johann. "We could not have accomplished so much so fast without him."

"You know that I'll want to go along," said Chris.

"Of course," confirmed Johann, but we're only going if we can solve this equipment problem. Until then, this entire rescue mission is somewhat problematical."

Chris followed Johann back to the Spirit. He watched for several hours as the three men worked with the incredible craft. He soon discovered where its various components came from. Just like the skilled craftsmen in the shops of Zion, Nick shaped the individual parts with his mind. They materialize before him out of thin air. Just at sunset, another test of the modified capacitor was conducted. The results were encouraging, or at least that was what Nick said. Still, it was not nearly good enough.

"You can't rush genius," said Nick, as the three researchers returned to Johann's study. The lights in the study were dimmed and a large holographic schematic of the device appeared in midair before them, spinning slowly. The holographic projection slowed, then came to a halt. Nick drew close to it, looking at one specific component. "We'd considered this problem some years ago, but its only utility was a trip into outer darkness. None of us had ever given any serious consideration to such a hazardous expedition. For that very reason, we've only given it serious attention during the past month. We've made incredible progress, far more than I'd expected, but as I said before, these things take time."

"But we don't know how much we have," objected Chris.

The holographic projection magnified, focusing on the component that Nick was interested in. "On Earth, none of us knew how much time we had. I understand your concern. If it helps ease your mind, we have had a series of major breakthroughs during the past three days. It has been, to say the least, miraculous. Before that, this engineering project had been mostly an exercise in frustration. I believe that we are very close to a solution." He pointed to a series of oddly shaped components. "I still believe that our problem is here, in the induction manifold."

David moved closer to the projection, until he stood at Nick's side. "Yes, I agree, sir. We need to find a way to open the gate even wider." He pointed into the floating phantasm. "I have an idea."

Chris realized that he was about as useful to this group as a third wheel on a bicycle. He didn't have the slightest idea what they were doing. He was only in the way. "I'd best be on my way. Please let me know if anything happens that affects my wife."

"Just a moment, Chris. I have something for you," said Johann, turning his attention from the schematic and walking to a desk in the corner of the room. From one of its drawers he pulled a large glass sphere, about 5 inches in diameter. It was attached to a curved black metallic base, flared at the bottom, to allow it to set upon a table without rolling off. "Walk with me."

Chris followed Johann into the main hallway and then through the front door into the open air. The sun had already set, and a curtain of darkness was descending upon the meadow. The sounds of the night were slowly replacing those of the day.

Johann handed the strange implement to Chris. "Send this to your wife the next time Aaron makes the journey. It is very important. Instruct her to keep it nearby at all times and under no circumstances allow it to fall with any force to the ground."

Chris was surprised to discover just how light it was. "What is this thing, a crystal ball?"

Johann smiled. "No, nothing as simple as a crystal ball. If all goes well, we might be able to use it to establish a direct link to her."

"You mean…I'd be able to speak to her, and she'd be able to hear me and reply?"

"More than that," replied Johann. "If all goes well, you'll be able to see each other as well. It hasn't been tested yet, at least not across the dimensional barrier, but I have high hopes that it will work."

Chris looked it over carefully. In the fading light, it seemed to emanate a faint blue glow. "I take it that it's very delicate."

"It is, but that isn't the only reason that it needs to be handled with care. To be used here in Heaven, it would only need a small receiver circuit to draw upon the power that is in residence all around us. It would even work on Earth, though not as well. In outer darkness, in Hell, there is no such field of power. The Spirit of God does not extend into those regions.

"For that reason, it has its own internal power source. It is a smaller version of the temporal capacitor in the Spirit. It doesn't hold a millionth of the power of that capacitor; still, within it is confined a tremendous amount of pure energy.

"I have done my best to safeguard its more critical components, but if it is dropped, if the housing of the capacitor is compromised, it could explode with disastrous consequences. You must emphasize the potential hazard to Aaron, but more importantly to your wife. Though she would survive the blast, the dispersion of that much spiritual energy, in the ethereal vacuum of Hell, might draw the attention of any demons within a hundred miles."

Chris held the sphere all the more carefully. He gazed up at the darkening sky. "Wait a moment, if this thing's energy could be sensed by demons, what about the Spirit? When it arrives, won't the demons sense it too?"

"Indeed they will," confirmed Johann. "That is the one drawback of our plan. That is why we'll need to get in and out in a terrible hurry. I'm hoping that Aaron and the angels who join him will be able to delay any demonic threats long enough to allow us to make our getaway."

Chris turned once more to Johann. "Do you really think that Aaron will be able to enlist the help of other angels in a wild scheme like this?"

"That all depends. If we don't manage to make this plan work, they probably won't. It would be a hopeless fight. They'd be outnumbered and fighting in hostile territory, and for what? To delay for but a few minutes the return of a lost soul to the sea of fire? But, if we could give them some measure of assurance that Serena could be rescued…well, that would be another matter. Then there would be hope." Johann paused, considering the state of angelic morale.

"You cannot begin to imagine the state of enmity that exists between the angels of Heaven and the demons of the pit. There are many who would give most anything for the opportunity to engage satan's minions in battle. Not just to put their wicked spirit forms to flight, but to do battle with the demon behind that spirit. It is not a desire for vengeance, but a righteous anger that drives them."

"But why couldn't they just rescue Serena themselves?"

"Because they could never reach the other world," said Johann. "Their only route to outer darkness is a narrow corridor formed by God Himself. It is carefully guarded so as not to allow anything unclean to escape the pit. The other world is out of their reach, and more importantly, out of the reach of demons."

"But not out of our reach," confirmed Chris.

Johann didn't immediately reply. "I hope not. I've calculated just how much energy will be required to execute the two jumps that Spirit will need to make in outer darkness. We won't attempt this rescue unless we have that much energy and then some. I hope you understand that."

Chris nodded.

"I'll be meeting with a delegation of angels in the morning," announced Johann. "Aaron has made the arrangements. I will explain our plan in detail to them; try to make them believe that it is possible. If this operation is to succeed, it will require a high degree of coordination. There will be many details to work out. But it will help my case if the problems associated with the temporal capacitor are solved or at least reduced by that time."

"I'd like to be there," replied Chris. "I've gotta make them understand just how important this is to Serena...to me. I can't let satan get his hands on her again."

"You are not going to be there," Johann said. His tone of voice left no doubt that his decision was final. "Do you know why I've kept you in the dark regarding our preparations up to this point?"

"No," replied Chris, "I don't."

"It's your state of mind. You tend to become irate and emotional in times of crisis. In those critical moments, you are prone to making very bad choices. I cannot take that chance tomorrow, Chris. You will not be there. You will respect my decision on this issue."

Chris nodded, reluctantly agreeing.

Johann placed a compassionate hand upon the young man's shoulder. "Go home now. I'll let you know when we're ready."

Chris stepped away, preparing to open the portal to home, then he turned. "Thank you, Johann. I can't begin to tell you how much I appreciate all that you've done."

Johann smiled broadly. "Thank me when your wife is safe and on the new world. Now, get some sleep."

A few seconds later, Chris vanished into the portal amid a flurry of glistening light. Johann walked back toward the house. He and the others would work through the night and into the next day. They would waste not a minute of precious time. They would strike a blow against the ultimate evil and deny satan that which he so much desired, the eternity of Serena Davis.

❈ ❈ ❈

The four angels sat around the table in Johann's study. They spoke among themselves, occasionally glancing toward Johann and Nick. They had seen the strange vehicle these curious humans had created, witnessed its potential. They'd heard the unique plan they had devised to rescue a single soul from the realm of satan. They'd listened to Aaron's impassioned plea regarding this human with the amazingly lucid soul. It was persuasive, if not incredible. They had even seen the mysterious world floating in outer darkness, a world hidden from the eyes of man and angel up until now. It was their leader, Moriah, who finally spoke out. He stood up, partially spreading his wings as he did so.

"You make a persuasive case for our intervention, Professor Kepler. It would seem that this condemned human has even reached out and touched the heart of one of our own. I agree that what you propose does not violate the principles by which we angels live. Still, what you propose places you and your companions in great jeopardy. In the event that we were overwhelmed by the demon hordes, and your craft were to prove itself incapable of returning you to the realm of Heaven, I could not guarantee that we would be able to carry you to safety."

"We understand and accept that risk," said Johann.

"Do you?" posed Moriah. "No one has ever attempted such a thing as you propose this day. I cannot guarantee what the Father's response would be if you were to find yourselves trapped within Hell. I do not know the mind of God. Have you considered what might happen to you if satan got his hands on you? You have no right to go where you propose to go. This one lost soul means that much to you?"

"It does," said Johann. "I know that it has no less meaning to you. Satan has taken far too many liberties with the human race. He has confused and deceived them, tricked them into believing that the Father did not care, yet we know that He does. Didn't Jesus speak of the shepherd leaving his flock and going out after the one sheep that had strayed? Jesus risked all for us, and I am willing to take this risk."

"As am I," said Nick, his voice resolute. "We have to go. We can do nothing less."

Johann and Nick were somewhat surprised when a smile appeared on Moriah's countenance. "I am surprised that you know the heart of the angels so well. So be it. I shall speak to the angels who I believe would consider such a bold venture." Quite abruptly, Moriah's voice took on a more solemn tone. "But know this; we cannot condone the removal from outer darkness of Serena, Abaddon, or any other soul…no matter how noble you might consider them to be. The Father in His righteous wisdom condemned them to that place, and it is there that they must remain."

"Of course," replied Johann, "that was always our intention."

Moriah nodded slowly. "Very well, then we are agreed. We shall assist you in this endeavor to the best of our ability. Let us discuss the details of our covenant that we may act as one, protecting each other from he who would seek to destroy us all. Let us shake the very pillars of Hell. Let us give satan but a taste of those things to come."

chapter twentyfive

AARON descended from the dark, starless sky, landing on the narrow ledge at the entrance of Abaddon's cavern fortress. This place had changed. There was a shattered boulder that partially blocked the entrance of the cavern. The tunnel beyond presented a realm of total darkness, only the presence of the luminous angel of God lent any light to the apparently dismal realm. Aaron walked in.

The floor of the cavern was littered with rocks and the air seemed musty and stale. Aaron moved cautiously forward, hoping that the changes he saw were the attempts of Abaddon and Serena to disguise the entrance to their subterranean sanctuary and not something more sinister. He proceeded through the winding tunnel, a growing sense of foreboding in his heart. He was relieved when he saw the faint glow of the great chamber before him and emerged into Abaddon's realm. All was as it had been before, though far more subtly illuminated. Only a few of the great crystals imbedded in the ceiling were glowing, and those that were did so with a dull sallow light, casting long harsh shadows about the room.

Aaron was surprised, nearly alarmed, when several dozen flying creatures similar to the one he had seen in the dark angel's garden emerged to greet him. They swirled around the room like bats, only far more swift and agile. After a moment they gathered together on the floor before him. They stood upright on their powerful back legs and gazed up at the angel in unison. Then they bowed, as if to honor him. Their ranks broke, to allow this servant of God to pass.

"They would make formidable guardians, would you not agree?"

Aaron turned to see Abaddon step from out of the gloom. Aaron was rarely surprised, but this was one of those rare moments. "Yes, my brother, they would."

"I found the advice you offered me during your last visit to be sound and took some precautions regarding the security of my domain."

"Yes," confirmed Aaron. "I see that. The changes were most convincing. Had I not been here before, I would have believed the cave to be deserted." It took the angel only a few seconds to fully regain his composure. "I am the bearer of important news."

"I see," said Abaddon, as the lighting of the room came back up to its normal levels. There was a look of concern upon his face, almost a frown. "I hope your news this day is not as dire as what you brought us two days ago."

"No," confirmed Aaron, "quite the opposite."

"Hello, Aaron."

Aaron turned to see Serena, dressed in white, emerging from the side passage that led to her chamber. "Hello, Serena. Your husband has sent you much this day. One of the things I carry is indeed wondrous."

"And you said you had news? Good news?"

Aaron hesitated, "Yes, I think so."

"Then let us hear it," Abaddon said, motioning to three chairs set in a circle not far away. "We could use good news right now."

"We could," confirmed Serena. "During the last day we've seen far more demons than usual in the sky over the island. It's a good thing that Abaddon disguised the entrance to the cavern. They might have dropped in on us if he hadn't. I'm starting to feel trapped. I feel like they're closing in on us."

"Hush, sweet Serena," bid Abaddon, placing his arm around her. "I've seen swarms of demons flying over the island before. It occurs from time to time, we just happened to be near the mouth of the cave when they passed by. They didn't stop; they didn't give this island a second thought. It was just a chance meeting, nothing more."

"I wish I was that certain," admitted Serena. "I'm starting to feel like I'm living on borrowed time." Then she caught herself. She would not talk like this, not before these two very precious friends. She managed a smile. "You were saying you had good news?"

"Indeed I do," Aaron said, returning Serena's smile. "Don't lose hope, child; your deliverance might be closer than you think."

Deliverance? It was such a wonderful word, sweet music to Serena's ears. If only it were true.

The three sat down facing each other. Aaron scanned the faces of his two dear friends before beginning. "When I last saw you, I was not certain that we had a plan of action. I can now tell you that we do and that I am very optimistic of the outcome." Aaron focused his attention on Serena. "Child, we are going to deliver you from Hell, and unto a place of refuge far beyond satan's reach, a wonderful green world. There you can dwell in peace, free from fear. It will even be possible for your husband to visit you there for days or weeks at a time."

No, this was too good to be true. "What about Abaddon? Could he come with me?"

Aaron turned to the dark angel, then back to Serena. "That is totally up to him."

Abaddon looked at Aaron incredulously. He was not so certain that Aaron was being entirely truthful with Serena. Perhaps he was endeavoring to raise her spirits, to give her hope in a time when it was in short supply. He pondered if, under the present circumstances, it was wise to challenge his bold statement. "What refuge are you referring to?"

"Another world in outer darkness—a world where neither angels nor demons, nor humans have ever trod. I have seen it with my own eyes; it is indeed wondrous."

Aaron outlined the plan to Abaddon and Serena in detail; and in doing so raised the hopes of their downtrodden souls. There were still some problems to work out. The Spirit's temporal capacitor, though vastly improved, was still not up to the task. Yet Nick and Johann felt confident that they were on the very threshold of a breakthrough; indeed, they might already have achieved it.

Then Aaron handed the strange glassy sphere to Serena, speaking of its potentials and its dangers. All was quickly moving into readiness, they could very well be rescued within the next 24 hours.

When all was told, Abaddon looked at his companions, searching for the words that he knew would be difficult for them to accept. He looked to Serena, took her hand in his. "Serena, I can't go with you to this new world, my place is here."

Serena's heart sank, her voice faltered, "But Abaddon, I need you."

"No, you don't, you'll be fine in this new world. You need to go there. I cannot protect you from satan and his minions if you remain. In the end, they would have you, do unspeakable things to you—I couldn't bear that. But I must stay. Someone needs to mind the garden, and more importantly, tend to my children.

Don't you see? They must grow and learn, and I must be here to teach them. I tell you this, one day they will be the undoing of satan and all those who stand with him. I will live for that day. I must believe that what I've worked for here has not been in vain."

"But you could take them with you," objected Serena.

"No, Serena," said Abaddon, "the time has come for us to part company. We will meet again. I am certain of it, but for now, we must go our separate ways."

"Perhaps you can speak of this later," suggested Aaron. "For right now, we must concentrate upon the plan. It will be difficult, but not impossible. Its success will not only be a victory for you, but for Chris and Johann, and all of the angels in Heaven. We all need this victory. We need to bring satan a defeat in the very heart of his empire. We need to bring him the message that he is no longer the master of outer darkness. He needs to know that his days of dominion are indeed numbered."

After Aaron departed, Abaddon spent the rest of the day in the vicinity of the cavern entrance. He needed to be alone with his thoughts, while at the same time evaluating their situation. His concerns grew ever greater as he spotted more and more demons in the sky over his tiny archipelago. Never had he seen so many. For the moment, they seemed uninterested in the small patch of land beneath them, but that could soon change. It was good that Serena was leaving. He would miss her, miss her terribly, yet to allow her to fall into the hands of satan was an even more appalling thought. No, she had to leave.

He returned to the depths of the cavern to find his lovely companion in the garden. Strange that she should be caring for a place that she would probably never see again. She was on her knees, cultivating around the vegetables, the crystal sphere Aaron had given her on the ground by her side. He stood there for a moment in silence, trying to burn the image of her into his mind. When he would recall her in the days to come, this is how he would remember her, working in the garden, caring for the last breath of life that this violated world still held within her bosom. Serena glanced up to see him and smiled.

"I'm going to journey some distance to the south," explained Abaddon. "There is an island there, the dwelling place of Batarel, a fallen angel like myself. He abides within a cavern there, one not nearly so grand as this. I've seen many demons flying from that direction in the past hours; I've become concerned."

"Would you like me to come along?" asked Serena, rising to her feet, and brushing off the dust from her dress.

"No, it would be far too dangerous with so many demons about. You had best remain here, it is the safest place. I shall not be gone long. When I return we can talk. It might be our last opportunity."

Serena smiled. "I'd like that."

Abaddon caressed Serena under the chin and smiled. Then he departed, leaving her to return to her labors in the garden. Abaddon didn't leave her by herself very often. She remembered that, on the first day, he had told her that he would need to lock her in her room when he left her. He never had. The door to her room had never swung shut since that day. There was a bond of trust between them. In a way she hated to leave him. He'd be here in solitude once more, and that disturbed her. If only she could convince him to come with her; still she would not question his decision. He was a creature of duty, and the task he had set for himself was not yet complete.

Serena returned to her work. She glanced at the crystal sphere like a teenage girl standing by the phone. She was waiting for a special call.

Abaddon reached the mouth of the cavern and scanned the realm beyond. He tarried for over a minute before spreading his wings and launching himself into the air. His wings beat rapidly as he accelerated into the black sky. Under normal conditions, it took about half an hour to cover the hundred or so miles between here and Batarel's island. He would try to make the trip in considerably less time today.

He climbed to a comfortable altitude, just above the turbulent air that swirled and tumbled above the flames of the sea. He was ever watchful for any sign of trouble, any traveling demons, yet none met his eyes. He'd find out if Batarel knew anything about the demon movements that he did not, then quickly return.

It took just over 20 minutes to cover the distance to the island. This place, where his fellow in exile called home, was a fraction of the size of his island. It was a small mound of jagged rock surrounded by flat lowlands that vanished beneath the black fiery sea when it ran high and rough. On the side of the mound, he had hewn a small cave for shelter from the cruel sulfurous storms. More than a few times Abaddon had bid Batarel to join him in his exile. This cave of his stood barely above the pounding waves when storms were at their worst. Eventually, with the steady rising of the sea, his home would be inundated.

Yet Batarel would not leave. He was more than willing to spend his eternity in seclusion and regret, and there was nothing that Abaddon could do to change that.

Abaddon landed on a level stretch of black rock, just below the entrance to Batarel's cave, and stepped in. He called out to him, but there was no reply. He walked through the narrow corridor to the only room in this meager lair.

The room was in a state of total disarray. The sparse furniture that his friend had fashioned so many years ago was shattered and scattered about. The grim scene made Abaddon's blood run cold.

He turned to see a pool of crimson near one corner of the room and a splattering of the same on the wall. The dark angel looked closely. It was blood, angelic blood—Batarel's blood. He had been beaten and thrown violently against the wall by a gang of vicious aggressors. No one or two demons could match the strength of the angelic warrior Batarel, one of the heroes of the Great War in Heaven.

Abaddon rushed outside, finding previously unnoticed traces of blood along the way. He stumbled down the steep slopes toward the lowlands below. The scattered rocks, the multitude of faint footprints, the traces of blood, all told a terrible story. The once great angel had been roughly dragged along this way by a small army of assailants, dragged toward the turbulent sea.

At the threshold of the island, the land plummeted some 6 or 8 feet to the swirling frothing sea below. Here he found the bloody fragments of a black-feathered wing. They'd dragged him here, shattered his wings, and cast him into the flaming fury. Powerful as he was, he would not escape this horrible fate for quite some time. It might take months, perhaps years before he could escape the fiery sea. Perhaps even longer.

The terrible truth lay before Abaddon. Satan was playing a new game. He had turned upon his own kind. Abaddon scanned the sea in hopes of spotting Batarel, yet in vain. Already his blood was dry upon the rocks. These things had transpired hours ago, and by now his friend might well be miles away. Abaddon knew not how to rescue him—the boiling ooze would ravage his body as surely as it ravaged that of the humans.

Only then did the terrible reality sweep over Abaddon. In his mind's eye he saw Serena, alone in the cavern, beset upon by this same armada of demons. Might Batarel have told them something? Batarel knew nothing of Serena, but he did know where he dwelled. Abaddon leapt into the sky.

Abaddon flew like he had never flown before. He had to get back before it was too late. He found himself doing something he had not done for centuries—crying out to the Father, not on his own behalf, but on that of his dearest human friend.

With a small basket of vegetables and the mysterious sphere in hand, Serena was walking back toward the main cavern room when she heard the footsteps. Had Abaddon returned so soon? She thought to call out to him, yet caution stilled her voice, something was wrong. She took several steps backward before she beheld a dark form in the tunnel at the threshold of the green cavern. Horror gripped her soul as it stepped into the light. Its bat-like wings were partially unfurled, rising above and behind a body largely draped in an ebon cloak. Its dark, gray hands bore long, slender fingers tipped with sharp, dark nails—its face was drawn and contorted, like that of a man of great years. She had seen such a being many times in the past; it was a fallen angel in the service of satan. This essence of evil gazed upon her, a cruel smile revealed sharp, angular teeth.

"At last we meet, Serena Farnsworth," he said, in a deep gruff voice, as he walked several steps into the cavern. "I hope that you have enjoyed your brief respite from the heaving sea, for now your fate shall be all the worse; I can assure you. Foolish you were to think that you could elude us indefinitely.

"I know not how you managed to escape your eternal torment within the great sea of fire, but your return to it must wait. As much as I would like to break every bone in your body and then throw you back myself, I have other orders. Lord satan is most anxious to renew his acquaintance with you. It is to him that I shall deliver you."

Serena took another step back, searching vainly for a plan. She carefully sat the crystal sphere aside, hoping that this minion of satan would take no notice of it.

"It was a dark angel, a warrior that granted you sanctuary," continued the demon, drawing ever closer. "That much I know. But which one, and why? What did one such as he have to gain by such an act?" The demon paused, then shook his head. "Well, it doesn't matter. If he wishes to be in your company, perhaps we shall allow him to join you in the sea of fire, which is very likely where you shall be when this is all done."

Serena didn't respond to the demon's query. It was no longer just her own safety that concerned her, but Abaddon's. She had become the source of his demise.

"I suppose I should thank you for wandering into my path. The master will surely reward me for bringing unto him that which he has desired these past months." The demon scanned his victim. "Ah, but first things first. You cannot appear before lord satan dressed as you are…no, that would not do at all. You have probably rid yourself of the clothing provided you by the master. Fortunately, I have thought of everything. I have brought a change of clothing for you." The demon tossed a short gray skirt and top at Serena's feet.

Serena searched her mind for a plan, anything, but it was in vain.

The demon's smile grew as two pairs of cruel black shackles materialized within his hands. He threw them on the ground in front of her. "Then there are these. Once you are properly attired, you will secure these around your ankles and wrists. They will restrain you during the long journey ahead of us, to say nothing of assuring your discomfort. I shall see to it that you do not escape again."

Serena stopped in her tracks. No she wasn't going to try to run. "And you think I'm going to cooperate? You're mistaken."

"Don't so much as think to evoke my anger," warned the demon, fire flaring in his eyes. "You will cooperate, wench. You are going to stand before the master. You will put those things on. You will do it now, or be all the sorrier for your foolishness."

"Never," retorted Serena, who took a bold step forward. "I'm not afraid anymore, not of you and not of your master, satan. I understand your kind now, all too well. You think inflicting pain makes you great, makes you powerful…well, it doesn't. What it makes you is pathetic, as pathetic as your master. You're a bunch of losers, all of you; and someday the one and only living God is going to put an end to the lot of you."

That was it; the demon broke into a rage. Never had any human spoken to him in such a way. He lunged toward Serena, yet he had scarcely touched her when a dark form swept in front of him. He was momentarily distracted. He turned to see it swing swiftly about and lunge at his neck. He felt the sting, like a red-hot poker being thrust into his throat. He howled in pain. He reached for it with his claw-like hand, yet it easily avoided his grasp. It stung him a second time, this time on the cheek. The demon swung completely around, its wings swaying wildly. For a second he was actually in flight, only to make a less than perfect touch-down some 15 feet back.

The tiny creature didn't give up. For a moment it hovered directly between Serena and her attacker, then it moved forward again, this time striking him at the leading tip of his leathery wing. It stung him and bit him again and again, just out of the reach of the demon's claws.

The demon flapped his wings again, dislodging his tiny foe. "What sort of sorcery is this?" he roared, flailing about at the air with his claws. "I'll get you, Serena! I'll get you for this!"

By now, Serena had her heavy garden spade in hand, the only weapon within her reach. She wielded it before her, trying to hold off her aggressor.

Bloody and enraged, the demon lunged at the young woman, only to be attacked again by the small, winged creature. It hit the crazed demon squarely in the face, clawing, stinging, and biting. Again the demon reached for his tiny tormentor, this time he succeeded. He pulled it away from his brutalized face, bringing a strand of bloody flesh with it. The small creature stung the demon twice on the hand before Serena heard the high pitched scream followed by a sickening crunch. The demon tossed the small mangled body to the side.

"You will pay for that Serena. I'll make you wish that you were still in the sea of fire."

The demon made a single step toward the young woman only to be struck squarely in the face by the heavy spade, not once, but twice. It rebounded both times with a loud metallic ring and a spray of dark, red blood.

He stumbled and felt a burning electric pain on the back of his right leg, quickly followed by another on the left. Within seconds he was in the midst of a cloud of tiny creatures, each as savage as the first. In desperation, the terrified minion of satan retreated into the tunnel, running toward the mouth of the cavern as his tormentors pursued him, lighting into him again and again.

Serena dropped the spade and rushed to that first small creature that had defended her with its life. Its wings had been practically ripped to shreds and its body was twisted and broken. Serena knelt before it, reached out to it with her hand. There were tears in her eyes.

The tiny creature looked up at her with dazed eyes, recognized her, and managed a slight smile. Serena was safe; it had accomplished its mission, now it could die.

Serena recognized this one. This was the same creature that had alighted upon her hand on that day when Abaddon had unveiled his creation before Aaron. It was the same creature that had departed rather than frighten her. Now, incredibly, it had given up its life for her.

"I'm sorry," said Serena, stroking its tiny face. "I'm so sorry."

For a moment it responded, rubbing its long hair against her hand, then its eyes hazed over as it went still.

"Thank you," whispered Serena, whose attention turned to the battle in the corridor.

This minion of satan couldn't be allowed to escape, couldn't be allowed to alert the others. She'd come too far to be defeated now. Serena reached for the spade and rushed to join the battle.

Serena ran as fast as she could through the tunnel, toward the great room. Demon blood was scattered everywhere along the way, giving testimony to the terrible conflict raging between the demon and her mighty defenders.

She joined the battle within sight of the cavern entrance. The demon had been reduced to a mass of flailing crimson flesh, enclosed in a tattered, blood-stained cape. Here and there she saw traces of grayish bone, so terrible had been the carnage.

The demon made a final rush toward the open air. It burst from the cavern and spread its leathery wings, yet they were tattered and wholly unsuitable for navigating the winds of Hell. The demon turned back toward the cavern to see Serena rushing headlong toward him, the sharp tip of the spade directed at him. Like some medieval knight, lance in hand, she ran him through.

So great was the speed and force of the impact, that the spade pierced his flesh, penetrated his heart, and emerged from his back. Blood oozed from his mouth as he stumbled backward, lost his footing, and plummeted from the edge of the cliff. He bounced off the rocks numerous times during the fall; and finally plunged into the waiting sea, which was just as willing to accept the body of a demon as it was the body of a human.

Serena barely managed to halt her forward momentum at the edge of the cliff, thanks to a dozen of Abaddon's children. They latched themselves to her in an attempt to check her fall. Serena could see the demon, still screaming, being swept away by the swift current. It was like no cry she'd ever heard, a high-pitched screech that hurt her ears, even from this distance. Within a minute, the intensity of the heat had silenced him as he began his endless journey into darkness.

On hands and knees, and with plenty of help, Serena crept back from the precipice. She gazed out at the burning sea, as the demon was carried farther away. "The shape of things to come," she whispered. She looked at the 20 or so tiny beings around her, surprised to see many of them nodding in agreement with her remark. She smiled at them. "Thank you, thank you all."

As the group began to reenter the cavern, another dark figure swept down. It was Abaddon.

"Thank our Father in Heaven that you are safe," he exclaimed, embracing the still shivering young woman. He took a careful look at her, saw the blood splattered on her dress.

"It's not mine," she said quickly, pointing toward the demon flailing in the fiery sea.

Abaddon was amazed as he listened to Serena's frightening story. When it was all told, he was visibly shaken.

"No human has ever accomplished what you have done today. It is a true victory for your kind."

"I had a lot of help," said Serena, looking at one of the tiny creatures, stationed on her right shoulder. She stroked its hair gently. She would never be afraid of one of Abaddon's children again. She owed more than her life to them.

As they walked back into the cavern, Abaddon told Serena about what he had discovered. What was happening was unheard of. A war was breaking out in Hell, yet it was a war that could have only one ending unless they escaped. The demons had Abaddon's kind outnumbered tens of thousands to one.

The green cavern bore the traces of the battle that had been fought. Abaddon reached down to pick up the small being that had given its life for Serena's. Abaddon shook his head sadly.

"She was the prototype, the first of this new generation. She was the leader, the queen, as it were. She was the link that allowed them to function as one. The others will be in disarray until they select a new focus, a new queen or king."

"How long will that take?" asked Serena.

"I'm not sure, but until it is accomplished they will be far less effective." Abaddon glanced at the small being on Serena's shoulder. "They may even bond with you for a time. I wouldn't be surprised. The purity of your soul will be nearly magnetic to them; but in the end, they will select a new center from among their own. It might well be the one on your shoulder. He was the first born."

Serena looked into the face of the small being that seemed oh so fascinated with her. He had a new friend, a friend who at last seemed unafraid of him. Serena's attention turned to the crystal sphere. It glowed faintly, as it had all along.

"I hope that your husband contacts you soon," said Abaddon, glancing at the glistening ball. "I fear we have little time. If things continue to deteriorate, we may have to leave this place."

Serena glanced at Abaddon incredulously. "But where could we go?"

Abaddon shook his head as they made their way back toward the main room. "I don't know; truly I don't. All I know is that there is change in our future. Things will never be as they were."

Abaddon and Serena sat together in the great room. Neither one said much. There was nothing more to say.

Then as if an answer to prayer, the total silence was broken by a soft hum emanating from nearby. Serena turned to the sphere that was nestled among vegetables in her basket. It was glowing within its depth—as if a small star had been born in its very heart.

"Abaddon!" she said, as she reached for the glowing sphere.

It was warm and softly vibrating in her hands. It felt wonderful. For the source of the glow within it was God's own Holy Spirit. In effect, God's own light had penetrated to the very heart of outer darkness.

Abaddon pointed to a white marble table several feet away. "Place it over there. We don't know what to expect. Aaron said it has never been tested."

Serena carefully placed the glowing sphere on the table. Yet despite Abaddon's warnings she remained very close to it, drawn in by its radiance.

Quite abruptly the sphere seemed to vanish, replaced by a portal of snow, several times the size of the original sphere. A chill ran up her back as she heard distant voices coming from within the swirling blizzard. She couldn't make them out, though she could tell that there were several different ones. Did one of them belong to Chris?

"Chris?" she called. "Chris, can you hear me?"

Her joy was nearly indescribable as she heard a voice from beyond call her name. It was Chris! It was really him.

"Chris!" she cried. "Oh my dear God, please let it be you."

Out of the snow an image was forming, a three dimensional image. It swirled and contorted as if viewed across waves of heat.

"We've got something," said another voice, more clearly this time. "We need more power, David."

A form materialized out of the snow, the image of someone leaning in her direction. His face was a blur at first, but rapidly clearing. "Serena, I hear you. I can actually hear you," he said, his voice becoming louder, more distinct. "I can almost see you from here. Oh, it's so good to see you."

"Chris," said Serena, in tears. "I can hear you. I can see you. It's a miracle."

"Not quite a miracle," said a figure standing directly behind Chris. "Not yet, at least." He turned to some third party outside the field of view. "We look a bit out of phase."

"I know, I'm working on it, Johann," came the reply.

The image almost instantly sharpened, only to blur once more. A few seconds later it sharpened to crystal clarity. Serena looked into the face of her husband for the first time in months. It was almost as if he was standing beside her.

"That's it," said Johann, looking over Chris's shoulder.

"This is taking a whole lot more power than I thought," came a warning from somewhere in the background. "I can't hold this wormhole open for very long. Let's make it quick."

"Serena, love, we're ready here; we're coming to get you," said Chris. "You've just gotta hang on."

"You had best make haste," said Abaddon, looking over Serena's shoulder. "Serena is in great danger here. You need to take her from here soon."

It took a couple of minutes to relay the seriousness of their situation. The faces on the far side did not fill Abaddon with a sense of encouragement.

Johann drew closer. "Very well, we had originally planned our arrival for tomorrow. We will move our timetable up. Can you be ready in two hours?"

"I hope we have that long," Abaddon said.

"We can't be there any sooner," replied Johann. "I'll have to contact Moriah immediately. We will need his help. Without the support of his angels, I fear that our odds of success will be considerably lower." There was a second's pause. "Nevertheless, we are coming, so be ready. There is a region of level ground along the southern fringe of your island. Is the land there stable? Will it support a heavy craft?"

"It is solid rock," confirmed Abaddon. "The only danger is from above."

"Our angel escort should take care of that," said Chris, his tone confident.

"Then that is where we shall land," said Johann. "Be there in two hours. I don't want to be on the ground for very long."

"We shall be ready," confirmed Abaddon.

Serena drew close to the vision before her, gazing into her husband's eyes.

"We're going to lose the signal in another minute."

"OK, Nick," confirmed Johann.

"So little time," said Serena, drawing even closer.

"Just for the moment," assured Chris, fighting back tears of his own. "But don't worry; we'll have the rest of eternity to be together. We're getting you out of there, I promise. In two hours I'll be able to touch you again. That thought will bring me through. Not even the gulf between Heaven and Hell will keep us apart. I love you, Serena."

His words sent Serena's head to swimming. "I love you Chris, more than ever."

"We're losing the link," warned Nick.

"See you in two hours," said Chris, his image beginning to fade.

Serena bid a final goodbye to her husband; yet she was not certain that he heard it, for the image dissolved before them, leaving a fading glow within the crystal sphere.

Abaddon placed his arm around the young human. "If there is anything you want to take with you, you'd best get it. We will need to leave here in ninety of your minutes. You don't want to make your husband wait for you, do you?"

"No," replied Serena, her smile growing.

"Then hurry up," said Abaddon, ushering her away. "Time is wasting."

Abaddon watched as Serena hurried off to her room. For once in his existence, he was unsure about what to do. Of one thing, though, he was certain; the next few hours would forever change his destiny. There was no margin for error. For the second time in as many hours he found himself reaching out to the Father for guidance. He only hoped that his words had been heard.

chapter twentysix

CHRIS wiped away his tears as the holographic vision vanished before him. If only they'd had more time. No, he couldn't think in those terms. He'd be seeing his wife again in less than two hours, touching her. He focused on that. Johann placed his hand on the young man's shoulder.

"There is nothing you can do here. We've loaded almost everything we need into the Spirit. All we need to do now is contact Moriah and let him know that we've had to move the timetable up. I want you to go home, visit with your mother for a time, then be back here in seventy minutes. Don't be late; we are on a tight schedule."

Chris hesitated, almost afraid to ask the question most on his mind. "Johann, are we really ready?"

"We will be," replied Johann. "We need to bring the temporal capacitor up to full charge. That will require about forty minutes. We'll need to recalculate our exit angle. All of our figures are based on a noon departure tomorrow. That could take about thirty minutes, but it will be done while the capacitor is charging. I just wanted more time to run through simulations.

"As best I can calculate, we will have about a twenty percent margin of error in terms of power. Not as much as I would have liked, but it is adequate." Johann turned toward the clock on the wall. "Chris, you need to be back here in sixty-nine minutes. I suggest that you waste no more of your wife's time."

Chris smiled, but said not a word. A moment later he vanished into the portal that led home.

Johann turned, surprised to see Nick behind him. "I thought you would be anxious to charge the capacitor."

"David is seeing to it. Johann, we have a problem."

"Serious?"

Nick shook his head. "I'm not certain yet. I didn't want Chris to know about it; he'd only worry. It took more energy than I had anticipated to open a wormhole of sufficient size to make the transmission possible. The density of the interdimensional barrier between Heaven and Hell must be denser than I'd calculated."

Johann's heart sunk. "Too dense for us make it back?"

"I'm not sure yet, but it is going to be frighteningly close. Even if we can make it, we won't have much of a margin for error. We'll need to get in and out as quickly as possible. I'll put as much power into the capacitor as it will bear. At this point, we might as well jump first and figure out how to get back later."

Johann nodded. He couldn't believe what Nick had just said. Nick was usually so cautious, but not today. They walked to the Spirit to make the final preparations for lift off. Johann thought back to their journey to the Tarantula Nebula eight years ago. It had been one of their first attempts at interdimensional flight. A miscalculation had left them stranded for several days in deep space. There'd been no band of angels to rescue them that day. They'd been compelled to rely on their own resourcefulness to repair their overloaded drive system and limp home. A similar failure on this flight might have far more serious implications. He tried not to think about it.

❧❖❧ ❧❖❧ ❧❖❧

Chris stepped onto the porch of the mansion where his old black cat had been waiting for him for the past two hours. He reached down and gave her a loving scratch on the head before heading inside. His mother was in her sewing room. She looked up and smiled.

"How did it go?"

"Not like we'd expected," replied Chris, doing his best to explain the situation.

What Jennifer heard left her with plenty of questions and concerns, yet she gave them no voice. They spoke of familiar things for some time, yet did their best to avoid any further discussion about the perilous mission. Jennifer knew that there would be no changing her son's mind. She wasn't even certain that to do so would have been a good idea. Perhaps he was right; perhaps he had to go.

As Chris bid goodbye to his mother and his favorite animal friend, he was full of optimism. "I'll try to be back by this evening," he said.

Jennifer stood on the porch, trying not to be too emotional. As she watched him vanish, though, tears came to her eyes. Within her heart a terrible dread was welling up. She had the feeling that he would not be coming back this evening or tomorrow. She wondered if she would ever see him again.

ᛝ❄ᛡ ᛝ❄ᛡ ᛝ❄ᛡ

Over 70 minutes had passed by the time Chris stepped from the portal and walked back into Johann's home. He found Johann, Nick, and David in the back yard making their final preparations. Johann turned to see Chris step out the back door.

"Two minutes late," he said, placing a metal case through the hatchway of the craft. "I was starting to become concerned."

"I still wish I could go," complained David, stepping back as the last piece of equipment was loaded on board.

Johann shook his head. "We've been all over this before. Someone has to remain here and monitor the landing site from my study. I'll need you to remain in constant contact with us and keep us informed as to the progress of the angels and any demons that might wander into the area. If you're not going to do that, then this mission is in jeopardy, we will be flying blind."

"OK, I'll do it," replied David, his tone apologetic. "I just wanted to see this place for myself."

"Maybe next time," replied Nick, climbing through the hatchway and into the Spirit.

Johann and Chris followed quickly behind. The main hatchway of the Spirit didn't have hinges, and it didn't close in the conventional sense. The rectangular opening simply vanished, replaced by smooth crystal. Within the craft, Nick had already taken his seat at the controls. The high-backed chair sat on a circular platform about 3 feet high surrounded by a railing of clear crystal. A steep stairway gave him access to this place of honor.

Before him, the control panel was amazingly simple. A large glass sphere and two smaller ones were built into the control panel. A wide range of complex readouts was suspended in midair in front of him like so many holograms. He scanned them carefully and apparently liked what he saw. On the lower deck level, below Nick's command level, there were eight chairs arranged in a circle. Chris noticed that none of the chairs had a seatbelt; but he decided not to question it. There just wasn't time to waste.

"The best seats in the house," Johann said, pointing to the two chairs before them.

Chris sat down, a bit nervous, and Johann sat in the chair to his left.

For nearly ten minutes Johann said very little. The only conversations were between Nick and David, who was monitoring the whole operation from the study. Chris turned to see a holographic projection of the youth among the other readouts; he was going over checklists, confirming readings, and so on. At least in that respect, this launch seemed similar to those he had seen on television. Yet right now, time seemed to be dragging on. Chris was anxious to get underway.

There was no announcement made, no fanfare, only a soft hum as the craft slowly lifted off the ground. The metallic landing gear retracted, rendering the craft a perfect sphere, moving swiftly into the sky. The trees fell away, giving Chris an unobstructed horizon. It dawned on him that he had never truly seen Heaven from the air. He wondered what it would look like. The answer—very much like Earth. The forested landscape dropped away quickly. They passed through a layer of widely scattered clouds. A river came into view and a large meadow to the north, yet no cities or towns met his eye.

"Passing 10,000 meters," announced Nick, momentarily looking away from the controls.

"Will we be able to see Zion on the way up?" asked Chris scanning the spectacular panorama below.

"No. Heaven isn't quite like Earth. For example, you couldn't reach Zion from either your home or mine if you couldn't form the portal. It is not a part of the same world. Heaven is many worlds, each a little bit out of phase with the other."

"Out of phase?" asked Chris. "I remember your saying something like that about the image of Serena in the crystal, yet I don't have a clue as to what it means."

"It's a bit difficult to explain," replied Johann, gazing up at the ever-darkening sky. Perhaps I'll go into it later."

"1,000 kilometers an hour, 25,000 meters," announced Nick, who seemed very busy flying the craft.

The sky above faded to black, making way for the stars of night, even as the daylight sky became a narrowing band of blue below them. The Spirit was hurtling headlong into space, yet Chris could barely detect any motion.

"A few words about going through the dimensional barrier," said Johann, turning to Chris. "I'm telling you right now that it's not the most pleasant experience. It can be visually stunning, but it can leave you feeling queasy in the stomach for a minute or two. Your up, your down, and your sideways are no longer what they were—they become concepts assigned to entirely different physical dimensions."

"At times, even some of the physical laws and universal constants change, and our bodies have to adjust to these changes. I'm not at all certain that our old bodies would even have withstood the shock, but our glorified bodies, they mange just fine."

Chris wasn't certain that he understood what Johann was talking about, but he did understand the queasy part. Flying used to do it to him all the time. He enjoyed the view, but he didn't like what it did to his stomach. He wondered why Johann had waited until now to break this news to him.

"We've never been through this particular dimensional barrier," continued Johann, "but I can't imagine it will be any different. Just don't become upset if it gets a little bit bumpy, we will get through."

Chris nodded, as he turned toward the incredible vista beyond the glass sphere. "Out of the blue and into the black," he murmured, remembering the words of an old rock song. That they were; the blackness of space was all around them now. He'd always wondered what it was like out here, now he knew. All he had to do was die, to experience it all for himself. The thought brought a slight smile to his face.

"We're two minutes to the dimensional barrier," warned Nick, glancing down at his two passengers. "This should be interesting."

"It is always necessary to travel into space when you form a dimensional corridor such as this," noted Johann. "We can't form one on the ground. The wormhole left momentarily in our wake would wreak havoc on everything around. Air, bushes, trees, nearby people, would all be sucked in and then deposited who knows where. It was one of the ground rules set by the Father before He allowed us to embark upon these ventures into the vast unknown."

"Right," confirmed Nick, "He didn't want His children leaving a mess behind when they were playing." Nick glanced at the readouts. "We're just passing an altitude of five hundred kilometers, speed eighteen-thousand kilometers per hour, one minute to go."

Chris was becoming increasingly nervous. "How does this thing fly? You know, it's strange, but I forgot to even ask."

"We create a very small spatial distortion directly above the craft, a tiny gravity well in the midst of space time," said Nick, keeping his attention focused on the displays in front of him. When we're on the ground it has to be a very small one, lest we disturb the surface around us as well. In deep space we can create a much larger distortion, accelerate to nearly the speed of light in but a few minutes. Crossing the barrier from one dimension to another involves very much the same principle, but on a far grander scale. Here we go."

Chris felt a falling sensation, yet it seemed as if he was falling upward. The world behind him dropped away at an accelerated pace, the hum grew in volume and pitch.

"Opening capacitor relays to standby," said Nick, "we don't want to lose power at a critical moment. Coordinates laid in. Making the jump, now."

Behind them, the globe of this version, this phase of Heaven, dropped away to insignificance. There was a momentary flash of light that seemed to come from everywhere. In that instant the stars vanished. Ethereal streams of light materialized out of the blackness, glowing tenuous clouds swept past them. They lent a range of kaleidoscopic color to the inside of the Spirit as they plunged deeper into the ethereal realm. Beyond the sphere, streaming clouds of color, clouds alive with coursing threads of lightning, shot past. With them came an increasing turbulence that made Chris sick to his stomach.

"Is it always like this?" he asked, closing his eyes for a moment.

"It is never like this," replied Johann, gazing wide-eyed at the awesome spectacle. "I can't even begin to explain what it is we are seeing."

"I am recording it," said Nick. "We can analyze the data later."

For several minutes they passed through the realm of ethereal storms. Yet the light around them, even the electrical power within these titanic maelstroms, was fading, giving way to profound darkness.

"The spatial energy field set up by God's Holy Spirit is fading," noted Nick, "we're switching to internal power. We're on our own from here."

Chris felt a queasiness in the pit of his stomach not associated with the turbulence that had now past. It was the sense of being without God's Holy Spirit, without His presence. They were moving into a realm where He was not. True, they had brought a portion of the power of that Spirit within the temporal capacitor, but that couldn't replace the actual presence of God. Chris closed his eyes. The absence of God's Holy Spirit was almost unbearable to him. It gave rise to a terrible sense of loneliness, even hopelessness.

There was a slight shudder as the sphere was flooded with amber illumination. Chris opened his eyes to see a disk of light ahead. It had the appearance of the sun yet far less luminous, far redder. Until recently, it was the only star in a realm of total darkness. Some distance to its right, Chris spotted a small thin crescent of a world, reflecting the light of the distant star. That crescent was slowly growing as they drew nearer.

"Gentlemen, I welcome you to outer darkness and the world of Hell," announced Nick. "We're right on schedule, right on course. Speed ten thousand kilometers per second and decelerating. Estimated arrival time thirty-seven minutes."

Johann stared at the world before them. "Let us hope that satan does not monitor the space around this prison world of his too carefully. Our entrance into this space would have been pretty hard to miss, wormholes usually are. One of our most important advantages is surprise. We need to get in and out as quickly as possible if we're to make this plan work."

Chris gazed out in silence at the rapidly growing crescent. Serena was down there. He offered a silent prayer for their success, yet he wondered if God heard it.

⁂ ⁂ ⁂

Serena had changed clothes, snatched up the few possessions that meant anything to her, and was preparing to make her way to the great room. She looked back on the tiny cavern room she had called home these past few months. She willed the crystal in the ceiling to fade a final time. She would not be coming this way again.

As she made her way back to the great room, she was certain that she heard voices. A bolt of fear shot through her as she cautiously peered around the corner to see Abaddon talking with five other dark angels. They were not demons with leathery wings, but angels with dark, feathered wings and faces not unlike that of human men.

"It is a terrible thing that has descended upon us," said one of the angels, speaking in the angelic tongue. "Satan has become completely obsessed with finding Serena Farnsworth. From north to south, from east to west, he has sent his minions in search of her. Then he became convinced that it was one of us who had aided her escape. Four days ago he issued an ultimatum. We were either to pledge our unconditional allegiance to him, or face a fate similar to that of the humans, eternal torment."

"Only a fiend like satan would advocate such a vile act against one of his own kind," said another.

"I, for one, do not consider satan and his minions to be our kind—not any more," said a third. "They gave up that right millennia ago."

"We have been carrying the word among our brothers that his minions are seeking us out," said the first. "Already thirty or more of us have faced a horrible fate—one usually reserved for humans. Few have accepted his alternative. We can't allow them to take us all down one by one. Those of us who are left must band together to oppose satan."

"It is this human female that is the cause of it all," said another. "Semjaza, you know that this is true. Humans have been nothing but trouble for us."

Semjaza seemed unaffected by this challenge from his compatriot. "Hold your peace, Ramiel, and your anger. Think you that satan was not disposed to do this thing anyway? To satan, the escape of this woman has been but an excuse to do that which he was already disposed to do. I believe it is a test of our resolve, of our character. It has made us choose who we shall serve. Though I have failed the Father and have been condemned to this place, and rightly so, I shall not betray him."

Serena hesitated then stepped out into the room. All eyes turned to her.

"Is this the face that launched a revolt?" asked one of the dark angels, turning to Abaddon.

Abaddon turned to Serena, stretching out his hand. "My brothers, behold the woman Serena."

"I am sorry that I have caused so much trouble for you. Truly I am."

It was not her contrite spirit that amazed the gathering but the fact that her words had been uttered perfectly in the angelic tongue.

The angels said nothing as Serena walked into their midst. They gazed upon her as if they were looking into her very soul. Some even placed a gentle hand upon her as if trying to sense something.

It was more than a minute before Semjaza broke the silence. "Abaddon, what manner of human have you found? Her soul is so pure. That one such as she should be cast into the sea of fire is indeed a travesty." Semjaza turned once more to Serena. "With a heart so pure, why did you not accept God's gift of salvation? Surely you must have heard his call."

Serena could offer no excuse; she remained silent.

It was Abaddon who told the group of the arrival of this most unique human into his existence. He spoke of her conviction, her purity, and her courage. He spoke of the rescue to come and the battle that would soon be waged in the skies above.

"In doing what I have done, I have brought great harm to my brethren, and I am indeed sorry. But you now see her for yourself.

What was I to do? There is something special about her. I could not return her to the agony that is the sea of fire. I had to take her in. I had to protect her. Now I must continue the journey I have started. The road ahead is difficult, but I must see this thing through to its conclusion."

Semjaza shook his head. "I can see that. I for one will not allow you to make that journey alone. I am with you, my brother." He turned to Serena and smiled, "and you too, Serena."

"I am Tamiel," said another of the angels. "I too will do my best to see you safely out of this place, if such is possible."

"I am Sariel," spoke yet another. "I too am at your service, Serena."

"And I am Asael," said another. "I am for you and my brother Abaddon. Today we shall stand against the evil one, as it was always intended. May God grant us strength."

Ramiel looked at the others. "I am tired of hiding, tired of running. I stand with you."

Abaddon looked at his fellows. It had been a very long time since they had stood together. "Then let us be off. We have less than thirty minutes before we deliver Serena to those who will take her to safety. Until then she is our responsibility."

Abaddon placed a black cloak around Serena to make her less visible to circling demons; then they moved out to face what might well be their final battle. Not far behind, but out of sight, 27 tiny creatures followed them.

❧❈❧ ❧❈❧ ❧❈❧

Satan sat upon his throne in the great hall of audiences. He had just sentenced a young, fair-of-face murderess to be frozen within the ice of the Continent of Darkness. Her sheer terror in his presence had made for a most entertaining sentencing. He was preparing to call forth his next victim when a demon captain stepped, no, practically stumbled into his presence totally unannounced.

"What is the meaning of this intrusion?" roared satan, rising to his feet. "Can't you see I'm busy?!"

The captain was shaking, yet he drew closer. "My lord satan, I must speak with you on a matter of utmost urgency."

By now satan's court was all astir with this surprising intrusion. For a mere captain to have dared to interrupt the master, something of great significance must have happened.

"You have one minute," said satan walking toward the quaking captain. "What you have to tell me had better be most important, for your sake."

"It is," responded the captain. "Just minutes ago a portal opened into outer darkness, a portal from Heaven. It remained open just long enough for a single object to pass through."

"And?" said satan, his impatience growing.

"The seers at the Gate of Sheol, report that they sense a great disturbance in outer darkness, a disturbance of enormous power, and that disturbance is moving swiftly toward us."

The captain now had satan's full attention. "What sort of power?"

"We don't know yet, we have never seen the like." There was a pause. "Well, maybe once, a very long time ago."

Satan didn't need to be told about that single incident. That disaster would be ingrained in his memory for all eternity. "And where is it going?"

"We're trying to determine that now. We believe it is headed for somewhere in the midst of the sea of fire." There was a pause of just a few seconds. "But there is something else."

"What?"

"Angels," replied the captain, "more than we have ever seen before, coming through the gate."

"How many?"

"Hundreds, maybe thousands, we're just not certain yet."

Satan was beside himself with rage and confusion. "Call forth my legions to intercept these angels."

The captain was confused by that order. "My lord, which legions?"

Satan grabbed the captain by the neck, lifting him into the air. "All of them, you idiot! All of them! Intercept these angels. Bring them down. Do you hear me?"

"Yes," gasped the captain, struggling to speak.

Satan released his grip on the captain who quickly scurried away. Satan turned to his regent standing by his throne. "I need my armor, my weapons."

"My lord?" said the regent, not at all certain as to what was transpiring.

"Do you not see?" roared the prince of darkness. "It is an invasion! It has begun. I shall lead my armies this day. We shall be victorious. I shall finally defeat the armies of God."

⊰❋⊱ ⊰❋⊱ ⊰❋⊱

David sat in Johann's study scanning three different holographic projections showing various aspects of Hell. It had been a routine, even dull assignment. The Spirit was two minutes from entering the atmosphere of Hell and there was still nothing to report. It seemed that they had caught satan completely by surprise. He had noticed the entrance of the angels nearly ten minutes ago. There appeared to be several hundred, more than he had expected.

Then he noticed a change in the movements of the demons in the vicinity of the island. Up until now they had been relatively random, but suddenly there was a pattern. They seemed to be grouping and turning toward the advancing band of angels. Then more objects appeared on the screen, entire legions of demons had taken flight and were moving toward the island. Suddenly this job wasn't routine or boring.

He turned to the crystal, his communications link with the Spirit. "Professor Tesla, we have a problem."

The disk of Hell had swelled to encompass nearly a third of the sky as seen from the Spirit. Chris looked down to see where day met night, down on the flaming sea. The bloated red sun began to sink beyond the distant horizon, and in a moment they were engulfed by the shadow of Hell. Only the flames provided any illumination. A chill shot up his back imagining his wife in that heaving maelstrom. The thought threatened to overwhelm his senses before he caught himself.

"There's trouble up ahead," warned Nick. "I think our secret is out. There are demons converging on the island, David reports several legions of them."

"More than Moriah and his angels can handle?" asked Johann.

"A lot more," confirmed Nick. "A legion of demons is how many...a hundred-thousand?

"About that," confirmed Johann. "How long until touch-down?"

"Eighteen minutes," said Nick, "and no we can't land any sooner. You know as well as I that we are tied to a schedule."

That comment raised Johann's eyebrows. "How long will it take for those demon legions to reach the island?"

There was a pause. "David figures we might have thirty minutes, maybe less. They're coming in awful fast, and the winds are probably in their favor."

Johann turned back toward the glass and watched the most dreaded world in all of creation growing closer. He noticed a storm far below, coursing with lightning. "That storm down there, how far is it from our landing point?"

Nick glanced at the distant tempest, then back at his holographic instrument panel. "Looks like about ninety to perhaps a hundred kilometers. Pretty far, it won't hit the island for at least two hours. It won't be a problem."

"But will it delay the demon legions? They would be coming from that direction, wouldn't they?"

That was a thought. Nick conferred with David. "Yes, the legions are coming in from Sheol. That storm is a wide one, and it's directly in their path. It will take them time to fly around it or over it. It might cost them twenty minutes or so. It won't affect Moriah and his angels; they're coming in from the west. We have another four or five legions coming in behind them from that direction as well, but they are at least an hour out."

Chris gazed down at the storm as well. "It looks like we got lucky."

"Perhaps," replied Johann, "or perhaps luck had nothing to do with it." He said no more. It wasn't a time for conjecture. Right now they needed to stay focused.

The Spirit swung around, positioning itself for final approach. Now Hell was literally under their feet. Nick scanned his readouts one final time to confirm that all was in readiness. This was it.

A slight buffeting and rushing air around the hull announced their entrance into the atmosphere. This operation was going to be trickier than they'd first thought. They had underestimated satan's response time. As it was, if nothing else went wrong, they just might be able to pull this off, just.

<hr />

Serena and her compatriots had reached the acid bogs along the island's southern plains. Their attention was drawn to the approaching storm in the east.

"We noticed that storm on our trip in," said Semjaza, gazing at the flashes of blue coursing through the clouds. "It's coming this way."

Serena shook her head. She looked toward the storm and then scanned the skies overhead, not quite sure what she was looking for; then she saw it. It looked like a faint star, high overhead, yet this star was moving, becoming brighter. "It's them!" She exclaimed, pointing toward the still faint luminary.

Abaddon drew a large luminous crystal from a pocket in his cloak, willed it to glow at its greatest brightness. It illuminated their surroundings in brilliant blue light. He hoped that there were no others to see it, save the humans descending from the sky.

Eight miles over their heads, the Spirit continued its rapid descent. Nick had a dozen things on his mind. They were entering a zone where attack from demons was a real possibility. He might have to react swiftly in case of trouble.

From his seat, Chris scanned the fiery sea below. "I see the island. It's a small patch of darkness setting in the middle of all of those flames. And wait, there's a light at the one end, a blue light. It must be Abaddon and Serena."

Johann pointed down and to the left of the craft, where a myriad of glowing figures was traveling in formation swiftly toward the island. "The angels; and they're right on time."

"Four minutes to touchdown," announced Nick. "We've got more trouble. David reports that we've got demons coming in several waves from the south, about five or six minutes out, several hundred of them. I hope Moriah and his forces can keep them busy. If our landing is delayed by more than ten or fifteen minutes, we will have about two hundred thousand more demons to deal with. This has to go perfectly."

Abaddon had selected a level site for the landing and had placed a series of three glowing crystals on the ground around it. The craft was now a softly glowing sphere in the sky, descending almost vertically toward the selected landing zone. From its sides, the four spidery legs extended and locked in position. It was almost silent, as three spotlights on the bottom of the craft bathed the plains below in brilliant luminance.

Overhead, the arriving angels moved to intercept the first wave of demons descending upon the island. The battle had begun.

The legs of the Spirit planted firmly on the rocky ground and the soft noise of the craft's engines went silent. From the craft's side, an opening appeared, and a small stairway emerged.

True to style, Chris bounded from the craft and onto the black rocky terrain without so much as a second look. Overhead, amid bright flashes of light, the angels had engaged their dark foes in combat. The glow of their mighty weapons lit up the sky.

"Chris!" cried Serena, running toward her husband and falling into his arms. "Oh, Chris, I was sure I'd never see you again, not for the rest of eternity!"

Chris hugged her tightly, kissing her on the cheek. "I'm with you now, my love, and I'm taking you out of here, I promise."

Serena gazed up at the escalating battle. More and more demons were entering the fray. "Chris, how many can that ship of yours take out of here?"

Chris turned to see the six dark angels. At first he was apprehensive.

Serena tried as best she could to dry the tears of joy that filled her eyes. "Don't be afraid, they're friends. Chris, I wanted you to meet Abaddon. I'd still be in the sea of fire if it weren't for him."

Chris stepped forward, extended his hand toward the dark angel. Abaddon accepted it. "I owe you more than I could ever say or repay. I saw the kindness you have shown my wife when I looked into her book in the Hall of Records. I thank you from the bottom of my heart."

"I am pleased to meet you," he replied. "Chris, you have a good wife, the very best. That which I did for her, she was more than deserving of. I now turn over the responsibility of her happiness to you. I am certain that she is in good hands."

Chris seemed surprised. "You're not coming with us? You are more than welcome."

"Abaddon smiled. "I am sure that I am, but I must decline your kind offer. There is much work for me to do here. I cannot leave it unfinished."

"But the demons will catch up to you eventually," objected Serena. "I can't bear to think of you in their hands. I wanted all of you to come with us."

Semjaza laughed out loud. "You give them far too much credit, child. We shall prevail."

"It is true," confirmed Asael. "Do not look at their numbers and judge us vanquished so quickly. We cannot come with you."

The others nodded silently; none would be joining Serena on her quest to the new world.

"Chris, Serena, we don't have much time." It was Johann who called to them from the doorway of the craft. Chris saw some sort of high-tech rifle in his hands. "Moriah is encountering greater resistance than we had anticipated. We need to lift off *now*."

Serena turned to Abaddon. "My ride is waiting."

"Yes, and you have a destiny to fulfill, of that I'm sure," confirmed Abaddon. "May the Father of all look kindly upon you, wherever you may go."

Serena embraced Abaddon one final time, kissing him on the cheek. "I'm going to miss you. I hope I get the chance to return your kindness someday."

Abaddon smiled, as a tear came to his eye. "One can never tell what the future might bring. Fair thee well, Serena."

Ramiel and Asael turned abruptly, their attention drawn by approaching danger. A second later a beam of brutally intense light flashed over Serena's head, followed by a loud report. Nearly a hundred feet away, it struck a shadowy black form, a demon had broken through the angelic defenses. The demon flailed wildly as it plunged to the rocks below, his body literally shattered by the blow of the weapon so skillfully wielded by Johann.

"Impressive!" exclaimed Sariel. "For a human, that is."

"Like I said, we need to leave," repeated Johann. This time he was noticeably agitated. "It is not safe here."

"Get clear, we're taking off," yelled Chris, as hand in hand he and Serena dashed toward the Spirit.

The black angels quickly scattered, not knowing quite what to expect. As Johann covered their retreat, Chris hoisted Serena into the craft, then leapt in after her. The portal swiftly vanished behind them.

"Let's roll!" Chris shouted, helping his wife into the seat by his side.

Nick was not as gentle on this lift off. Amid a whirlwind of swirling dust, the Spirit hurtled skyward.

A demon swept just below them as the Spirit made an evasive maneuver. The ground swirled below them before Nick regained control and continued skyward. On the ground far below, the six black angels had already taken to the air, making good their escape from the growing demonic threat.

Already Moriah and his angels had broken off their attack. They had done what they could. Yet they were rapidly being outnumbered as demons by the scores continued to join the battle. Now with their objective accomplished, they would need to make their way home. For the first time in many centuries they had engaged a demon army in the flesh. They had made the demons feel the sting of their weapons, brought to their remembrance the Great War in Heaven, the war in which they had been defeated. It felt good to strike a blow against the greatest foe of them all, even though the battle was brief.

Yet even as they flew for home, they realized that this was only a taste of things to come. They would fight again; and next time they would have the resources to vanquish the army of darkness once and for all. It was something to look forward to with great anticipation.

The Spirit punched through the sound barrier as it raced toward the upper stratosphere, leaving any opposition far behind. Serena and Chris sat there, hand in hand, watching the vile realm of Hell dropping farther away. The dull star that was the center of Hell's orbit materialized along the horizon, bathing them in its amber glow.

"We pulled it off, Johann," said Nick, beaming with pride. "There were times when I had my doubts, but we really did it." He glanced at his readouts. "We're crossing into space now. Preparing to set course for the jump. Next stop, the new planet."

"Wait till we reach five hundred kilometers before you make the jump," cautioned Johann.

"Of course," confirmed Nick. "Three minutes forty seconds to the jump."

"Jump?" asked Serena, still overwhelmed by the events of the past hours.

"Yes," confirmed Johann. "We have a long trip to the new world. If we attempt to cross such a distance in normal space it would require twenty-two centuries. I'm not that patient. By creating a hyperspace wormhole, we can reach it without traveling through any of the space in between. You see, the shortest distance between two points is not always a straight line."

Serena felt certain that she should have understood that explanation, but she really didn't. She looked to Chris.

"It's a physicist thing," he replied.

Serena broke out into laughter. It felt so good to laugh again, yet her happiness was short lived.

"I can't get a lock on the new world," announced Nick, his frustration apparent. "I've tried three times. According to my instruments, those space time coordinates do not exist, at least not in outer darkness."

Johann rose from his chair and joined Nick at the controls, only to confirm their worst fears a few minutes later.

"What now?" asked Chris, who, with Serena walked toward Nick and Johann.

"Well, for the moment we drop into a parking orbit until we can evaluate our options," replied Johann. "We have time."

"Some," cautioned Nick. "The capacitor won't hold its charge indefinitely. If we can't come up with a solution in about eleven hours, we will lack the power to escape outer darkness. We'll be stuck here."

"Why can't we just set course back to Heaven," suggested Chris. "Maybe we could negotiate a pardon for Serena."

"We can't do that," said Johann. "You know that."

"How do you know," objected Chris.

"Look, this is not something I've contrived," objected Johann. "I've spoken to Aaron regarding this issue. I gave my word to Moriah that we would not resort to this. What would you have me do, Chris?"

Chris did not get the chance to respond.

"Johann is right," interjected Serena. "I was condemned to this place by God. I deserve to be here." Serena drew closer to Chris, placed her arms around him.

"And there is more to it than that," continued Johann. "Serena's reality is in outer darkness. There is no way out. Even if we were to try to return to Heaven with her on board, she would not survive the trip. Her physical body would evaporate like a mist, leaving her spirit to float in outer darkness for all eternity. She can't go with us."

"I love you, Chris, more than anything, but we can't do this," said Serena. "We have tried to cheat my destiny. You've got to take me back. Maybe you could just release me into space."

"No!" cried Chris, drawing Serena closer. "There has to be another way, there just has to be."

"Don't make a decision yet," Nick said, rising to his feet and turning to the couple on the deck below him. "Look, I've tried not to interfere in any personal affairs up to this point. I've just made what talents I possess available to all of you, tried to offer what solutions I can. I was never in love as you, and I can't claim to fully understand what the two of you are going through. What I *will* tell you is not to make any hasty decisions right now. You are too emotional. Let it rest for a time, think things out for a few hours. Weigh out your options. Only then commit yourself to a decision." Nick sat down and scanned the readings. "I'm placing us in a one thousand kilometer-high parking orbit. I truly believe that there is a solution to your crisis, but you will need to find it together."

Chris and Serena did not return to their seats, but rather sat on the floor together, arm in arm. As they did, Nick and Johann continued to explore their options. They had not come so far, braved so much, to give up now. They couldn't abandon Serena. If there was a way out, they would find it.

chapter twentyseven

THE Spirit swept high above the brutal sunlit deserts of Hell, above swirling dust storms, roiling lava pools, and other unseen horrors. The coming of night an hour later offered no solace, for it brought forth a panoramic view of the glowing sea which Serena knew too well. Through it all, she cherished her time in her husband's arms, dreading the hour when it would come to an end.

Chris prayed fervently for guidance, though he still wondered if prayers were heard from this place. Serena joined him in those prayers. For the first time they were of one mind in the spirit. Chris and Serena spoke of their happy years on Earth. They cherished those wonderful times; yet here and now, their togetherness seemed all the more precious. These few hours together were like no others.

Meanwhile, Nick and Johann worked feverishly, conferring with David, running simulations, trying to figure out where they went wrong. In the end, there were more questions than answers.

They were moving into their third orbit with the swollen sun rising once more above the horizon, when Chris rose to his feet. "Johann, what can you tell me about this corridor that the angels use to travel to and from Heaven and Hell?"

"It's what we call a stable wormhole," replied Johann, stepping to the railing that encircled the command console and looking toward Chris. "Using it, angels can travel back and forth at will, expending very little energy of their own in the process."

"Yes, but where in Heaven and Hell does it lead?"

"To several places, as I understand it," said Johann.

"Between the Judgment Hall of God and the waiting cells of Hell for one," said Serena, rising to her feet. "Believe me, I know."

"Yes, but where did the angels who supported us enter and exit from?" asked Chris.

"That place is located on a vast plain right where the daylight meets the darkness. I suppose you might say that it has some historical significance. It is the gateway through which satan and all those who followed him in the Great War originally entered into Hell and their eternal exile. It is a sort of gigantic stone archway, by my understanding."

Abruptly, a large sphere materialized in their midst, a representation of Hell. Johann drew their attention to a great peninsula of land jutting out into the sea of fire. "It is here, nineteen-hundred kilometers west northwest of Abaddon's island."

Chris appeared to be onto something and he had everyone's attention. "How long would it take to get us there?"

There was a moment of silence. "If we follow our current orbit, make a trajectory correction, about two hours and ten minutes," said Nick, consulting the readouts.

"And how much time do we have left before we have to return to Heaven?"

"Just under six hours," said Nick, who had now turned toward Chris as well.

Chris hesitated, then continued. "I need to speak to David."

Nick motioned to Chris to join him and Johann on the upper deck. Amid the cryptic readouts suspended before Nick, an image of David, still sitting in the study, appeared.

Chris leaned forward. "David, you need to go to Zion, to the holy place, to confer with God. How long would it take you to get there?"

At first David seemed confused. "About two hours, maybe less if I run."

"Now listen carefully; I need you to relay a message from me to the Father. You've got to convince Him to intervene on Serena's behalf, to reconsider her sentence to outer darkness. I should have gone to Him long ago with this petition, but I didn't. Now I must depend on you to deliver it to Him. Will you do this for me?"

David seemed nervous. He looked at Chris, a trace of fear on his countenance. Then he saw Serena standing behind him. She desperately needed his help and he couldn't deny it to her. He'd witnessed her suffering, strength, and courage from the unique perspective one gained in the Hall of Records. His resolve was strengthened. Until now he'd been a minor character in the incredible drama, largely relegated to the sidelines; but now he had the opportunity to make a real difference. "Tell me exactly what you want me to do and say."

Chris took only five minutes to prepare David for his most important meeting. Then David made his last report to Johann and departed for the City of Zion.

Johann looked at Chris. "I know how you feel, but I must tell you that I don't see how this is going to help. Going back down there into harms way and waiting at the gate for a decision from God is a very reckless course of action. It is most unlikely that God will reverse His decision; surely you must realize that. There has to be a better way."

Chris remained uncharacteristically calm. "Johann, you've had nearly five hours to come up with a plan. If you've got something, I wish you'd let the rest of us in on it."

For a moment, Chris's challenge met only with silence. "They'll be monitoring our movements; you realize that."

"Yes," confirmed Chris. "I'm counting on it."

"We go down there and they'll be on us in a matter of minutes."

"I suppose so."

Johann threw up his arms in frustration. "So why are we doing it?"

"I have a plan," replied Chris, with a growing smile. "I'm not telling you it isn't risky for all of us…it is, but I think it's our only shot."

For the next ten minutes Chris laid out his proposal in detail. Johann heard him out, yet when the telling was through, he was even more skeptical.

"Look," Chris said, placing his arm around Serena, "I have no right to ask so much. You don't have to stay. If you want, you just put the Spirit down long enough to drop Serena and me off. I wouldn't blame you for a second, but this will work better if we all pulled together."

"You realize what you're asking of me?" confirmed Johann.

"I do," Chris said, "but I really believe that it won't come to that; this is going to work."

"It's absolutely reckless…but I'm with you," Nick said.

Johann turned and walked down the steps to the main deck. He sat in his chair gazing at the barren world below. He didn't much relish spending eternity here. He'd seen too many of its horrors from the safety of the Hall of Records. Yet, if they did succeed; what an incredible concept it was. It might be well worth risking one man's eternity. "Very well, Chris, we'll do it your way this time. I only hope you're right."

"OK everyone," announced Nick. "Return to your seats. We have a course correction to make in a little less than three minutes. Then I suppose you'll need me to come up with another technological miracle."

"That was the general idea," said Chris, sitting at Serena's side.

"I'll have it ready for you when you need it," Nick said. "The rest is up to you."

⁂ ⁂ ⁂

Satan paced back and forth in his audience chamber like a restless lion in a small cage. He had dismissed nearly all of his entourage. Only Governor Moloch and General Krell remained. "What is it that we have seen this day?" satan asked, his frustration only too obvious.

"I believe that it was a rescue, not an invasion," replied Krell, approaching the master. "Less than six hundred angels were involved in the attack. They engaged our forces for but a brief time before withdrawing once more through the great portal. The battle was fought above a remote island in the great sea of fire, an island suspected to be under the dominion of one or more dark warrior angels. A human female dressed in black was spotted by several of our soldiers. We believe that human was Serena Farnsworth. She was, in fact, seen in the presence of a group of dark angelic warriors. We believe two of them to be Semjaza and Abaddon, the highest ranking members of this fallen clan. Apparently it was one of them who rescued her from the sea of fire."

"And the strange intruder from the sky, the one that radiated so much of the Father's power, what of it?"

"It appeared to be some manner of crystalline sphere. We believe that it was some sort of vessel, under the command of a group of humans."

"Humans?" roared satan. "That is utterly impossible! They are weak; they do not possess the wisdom or power to create such a thing!"

Moloch hesitated to challenge the wisdom of the master when he was in a mood so foul. "Apparently we have underestimated them."

"Yet this thing, this sphere of power, has not departed our realm?" observed satan.

"No my lord," confirmed the general, "it has not. Even now it whirls about our world."

Satan turned to Moloch who was deep in thought. "What thing are they up to? Why go to so much trouble to rescue one insignificant human wench?"

"Is she insignificant?" posed Moloch.

There was a moment of silence in the chamber. "No, perhaps not," replied satan.

A lieutenant of satan's imperial legion entered the chamber. He bowed before the master.

"Yes," replied satan, "you have something for me?"

"Yes, my Lord," he replied. "The sphere has changed course. It is descending and decelerating."

"Where is it heading?" asked the general, approaching his subordinate.

"We are not certain as yet, but we believe that it is preparing to attack again."

"We had best be prepared for another angelic assault," suggested Moloch.

"The first one might have been no more than a ruse. A full scale attack could come at any time."

"None of this makes any sense," complained Krell, "at least not from a military standpoint."

"They're playing with us," insisted Moloch, "prodding us, probing our defenses, searching for weak points. I fear this is only the beginning. We need to move as many legions as possible to the portal so as to fend off any future attacks."

"Calm yourself, Moloch," insisted the general. "We are in no immediate danger." Krell turned to the master. "Shall I order our legions to attack this sphere once it is within our range?"

Satan stood in silence, twirling his goatee with his left hand. "No, let us allow them to make the first move. Let them land, then we shall see what happens. Only when the enemy's intentions are clear shall I respond. For the moment, the move is theirs."

⊱✳⊰ ⊱✳⊰ ⊱✳⊰

The Spirit descended over the darkened hemisphere of Hell. Below them stretched the insidious Continent of Darkness.

"Two hundred and ten kilometers altitude, three thousand kilometers to target," announced Nick, who had the sphere aimed forward toward the point where the sun would rise in another twenty minutes.

Chris, Serena, and Johann sat facing the planet's cold, darkened surface. Here and there they could see an area engulfed in a red glow, lava pits in a realm of unimaginable cold and eternal night.

"Do you figure that David has reached the most holy place yet?" asked Serena.

Johann pulled his timepiece from his pocket. "Probably not. He'll arrive in another twenty minutes or so."

"About the same time we will arrive," noted Serena.

"Approximately," replied Johann.

Serena looked deep into Kepler's eyes, as if trying to discern the contents of his soul. "You have great doubts about what we're about to do, don't you?"

There was a pause, and it was not reassuring. "Yes, I do."

Serena's countenance took on a greater intensity. "Professor Kepler, if you don't believe this is going to work, why are you going along with it?"

Johann smiled. "I'm not really certain. It could succeed, I don't know the mind of God; no one does. Yet I feel that this quest must come to an end by one means or another. There must be some closure; and as I see it, this is the only way by which it may be obtained. Otherwise, your husband will continue to pester me throughout all eternity."

Johann's comment brought a much needed hearty round of laughter from everyone.

Fifteen minutes later, the light of day flooded into the vessel, even as they swept in low over the coast. The skies around them seemed free of demons, at least for the moment. Apparently their landing would go unopposed.

The Spirit once more extended its metallic legs and hit the rocky ground about 50 feet away from the great portal. It was more than Serena or Chris had expected; a great arch of dark gray marble over 100 feet wide and 80 feet high stood before them. It seemed strangely incongruous, a lone structure on the barren rocky plains. The hatchway opened, and Chris and Serena wasted no time stepping from the Spirit and back onto the rocky wasteland of Hell.

"I didn't think I'd be back here this soon," Serena said, looking around nervously.

"With any luck we won't be here that long," replied Chris, walking toward the arch.

"I don't think luck has anything to do with it," said Serena, walking by his side.

The archway in no way appeared unusual. It was not the end of a tunnel of light, not a corridor pulsing with energy, the background of the plains, and the distant mountains beyond, could clearly be seen through it. It looked like a relic of the past, a monument to the futility of those who had turned their backs on the Creator of the universe.

Serena looked up to see an inscription etched deeply into the stone along the top of the arch. She recognized the symbols as those associated with the ancient angelic language. She was far from being an expert in that language, yet the inscription was simple enough to translate. "Abandon all hope, ye who enter here," she said.

"Dante was actually here," gasped Chris, "at least in spirit. He spoke of seeing this inscription at the very gates of Hell."

Johann was the next to disembark. He held the powerful rifle in his hand, the one that had ripped a demon to shreds during the battle. "What now?" he asked, looking around to verify that they were alone.

"Now? Now we wait," Chris said.

Their wait was short. Scarcely a minute passed before a dark portal, perhaps 10 feet in diameter, appeared about 30 feet away from where Chris and Serena stood. It was like a doorway into nowhere. Through it emerged an entourage of perhaps a dozen demons accompanied by satan himself. The portal dissolved behind them. Satan scanned the humans before him with interest.

"I've missed you, Serena," he said, a smile on his face. "I'm so glad that you've decided to return to the fold." He paused for effect. "Or is it that you didn't have a choice? And look, you've brought some friends along with you. This is indeed a surprise, so unexpected."

Satan crossed his arms and turned his attention to Chris. "Well, who do we have here? Why, I do believe it is your husband. Could it be that even in Heaven he somehow remembered you? How very interesting. Surely you must realize that this wench is no longer your wife, she is my property, to do with as I see fit. No one escapes my domain, no, not even one. Did you truly believe that you could cheat me of a soul? If you did, you were very much mistaken."

Throughout satan's ravings, Chris and Johann stood in silence. Their countenance bore no trace of emotion. They were not afraid of this braggart, for they knew that he would not be the one to decide their fate this day. Hopefully, the last word would be theirs.

"Young man, if you truly wish to be with Serena throughout eternity, I think I can accommodate you. Yes, I think that we can find a place in Hell for *both* of you. The question is where. Should you be made to suffer apart, denied each other's company throughout all eternity, or should you endure a common fate, each doomed to watch the one you love in excruciating torment, unable to intervene, and eventually coming to despise them? Interesting question, is it not? Well, we have plenty of time to decide that, don't we? Perhaps after you are all properly attired, I can arrange for each of you to receive a special tour of my domain, as I did for Serena. Yes, that would give me time to prepare a place for all of you, an ordeal most appropriate for your crime. Yes, that is what I shall do."

"Are you quite finished?" Chris asked.

"Not nearly," laughed satan. "I have all eternity, and so do you. The difference is that my role shall be that of the master and yours that of slaves. You will suffer for my amusement."

"I wouldn't be so sure of that," Chris said, his tone absolutely calm.

Again satan laughed and his entire entourage with him. "You are in my realm now, young human. You and your friends are no longer protected by the hand of God, not here. When you crossed into my domain, you gave up those rights. Here you are no better than any other damned soul—here you belong to me."

This time it was Chris's turn to laugh.

"Not very likely. I have listened with much patience to your ranting. Now you will hear my terms, there are only two. One—you shall renounce any claims you have on Serena and trouble her no more. As long as she leaves you in peace, you shall do the same. Two—you shall make peace with Abaddon and his fellow dark angels. You shall grant them their own homeland within the bounds of Hell and trouble them no more. They, in turn, will be obliged to not interfere in your affairs."

Satan looked at Chris dubiously. His rage was mounting, though he managed to keep it in check. How dare this human dictate terms to the prince of Hell? This being was as stupid as he was bold. "I see…and what if I choose to reject your terms? What is it that you shall do?"

Chris smiled, further angering satan. "Something very simple, really. My colleagues and I shall conduct a most interesting scientific experiment. We shall determine if a so-called immortal being can survive being reduced to vaporized atoms and having those atoms scattered over approximately five hundred square miles."

"Excuse me," interjected Johann, "you are underestimating the device. It would be more like *eight* hundred square miles. The energy released would, after all, be three hundred and ninety one megatons, plus or minus two percent."

Chris turned to Johann and bowed ever so slightly. "Excuse me, professor, I stand corrected."

Now satan was furious. "What are you talking about, human?!"

"Oh, excuse me," Chris said, turning back to the enraged monarch. "I was speaking of a breach in the core of a temporal capacitor. It takes a lot of energy to punch a wormhole from Heaven into outer darkness and push this baby through, yes indeed. Even you lack the pure power to accomplish a feat of such magnitude. Fortunately, we don't. Tell me, do you think you could survive a blast that would remove this entire peninsula from the map of Hell, and change the face of this entire planet?"

Satan glared at Chris. "You expect me to believe that?"

"It doesn't matter what you believe," said Nick, stepping from the Spirit. "It happens to be true. I built it. I should know."

"Our proposal is completely reasonable," said Chris, "far more reasonable than the alternative. Still, it's your decision. If you choose the alternative…well, that's your choice. In that case, there will no longer be a prince of darkness to rule Hell. I have more than a few reasons to see you wiped from existence. Go ahead, make my day." Chris smiled; he had always wanted to use that famous old movie line.

A tense deathly silence fell over the group of protagonists. It was satan's move. For a moment, perhaps for the first time in a millennium, he was unsure about what to do. He stared into this bold human's eyes. Eyes nearly as cold as his, returned his gaze. Was he bluffing? Satan knew well the love of humans for games of chance. He had lured so many of them to their doom through that compulsion. Try as he might, he couldn't read this human.

Should he play it safe, agree to this human's terms, or call his bluff? Could this human really do what he claimed? He couldn't ignore that possibility. No, it was against his nature to make a pact with these loathsome beings. "An admirable attempt, young man, however I must decline your generous offer. You shall surrender to me, you and your entire party. You are a part of my realm now, and you shall be for all eternity."

Chris's heart sank, though he did his best not to show it. His bluff had been called. Yes, he had anticipated this possibility, though he had prayed that it would not come to this. Now he had to make good on his threat. He dared do nothing less.

He turned toward Nick to see the detonator in his hand, his thumb on the trigger. There was no doubt in his mind that Nick would push the button if the situation forced it.

Chris turned and faced satan. He had one more card to play. "I would be doing the human race a great favor by removing you utterly from the face of existence. The universe would be a far better place without you. Still, I will give you one last opportunity to reconsider. Is that your final word?"

"It is," said satan, a growing evil smile on his face. "You were a fool to think that I would fall prey to your lies."

This was it. Chris looked to his wife. She returned his gaze and nodded in agreement to the decision he had already made. Simultaneously they reached out and took one another's hands. Whatever would happen now would most certainly be better than what satan had in store for them. Chris turned toward Nick—it was time.

But Nick was focused on the portal to their left. The barren scenery beyond the great arch had taken on a rippling aspect. Suddenly it vanished, giving way to a deep swirling vortex. There was movement beyond, someone or something was approaching the threshold. The vortex vanished as quickly as it had appeared, and a figure dressed in white stood upon the rocky plains.

"It's You!" cursed satan, in a snarling tone. "What business do you have in my realm, Nazarene?"

"The Father's business," said Jesus, stepping toward the tense gathering.

"I have grown much stronger than I was the last time you dared to set forth in my realm," said the devil. "You would find me a considerable adversary."

"Hold your peace, satan," said Jesus, His tone surprisingly calm. "Your time is coming, but that appointed hour is not yet. You shall depart from my sight."

"But these humans are mine!" roared the devil. "They are in my realm. You cannot take them from me!"

"You have only that which the Father gives you," replied Jesus, advancing several more steps, "not all that you desire. Now, go." The words of Jesus remained calm, yet undeniably firm. Satan had to obey.

"I shall yield to your will this time, Nazarene," the devil hissed angrily, "but I assure you that my day of retribution is coming."

Jesus did not respond to satan's threatening tone, yet his eyes never left him.

A moment later the dark portal materialized, and satan and his minions retreated within. The portal vanished.

Jesus turned to Nick and Johann. "It will not be necessary to destroy your ship. I have come here on behalf of our Father. The two of you should not be in this place, it is not meant for God's children to journey here. It is His wish that you depart at once and never return to this realm of outer darkness. His loving hand is upon you, and your return journey will be a safe one."

"But Lord, what about Chris and Serena," objected Nick. "We can't just leave them here."

"You must," replied Jesus, "The path of these two shall not be the same as yours. Now, go in peace my friends."

There was nothing more to be said. Johann walked to the reunited couple; they all embraced.

"I pray that our paths cross again," said Johann, trying his best to smile. "The two of you have taught me much about love and devotion. May God bless you, both of you."

With those words he walked toward Nick and the Spirit.

"It has been a pleasure to have known you," said Nick, standing there stoically. "I pray that you shall find happiness, wherever you may go."

Nick and Johann stepped into the Spirit, the hatchway closed and vanished. Jesus, Chris, and Serena stood on the rocky plain as the craft rose almost without sound into the dusty brown sky. Within a minute it had vanished from sight.

Jesus turned to the loving couple who stood arm in arm. "The time has come for us to part company," He announced.

"Has the Father come to a decision about Serena?" asked Chris, his voice faltering and uncertain.

"He has," confirmed Jesus. "I only wish that He could have decided in your favor, but such is not the case." Jesus focused upon Serena. "You decided not to accept the path to salvation that I offered you. For this reason, you have no place in Heaven. I am sorry."

"But what about the new world I saw in Johann's study?" objected Chris. "Why couldn't she be sent there?"

Jesus shook his head. "It's just not possible, Chris. That world, and the others you saw, are hidden worlds. They are not ready for humankind. That world you speak of is the new Earth. God has held it in trust until the day that humanity will be ready for it. There too is the new Heaven. It awaits the day when humankind shall shake off all remnants of their old nature.

"On that day, they shall become like unto the angels, celestial beings, not terrestrial ones. Yet, that day is still afar off. The third world, the one of pure fire, is that which awaits satan and his angels following the final judgment. All of these worlds are beyond your reach for the moment."

"What about Abaddon and the other dark angels," asked Serena. "Surely they don't deserve the same fate as satan and his angels. They're nothing like them."

"They are in the hands of the Father," replied Jesus. "I cannot tell you what fate awaits them, but it lies along a different path from that of satan and his followers, that much I can tell you."

"And what about us," objected Chris.

"You too have a destiny, both of you. It is the Father's wish to send each of you to the place where you belong. Things must be set right. Chris, God loves you, you are His son, but you cannot continue to act so irresponsibly. You must learn to live within the limits of His will, to always seek His council. The end times draw very near, nearer than you might imagine, and we must remain committed to Him who has done so much for us."

Jesus paused before continuing. He turned to Serena. "As for you, child, you have forged your own path. Everything we do in life carries with it a set of consequences. You created your own destiny. The time has come for you to step back onto that path, to continue the journey you have already started."

A pair of portals opened up before Chris and Serena, one light and one dark. It was time to go.

Chris realized that there would be no arguments, no further appeals, God's decision was final. For a moment they embraced, exchanging one final kiss.

"Please, don't try to remember me again," said Serena, tears in her eyes. "I'm not worth an eternity of sorrow. Be happy, Chris. Love God with all of your heart; become the best son you can be. I'll carry enough of our love in my heart for the both of us."

"It's time," Jesus said, placing a hand upon both of them and leading them toward the portals.

Their hands slipped from one another, and Serena entered into the dark portal even as Chris entered the light. Their journeys had begun.

For Serena, the tunnel was mercifully dark and calm. There was no sense of cold or heat, peace or fear, it was a realm of nothingness. A faint point of light appeared ahead, only to slip quickly past. Then there was another one, and another. Within a few seconds Serena was surrounded by a shower of falling stars coming out of the darkness before her. Stars? No, not stars, snowflakes, thousands of them. Her mind was bombarded by a dozen conflicting sensations, then it cleared. She was wearing her favorite medieval dress, the one she often wore to renaissance events.

She looked to her right to see telephone poles passing by. Ahead she saw parallel lines of yellow that stretched out to meet the snowflakes. She was in the car, the car she had died in on that fateful night. To her left she saw Chris at the wheel. What was going on? Then she realized—the turn, the black ice, the huge truck.

"Chris, pull over!" she gasped. He was braking even before she had spoken.

Still, the deadly turn loomed ahead, and within seconds it would be too late. She couldn't bear to go through this all over again.

"I've got it," said Chris, applying as much brake as the slick road would allow.

They hit the turn with its deadly black ice. The small car began to slide. Chris wrestled for control, turned into the skid. They began to cross the double yellow line, only to swerve back into their lane once more. All the time they decelerated. They swung out of the curve and onto the snow-covered shoulder. There was a slight bump as the car nudged into a large drift.

Then they saw two bright lights—an 18-wheeler thundered by in the far lane. Within seconds all they could see through the driving snow were the truck's tail lights. For a moment they sat in total silence. Chris put the car into park and turned off the engine. They fell into each other's arms.

"What happened?" gasped Chris, holding onto Serena tightly. "I just had the weirdest dream…but I was awake, I had to have been."

"Chris, I want to pray the prayer of faith," Serena said. "I want to do it here and now, before I do anything else. I want to place my faith, my life, in the hands of Jesus. I can't go to Hell again, I can't!"

The realization swept over Chris like a gigantic wave. "Then it was all true, it really happened."

"We have to pray now," insisted Serena.

And they did, several times. It was over half an hour before Serena was satisfied and they pulled out onto that country road once more.

"Was it some sort of vision, or were we actually there?" asked Chris, as they stepped from the car and made their way toward the old rock house. "I mean, will anyone ever believe us?"

"It doesn't matter, we've got a job to do," Serena said, as they walked through the snow to the front door. "We've got to warn everyone about what we've seen. I don't want anyone to go through that. I promise that I will spend the rest of my life carrying my warning to all who will listen. It is, after all, a small price to pay for the sake of eternity.

Epilogue

CHRIS and Serena looked out across the congregation of the large church in San Diego as they completed the story of their harrowing journey beyond the world of the living. Several had been moved to tears. There would be many at the altar call tonight, there always were. Satan would again be cheated of that which he most desired, new souls to desecrate.

Chris and Serena had told the story hundreds of times, yet they never grew tired of it. It was always rendered with the same enthusiasm, the same intensity, as it had been on that first morning to the congregation of their own church.

Two and a half years, three crusades, and a book later, they were still on the evangelism trail, talking to anyone who would listen. Along the way, they had generated plenty of controversy. Some said that they had made up the entire story for their 15 minutes of fame. Others said that their journey had been a divine vision, but that it had never really happened.

Yet, Chris and Serena knew better. They did not let their detractors dissuade them. They would continue on; they could ill afford to do anything else.

In the months immediately following their return, they had often questioned whether their experience had indeed happened or whether it had been nothing more than a vision from God, a warning of things to come. They had looked for any evidence that the people that they had encountered in Heaven and Hell had indeed lived on the green Earth. The results of their search had been chilling. From the records of the 9-11 tragedy, to old copies of the *Wall Street Journal*, the reality of their experiences were confirmed again and again.

This was the last night of their southern California tour. They'd be moving on to Arizona in the morning, then up through Utah and Idaho, and finally back home. As always, the meetings were scheduled back to back. There was a sense of urgency about their mission. Time was running short for the world's people. The inevitable final battle between the forces of good and evil was approaching. Chris and Serena viewed each night as possibly their last, the last chance to bring souls into the Kingdom of God, the last chance to deny satan another victim.

The crowd was thinning out as a slight, dark-skinned man stepped up to the table where the couple was autographing their book. At first Serena didn't notice him; she was too busy speaking to a young woman and her son directly ahead of him. When she looked up and saw him, her heart skipped a beat.

"Hello, Serena," he said, smiling broadly.

"Benny?" she gasped, rising abruptly to her feet. "Is it really you?"

"None other," he confirmed. "A man renewed and consecrated by the Spirit of God through the sacrifice of His son, Jesus. I've read your book, Serena, it's incredible, but I believe every word."

Serena reached across the table and hugged him, "I thought I'd never see you again. It's a miracle, but how?"

"My story is not as incredible as yours," assured Benny. "I never even reached satan's audience chamber. As that demon stood there before me, as those burning shackles went shut about my wrists, all I could think of was another chance and what I'd have given for it.

"The next thing I knew, I was in a hospital bed in intensive care. I'd suffered a tremendous heart attack. I'd been dead for nearly three minutes during my ride in the ambulance. During those three minutes, I'd lived two days in Hell. God had given me a second chance, and I wasn't about to waste it.

"There was this nurse, right there in intensive care; she listened to my story, and when I had finished, she told me how to pray. She told me how to invite Jesus into my heart, and I did. That was the beginning of the new Benny Patel. Ever since then, I've done everything within my power to spread the gospel. I didn't much care what people thought about it."

"Fantastic," gasped Serena.

By now, Chris had taken notice of Benny as well. He had seen him in Serena's book in the Hall of Records—now he was here.

"But there's more," Benny said. "When it came time for me to thank the nurse who had prayed with me, she was nowhere to be found. In fact, no one in the ICU had the slightest idea who she was, but I did, at least I do now. She was an angel; there's no other explanation."

Rarely had such a joyous reunion been orchestrated. Chris and Serena met Benny's wife and children, a family restored by the love of God. They spoke for hours about the precious gift they had received, a gift of knowledge and life.

"In these last days, God has granted us a precious gift," Benny said, as they prepared to part company. "He has given us the opportunity to change the path of destiny, not just for ourselves but for others. He has allowed us to peer beyond the veil of death, to glimpse the horrors that it might hold for the unwary, and return with a warning for all humanity.

"We must go into the world and warn people of the darkness we have seen; and at the same time, we must bear witness to the Light. It is our mission to see the world through the dark times ahead and into the Light of God beyond."

Chris and Serena continued on to Arizona with a renewed spirit and clearer vision of their task.

The age of miracles had just begun.

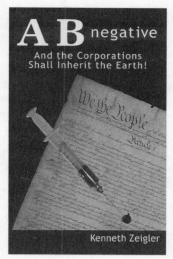

A B NEGATIVE

Welcome to America 2052. The Corporate Collective, a mighty alliance of mega-corporations, dominates every aspect of American life. Its elite military force struggles to suppress the growing discontent spreading across a nation in the midst of the darkest economic depression in its history.

In this America of broken dreams, Kendra Olson faces a grim decision. Soon her parents and younger brother will be compelled to leave the homeless shelter, their only source of food and warmth, to face a cold and lingering death on the streets of New York City.

Her only hope pf escape rests in the hands of her older brother, Lieutenant Kenneth Olson, of Army Special Forces, and a small group of unlikely rescuers. Yet there is more at stake than just her life. One of the Collective's most terrible secrets awaits Liuetenant Olson upon a surgical couch at the very gates of the Collective's own private hell. AB negative carries you on a roller coaster ride through the world of the not too distant future. Welcome aboard!

- Paperback: 266 pages
- Publisher: Windsor House Publishing Group (September 18, 2003)
- ISBN: 1881636429

Available through Amazon.com

Kenneth Zeigler was born in Harrisburg, Pennsylvania. He earned a Master's degree in chemistry from Shippensburg University, with thesis work in the field of quantum chemistry. He is a research scientist who has taught secondary and college-level science and mathematics for 30 years. He is married and currently lives near Phoenix, Arizona.

IN THE RIGHT HANDS, THIS BOOK WILL CHANGE LIVES!

Most of the people who need this message will not be looking for this book. To change their lives, you need to put a copy of this book in their hands.

> *But others (seeds) fell into good ground, and brought forth fruit, some a hundred-fold, some sixty-fold, some thirty-fold* (Matthew 13:8).

Our ministry is constantly seeking methods to find the good ground, the people who need this anointed message to change their lives. Will you help us reach these people?

> *Remember this—a farmer who plants only a few seeds will get a small crop. But the one who plants generously will get a generous crop* (2 Corinthians 9:6).

EXTEND THIS MINISTRY BY SOWING
3 BOOKS, 5 BOOKS, 10 BOOKS, OR MORE TODAY,
AND BECOME A LIFE CHANGER!

Thank you,

Don Nori Sr., Founder
Destiny Image
Since 1982